JUDGE-

REVELATION

by Roy Bright

Cover Art by Barry Renshaw with
thanks to

Null Entity (Kyle Ross).

Copy Editing by Ben Way.

Line Editing by Mike Harris.

.

For Reece, Tyler and Lily.
We did it guys. The series is complete. Next stop – the silver screen.

Special thanks to:
Judge Meister (for the 'continued-longer-than-anticipated' lend of your sword - you'll get it back, I promise), Alyssa Craig (for being Charlotte's body model for the cover), Andrew Wood (for the cover art reference photos), and my amazing beta readers: Louise Rhodes, Stephanie Farrant & Simon Leonard.

Also, super special thanks to Louise Rhodes for being immensely patient and putting up with all my crap, especially with regard to me taking ages to give you all the info needed to promote my online presence. You are an angel.

Immediately after the tribulation of those days the sun will be darkened, and the moon will not give its light, and the stars will fall from heaven, and the powers of the heavens will be shaken.

Matthew 24:29

ONE

Gentle waves lap against the side of a small wooden boat and ripple away, their trajectory altered by its interruption. The vessel creaks its way through the murky and pungent river, slipping through the eerie and noxious fog bank that surrounds it.

At its head, behind a lamp mounted on a pole shining far brighter than its size would suggest, stands a figure draped in a tattered, dark cloth gown, a hood covering its face. And with good reason, as few would ever wish to see what lies within the darkness of the hood's folds. From out of the gown's cuffs, skeletal hands grip a long wooden staff, and poke it into the murky depths below slow, and methodical, pushing the boat forward with each stroke

Somewhere, a crow caws and others join in, theirs the song of the dead, an anthem to welcome new arrivals transported down the river of the damned to take their place within Hell's everlasting torment.

The boatman pays them no heed as he continues his journey, his attention fixed steadfast ahead, focused.

Not far now.

Around him, the fog dissipates little by little leaving in its place open pockets of clear air that reveal a larger area of the river and the gigantic, rocky tunnel within which it flows. More of the boat clears the mist and the boatman stabs his staff into the water with increased force, spurred on by the notion that he is close to his destination, the journey almost complete.

The sound of rattling chains drifts on the air from behind him, their metallic jangling sounding close and as the Boatman clears the final remnants of the fog bank, the rest of the small vessel comes into view, trailing three chains that start small then grow in enormity, stretching far up from the boat's stern and at angles to each other, attached to and dragging a gigantic galleon from Hell with a grinning, demonic face forming its figurehead.

Piercing and terrified screams cry out from the ship, full to the gunnels with the damned – men, women, and children, all bound for eternal torture as demon's swarm over the vessel's deck, clawing, biting, and tearing them to pieces. Gore and viscera wash over the sides, staining the water crimson, and human body parts are everywhere, with people ripped apart only to find themselves knitting back together seconds later. The process then repeats, their horrific and painful torture continuous.

A young boy, no more than 11 years old, frantically claws at the deck of the ship as a large demon drags him toward the galleon's stern. His face is a mixture of pain and confusion as he struggles to comprehend the insanity he endures. He manages to wrap his arms around a piece of the structure and hold on, but it proves fruitless as the demon turns back to him and laughs, deep and demented, then drags him forward once more with a quick flick of its wrist.

The child screams in terror, his arms flailing against the deck, fingernails clawing at it, unable to prevent himself from being drawn toward the fresh fate that awaits him.

The other demons howl into the air, reveling in the terror and slaughter. It feeds them, fuels them even, and they take great delight in it. This is what they were born to do, their purpose being to gorge on the devastation of human souls, and within this domain they excel at it.

3

But, for all their terrifying dominance, for all their ghastly actions, there are two on the boat that do not fear them.

Charlotte Hope and Judas Iscariot stand side-by-side on the raised deck of the galleon's forecastle, their attention fixed ahead and ignoring the carnage behind them, or at least Charlotte is doing her best to.

In her hands, she grips her swords – the Katanas of Destiny. Devastating holy weapons that no demon can withstand, infused with the power of the spear that pierced Christ's side, and passed down to her from Judas whom she adores as her surrogate father. Her fingers tighten around them as she listens to each scream, every cry, and her heart sinks. She knows that people do and have done terrible things to one another upon the Earth, and that for many those actions warrant a place here among the damned, but still this is too close, too real and she can feel every ounce of their pain, and it is damaging her soul. She grinds her teeth as she listens to the young boy's terrified shrieks and is about to turn around when a clearing of the throat from Judas halts her. She glances toward him in time to see him shake his head, not much but enough to be missed if one wasn't paying attention. With a sigh she focuses her attention ahead once more.

"That is not why we are here," he says, his face solemn, stone-like, and emotionless.

She remains stoical for a moment longer, staring ahead, the pain of each human soul behind her causing her to wince. Closing her eyes, she exhales through her nose. She can't. She won't. No matter what these people have done, she will not idly stand by and let it happen around her. Despite Judas' warning, she caves and turning around stomps toward the demon, still toying with the child as it drags him screaming along the deck.

Up until now, they had remained invisible to Hell's minions, masked by a protective cloak of Dark-Divinity emitted by Charlotte, a unique variation of her holy power, received from defeating The Horseman known as Pestilence in the sky above Vatican City. But that protection only lasts if there is no interaction with the crew of the demonic vessel and so, motion-blurring toward the creature covering the distance in the blink of an eye and slicing its head in two with one quick flick of her sword, the camouflage dissolves.

Howls and screams permeate the air as the intruder's presence is now alerted to the hellish crew of the galleon.

To her right, a demon's claws click upon the wooden deck as it makes its way toward her, open mouthed to reveal rows of razor-sharp teeth flecked with blood and saliva and viscous crimson liquid dripping from its jaws.

The boy looks at her, his face locked in the action of crying, his eyes full of fear and confusion as she holds a hand out to him, signaling for him to get up and make his way to her, all the while keeping the creeping demon in her sight. She senses that its attack is imminent and readies herself.

But it doesn't, the reason being Judas turns around to stare at it, his movement slow and deliberate. He doesn't draw the massive sword fixed upon his back, instead he glares at the creature with such furious intent that it backs down and creeps away, unwilling to challenge him, in no small part due to the fearsome holy energy that pulses from him. For a lesser demon such as it is, the angel ahead is terrifying enough for it to cower before him, even within its own domain.

Ahead of Charlotte and Judas and a deck above, an enormous, muscular demon humanoid in form and draped in rags, with a sackcloth covering his face and a gigantic cleaver held in its hand stomps toward them, his footsteps thundering upon the deck. He raises the weapon, blood dripping from it, and points it at them.

Charlotte feels a shiver snake its way down her spine. The sackcloth upon the butcher's head may be mundane and featureless but it conveys a level of disturbing creepiness that is rare even for her, having fought the many creatures she has up to this point. Her eyes dart around, identifying and prioritizing targets as more demons close in on them from every angle, emboldened with a newfound bravery from the presence of the butcher.

A sudden lack of screaming and sounds of mutilation from the damned within the holy pair's immediate vicinity adds to the eeriness of the standoff and she grips her swords tighter, readying herself for the certain carnage that is about to be unleashed.

Judas stomps forward and draws Ikazuchi from off his back, the name he gave the weapon so that he was able to claim the demon sword Azazel while within his realm, and all around the demons stop and cease creeping toward him and Charlotte.

The butcher lowers his weapon and lets out a blood-curdling cry, but to Charlotte's amazement the scream doesn't signal an attack, instead the opposite, as the demons retreat and head back to whatever torture they had been inflicting prior to being disturbed.

She glances at Judas and shakes her head a little.

He looks at her for a moment, then offers a cursory shrug and focuses his attention back to the butcher as he turns and stomps away.

Stowing her swords back into their scabbards upon her back, the tip of the blades uppermost, she takes a deep breath and looks down to offer a hand to the boy once again, but he is gone. She looks up in time to see him ambling away after the demon that had dragged him across the deck, and in that moment as she watches the child follow what she can only assume is a preordained path, she understands: she doesn't possess the power to alter the fate of those onboard, and she wonders if she ever will.

Turning back to face the direction in which the ship travels, her eyes widen, and she takes a deep breath. "So. Those are the gates of Hell then." She nods ahead.

"No," Judas replies with a sniff, turning to face her, and returns his sword onto his back as metallic arms snake their way out of the side of the weapon's hilt and wrap themselves around his torso, holding it in place. "That is Port Dominion. From there, the damned are herded together and taken to the gates a short way from the port. There they are judged and then transported inside to the particular region within Hell in which they are to be tortured for eternity."

"Region?" she says, her eyes narrowing, "Hell is Hell, isn't it? What does it matter where in particular they are sent?"

Azazel's serpent-like voice whispers out from the sword. "May I answer?"

Rolling his eyes, Judas holds out a hand allowing the weapon to shift from that of Ikazuchi into its demon, humanoid form of Azazel.

"Ahh," Azazel says, placing his hands upon his hips and thrusting them forward, "it's good to get on one's feet again and stretch the old legs. Also, kudos guys," he says, motioning backward with his head, "those lesser bastards were genuinely terrified of you. You won't have any trouble from those little fuckers for the rest of the journey." He grins and then takes a deep breath. "Oh my, that is a flavor I never thought I would taste again. So, so sweet, the fresh scent of Hell."

"If you say so," Charlotte says with a shake of her head and her voice dripping with sarcasm.

Sighing, Azazel turns toward her. "Come now my dear. Are we to do this dance all over again? Are we to fall out the length and breadth of this journey? Have we not been through so much that we can now trust one another and work together effectively?" He raises his eyebrows.

She stares back at him, her eyes narrowing. "I will never trust you, demon. So dispense with the pleasantries and just get on with what you have to say."

"Very well," he says, the corner of his mouth twitching, then bows, the action bordering on the petulant. "To answer your question regarding the destination of each damned soul, Hell is split into vast and varied regions. Each region has a specific theme to it, much like an attraction park." He grins but stops as Charlotte's cold stare indicates she doesn't share his sense of humor. He sighs. "Well, each region carries within it certain methods of torture, focused on the sin or collective sins that the damned soul has been cast down for. Furthermore, the experience is tailored to the individual – personalized, if you like. Peoples' sins are vast and multifaceted, you see, and therefore Hell has a lot to cater for. Now all that I have just told you is in itself quite unimportant. After all, we are not here to save the damned. But to get to our destination of the Temple of Belial, we must pass through some of these regions."

"Great!" Charlotte says with a sigh.

Azazel chuckles. "Come now, you knew that this was never going to be a walk in the park my dear." He winks, further exasperating her. "What is also very important to note is that Hell is a battleground – it is in a constant state of civil war. Always has and always will be."

Charlotte frowns and turns toward Judas for a second before returning her attention toward Azazel. "Civil war? Why?"

Taking a moment to consider his reply, Azazel scratches the side of his head. "Lucifer is the Commander-in-Chief of Hell, this much is true, but each region is controlled by its own hierarchy, its own Lord, not to mention all of the crap that goes on within the Nine Circles. Many of them serve Lucifer without question. Malphas, for instance – a good and loyal lapdog to the King of Hell in every way. However, many others are not as obsequious and are constant in their attempts to usurp his control over the Underworld. All in all, it is quite pathetic and pisses Lucifer off to no end, as it serves to do nothing more than divert his energies and attention away from his true goal – that of conquering the realm of man and the White Kingdom. But now everything has changed."

"How so?" Charlotte's eyes dart back and forth.

"Because of you." He stabs a finger at her.

"Me?"

"Yes – you."

Azazel smiles. It is not a welcoming gesture.

Judas sighs and turns toward her. "Lucifer knows we're coming, of that we can all agree, but to make matters worse our arrival here will clearly not go unnoticed. It won't take long for the Lords of Hell that are not within Lucifer's inner circle to realize why we are here and where we are going, and undoubtedly they will try to use that to their own advantage."

Azazel moves around them both, almost dancing. "Exactly. This will provide the perfect opportunity for them to make their move. They may not know the ins and outs of Lucifer's plan, nor understand exactly what you represent my dear, but they will know that capturing 'The Light' will give them a much-needed edge over him and they will use that the best way they can. In short, our journey to the Temple will not only be hindered by those loyal to Lucifer, but by those wishing to relieve him of his command." He smiles, a wicked and teeth-filled one. "This is going to be so much fun."

"Fun?" she says, anger burning within her eyes. "People… are… dying. The fate of everything and everyone we love rests with us, and you think this will be *fun*?"

Azazel smirks.

Judas closes his eyes for a moment and then looks down, drawing in a tired breath. He glances over the front of the ship as it draws closer to the bank where it will dock. "Ika," he says, calling Azazel by his conquered name and glancing toward him. "It's time."

Azazel nods and bows his head then holds his arms out to the side. A moment passes, and he lifts his head then looks at Judas in confusion.

"Well?" Judas says, his brow creasing to the center. "Transform."

Azazel bows his head once more, his face steeped in concentration. After a few more seconds his lets out a sharp breath and looks up again, his annoyance evident. "Huh! It seems I can't."

"What? Why not?" he asks while shaking his head and scowling. "A Thŭramré shouldn't affect you, you're of demonic origin."

"Well, yes indeed," Azazel replies, then takes in a deep breath, "how curious. It seems Lucifer has a few tricks up his sleeve that I don't know about."

"What's going on?" Charlotte says, glancing at them suspiciously.

Judas grunts. "It seems Azazel cannot transform into anything but his sword and human guises. I needed him to change into his flying serpent form and transport us to the down-well that leads to the lower levels of Hell. Thŭramré curses prevent angelic beings from using their wings and from creating portals, but it shouldn't affect demons. It would seem Lucifer has something else in play here, specifically targeting Azazel's abilities. Looks like we are on foot all the way. Dammit!" He utters the last word with such venom he is almost spitting it onto the ground.

A voice stirs within Charlotte and calls out to her.

Use me, young one. Use my gifts.

A dark energy swirls from out of Charlotte and surrounds her. Without thinking, she grabs a hold of Judas and Azazel under their arms and with a powerful leap propels them up and off the boat toward the bank where they crash-land with an unceremonious thud, forward rolling across the dusty ground.

"What the shit was that?" Judas says, righting himself up into a sitting position from off his back and spitting out dirt.

"I'm sorry," she says, rolling over onto her side in much the same manner, "I thought I would be able to control that a bit better."

Still confused, he spits out more dirt while patting more off his face and hair. "Fine, but again, what the shit was that? How did you leap so far? That must be half a goddamn mile!"

She offers him a small and tight smile. "Pestilence spoke to me and, well, I just knew how to do it."

Having defeated Pestilence during their battle, Charlotte had absorbed the essence of the Horseman and in turn many of his abilities. And she had intrigued the ancient one so much he had decided to remain and not return to the creator of the universe and of all things, the Alfather, instead attaching himself to her essence (admittedly only for as long as she still amused him). Having spoken to her on the boat, he had given her power a boost thus enabling her to complete the impossible jump from boat to shore.

She stands and dusts herself down then takes in a deep breath. "Whoa!" she says staggering, momentarily unsteady on her feet.

Swift to rise, Judas takes a hold and steadies her. "You okay sweetie? What's the matter?"

"It's nothing," she replies, regaining control of her breathing, "I'm just not used to having this much energy running through me. Even compared with my own Divinity levels. It's nuts. Masking us on the boat was one thing… but this!" She grins at him, more to reassure than to be funny, then pats his arm. "Don't worry about it, I'll be fine."

He stares at her for a few moments, unconvinced, then turns around. "Gate's this way," he says, with a nod of his head. "We gotta go through Dominion, so it will be best to keep our profile as low as possible. Most demons won't bother us since they have the herding and butchering of human souls to keep them occupied, but since they know we're here I'd take no chances and be prepared for a fight." He looks at each of them in turn. "But only if there is no other choice, understood?"

Glancing at Charlotte, Azazel smiles then shrugs. "Hey, you're the man who'll be holding me. I'll do as I'm told."

Judas focuses his attention on Charlotte.

She nods. "Yeah, of course. We may be brimming with power, but I see no point in expending it on low-level shits in this neck of the woods."

Judas turns back to face their intended direction. "Good." He holds out his right hand. "Ika!"

Feeling the pull of the call from Judas' outstretched hand, his feet sliding against the dusty ground, Azazel thrusts out a hand of his own. "Master, wait! Please."

Judas snaps his hand shut, halting the symbiotic transformation.

"This is my domain, this is where I am at home. I can better serve you in this form while we travel. I can offer much assistance and counsel. Please master. Allow me to remain in my human form and be your guide."

Judas grunts. "I don't need a guide. I know all that you know, remember? We both absorbed Barachiel's knowledge."

Azazel edges closer to him. "Ahh, that is true, but we only absorbed what Barachiel and my brother Leviathan knew. Believe me, master, they didn't know all that I do. I can and I will be of great use to you – but in this form. Besides, isn't it tiresome for us all? Me constantly asking for permission to become human so that I might dish out valuable information? I know this one grows weary from it." He points toward Charlotte and grins.

Judas draws in a deep breath through his nose, his gaze fixed on Azazel, then purses his lips together and exhales it in the same way. He glances at Charlotte who raises her eyebrows, and he nods then turns his attention back to Azazel. "Okay. But no bullshit, and you're back in the box the very second I need you for battle."

Azazel's grin eases into a warm smile. "Master, of course that goes without saying. You won't regret this."

"For your sake, I had better not." He glances toward Charlotte once again. "We don't need any of your crap right now. Especially since we are gonna have enough problems with the Gatekeeper."

TWO

Sarah lifts the edge of the scarf covering her mouth, the brown and tan material having slipped down a little. Again. So annoying. And then adjusts her goggles as dust whips up from the force of the wind, causing her to squint to see ahead. She cannot, and so rests her back against the concrete slab then slides down it and sits on the ground. She grabs the water bottle attached to her combat webbing, opens it, and pulls her scarf down, aware of the irony of having just adjusted it so that it covered her mouth once more. She drinks deeply, and the tepid water tastes funny and metallic but nonetheless refreshing, then she pulls the scarf back up and clips the bottle onto her webbing as a male voice squelches into life through her earpiece.

"Angel-point this is Tartan-1, what's the hold up? Over."

"Uggh," she says, rolling her eyes behind her goggles. "Must we use these ridiculous codenames? I'm pretty sure the demons are not tapping into our conversations in the same way that the, errr, I dunno, Russians or someone might."

Muted laughter follows then the male voice once again. "Fair enough. Recruit Sarah Fisher this is Sergeant Aaron Jones, what is the hold up? Over."

More laughter from her earpiece and more eye rolling from her.

"You don't have to be a jerk about it Jonesy. But point taken, I guess codenames are quicker." She giggles.

"But seriously Sarah. Are you okay? What's the matter?"

"Nothing. I just can't see, the wind is too fierce, too much dust. Just give me a minute, yeah?"

"Okay, just a minute, but we cannot stay here as our position is a little… exposed."

A new voice joins the conversation.

"Sarah, this is Isaac. I am coming to you. Hang on."

"NO!" she commands, "you'll blow my stealth. They see you now Isaac, or had you forgotten?"

"The only thing I have forgotten, sister, is my promise I made to father to keep you safe. Now stop backchatting me, I'm coming to you."

"No, you are not, and don't talk to me as though I were a child. I am my own person and I can take care of myself. Just you stay there and carry out your orders as assigned."

"Don't argue with me Sarah I am com—"

"No, you are not! Stay there for the love of all that is holy, just… stay there."

Sarah and Isaac squabble over the comms, bickering at one another in the way that only siblings can, each unwilling to listen to the other, or to reason for that matter and it is Colonel Nathan Taylor's stern voice that brings the argument to an abrupt close.

"*Enough!* Cease your incessant jabbering. You asked that I bring you along on scouting missions, so you will act and behave accordingly: like soldiers and not bickering teenagers. Am I making myself perfectly clear?"

"Yes sir," comes Sarah's quick and compliant response.

Isaac says nothing.

"Very well," Nathan continues, "Isaac, I will take your petulant silence as an indication of your full cooperation. Now, keep the chatter down and your attention up. Angel-point, we move on your signal. Understood?"

"Understood, sir," she says.

"Good. Now act like goddamn professionals."

Nathan's closing remark meant that there was to be no more messing about, no more goofing around, and no more taking the job lightly.

She lifts her head up and sighs, closing her eyes as she does. She scans the area, the ruins of the once beautiful city of Saguenay, Québec, a former tourist destination where people would travel to revel in Canada's majestic scenery, much of it located upon the banks of the Saguenay River and its surrounding area, now nothing more than a barren wasteland and a shadow of its former self.

Gone are the beautiful forests, stunning mountains, and temperate shoreline that was perfect for all manner of water activities, and in their place a hell-rot that has covered much of the planet accompanied by desert-like conditions. Ramshackle homes and devastated buildings complete the post-apocalyptic landscape with most of the area now lost to the sands, and unless people had been here before or seen it in pictures, no one would ever know of the beauty that the area once had to offer.

It has been nine months since the fateful day when Sarah, Isaac, Gary, Nathan, and the others were forced to leave Selfridge Air Base in Michigan and search for new accommodation; the same day her little sister Abigail lost her life at the hands of the former Archangel, now turned demon, Samael and her thoughts turn to her once more. She closes her eyes and a small tear beads causing her to blink them open and take a deep breath.

Abigail's death hit Sarah hard and she had struggled for a long time to come to terms with it. She blamed herself for not taking better care of her, for not being there when she had needed her the most. True, Abigail had been a brave one, with a calm exterior that always looked for the best in any situation no matter how dire it seemed, but on that day she had needed her big sister and their brother to protect her and they had not been there, instead imprisoned within a storeroom inside the mall infested with diabolical cannibals.

A cold sensation snakes its way up Sarah's spine and she shudders, not wanting to think of that place and the horror that had been within. But as hard as it had hit her, it had impacted Isaac tenfold.

Following his sister's death, he had allowed a great darkness to enter his heart, filling it with hate and loathing to such an extent that he had been of great concern to the others and their new allies, the residents of Bagotville Air Force Base near Saguenay, Québec, the site of their new home. They had discussed whether to quarantine him or worse, exile him in the barren wasteland, such had been his evident bitterness. They all knew that such deep-rooted anger and fear could lead to a person turning, lost to the whim of Lucifer and transformed into a 'Taken', the soulless hive-mind creatures under his control. But in the end, the Archangel Michael had put an end to such conversations. He had spoken up for Isaac, and a glowing recommendation from an Archangel was something that no person was going to take lightly. He had stated that although Isaac's grief and subsequent anger were at extreme levels, he sensed no malice in the boy and didn't think he was in danger of turning. He had reasoned that he saw the exact opposite: an innate desire to eradicate the demon scourge and by doing that he would be a much more useful part of the solution. Michael's testimony had been enough for Gary and Colonel Taylor, and they had made it quite clear that Isaac was to be left alone and allowed to operate as part of the military contingent, something the boy took to with great aptitude.

Prior to the onset of the Apocalypse, Isaac had been a person of peace, love, and harmony. A devout and practicing Amish who had wanted to follow in his father's footsteps, hoping one day to become a bishop and guide his community in the right and proper ways to lead their lives. Now, however, his behavior was more akin to fearless warrior than priest, although Gary had once remarked that fearless and reckless shared the exact same DNA and that at times Isaac needed to curb his eagerness for destruction, less it walked him down a path from which he might never return. Becoming a Taken wasn't the only way a person could destroy themself.

Isaac hadn't listened though, he rarely did any more and although he wouldn't admit it in front of the others, his disdain for Gary and the Archangels was almost as high as it was for the demons, having blamed them for Abigail's death. In his mind, Gary had meant to protect his sister, having had been with her almost up to her final moments. His mind had been unable or unwilling to comprehend how he had managed to lose her, an event that had resulted in her death. Even after Gary had explained that he and Conrad had been forced to make Abigail run from that terrible room where they had battled the cannibals and powerful stalker demon, Isaac had refused to listen, instead insisting that the former detective should have done more, should have stayed with her no matter what. But Isaac's grief had blinded him to one important fact – Gary agreed with him entirely, something he had confided in Sarah. He had told her that Isaac was right, that Abigail's death was his fault, that he had been responsible for her, and that he should never have left her alone in that place. Of course Sarah had argued the opposite and tried to reason with Gary. That nobody could have known what was going to happen on that terrible day, nor prevent it. It had been one of those things. One of those terrible, horrible things. But at least Abigail was with God. Her ascension within the loving arms of Gabriel saw to that and it was a memory burned deep into Sarah's psyche, and one she turns to often, cherishing the knowledge that her baby sister is in the holiest of all places.

A squelch in her earpiece brings Sarah out of her painful reverie that threatened to overwhelm her and cause a crying fit, and she is grateful to the interrupting voice that follows it.

"Angel-point, hold position. One of our spotters is reporting movement extremely close to your location."

Her eyes snap open and she flattens against the stone slab. Fighting the panic and trying to control her breathing, she focuses her attention into listening, attempting to identify the sound of movement but the fierceness of the wind makes it difficult. She is about to speak, to respond into her comms unit when she feels the dripping of liquid onto her left shoulder. Her eyes shift toward it, slow without moving her head and she holds her breath. She sees it: the snout of a scouter demon.

Although this variant is much smaller than most of the creatures that the group had encountered, they are to be underestimated at one's peril. Fast and ferocious, the oily black-skinned creatures are pack-hunters, and where one was, others would not be far behind. To further compound matters, they seemed to operate with a hive-mind mentality, meaning that as soon as any fighting started, the pack would follow quickly no matter the distance between them or the length of the odds.

She feels her heart pounding within her chest from holding her breath for so long. Loud thudding, and she fears the sound of it alone will alert the demon to her presence. Her pure and Amish ways had provided her with a defense mechanism, an invisibility to the creatures that would break only from interacting with her environment. But lately she had been growing less confident in that ability, sensing that the demons were growing stronger, that their hold on the Earth was tightening and she knew that once they owned it, no one would be safe… not even her. Isaac had also once possessed the skill, but his violent breakdown and unadulterated rage at the sight of his sister's murder had collapsed the gift and he was no longer able to hide in plain sight from them.

The demon slinks down over the concrete slab Sarah is pressed hard against, forcing her to slide to her right and away from it as quietly as she can. Its claws click against the surface and it continues to sniff the air, zigzagging its snout up and down.

It senses something. She knows it. And whether that be her or the rest of the team roughly two clicks away, she cannot stay here because if the others come – and they will – she cannot risk one of them creeping over the concrete to the right of its associate and thus straight over her body. The thought that it wouldn't detect her while crawling over her would be a stretch too far, and so she does the one thing she does not want to do: she moves, and as she does she disturbs rubble at her feet and it clatters away.

The demon's attention snaps to the tumbling rocks and dust and it growls, then turns its body to the right and readies to move toward it.

She must move, otherwise it will climb on top of her and so she leaps to her feet and bolts, running toward an abandoned shack that was once a home; one of the few remaining that had not been devoured by the sand. Her heart pounds once more, her breathing erratic as she makes a journey she was not prepared for and in turn neither was her respiratory system.

Fortunately she is an excellent runner, possessing great speed and agility and she clears the moderate distance in a matter of seconds, ducking into the building and navigating through it to find a wall to flatten herself up against. She takes a deep breath, closes her eyes, and breathes out slow and steady, attempting to get her exhalations under control. It is not working and does more harm than good, her lungs locked in stalemate, forcing her to blow out hard and then reciprocate the action with a deep inhalation.

The demon skids into the building and then raises its head and offers up a terrifying scream, piercing and shrill, one that fills every square foot of the ramshackle structure.

Sarah throws her hands up to her mouth and shuts her eyes, the action causing a tear to roll down her cheek. And then more screams. A lot more. Not close though, further away, much further than from where she had run from, and she reasons that she may have a little more time to evade the beast within the building in the hope that it loses track of her.

But today luck and fortune aren't on her side, and the demon speaks.

"I know you're in here. You are a curious one, aren't you? Fast and unseen, but all the same you are here. I have experienced this before in a mall just outside of Detroit. Knowing that something was there but unable to see it." It slinks further into the building, searching left and right with eyes and snout alike. "But even after all her tricks, that one could not hide forever… and neither will you."

She closes her eyes tighter. It is her sister Abigail the creature refers to, and it takes all she has not to burst into tears. She gathers herself, just enough to retain her calm.

She can hear it creeping around just outside the room in which she is hiding, getting closer, and so with the grace of a ballet dancer she moves and pivots around the doorway on the opposite side of the room, thankful that the door itself is in pieces upon the floor.

The demon locks its attention on the slight sound and tears into the room with a loud growl. It searches, scrambling within, and then darts into the larger room, rubble and trash scattering under its clawed feet.

Sarah wastes no time. She peels away from the wall to the side of the doorway and back into the room she has just come from, using the demons noise and fury to mask the sound of her own movement as it passes her by. Hurrying toward a door in the far-right corner, she passes through it, her movement swift yet purposeful, taking great care to make as little a sound as possible, and as she sneaks into the next room her eyes widen. Within it is another scouter demon and it is looking right at her. But this one is different, larger, its eyes black and not yellow. She freezes, not knowing what to do. *This is it, this is the end,* she thinks. Two minutes ago she was alone, resting, contemplating the death of her little sister and now she is staring her own demise straight in the face. She almost laughs at the thought of how ridiculous the situation had become but that would be a silly thing to do and so she remains perfectly still as she watches the demon cock its head to one side, knowing something or someone is present but cannot pinpoint what or where. It barks toward the corner of the room to her right, the sound akin to that of a whooping cough and then narrows its eyes and forces its head forward as though searching for more information. Then, turning its head right and toward her, it cough-barks again and focuses its attention on the sonar-like blast that rockets away from it.

The wave passes over a shape, leaving the outline of a human. "There you are," it says, sneering. It cackles.

Sarah takes in a sharp breath and her eyes open wide. They have evolved. They know how to see her by directing their bark at her in a type of sonar detection. She doesn't know what to do. She cannot run as it would pounce, but she cannot stay where she is as it now stalks toward her. This is her end, she knows it and closes her eyes in preparation.

As the demon closes in a male voice screams, and the demon turns toward the sound. Isaac dives through the glassless window to the left of the demon and grabs a hold of it and rolls it over. He digs his knee into the beast's ribs, now on its back, and rains blow after blow into its face with his fists.

Unaffected by the pathetic punches, it snarls and gnashes up at him, its appendages flailing in the air as it attempts to right itself, then draws up its hind legs under him and kicks out, sending Isaac flying into the wall behind him. It scrambles to its feet and prepares to pounce upon the foolish attacker, the stupid human who has been rash enough to engage in a wrestling match with it, knowing it will enjoy ripping him to pieces and so launches at him.

A loud bang rings out and the demon propels into a wall to the side of Sarah as a powerful shotgun blast rips into its side, obliterating its body. The creature screams in pain as Conrad Bzovsky leaps over the window sill and into the room, firing for a second and third time. His face is a chiseled mass of hatred and determination as he explodes parts of the demon. With a growl, he closes in on the beast and continues to fire, his one good eye focused upon it, the other covered by a patch, damaged beyond repair at the hands of the cannibal leader Colt during their fight in the mall nine months earlier. It was an encounter he had been lucky to survive, saved only by the solo rescue attempt of Colonel Taylor – an act he will never forget. He turns to his right at the sound of the other demon scrambling into the room and fires the autoloading combat shotgun again. The weapon's recoil would be difficult to control for most people while firing it as rapidly as he does, but Conrad Bzovsky is no normal soldier and he intensifies his attack upon the beast entering the room.

Shot rips into its face, causing it to tumble to the ground and skid toward Conrad's feet, its fierce momentum carrying it forward, and he brings up a massive leg and drives it into the creature's face, opening the wound of the shotgun blast even further. It gurgles and hisses at him, confusion swimming in its one remaining eye that darts back and forth attempting to make sense of the situation.

Conrad lifts the shotgun up to his face and admires it. "This," he says in his thick Ukrainian accent, "this is good weapon. Young Daniel did well creating shells for it."

Across the room and against the wall, Isaac gets back to his feet. "I don't think we have time to admire the qualities of modified holy bullets right now, Conrad. There will be more coming, we must get out of here."

"Shot," Conrad says, very matter-of-fact.

"What?" Isaac replies, his eyes narrowed and his head cocked to one side.

"Is shot, not bullet."

Isaacs eyes open wide and he shakes his head. "What the fuck ever man, we need to be gone – now."

"Agreed," Conrad says, with a sharp nod, then turns toward Sarah. "You okay, little girl?"

She nods back and attempts a smile but fails. Her legs feel like jelly.

Conrad places an arm around her shoulder and attempts to move her only to have it slapped away by Isaac.

"I'll take care of her, you just make sure our path is clear," he says, then puts his left arm around Sarah and with his right, swings the assault rifle dangling from his back around to his front and raises it. He leads Sarah through the building, supporting her as they move, joining Conrad outside who has stopped to scan the area. Isaac sees what the huge man is looking at.

Outside, around 50 feet away from them, stand dozens of scouter demons, all perched upon the rubble and ruins, their eyes fixed upon the trio.

"Shit!" Conrad says, sniffing.

"Fuck, more like," Isaac retorts, his speech breathy, his mouth wide open, and his eyes darting back and forth as he assess their numbers. "We are so screwed!"

"Hmm. Would seem so," Conrad says, then spits on the ground, marking his defiance.

Isaac removes his supporting arm from around Sarah and raises his weapon, following Conrad's lead as he raises his.

One of the demon's screeches into the air and the rest follow suit, their terrifying sounds filling the humid midday air.

Sarah throws her hands up over her ears. She hates the sound. And although she presses them tight against her head, it does little to prevent the hellish screams penetrating through and filling her mind, destroying what little calm she clings onto. And as she wrestles with the toxic noise, another sound spikes in from out of her earpiece, a hurried voice that brings her back into the moment.

"Angel-point, this is Dragonhammer… grab some cover."

Sarah removes her hands from her ears and screams, "Back inside, *now!*"

Isaac and Conrad turn to face her having heard the same command, then dive back inside the building right behind Sarah.

Directly behind the shack, two Apache gunships rise above a sandy bunker, their rotors roaring, the sound quickly followed by bursts of their 30mm M230 chain guns, and the bullets ripple into the demons, exploding some and launching others backward and into the ruined buildings behind the horde.

As their comrades are obliterated by the high-velocity weaponry, the remainder disperse in all directions, howling and screaming, running from their doom as while they remain upon the Earth, their bodies are susceptible to their prey's weapons, especially since the humans have somehow managed to infuse them with holy power.

From inside the building, flat on the ground, Isaac pulls himself forward to the doorway so that he can witness the creatures' demise. He grins as they scatter in panic. "Yeah, fucking run you fucking cowards. Fucking… COWARDS!"

As the last of Isaac's insults are unleashed, they do so with such a biting venom it causes Sarah to look at him with concern. But since she is grateful to the air support's intervention, and saving their lives, she pushes it from her mind as quickly as it arrived.

All three react when one of the gunship pilot's voices sounds in their earpieces, their hands moving to the comms, the action automatic.

"Okay guys, the area looks clear. Vacate with haste and rejoin your group."

Conrad stands. "Thank you. I owe you big beer."

The pilot laughs. "It's all part of the service my friend, but we'll take the beer regardless. Dragonhammer out."

"You got it," Conrad replies with a laugh of his own. "Okay," he says, turning to Isaac and Sarah Fisher, "We go now. We move fast and keep eye peeled. Demons may run, but are not cowards," he glances at Isaac, who scowls back at him, "they regroup and return."

"Got it," Sarah says, nudging Isaac, causing him to look at her and then nod.

Conrad glances out of the door, looking left and right, his enormous frame barely allowing him to fit through the doorway. He looks back at Sarah and Isaac. "Is clear. We go."

They run out of the door and turn right, moving back to the scouting party's last position.

"Fun day!" Conrad says, without looking back.

Sarah and Isaac look at each other, their eyes wide.

THREE

Gary raises a hand to the young soldier as she passes, acknowledging her salute. "Good afternoon," he says with a smile.

"Sir," she replies with a small nod of the head and a warm smile of her own.

The Former West Babylon P.D. detective isn't military trained, nor would he ever claim to be, but since arriving at the base nine months ago he has become something of a celebrity given his close and personal relationship with Charlotte and Judas, and people believed he has as much say in holy matters as The Light and her protector do. As such they treat him as an honorary member, an officer of sorts. He knows he isn't, in fact, but truth be known he's enjoyed the small amount of prestige the notion (albeit a misplaced one) has brought him, with his opinion and counsel sought often during military meetings, especially with regard to whether the angels intended to return and how long it would be before Charlotte and Judas also did the same. But on every occasion his answer had to be as before – he didn't know. And his lack of knowledge or ability to provide answers had begun to create an air of unease when he talked with the senior officers. Military personnel do not like uncertainty – they loathe it, and it is for that reason he is a little concerned to be called to the office of Major-General Peter Dawson, the highest-ranking officer within Bagotville base and its present Commander.

Gary and the rest of the survivors of the horrifying events at the mall had been welcomed with open arms by Dawson and his staff, not least upon learning who his closest friends were. Like Colonel Nathan Taylor, Major-General Dawson had up to that point been struggling to keep the morale and spirits of his men lifted, so the news that a group of survivors were being brought in who were accompanied by angels had sent a substantial wave of euphoria around the base.

Without warning, and hours before the transport helicopters that had been sent to the location of a distress call had arrived back at base, portals had opened, and through them strode majestic, holy beings ferrying tired, frightened, and hungry people – many of whom had been subjected to their worst 24 hours of their lives since the Collapse. Those watching stood in awe, at last confronted with undeniable proof that Heaven had finally joined the fight and that they were not alone and left to die like animals.

And on that day, fervent religious emotion was at its highest with people crying, children rushing to the angels to touch them, the devout falling to their knees with hands clasped together, their faces turned heavenward; yes, that day had every joyous emotion conceivable. And as people poured through the portals, the base inhabitants went to them to offer support and comfort, to tell them everything will be all right, that they were safe from whatever horrors the angelic beings had rescued them from. It was a moment that defined what it was to be called human.

During the event, the Archangel Michael had introduced himself to Major-General Dawson, advising him that more were to follow – souls who had been too scared to use the divine wormholes, opting instead to return on the helicopters, their trust in man-made machinery higher than mystical power. And shortly after Michael's arrival, Gary and Nathan stepped through another portal and made themselves known to

Dawson, who from his posture and tone had been easily identifiable as the person in charge. Following handshakes and spot briefs, they had been guided to a room to be debriefed in full, and it was during that session that the horrifying events of their tragic day were described. Major-General Dawson and key members of his staff had listened to Gary and Nathan's account of the last 24 hours with mouths agape and eyes wide. When they finished, it had been Dawson to remark that he thought he had seen and heard it all, but what had transpired at 'Cannibal Mall' (a term coined by Gary, and one that had stuck) sickened him and the rest of his staff deeply. The fact that people could devolve into such terrible and murderous creatures so fast had been a notion that worried Dawson a great deal. It had been Gary to remark he was sure those people had always been that way, the clear majority at least with other stragglers having succumbed to the murderous congregation's peer pressure out of fear and a sense of belonging no matter what the cost. He had surmised that the group, led by their vicious leader Colt, had probably existed as they were long before the Collapse and the Apocalypse had been nothing more than an opportunity, without restriction, to practice their dark ways. It was a thought that had been even less comforting to Major-General Dawson.

And so in time over the following months, Gary and the rest of the survivors had pitched in and done their bit to maintain the community that they had been fortunate enough to be rescued by.

Nathan had gone on to do what he does best: command advance reconnaissance parties, and not long after his appointment he had been regarded as Dawson's second in command on all matters, something Gary had known to have been an inevitable outcome, such was the man's presence and military skill, while he himself had been assigned as the leader of the community patrols. Up until his arrival, those patrols had been formed out of various military personnel, but at his request they had been relieved of their duties and reassigned to matters more suited to their skill sets so that he could build a force out of the civilian members of their group. His reasoning was that keeping the status quo and maintaining law and order was something best undertaken by non-military types, as over time the survivors would want to lead as normal a life as possible and the notion that their day-to-day affairs were purely in the hands of military personnel would lead to dissent. This point of view was something Major-General Dawson happened to agree with, and so Gary had talked himself into a role that was for all intents and purposes the Chief of Police (although he hated being referred to as 'Chief').

As he walks the corridor, Gary scratches his beard, annoying as the thing is, never having been one to let facial hair grow unkempt. He is about to take a right turn at the end of the corridor when he stops and looks to his left as the sound of cursing and things being thrown draws his attention. Walking over to a door labeled 'Lab 1', he peers inside and knocks lightly against the framework. "Hello... everything all right?"

Toward the back of the laboratory, a teenage boy's head pops up from behind a work surface littered with scientific equipment. Standing up straight the boy sniffs and then brushes back his long curly auburn hair.

"Ahh, Detective Cross, impeccable timing. I want to report a theft."

Gary's head drops forward and he sighs. "What is it now, Daniel? What's today's issue?"

A child-genius Daniel Holtz may be, but he is also one of the more frequent pain-in-the-ass characters that Gary must deal with, and time spent around him can be energy draining.

In the beginning, he had been taken aback when first introduced to Daniel, a 14-year-old boy with an estimated IQ to be in excess of 300, who for the previous 12 months had been responsible for the improvement of many of the base's weapon systems to help better combat the demonic threat. His specialist area was detection, where Daniel had modified a certain amount of the base's radar equipment to scan for particular frequencies that only demons exhibit, effectively giving them advance early warning keyed specifically to the denizens of the underworld and thus removing the need to scramble scouting parties to check out contacts outside the base's perimeter. More often than not they turned out to be scavenging members of the area's wildlife. He had also made improvements to the base's supply of hollow point ammunition so that it could carry blessed water in the tips. Many had ridiculed Daniel for his idea stating that as smart as the kid was, he should leave the 'Buffy' crap well alone. Those people had to eat some serious humble pie when he had proven his idea to be not only correct but also effective at stopping demons using much fewer bullets. His ingenuity had seen Major-General Dawson appoint him to the position of head of Research and Development for the base. The title was grandiose, the actual position not so much, and the appointment had felt much emptier than it should have since he was the only one working on R&D.

Daniel folds his arms across his chest. "There is no need to address me as though I were a reprehensible imbecile worthy of your condemnation, Detective. You are the head of the community patrols are you not?"

Lifting his head back up, Gary takes a deep breath and exhales. "Yes, yes I am. But I am very busy today Daniel and I don't have time to listen to you complain about one of the aircraft service techs taking items from their *own* workshop."

"It isn't one of *their* workshops Detective, it is now a laboratory, *my* laboratory to be precise and well they know it. If you wish for me to continue researching and modifying weaponry to assist you in your fight against the creatures of the underworld, then I suggest you make it clear to them that they are not to come in here and steal *my* things."

Daniel's tone and anxiety rises as he finishes the last part of his sentence, causing Gary to raise his hands up to placate him. Unconvinced, he says, "Look, I'm sure that nobody came in here with the intention of messing with you or your stuff, and with the express purpose of winding you up to get you to complain again. So please just calmly tell me what's missing and I'll attempt to retrieve it for you in a timely manner so that you can get back to… whatever it is you are doing. Okay?"

"Portals!"

"I'm sorry, what?" Gary's facial expression matches the confusion in his tone.

"Portals. The demon portals. I am doing research into how they work in the hope that we might find a way to stop them, or at least prevent them."

Gary's eyes widen and then he blinks several times. "You want to... stop portals?"

"Yes. Which is why I need my oscilloscope and it is bloody annoying when they come in here, rummaging around, messing with my systems, taking stuff that doesn't belong to them, and just—"

"Okay, okay. Fine, Daniel – I get it. I'll look into finding out who came in and *borrowed* the oscilloscope."

"Stole! And it is *my* oscilloscope, Detective."

"Oh, for the love of God—"

"And when is the scouting party due to return, Detective? I really need to speak with Colonel Taylor."

Gary rolls his eyes. "I don't know, Daniel. I was on my way to see the Major-General when I stopped here and will you please just call me Gary instead of Detective? I have lost count of how many times I have told you this."

"You are a police detective and the head of the community patrols. That may not mean something to other people, but it does to me so I will continue to address you in the correct and proper manner."

Gary stares at him for a moment, his mouth open a little, then concedes. "Okay, whatever." He turns and walks away, raising his right arm into the air. "And I'm all over the case of the missing oscilloscope, just gonna grab my posse as soon as Velma finds her glasses."

"Sarcasm doesn't become you, Detective."

"Oh, I think it does. A bit," he replies as he continues to walk away.

FOUR

"Thanks for coming Gary," Major-General Dawson says, greeting him with a firm handshake.

"No problem General. You seemed kinda keen to get me down here, I hope it's nothing too serious?"

Dawson indicates for him to sit in a dark red leather Chesterfield opposite his and takes his own seat.

Glancing around, Gary remarks to himself how he always enjoys his trips to the General's office, not least because there's usually a drink in it for him. An office interior typical in every way, with pictures of Dawson decorating the walls and cabinets, a visual reference to his time served in the military and Gary always finds himself drawn to a particular picture of the man shaking some important person's hand, a Governor or Senator perhaps? He could never be quite sure and didn't like to ask.

Around the rest of the room and bordering a huge rug bearing the Royal Canadian Air Force insignia atop a modest cream carpet stands large wooden bookcases filled to the brim with literature of all kinds:

Shakespeare, Tolstoy, Hemmingway, Sun Tzu's The Art of War, and Gary even spied a Tolkien work or two. At the head of the rug and to his left in front of a wide, wood-framed window sits a large oak table with a green leather writing surface, adorned with trays brimming with copious amounts of paperwork. On the right-hand side of the desk just behind one of the trays stands a small Canadian flag sat in a round black base, and behind that is a picture of Dawson's family, his wife and two young sons.

Gary studies the picture for a moment, realizing that in all this time he had never discussed Dawson's family at length with him.

"Felicia, Jack, and Harvey," Dawson says, with a modest smile, interrupting Gary's thought process. He motions toward the picture. "The boys would've been six and nine when that was taken." He offers a small laugh. "Oh, how the world was different back then." He stares at the picture.

Gary nods, his mouth curling at one edge into the beginnings of a smile that doesn't quite materialize. "Indeed it was General, indeed it was." He glances toward Dawson and considers asking about his family, perhaps coax out of him what their fate might have been and then dismisses it as a morbid and foolish curiosity.

Sensing his interest, the General satiates Gary's desire for knowledge. "Funny that we have never talked about either of our families, especially given the amount of times you have been in this office." He smiles. "Like most out there, they were lost to the Collapse. Felly had taken the boys into town to buy a video game they had been pestering us for, one of those shooting games – Black Ops I think they called it. Despite the realities of my day job, I never approved of those types of games, and nor did Felly," he expresses a laugh, his head rocking back slightly, "but since they had been so good with their studies that week, she had picked them up from CFB elementary and then drove them into Saguenay. Breakfast that morning was the last time that I ever saw my family." Pursing his lips together a little, he smiles. He looks toward the window for a moment and then back at Gary. "Did you have a family? Y'know, before all of this?"

Half-smiling, Gary lowers his head a little and sighs.

"Bah!" Dawson says, with a wave of his hand, "Enough of that I dare say. No more dwelling on the past, it's the future that concerns me."

Gary nods and raises his head, turning his full attention toward the man.

"So tell me Gary, have you had any word at all from Charlotte and Judas?"

He ponders for a moment. "I'm sorry, I haven't General."

"Oh please. Let us dispense with the formalities. I know we haven't spent every waking moment together, but we have known each other for a little less than nine months now, Gary. Please call me Peter."

Gary smiles and nods. "Very well Peter. But no, I haven't heard anything from them. And to be honest, if they do make contact then I'm sure everyone will be aware. Sneaking in and out like a ninja isn't quite Judas' style." He raises his eyebrows and smirks.

Returning a smile, Dawson gazes at him for a moment, then stands and walks over to a cabinet. Taking out a whisky glass, he presents it to Gary while raising his eyebrows, and the smile and gentle nod from the man prompts him to go ahead and grab a second glass then pour them both a Scotch. Placing the bottle back, Dawson takes the lid off a silver ice bucket and grabs one cube for each glass with silver tongs, dropping it into the light brown liquid, then tosses the tool back into the bucket and replaces the lid. Walking back to his seat, he swirls the liquid around inside his glass and hands Gary his.

Taking it, Gary performs the customary sniff while circling the Scotch around in the glass. "Hmm," he says, closing his eyes, and smiling, "wonderful... and oaky."

Dawson smirks as Gary opens his eyes and then raises his glass to the man and drinks, the deliciousness of the liquor evident upon his face.

Gary responds in kind, savoring the flavor in the same way.

They sit that way for a moment, each taking turns at sipping their drinks, relishing the feeling of freedom from the troubles of the world outside with all that they entailed for now being the furthest from their minds, and then Dawson leans forward in his chair.

"I'm worried, Gary. A great deal."

Frowning, Gary sits upright, feeling the need to adjust himself so that his posture asserts himself as fully attentive. "Oh, how so Gener— I mean, Peter?"

"Demon incursions are getting closer and closer with each passing day. Just this afternoon, not more than a couple of hours ago, Nathan radioed in the position of a large group of scouters that they were forced to engage."

Before he can continue, Gary interrupts him, shuffling forward in his chair with abrupt force. "Is everyone okay? Did anyone get hurt? Are Sarah and Isaac all right?"

Having taken another sip of his Scotch while Gary spoke, Dawson nods his head, drawing the liquid back within his puckered mouth. He swallows and pats the air with his hand. "Yes, yes all are fine, thankfully. Some minor scrapes and bruises I believe but nothing too serious. He didn't go into much detail mid-op, but of course we will receive a much more comprehensive debrief when they return shortly. But this is the second incident in as many weeks where a large force of creatures has been encountered, and this time they were much closer. They're looking for something or someone, Gary, and if I had to guess I would say they are looking for you."

"Me?" he says, his eyes wide, the drink he was about to take halted, the glass lingering in the air in front of his chest.

"Who else could it be? Certainly they wouldn't bother themselves with any of us, we hold no importance for them other than cattle to slaughter so it must be you. I can only surmise that they need you to find the location of Charlotte and Judas."

"Well then, they're shit out of luck cos I ain't got a clue."

"But they don't know that Gary, and I'm fearful that a lot of people may get hurt in the process."

Gary stares at him for a moment and then takes another drink, looking into his glass as he does. "You asking me to leave, General?" Formality has returned.

"Oh, no no no, of course not – nothing like that Gary, nothing like that at all."

He looks suitably relieved.

"I wouldn't dream of such a thing. No, my concerns and the reason I have brought you here is to discuss alternatives and strategies. A plan as to how we either stand our ground or evacuate our people."

"You think it's that bad?"

"Well, it's better to assume that to be the inevitable outcome and be prepared for it rather than to assume it only a possibility and be woefully underprepared. Don't you think?"

Gary smirks. "Yeah. Yeah, I do. Funny, someone once said something very similar to me. I think you and Judas would get on very well." He takes another drink of his whisky, only this time a large gulp that empties the glass.

Dawson does the same, then raises his glass toward Gary while the liquid is still in his mouth, silently asking if he would like a refill.

Gary nods and hands it to him, then wipes his mouth with the back of his hand, cleaning up a minuscule amount that has dribbled from the side. "So, what's your preference? Fight or flight?"

Dawson muses for a moment. "Well, both have their pros and cons. On one hand, fleeing might ensure that most live to fight another day, but the uncertainty of the unknown and what we might run into in the wilderness terrifies me. Plus, we also lose the solid home we have built and maintained. However, if we stay put there is a chance we can dig in and repel any invaders, but we might lose many in doing so and how long do we keep that up for?" He sighs. "It's a real conundrum, Gary."

"Perhaps I can be of some assistance in making up your minds on that one, gentlemen?"

Both men stop mid-drink and turn toward the doorway to see Daniel stood there.

FIVE

"You're gonna have to help us out here, Daniel, because I am struggling to get my head round it," Dawson says as he paces in front of the seated boy.

Gary leans forward in his chair. "Are you saying you can create a force field around the base to keep the demons out?"

Daniel sighs. It is his fourth in as many minutes. Despite being told on many occasions that his level of intelligence would be his downfall within normal social situations – that over time, his gift would mean that interacting with people of normal or lesser intelligence would be indomitably frustrating for him – Daniel has never felt that to be the case nor uncomfortable with or unable to effectively communicate with those around him. However, that has always been down to him and his ability to take deep breaths and repeat information clearly and concisely, to not let it affect his frustration levels. However, he has always been aware of his need to slow down his dialogue at times. Not out of a sense of patronization, more so that he tends to ramble, to blurt, forgetting that very few are up to his level of information deciphering and processing speed.

It was clear from an early age that Daniel was special. His ability to formulate coherent words at six months old was the first indication of his acute eidetic memory, and a gift that had stuck with him and not dissipated as is common in young children. At the tender age of three, he had aced the John Hopkin's diagnostic for a precocious math test without even studying for it. But his level of brilliance, astonishing as it was, had not been hard to understand. His mother Patricia and father Victor had met while working on a project at the California Institute of Technology, where they had both been professors in their fields of pure mathematics, harmonic analysis, and algebraic combinatorics and their genetic excellence had clearly found the perfect fusion in Daniel. His abilities had seen him graduate high school at six years old and had been responsible for him enrolling at Caltech at the age of eight, one of the youngest students in the university's history. His exceptional talent had also led him to be awarded his Bachelor of Science at the age of 10, which saw him then go on to study for his PhD in physics with a keen interest in the quantum branch. His genius had not been limited to mathematics and physics, however, as he had also shown immense prowess in the field of engineering, another of his father's hand-me-down traits.

Victor and Daniel had possessed an incredibly strong bond, spending many hours in Victor's workshop and garage at their home close to the campus. Daniel loved fixing up just about anything – engines, motors, computer systems. If it had a technological aspect to it, he would want to open it up and see how it worked, then more to the point ensure he could put it back together in a better state than before he took it apart. It was a pastime that had seen both him and his father get into trouble on a few occasions, one such time being when they had built a small fusion reactor in the garage that malfunctioned and knocked out the electricity grid around them for 12 blocks, an event that not only annoyed their neighbors but also the senior faculty staff.

Thankfully, despite his genius and brilliance, no one would have known about it without being told, as he had been able to arrest his abilities and get along with people just fine. He was even deemed cool by some of those older than him at high school who had become his classmates and also the significantly older ones he had come to know at Caltech, despite the quirky and gentlemanly way in which he talked.

All of that changed, however, during the Collapse when Daniel and his family had been visiting a close friend of Victor at Concordia University in Montreal. He had watched in horror as his father had transformed into a terrifying creature and ripped his mother apart before his very eyes while they had been having lunch in a restaurant. Barely escaping with his life, panicked and distraught, it had been the first time ever that he could remember feeling like a child, unsure of the world around him, unable to comprehend things that he had taken for granted. And so he had run like he had never before, until his chest heaved and his lungs had been fit to burst. And he had stumbled, and he had fallen, skidding across the ground, scraping his elbows and knees. But there had been no one to pick him up, no one to tell him that everything would be all right; that mother was there for him. He had crawled to a doorway, had drawn his knees up to his chest and buried his teary face in between them.

It had been gunfire that had brought Daniel out of his trance. A firefight between soldiers and the Taken. And as he raised his head up at the approaching footsteps, he had burst into tears at the outstretched hand of a soldier, telling him that everything would be all right, that he should go with him. And that had been how he had come to be in the service of Major-General Dawson at Bagotville Air Base.

Daniel sighs for a fifth time, preparing to explain yet again what he thinks is a simple concept to two men he considers to be relatively intelligent. He feels drained from having to suppress irritation, to resist deriding them with condescension. "No gentlemen, I am not saying that I can create a force field around the base in the manner that you are thinking, all blue and shimmering. This is not Star Trek, and I am not intending to raise forward shields or engage warp drive. What I am saying is that I think I can create a magnetic layer that will systematically interfere with the demons' ability to portal into the base. We will still have a huge problem if they decide to send everything they have in the shape of a physical attack, but I think I can stop them getting in behind our lines and on our flanks."

Gary looks toward Dawson and raises his eyebrows, with the General returning the gesture. "Stopping a full-frontal attack is a discussion we need to have, without a doubt, but this… this is huge if it can be pulled off."

"Indeed," Daniel says, while reaching over to grab Gary's glass of whisky, an action cut short from Gary's sharp slap, causing the boy to retract his hand with an 'ouch!' and an awkward smile. He clasps his hands together. "Although, I am probably being a little facetious when I say this is not Star Trek, because I believe if I can square away a portal jammer, I may, given time, be able to provide a harmonic weapon that specifically targets demons." He grins and double flicks his eyebrows up, as though awaiting and expecting their applause. It doesn't happen. He harrumphs, his eyes narrowing, his lips tightening and puckering, then sits back in his chair.

"Well, Daniel," Gary says, getting to his feet, "let's just put the 'possibles' on the back-burner for the time being and concentrate on what you believe you can do. What are you going to need to make this happen?"

"Data, Detective Cross.

"Gary!" he says, correcting the boy again with a sigh, then closes his eyes while lowering and shaking his head. "How many times must I tell you, it's just Gary."

Daniel throws his hands up into the air. "Uggh, Gary, Detective Cross, what does it matter? The point is, I am going to need data and a lot of it. I need to understand the nature of the demons' portals and for that I need information."

"What kind of data?" Dawson says, stepping forward.

Daniel regards them for a moment before answering, his facial expression apologetic. "The kind that can most likely get people killed, General."

Gary and Dawson look at one another.

Turning back toward Daniel, Gary's brow furrows and he speaks through tightened lips, his words pointed. "What kind of data, Daniel? No more pissing around – be specific."

Daniel eyes him. The man is annoyed and in no more mood for games. He cannot have an angry Gary, he needs him on his side for the plan to work as he knows that with his standing within the base, the way that people respect him, it is his only hope of convincing them to comply with what he is about to ask. He takes a deep breath, his shoulders rising, then speaks at speed. "I am going to require a small force to accompany me to a portal event, then record its harmonics and quantum state so that I can isolate how it behaves in our world thus being able to prepare counter frequencies and harmonics to prevent the event within a specified area relative to the telemetry equipment in place."

Gary stares at him for a few seconds without saying anything, then takes a deep breath and draws his fingers across his eyes to the bridge of his nose. "Okay. I don't pretend to have the first idea what you're talking about in terms of the science of it all, but what I do understand is the combat element and you are telling us that you want to get close to a portal, when demons pour out of it, take scientific measurements, and then skip off into the night with everyone daft enough to accompany you on this project at risk of being ripped to shreds. Is that about right?"

Daniel's mouth twitches as his gaze bounces between that of Gary and General Dawson. "Yep. That's about the size of it."

Gary stares at him for a few seconds longer, his eyes wide and his mouth open. "Okay, okay okay," he says, waving his hands in front of him, "let's just say all of that is possible, how in the world are you gonna get or even predict a portal event happening? We have no idea of knowing when those things are gonna take place."

"Well… it's a hunt, isn't it? And what's one of the best ways of drawing your prey to your designated hunting ground?"

Gary's shoulders drop and his head flops forward. He then sits back down with a sigh. "For fuck's sake Daniel. Baiting a hunting zone with dead meat is one thing, using a person is quite another."

40

"I understand that, Gary, believe me I do, but we need more protection than we have at present and if what I heard from your conversation with General Dawson just now is correct, we are up against the clock on how quickly it will be before they come knocking on our front door."

Gary and the General shift in their seats, Dawson having sat down almost at the same time Gary had, and Gary throws his arms into the air.

Daniel's attention bounces between them again. "Look. I don't have all the answers on this one gents, and I certainly don't understand why Lucifer's army has, as of yet, not bashed down the door and killed us all. Maybe your superhero friends are battling him right now and keeping him busy, I don't know, but one thing is for sure if the General is correct. A heightened amount of demonic activity is happening relative to us and it is getting closer and closer with each event. So it is only a matter of time before they find us and I for one would like to be a little more prepared than we are right now. And who knows? Maybe this tech could provide us with a significant turning point and give us an advantage against them if this is to be what the rest of our lives look like."

The last words uttered cause Gary to look up sharply at the boy. In all the time that this has been going on, that he, Charlotte, and Judas have been fighting the forces of Hell, he had never once considered the fact that his friends wouldn't succeed, that the way the world was now was the way it was going to be for all time. He sighs. "Look, you're right Daniel, we should be more prepared, but I have no doubt in my mind that Charlotte and Judas will succeed, that they will restore the balance and set the world straight. This isn't what we are or what we can expect for the rest of our existence." He takes a deep breath. "Okay. This is worth looking into and drawing up a provisional plan. But I ask you now, do you honestly believe that you can come up with such a device?"

Daniel takes a moment to consider his response, taking deep breaths of his own. "Yes. Yes, I do."

Gary looks at General Dawson who signifies his approval by raising his eyebrows, nodding his head, and gesturing with an arm that was folded in front of his body. Turning back to Daniel, Gary is about to speak when a knock at the slightly ajar door interrupts him.

"Come in," General Dawson says, his attention drawn to the sound.

A hand appears on the doors edge and pushes it open and Nathan steps into the room.

The stature of the man, his physical presence and assertiveness even when talking in general conversation always influences Daniel and the teenager straightens up as though an unheard voice has told him to do so.

Gary stands and strides over to Nathan, his hand outstretched. "Hey brother, how are ya?"

"Yeah, good my friend, good. Bit of a wild one today, nothing we couldn't handle or at least nothing Conrad couldn't handle." He smirks at Gary who returns the gesture. "However, incursions are getting closer and more frequent, so that's a tad worrying." He motions toward Daniel. "So what's going on here?"

Opening his eyes wide and taking a deep breath, Gary places an arm around Nathan's huge, muscular shoulders and guides him over to a seat. "Well, it's funny you should ask. Daniel has a request I'd like you to hear…"

SIX

"How long have we been here? Since we left Earth time, I mean?" Charlotte says, tucked in close behind Judas, as they stealthily walk the deserted streets.

Judas shakes his head. "I'm not sure. Couple of days perhaps."

"Three days. Give or take," Azazel interrupts, correcting him.

"Huh!" she says in surprise. "So weird. I'm not feeling hungry or anything."

"Your body won't work like that down here sweetie in a realm such as this," Judas replies, glancing back at her.

"Oh, I know," she scratches the side of her head, "it's just weird, y'know? It feels… strange."

Judas stops for a moment to survey their route, then continues ahead.

"So what's the time dilation situation here, Azazel?" she asks, without looking at him and still moving with Judas.

"Well," Azazel says, rubbing his chin, "each day here will equal around three months up there, or thereabouts."

Charlotte sighs. "Nine months! Nine bloody months! That's how long we've been down here in their time? Nine whole months! Gary must be worried sick." This time she does glance toward the demon. "How come I know so many things following what happened in Vatican City, yet remain a relative stranger to this land and all its comings and goings? I should know these things… I feel like I should know these things for sure."

Judas stops and looks back at her, then glances toward Azazel.

The demon eyes him for a moment, taking his time to reply.

Noticing an exchange between them, Charlotte become suspicious. "What? What are you not telling me?"

Azazel smiles a little. "There is nothing that we are not telling you. We are equally surprised ourselves that you do not know more about Hell than you appear to. Especially since your assimilation with the Seventh Seal and The Book."

She puts a hand to her chest, the memory of the moment in the catacombs where she melded with the Seventh Seal and The Book having taken them from their resting place within the Ark of the Covenant; remembering how she was bombarded with knowledge, how many of the world's memories were bestowed on her – vast knowledge deposited within from that final awakening event. Yet despite receiving the ultimate prize, she knew that some things had eluded her within the data transfer, that certain fragments of knowledge remained out of her grasp, teetering at the edge of her mind, her reach not sufficient enough to take hold of them. And she wants to know. She wants to know everything.

Since the symbiosis, she had begun to feel increasingly unwell and it had been getting harder and harder to keep it from Judas. She knew that if he found out that The Seal and Book were slowly killing her, he would do everything in his power to try to remove them. Not that he could, and they would waste time they didn't have while his paternal desire to protect her raged within him. So she had kept it from him in the hope they could accomplish their mission before her own time ran out, because despite the gaps in knowledge she has from The Seal and Book, her impending doom was not among them, and she didn't want to die – not at all. Martyrdom was not on the cards as far as she was concerned, despite what her brother Jesus Christ had gone through an age before her. And the one thing about her lack of access to all knowledge that bothered her is that she still does not know what to do when they reach the Temple of Belial. She knows full well it is where they need to go, but so far the instructions of what she must do at the site elude her. Of course she has told Judas that she does indeed know; a little white lie to prevent him from worrying further, given she was sure the knowledge would flood in once they were on their way, but it has not and that is another factor that has added to the concern growing within her.

She is dwelling, and aware that if it goes on for too long Judas' suspicions will be aroused so she changes the subject. "It's not how I imagined it."

Hugging a wall with his right shoulder, he turns to look at her. "Why, what do you see?"

She shrugs. "Y'know, all medieval and stuff. I thought it would be, I dunno, twisted and rife with corruption or something."

He lets out a laugh.

"How strange," Azazel says, interrupting Judas' smirk. "She sees the same as you. You two are truly symbiotic."

"What does he mean by that?" she says, furrowing her brow.

Judas peers ahead and around the corner for a moment, eyeing up their route. The way looks clear and so he beckons them forward, trotting off to the next wall of cover and answering her as he moves. "Well, basically everyone's vision of Hell differs greatly. Usually, what one person sees, another does not. Your experience is tailored to you and your sin, until you wither and perish to be reborn anew as a demon."

Catching up to him, she grabs his shoulder and turns him round. "How do you know so much about this place? I thought you'd never been here?"

"I haven't," he says and cocks his head toward Azazel, "but since he and I bonded with Barachiel's essence, I now possess his knowledge so I know a great deal and a lot about Hell in particular. I probably know

45

more than him." Again, he motions toward Azazel, whose sly smirk makes him look overconfident bordering on smug.

"Okay," she says, sliding her hand off his shoulder and motioning around with her head, "If you know so much then where are all the people? The demons? You would think Port Dominion would be bustling with them, wouldn't you?"

Judas looks at Azazel and raises his eyebrows. "She's got a point. Why is it so quiet?"

"You tell me master," Azazel says, cocking his mouth into a rictus smile. "You're the one who knows more than me." The smile grows into a grin.

"Yeah, very funny dickhead," Judas says, refocusing his attention on the deserted streets ahead. Just as he sets off again, Charlotte grabs his elbow.

"Dad, wait. We've been here before."

"What?" he says, narrowing his eyes at her.

"We've been in this spot in this street not five minutes ago. We're going round in circles."

He glances around and then looks back at her. "Are you sure? This looks and feels different to me."

"No, definitely. I remember that door over there. The crescent moon carved into it with the gory mess of I-don't-know what-hanging off it... we've definitely been here."

He looks in the direction she points in but doesn't see what she sees. "There's nothing on it sweetie. It's just a wooden door."

Snapping her attention back on him, she looks surprised. "You're messing with me right? You can't see the blood on it?"

He shakes his head.

She strides over to the door. "But it's right here. *Here!*" She jabs a finger at it.

"Shit," he says, looking around, "we're not seeing the exact same thing, only parts of it."

"What? Shit!" she replies, glancing around.

Judas looks at Azazel, urging him with his eyes to offer up a plan, an escape route.

"Don't look at me," the demon sword says, "I'm having just as much fun as you with this."

"Fun!" Charlotte screams at him. "You think this is fun? We're being fucked with and you're having a good time?"

"Well… yeah," he responds, his eyes wide.

Judas strides toward him, his eyes annoyed.

Azazel holds up both hands. "Look, you have to relax and take Hell a little less seriously or it'll be your undoing."

Judas grabs him by his lapels. "Stop fucking with us Azazel and show us how to get out of this. I command it."

Azazel turns his head to one side to avoid the spray of his angry spittle. "Very well, master. Very well." He points to his right. "Run in that direction aimlessly."

Judas roars, lifts him up, and slams him into the ground on his back, causing Azazel to speak with haste.

"I'm serious, just do as I say. Run in that direction as aimlessly as you can and when you get to the edge of your despair, think of the exit, of how you imagine the gates to be, and it will bring you to them."

He screams into his face. "What do you mean, *it* will bring me to *them*? What fucking *it*?"

"Hell," he shouts back, aware that he is on the cusp of receiving another blow from Judas. "Hell will bring you to her gates. She is a living, breathing entity. She is Lucifer's bride, his mistress, his lover. He has given himself to her and that is how he commands her at will. Hell *is* alive, but you must know how to manipulate her if you wish to make your way through. Now please, do as I ask."

Judas lets go of him, but with an aggressive shunt that causes Azazel's head to bounce off the ground. "You'd best be right about this, or so help me—"

"Trust me, master. I have nothing but your best intentions at heart." There's a forlorn cast to the demon's gaze, partially hiding behind a hand raised in front of his face.

Judas stares at him for a moment then turns toward Charlotte. "We do as it says. We will have to trust… it." He glances down at Azazel, now getting to his feet, then back to Charlotte. "You ready?"

She nods, an uncertainty about the action.

"Okay. Get set."

He takes a deep breath and grabs her hand.

Before he sets off Charlotte turns toward Azazel.

"You're not fooling anyone you know. You're messing with us. One slip and I will send you back into the pit myself."

As she turns around, Azazel's smirk slowly unfurls into a grin.

Gripping her hand tighter, Judas counts to three and darts off with Azazel sprinting after them.

They race through medieval streets, turning and twisting, changing direction left and then right, unsure of where they are headed as wooden doors stream past. They pass street after street, and the area appears to close in and oppress them as they struggle to find an exit in the endless cycle that grows ever more disorientating.

Judas is the first to lose control.

"This is fucking pointless. It's not fucking working," he screams out loud, his frustrations boiling to the surface as he continues to drag Charlotte along, his gaze flitting from one point to the next.

"Patience, master," Azazel reassures, "all will reveal itself in good time. Channel your aggression, let it drive you forward, let it feed you. Bend this place to your will."

"What the fuck are you talking about?" he shouts, his anger growing. "You said to run aimlessly then focus on where we needed to be, and it would happen. WELL, NOTHING'S FUCKING HAPPENING!" His anger peaks, and forgetting that Azazel is in his human guise, he refers to him by his conquered name. "Ikazuchi, tell me what the fuck is going on?"

Judas is losing control.

"Just a little more, master. Just a little further," Azazel says, urging him on.

Pestilence's voice sounds inside Charlotte's head. *This is wrong. Something feels wrong.*

She agrees. She knows it. Seeing Judas like this, his teeth gritted so tight it looks as though they might shatter, his hand wrapped around hers with such force it now hurts, his breathing fast and shallow, and she becomes seriously concerned for him.

"Stop this," she cries out, attempting to bring him to a halt, to stop the panicked rush through Port Dominion's streets. "We need to stop this!"

But it is too late.

Judas comes to a halt and releases her hand while screaming into thin air, as though at someone or something. But nothing can be seen where his maddening eyes are glaring. Around him a vicious wind whips up, as it would in the early stages of a tornado. Small at first but gathering speed, force, and momentum. It encircles him and grows, its magnitude expanding, collecting dust and dirt as it spins around and he continues to scream into it, his face demented and insane. Having ceased gritting his teeth, his mouth is now open and stretched into a sick smile, and his hands are planted on the side of his head, fingers outstretched but bent slightly as though they could tear and claw at the skin on his face at any second. His screaming changes into an insane laugh, rising in intensity, and all the while Azazel screams at him, encouraging him to further let go, to channel his rage, his violence, his darkness.

Charlotte shields her face from the cyclonic frenzy, while at the same time the fierce wind causes her to lose her footing, pushing and moving her further away from him, giving her the distinct impression that the anomaly is designed to separate them. She draws her swords and slams them into the earth to create anchors to prevent herself sliding any further as the tornado's force peaks and she feels her feet rising off the ground. She is running out of time to stop this and without knowing what is causing this sudden burst of violent energy from Judas or why, she realizes she must do all she can to put a stop to it; to bring him down and back to her.

Pestilence's voice once again affirms her own thoughts. *Stop this. You must stop this, NOW!*

Before her feet leave the ground entirely, she closes her eyes and focuses, drawing upon her Divinity and then allowing it to wrap around that of Pestilence's dark energy, intertwining with and strengthening it. She opens her eyes and they glow, not white but somewhere between that and darkness, a shimmering grayish-silver, splattered with tiny beads of light within, their formation such that they could resemble a distant galaxy. She cries out, and an enormous burst of energy explodes from her, destroying the cyclone and dropping her down to the ground where she lands on her feet.

Ceasing his sardonic laughing, Judas falls forward onto his hands and knees, his chest heaving.

Retrieving her swords from out of the ground with a small grunt, she casts them to the sides where they mystically twirl in the air and then slide themselves back into their inverted scabbards on her back, then runs toward Judas, skidding to her knees at his side and wrapping her arms around him, pushing her face close to his. "Dad! Dad, are you okay?"

He continues to look down at the ground and his breathing slows, returning to normal, while spittle dangles from his mouth.

She repeats her question, then asks if he can stand while placing an arm under his and guiding him to his feet. He looks dazed; not himself, as though unaware of his surroundings. "What have you done to him you fucking monster?" she screams at Azazel.

"Me?" he says, eyes wide, mouth open, and a hand upon his chest. "I have done nothing. He did it all. I merely guided his rage to the place it needed to be to bring us… well, here." He motions to his right with a sweep of his hand.

Her sight follows the flow of his gesture and her eyes widen, seeing that they are no longer amid the medieval wooden huts, but instead in a canyon, and that they are around 300 feet away from a gargantuan demon who is knelt within a rock wall that stretches up far beyond the reach of the human eye. The creature's back is embedded into the rock face, its blistered skin almost transparent with every vein and piece of muscle and sinew visible. Between its legs swirls a maelstrom of dark energy – the gate into the heart of Hell itself. From out of the side of its hairless body protrude six arms, with four of them dedicated to grabbing as many of the damned and tortured as he can, lined up in front of him to be thrust between his legs and into the portal, each into

50

their own personal Hell, where they will spend a terrifying eternity. His other two arms scoop up more terrified bodies, tossing them into his mouth, as though engorging on a buffet where manners are not required. And as she stares at the creature feasting upon the damned, she realizes that it is blind, a mottled blindfold covering its eyes and she wonders if it ever possessed eyes upon its chalky white face. Despite the carnage, it is Judas' voice that startles her away from the scene.

"So… this is the gate to Hell then is it?"

"Oh my God, are you okay?" she says, her hands racing to the sides of his face, cupping it. "I thought I'd lost you."

His puzzled expression causes more dread to rise within her.

"What happened?" she asks, with a deep frown.

"I don't understand what you mean?" he says, shaking his head.

His response startles her. "You can't be serious?" Her eyes widen. "Just then, losing it? The screaming?"

Again he shakes his head.

"Are you telling me you don't remember going bat-shit crazy and creating the tornado from Oz?"

"What?" he says, narrowing his eyes and glancing between her and Azazel. "The hell are you talking about? We were running and running and then we turned a corner and ended up… here?" He motions around them.

"No, that is not what happened." She turns toward Azazel. "What the fuck have you done to him? What just happened?"

Azazel leans his head to the side a little and shakes it, while raising his hands, his mouth screwing up in the process.

The sarcastic expression is not lost on Charlotte and she advances toward him, snapping a hand to her side where one of her swords releases from its scabbard and flies into it.

Azazel takes a step back.

"Tell me or so help me God I will take off your bastard head."

Finding his defiance, Azazel steps back up to her, his face contorted into a snarl.

Judas inserts himself between them. "Hey, *hey!* I believe you sweetie, I do. Honestly. But we need to deal with that first and him second." He motions toward the Gatekeeper with his head and then Azazel.

Ahead, the Gatekeeper ceases his dining and turns his sightless gaze upon them. He speaks, his speech slow and labored, a deep boom to it. "Ahh, how honored I am to have such distinguished guests. Although I am surprised to find the infamous Judas Iscariot walking into Hell, and not being dragged in by his feet as Lucifer once promised."

The Gatekeeper roars a laugh, one that follows the same pace as his monotonous talking.

Charlotte glances at Judas, separating herself from Azazel's snarling glare, and then adjusting her clothing, she strides a few paces toward the Gatekeeper.

"And look who we have here," the giant demon continues, "Heaven's own little darling. The child who changed her... destiny."

Another booming laugh.

She frowns, her eyes narrowing. "What do you mean by that?" She looks at Judas. "What does he mean by that?"

Judas steps forward to her side. "Nothing sweetie. Like everything down here, he's full of shit."

The Gatekeeper bellows another laugh and then focuses upon Azazel.

"And you have the Architect with you also. How fascinating. Fascinating and yet queer. It is a truly strange day when the mighty Azazel stands at my gate."

Now it is Judas' turn to look confused. He edges his gaze toward Azazel. "And what does he mean by *that?*"

Azazel glances at Judas and snorts a small laugh. "Ignore it, master. Damn thing's been here that long it hasn't a clue of what it speaks." His head turns toward Judas. "I mean, are we to listen to its ramblings of destinies or shall we just kill it?" A wry smile spreads across his face.

Judas refocuses his attention back on the Gatekeeper, his action noticeable by Charlotte as one of shrugging off and dodging Azazel's question.

She glances at the two men. "Something's going on here and we will talk about it later. But first…" She strides forward and holds out her other hand forcing the remaining sheathed Sword of Destiny into it.

Before she can get away from them, Azazel reaches out and grabs her by the arm, an action that garners a stern reaction from her causing him to let go and hold up his hands. "Look, just wait."

"For what!"

"For the realization to hit you that you cannot kill him."

"Watch me," she says, turning back around.

"No. I mean, I know you can," he says, stopping her from moving once again. "But you must not if we are to have any chance of getting through that gate."

"He's right," Judas says, stepping up to and standing next to her. "I have to kill him while Azazel is Ikazuchi. While he is my sword. We have the power of Leviathan, Azazel's brother, remember, and with it we absorb the energy and knowledge of anything we kill. That way I will be able to understand how to unlock the gate and let us pass through."

"Besides," Azazel says with a sly grin, "you will have enough to worry about without fighting the big guy."

Before she can answer, the Gatekeeper laughs once again causing them to look to his direction. "So, a fight then! Good! I haven't had one of those in a Mazorakor's age."

She glances at Judas while frowning, cocking her mouth to one side, and in return he frowns and shrugs his shoulders. Neither have a clue as to what the Gatekeeper is referring to.

In a surprising turn of events, and catching everyone off guard, the Gatekeeper sprints out of the wall in which he had been partially embedded, his gigantic feet thundering across the barren ground and comes to a sliding halt around 50 feet in front of them, spraying up dust and dirt into a massive cloud, forcing them to turn their heads and shield their eyes. As the dust clears, he spreads his six arms wide and roars while moving his head from side to side, and from out of his mouth cascades the dead, dozens of them, hitting the ground with sickening, unceremonious thuds, causing some of their diseased bodies to burst open. From where they land, they rise to their feet without the use of their arms, some with their bodies bent almost double at their lower backs, their heads arcing up almost from their ankles. The action is slow and grotesque.

Charlotte shudders. "Now that is fucking creepy."

Judas looks at her and half-smiles. "You take the adds, I'll take the boss."

She returns the gesture, adding a nod at the end and then motion-blurs ahead into her assigned enemies where she starts to cut them down.

Seeing how quick she dispatches her foes, the Gatekeeper spews forth another batch of dead, only this time their numbers stretch into the hundreds.

It is now Judas' turn to attack. He looks at Azazel, nods, and then motion-blurs ahead.

Despite his massive size, the Gatekeeper is fast, incredibly so, and he launches all six of his fists at Judas punching them into the ground. Motion-blurring and weaving in between them, Judas avoids the earth-shattering attacks until one is too fast for him and lands close, catapulting him upward, the dusty surface around him splintering and exploding from the force. He spins through the air and spreads his wings, which have been turning blacker since he conquered Azazel. The Thŭramré may prevent him from flight and from using his portal ability but it does not stop him from utilizing his wings as an air break and he thrusts them forward to halt his airborne tumble and then spreads them wide again to glide to his target. Holding out his right hand he calls to his sword. "Now Ikazuchi!"

Azazel bursts forward from where Judas left him, with a motion-blur effect of his own and leaps into the air, twisting while crossing his arms across his chest. He transforms into the demon sword and lands in Judas' hand.

With a roar, Judas drags his sword arm from back to front, and brings the might of his attack to bear on the top of the Gatekeepers head.

The devastating blow cracks a small part of the Demon Lord's skull and the force sends him reeling backward with all six arms flailing as he topples to the ground.

While the Gatekeeper receives Judas' hammer blow, Charlotte cuts down what feels like her 200th walking corpse, but for every bit she cuts off her demonic foes, another corpse generates out of the detached piece, bubbling into existence at a rapid rate and scrambling toward her, sometimes while in the throes of transformation, their arms and legs circling their bodies unnaturally, moving the creatures toward her at high speed.

To not allow them to swarm her, Charlotte increases her movement and zips between them, almost like a beam of light tearing into each one, her swords impossible to follow even by a demonic eye as she moves at an inhuman speed through the ever-increasing numbers of the dead. She understands her role is to keep them busy while Judas dispatches the Gatekeeper, but she is acutely aware that she is running out of time and if she doesn't thin their numbers fast, they might overrun her and force her to expel more energy than she can spare. And that would not be a good thing as she wishes to retain as much Divine power as possible for the traverse across Hell.

But there are so damn many of them.

Nothing for it, she will have to deal with them now.

Skidding to a halt in the middle of the demonic horde, she slams both swords into the ground and brings her hands together at their fingertips in front of her body. Closing her eyes, she inhales deeply and calls upon as much Divinity as she can muster, and between her hands a powerful ball of energy forms. She moves them further apart and the pure white lightning ball increases in size and mass, much like the one she created outside of the US Bank when she first materialized back into Earth's time at the age of 18. That was just over a week ago, and the rate in which she now forms the energy weapon within her hands is testament to how far her powers have grown since then.

The ball lights up her face and causes her hair to whip around it as it crackles and fizzes within her hands, and now the size of a basketball she grits her teeth and digs her fingers into it, ripping it apart as masses of demons swarm her. She raises her face upward and screams as it explodes, incinerating the creatures before they can lay a hand upon her.

An explosion of Divine energy causes Judas to glance to his left, just as the Gatekeeper crashes into the ground beneath him, and he smiles for a fraction of a second before refocusing his attention upon the sprawling demon boss, whom he is falling onto.

But before he can land upon him, the Gatekeeper lashes out and catches Judas with a devastating backhand that catapults him into the rock wall close to where he himself resided, half-buried, moments earlier, the force of the swipe embedding the angel into the rock as it splinters and cracks around him.

Wasting no time, Judas drags himself out of the crater, but much to his amazement the Gatekeeper has already gotten to his feet and is thundering across the 200-foot gap between them, and before he can fully peel himself out of the wall, the demon slams a palmed hand into him, pushing him further back into the rock, then repeats the action, again and again, forcing him deeper and deeper into the wall.

Eventually, the demon stops, reaches in, and takes hold of Judas. He pulls him out and drags him toward his blindfold, and what would have been his eye line if he had ever possessed the power of sight.

Struggling within the Gatekeepers grip, Judas groans as the demon tightens his fist around him and, staring into his blank face, he now sees that it is burned and scarred having caught some of Charlotte's Divinity blast moments earlier. The Gatekeeper snarls at him, baring thousands of razor-sharp teeth.

"Her pathetic attacks are no match for me. These wounds will quickly heal, and you will be dead even sooner than that, rotting within my belly like the putrid shit that you are."

Judas laughs, although the action is made difficult by the crushing force surrounding his body. "Stupid fucking demon. She wasn't meaning to kill you. Believe me, if she had tried, we would not be having this conversation."

The Gatekeeper roars with laughter. "Is that so? Wretched creature."

A sudden, biting pain in his stomach causes Judas to screw up his face and grit his teeth, and he breaths in deep and closes his eyes. He feels something stir from within him without his permission, a power he did not wish to call upon and one that does not belong to him, yet there it is – attached, like a limpet. It circles and intensifies, building from his core, stretching out all over him. The power of his defeated Horseman, Lady Famine. Yet unlike that of Charlotte's contained entity, this one does not play well with others and it refuses to form a symbiotic relationship with its host. It spreads out from and over him like a rot, a particularly vicious cancer, and it seeps into the Gatekeepers fingers and, in turn, his hand causing it to shrivel and wither like a dead plant.

The Gatekeeper shrieks and releases him, the angel falling to the ground with a thud.

As the last remnants of the attacking demons flutter to the ground around her like snow, Charlotte casts an eye toward Judas as he hits the ground on his back, and concern grips her as she witnesses a diseased energy spread over his body. Wasting no time, she motion-blurs to him while charging her hand with pure Divinity then slams it against his body. "Oh no you don't, you bitch," she calls out as her holy light chases the demonic rot back into him and he sits bolt upright with a sharp intake of breath.

He stares into her face, confused. How had he let Famine get the better of him? How had that been possible? He shakes his head, willing his senses back into action. Ahead, he sees the Gatekeeper writhing in agony on the floor, Lady Famine's disease threatening to engulf him.

"Not like this," Charlotte says, glancing toward the demon and then back at Judas, "he cannot die like this or we will not get in."

He looks at her for a moment, not quite understanding what she is saying to him.

"DAD!" she screams, "are you listening? You can't let her disease kill him. You must strike him through with Ikazuchi. Remember?"

He looks to the ground for a second and then back at her, startled. Finally, understanding returns and he scrambles to his feet and holds out his hand, Ikazuchi clanking across the ground and then streaking into it once more. Gritting his teeth again, he motion-blurs toward the Gatekeeper and leaps into the air, his face focused into a grimace of power and might, Ikazuchi held aloft in both hands, then drives the demon sword down toward the wailing demon as the creature flails around on bended knee, clawing and tearing at its skin that blisters and boils. The devastating weapon slams into his skull, splitting it open and Judas powers through and into the Gatekeepers head, into his brain and the demon screams with countless others melding with it into a dreadful cacophony of suffering.

The Gatekeeper rakes at the side of his head, and thrashes it from side to side, spraying dark, viscous liquid out of the wound and onto the ground in large puddles. He screams again and again, a continuous roar, and scrambles to his feet, all the while scratching at the side of his face. Out of control, he runs toward the rock face and head-butts it with as much force as he can muster and the blow stuns him, bouncing him back off it, staggering, and the screaming ceases.

Judas erupts from out of his head, somersaulting and spreading his black wings, gliding to the ground then walking away from the Gatekeeper as he falls forward onto his face. The very instant he hits the ground, his body spasms violently, causing Judas to turn around and prepare himself for more battle. But the demon is dead. He can see that much is certain, even though his body continues to jerk and writhe on the floor. Eventually, the spasms cease with one last convulsion.

Judas looks toward Charlotte who stares back at him with a blank expression.

Without warning and causing them both to jump and snap their attention toward it, the Gatekeeper's corpse slides toward its original place in the wall at great speed and slams into the rock with such force it causes the body to splatter.

Within Judas' hand Ikazuchi vibrates, the action growing ever more violent and with greater intensity as each second passes, and he must place both hands around it to hold on as the kinetic energy transfers into him. Then, a glow envelops the sword, a dirty yellow color and he feels a strange energy pulse from it and work its way into and up his arm, and not knowing why, he lets out a fearsome scream and points his sword toward the splattered remains of the Gatekeeper. From out of the weapon, a dark yellow beam erupts and explodes onto the ruined corpse and as Judas continues to scream, the beam draws the body back together, circling it within the rock. It swirls like a whirlpool, dark and foreboding, growing in speed and intensity, and then as quickly as it had appeared the beam of light blinks out, and Judas stumbles forward a few steps and then bends over double, his breathing heavy with his hands upon his knees.

Ahead, the swirling mass that was once the Gatekeeper's body erupts with a low-yield explosion that sprays outward to a point and then sucks back into itself, settling into a gently revolving black mass portal.

Judas looks up at Charlotte as she joins him at his side. "Piece of piss," he says with a grin.

Charlotte laughs and shakes her head.

SEVEN

Striding into his war chambers and greeting his Generals, Lucifer's mood is cheery and his demeanor confident, pompous almost. Gone for now is his true demon form that he had remained in following his defeat at the hands of seven-year-old Charlotte in the New Mexico desert a little over two years ago, and in its place is his human guise of the well-dressed, chirpy British fellow.

Today, he has much cause to feel jubilant and is lifted by the notion that his plan is finally taking root and moving in the direction he had first intended. Sure, there had been a hiccup or two along the way; Masakai and Kento's awful handling of the initial extraction of Charlotte; her first Awakening event happening earlier than he had intended thereby allowing her to sneak up and deal with him during the desert encounter; Judas conquering the demon sword Azazel (an event that was most unexpected); and him subsequently dispatching Barachiel (again, unexpected). There was also the loss of two of the Four Horsemen to Iscariot and the Jew bitch who have really made a habit of being irksome, but all in all the right result seems likely to prevail in the end. True, he still doesn't possess the Seventh Seal, the final piece of the puzzle required to unlock The Book, nor that item itself, the relic that will make him all-powerful to allow him to finally begin his reign upon the Kingdom of Man and facilitate his assault on The White Kingdom, but that's irrelevant as everything is now in hand given that Iscariot and the girl are moving to exactly where he wants them to be. Yes, today Lucifer is beside himself with delight and it is written all over his face, a face that still bears the outline of Charlotte's hand prints and a mark no demon in Hell dare mention in their master's company. He claps his hands together as he approaches his counsel.

"Hello and good day to you all. And what a fine time it is too." He beams a smile, moving toward them as they stand on his side of a large, oval oak table, around 20 feet in length, twisted and macabre in design with the table's skirt formed from the carvings of hundreds of souls in various depictions of torture or being devoured by demons. On closer inspection one would see that it is a living, breathing piece of art, the damned writing and thrashing being actual living entities within the cruel and murderous design.

Around the vast and darkened hall stand various works, all with a slant to the dead and the demonic and dotted amongst them all manner of weapons and armors from every corner of man's history. On the other side of the table to Lucifer's approach sits a huge, decorative fireplace within an enormous wall and above it hangs a grandiose painting depicting Louis Boulanger's 'The Round of the Sabbath,' one of Lucifer's favorite pieces. He notices Samael admiring it as he approaches.

"Marvelous, isn't it brother? That Boulanger really knew how to capture the romanticism of a subject and show the beauty within its horror, don't you think? Shame his popularity in his time never reached any significant height, but the same can be said of many artists we hold dear today."

Samael, the former Archangel but now with his transformation to demon complete, looks at Lucifer for a moment and then turns his attention back to the work of art. "Personally, I prefer Thomas

Stothard as he seemed to like painting you in tights." His voice is deep and resonant, and he glances back at Lucifer with his eyes mischievous and full of sarcasm.

Lucifer bellows a laugh and holds out a hand to greet Samael and he takes it, the two exchanging a firm handshake.

Samael may be a new addition to the high ranks of the demonic but none in the room and few others in Hell would ever look or talk down on him. During his time as an Archangel, he was one of the fiercest warriors the realms had ever borne witness to and his transference to demon had done nothing to undermine that. In fact, the very opposite – it is probable that Samael is now the deadliest and most revered of all Lucifer's Generals, even that of Malphas who stands beside the recently fallen angel.

Lucifer smiles. "Brother, *dear* brother. How wonderful it is to finally have you among our ranks. And look at you." He takes a step back to admire him. "You look more like I should to the humans than I ever could. The large, black sweeping horns, the terrible clawed hands, and not to mention your wonderful muscular red body."

Samael glances down at himself. "I would say it is more garnet than red, but I can't say I dislike it. Anything is better than endless white. Fucking white… everything fucking white. I was sick of it. And His bullshit."

Lucifer laughs again. "I am sure you were, my friend, as were we all. Although I was certain you would have followed me during the days of the rebellion." He ponders for a moment. "Alas that is behind us now and you are with us at last. Oh, and thank you for the gift." Lucifer motions toward the Sixth Seal upon the oak table, sat next to the Fifth. "I trust you had little trouble obtaining it?"

Samael grunts and smirks. "Candy from a baby."

Lucifer grins back at him for a moment and then turns to his other Generals who, unlike Samael, have decided to adopt their human guises in line with Lucifer, and he greets them each with a handshake. First and to his left is Lord Malphas, the highest ranked General in his army and the demon responsible for gathering most of The Seals together that allowed Lucifer to summon forth The Four Horsemen. Next and to his right is Lord Astaroth, the Commander of The Infernal – Lucifer's Special Forces and espionage division. Next to receive his greeting are the Demon Lords Oriens and Amaymon, the Commanders of the heavy demons and winged contingent respectively.

He then shakes the hand of Asmodeus, the Commander of The Defile, Lucifer's elite guard and Hellwatch's direct equivalent. Finally, Lucifer looks toward the Horsemen War and Death, stood further down the room away from the table, and raises a hand in greeting.

"And welcome to you, auspicious guests, the remaining Apocalyptians," he glances toward Samael, "is that a word? It feels like it should be a word."

Samael raises his eyebrows and shrugs his shoulders just a tiny amount, suggesting he neither knows nor cares.

Cocking his head to one side slightly and scrunching up his mouth, Lucifer turns back toward the Horsemen. "I hope you two will fare better against our prey than your brethren did?"

Death says nothing, hunkered down, his elbows on his knees, his gaze focused upon Lucifer, his golden glowing eyes set in a slate-gray mask.

Lucifer makes a show of shuddering. "Chilling indeed, Master Death." He smiles.

War's voice causes Lucifer and the rooms other occupants to pause and listen.

"You should not underestimate Iscariot and The Light. We did not, and yet they still proved to be… difficult."

Lucifer throws his hands into the air. "Oh, my friend. I fully intend to not underestimate them. I have done so before to my own detriment. Which is why I am taking a decent contingent along with me this time, and you two are to be my crowning weapons – the very tip of the spear." He turns and picks up the Fifth and Sixth Seals, then half-stands, half-sits against the table, facing his subordinates once more, all of whom reposition themselves so that they are stood in front of him. "My friends, it is time. Iscariot and the girl have defeated the Gatekeeper as expected and have now entered Hell. There is to be no personalized experience for them, they will see the realm as it truly is, and since they have Azazel with them…"

The Generals shift in front of him and groan lightly.

"…I know, I know," Lucifer says, while patting the air with his hands, "but since the Architect is with them, he will know which down-gates to approach to get them to the temple in the fastest time. I would like to be there ready for them when they arrive, something I am sure Iscariot will anticipate, so therefore let us portal down and get ourselves set for the beginning of our glorious victory."

His Generals shift in their standing positions again but this time there are no groans, instead only grunts of agreement.

All except one, Malphas, who raises a hand. "My Lord!"

"Yes Malphas, what is it?"

"Well, and I am sure I mentioned this, but while we are in possession of The Seals, portals seem to be… problematic, even here due to the bizarre holy energy they possess. It is why I had to walk the land when I first brought them to you."

Lucifer looks taken aback, but then adopts a wry smile. "Malphas. Brother. I am the mother fucking King of Hell, Seals will not prevent me from going where I desire."

Bowing a little, Malphas edges back as Lucifer strides past him.

Thrusting his hand forward and then clenching it into a fist, Lucifer summons a dark portal, one that explodes into life, swirling, crackling, and fizzing and then as fast as it appeared it disappears, causing Lucifer to purse his lips together and frown. Drawing in a deep and agitated breath, he repeats the action and gets the same result. He tries one last time, and again the same outcome. He blows out, hard, rippling his lips in the process. "Well… fuck it."

Samael laughs.

Lucifer turns to face his men once more. "Fucking fuck it. Looks like we are on foot boys."

Lord Astaroth steps forward. "In that case, my Lord, I will deploy Infernal Agents to intercept Iscariot and the girl."

Lucifer dismisses his suggestion with a wave of his hand without looking at Astaroth. "No, no, that won't be necessary. I will close the down-gates and leave open only one." He ponders for a moment. "Hmmm, the one close to The Well of Souls will be perfect I think."

"Why that one, Master?" Lord Oriens says, moving a little closer to him.

"Because I have a feeling that once she is there, the little bitch will want to try to retrieve an old friend. And that way, I get to fuck with her all over again." He laughs briefly at the thought.

Looking around at his compatriots, Lord Oriens raises his arms a little, "but Master, shouldn't we just descend on them now, take the Seventh Seal and The Book and be done with all this?"

A ripple of agreement circulates among the Generals.

Lucifer walks over to Oriens. "You just don't get it, do you Scott?"

Oriens looks around at the others once more, his frown deeper than ever.

Lucifer sighs and shakes his head. "Never mind, it's… it's a Dr. Evil thing." He breathes out hard through his nose. "Iscariot would get it."

Oriens glances toward Asmodeus and his mouth forms a puzzled smile.

Lucifer places his hands on his shoulders. "Thing is mate, I cannot do anything to them outside of the Temple. I must extract The Seal and The Book while she is in the Circle of Belial, right in the heart of the Temple. Apparently, it's the fucking rules." He sighs again. "Despite everything that I know, and for some reason, there are rules, always there are rules, processes, procedures. It's that dickhead above and his weird sense of humor," he motions upward with his eyes, "fucking pisses me right off. But the bottom line is we cannot extract the relics from her unless she is compromised under the sign of Belial. Fucked up, I know, but thems the rules. Once that happens, however, I will be able to unlock The Book using the last three Seals and we go to work." He smiles. "Besides, I'm having fun," he looks around at the others. "Are you not having fun?"

They gesture in different ways, ranging from agreement to bewilderment.

"This is a once in a lifetime experience for them, lads, so shouldn't we allow Iscariot and Charlotte to enjoy themselves a bit?" He smiles once more. "Lord Astaroth?"

"Yes, my Lord?" comes his swift reply.

"Close all down-gates with the exception of the one near the Well." He clicks his fingers. "Oh, and also the one by Dermigons Fountain, we will use that one ourselves."

Astaroth nods and takes his leave.

"Lord Asmodeus?"

Asmodeus walks over to Lucifer.

"My friend, I have a special mission for you."

"My Lord!"

"There is a particularly annoying person on Earth that I wish you to remove for me, a professor. He is about to make a discovery that would reveal certain... facts, and I would rather that information were not made public for now at least. It might ruin a surprise I have in store and I don't want to take *any* chances this time." He grins. "So, be a dear and have The Defile rip the cunt apart for me, would you?"

"Of course, my Lord."

Asmodeus turns and starts to leave, but Lucifer stops him. "Actually, on second thoughts wait until he makes the discovery. By all means toy with him first, but I would like him to have found the information but be unable to pass it on, and for him to know his life's work was all for naught as he is torn limb from limb." Lucifer grins, an unnerving one even for the Lords of Hell. "Oh, and when you're finished take the boys to Canada and be done once and for all with that fucking Gary and his crew. In fact, take the new boy with you. I have a feeling he will prove to be most useful."

It is now Asmodeus' turn to smile, albeit one not as intense as Lucifer's a moment ago. "My Lord, it shall be done." He bows and walks away.

Lucifer turns to face Oriens and Amaymon. "Assemble a force to move through Hell with us, nothing too large but enough to ensure victory – especially in case any of the sub-level Lords get any funny ideas. I really don't have time for their rebellious shit right now."

"Yes master." They reply almost in unison, each with a nod of their head and then stride off to carry out their tasks. They then stop and turn to face him as he clicks his fingers.

"But guys, put the word out: I do not want any interference from the usual suspects. We need a united front on this one and the bullshit needs to end... for now at least. The girl and Iscariot must make it to the Temple. By all means they can make it difficult for them and... well, interesting," he grins, "but make sure the Lords know they need to toe the line this time, especially that big bastard." He winks, and the Generals smile slightly and nod, then continue off in the direction they were headed.

Malphas sidles up to Lucifer. "You think Cthulhu will give you problems, my Lord?"

Lucifer glances at him. "He'd better not. I'm in no mood for him. No matter how big he thinks he is he will taste the wrong end of an arse kicking if he gets up to any shenanigans." Lucifer glances at him once more, "Good work on this one, Malphas. You really came through."

Malphas smiles a little and transforms into his demon form, his dragon-like features still displaying remnants of the smile. "It was an honor, my Lord. Your time has truly come."

Lucifer places his hands on his shoulders. "That it has my friend, and you will be right there with me when it happens."

Malphas nods, glances toward Samael with a wry smile, and then walks out of the chamber.

Pushing himself away from the table he had been leaning against, Samael moves to Lucifer's side, his gaze fixed ahead and not on him. "That one is weak. He has used others to manipulate his position and is not worthy enough to be your High Commander."

Lucifer's gaze remains fixed upon the departing Malphas. "And you think you are?"

"The fuck do you think?!"

Lucifer glances toward Samael with a smile. "But Malphas has been my most trusted General for a very long time and has won many battles for me."

Samael scoffs. "Yeah, against fucking humans and shit demons, never against anything that would truly test him like, say, Iscariot for instance." He glances at Lucifer. "Got his ass handed to him by Judas at the airbase, didn't he?"

Lucifer ponders for a moment and then smiles a little. "Do what you will, but only when this is over and done with. Understood?"

Samael grins.

Lucifer smiles broadly and takes a deep breath, then exhales it through his nose. "It really is good to finally have you here, brother."

Samael offers him a dutiful nod.

Patting Samael's shoulder, Lucifer then clicks his fingers at War and Death, summoning them and walks around the table toward the fireplace, all the while staring at the painting above it.

EIGHT

Ibrahim Yali rubs his tired old Turkish eyes with a thumb and forefinger, then puts his bi-focal spectacles back on the bridge of his nose. It's been a long day. A very long day. He sighs, then taps the open page of the large book sitting in front of him. "Come on, Ibi," he tells himself, "just one more chapter, I'm sure it's here somewhere."

Ibrahim, or Ibi as he is known to those closest to him, has spent the last two and a half years holed up within a secure compound inside Angkor Wat, the temple complex deep within Cambodia and the world's largest religious monument. A month prior to the Collapse, he had travelled to the ancient site to study a new find beneath the complex – part of an expansive and lost city that some of his colleagues had believed to be part of the largest empire on Earth if their findings were to be proven correct. His position as Hershey Professor of Buddhist Studies at Harvard Divinity School meant he was near the top of the list of people invited to study the site and he had been delighted to have been selected as a member of the lead team of researchers. The research had been expected to take years, but Ibi hadn't given the invitation a second thought. His work had been his life and unfortunately, like many dedicated to their career, his passion had grown inside him like a cancer, a disease that had eaten away at everything other than his physical form – his marriage, his relationship with his children, everything. And so when he got the call he went without a moment's hesitation, because that is what Ibrahim Yali did. But his extensive research into the site was not to go as he, or anyone else for that matter, had planned.

During an early evening meal following a long and fruitful day of discovery, many of the people present within the camp – researchers, archeologists, parts of the security detail – began to feel strange and unwell. Before long, the horrifying reality of the apocalyptic events presented themselves to those unaffected by Lucifer's will and so the Taken sprang forth and proceeded to tear everyone to pieces, limb from limb, without hesitation or mercy. At first, Ibi was stunned into a terrifying paralysis, unable to move, to only observe as the horror unfolded before him. It was Jerry Conroy, a former US Army Sergeant and head of site security that snapped him out of his trance, screaming into his face to move as he unleashed fury from his automatic rifle into one of the blood-lusting creatures. With Jerry and a handful of the dig team, plus several of the Cambodian staff's help, they had managed to fight their way into the main complex of Angkor Wat and secure an inner chamber from the rampaging horde outside. Following a couple of days of what was thought to be no activity from outside, and the fact the chamber had begun to become unbearable from the stench of urine and feces, Jerry had made his way outside to assess the situation. The scene that greeted him was something that would be burned into his psyche for the rest of his life. And Jerry had been no stranger to death and destruction with tours of Iraq and Afghanistan under his belt.

So after a thorough investigation, Jerry had given the all clear and the survivors had set about scavenging and securing the area to plan their next move. It had been during one of their searches that Ibi had accessed a radio in one of the camps, and as fortune would have it they had caught the broadcast of a message from another site further up country, although many had wished they had not as prior to the battery finally giving up, the team had learned enough to know that attempting to move into a city to seek help and rescue would have been pointless. The team member on the other end had told them that the event had been global – it was the end of the world and that he had seen demons and monsters roaming, hunting, and killing. He had advised them to stay where they were, as their remote location in the temple near the city of Siem Reap would most likely serve them longer in their chances of survival. Of course, not all within the survivors group had taken kindly to the suggestion and had left the site to attempt to return home, to search for loved ones. But not Ibi and not Jerry. For as unalike as they were in their chosen fields of expertise, they shared great similarities in terms of life choices and dedication to their jobs, and so they stayed, Jerry putting his decision in the bluntest of terms: "who the fuck have I got to go back to!" But Ibi's had been more out of the sense that he didn't know where his children or ex-wife were and any attempt to find them would be pointless. And so they made the best they could of a hopeless situation, Jerry putting his survival skills to great use, along with the two Cambodian members who had remained, and then with everyone's help they secured the central complex into a fortifiable place of refuge.

A few months into their new home, Ibi had called a meeting and stated his desire to get back to his work of studying the ruins beneath the complex. Of course, Jerry had protested a great deal, but in the end he conceded that death could come at any time, and that the team might as well keep busy with what they loved doing while they wait for it – a rare outbreak of humor from Jerry that had made Ibi chuckle a great deal. And so Ibi had set about his work once again, the call of his passion proving much too difficult to ignore and it was on an excavation into one of the deep catacomb tunnels that he had made an incredible discovery. Like many important finds, this one had been out of pure luck. An untied shoelace, a foot raised up onto a jut of rock, a push too hard to return to a standing position, and a collapsing wall. The hole created by the small cave-in had revealed a large room on the other side, containing candles that somehow had remained lit, a sight that had both intrigued and frightened Ibi and Jerry in equal measures.

Within the chamber, which was pristine in its presentation, sat a vast library of large, gold-leafed books on huge wooden shelves. Upon opening and inspecting one of them, Ibi discovered a language that he was unfamiliar with, told in pictures but with symbols that he could not interpret. The text had a style of presentation similar to hieroglyphics, but with detailed pictures sat within them, with smaller symbols that arced all around the drawings and when he ran his fingers over them, he felt a mixture of euphoria and revulsion that caused him to drop the book. Upon picking it up and reading the spine, it read in gold leaf 'Barachiel' with a series of symbols next to it that Ibi's keen sense and formal training told him was a numbering system.

Unwittingly, they had found the Library of Barachiel within one of his old strongholds; one that he had never felt the need to shield from human eyes in the same way he had Castle Corvin, the site of his battle with Judas where he and Azazel defeated Barachiel and Azazel's brother, the second of three demon swords known as Leviathan.

The find had instilled a deeper desire for knowledge the likes of which Ibi had never experienced before, and so he set about ensuring the room was secure, then began cataloguing the archive as best he could. His progress was slow at first, but gained momentum as he put his competent code-breaking skills to the test and began to work out patterns, enough to put certain books into order. His studies had been relentless, exhausting.

And six months ago, after almost two years of hard work, he had made a breakthrough, a small understanding of the basics of the language, and since that time he had been translating the text at a furious rate as though his life depended on it. He couldn't explain it, but he knew he had to get through the knowledge, to understand what it meant, that something very important hinged on his discovery. From what he had been able to decipher, he had come to understand that he was within a library created by an Archangel named Barachiel and that the divine entity had been entrusted with holy relics of enormous importance. Through much intelligent guesswork, Ibi had concluded that he had been entrusted with Seven Seals and The Book. Despite understanding what the first four Seals were for, he had been unable to determine the purpose of the remaining three, nor the importance of The Book. And that had been his passion for the last couple of months – trying to determine the meaning of the last four relics.

And it is that passion that has him yawning once more. He decides to call it a night. His search for the meaning into the purpose of the last three Seals and The Book would have to wait. His eyes and brain had nothing more to give. He stands and, thrusting his hands into the center of his lower back pushes his hips forward, accompanied by a gratifying groan. Running his hands through his gray, bushy hair, he grabs a small black cloth and drapes it over the open book, ready to pick up where he left off tomorrow. Looking around, he studies the room as he does every night before leaving to go topside. The fact the candles continue to remain lit after all this time is still a mystery to him, although after the events of the last couple of years he wonders if anything should surprise him anymore. Releasing a small laugh, he prods his glasses back up the bridge of his nose and leaves the chamber.

Making his way through the narrow corridors, lit with small, oblong shaped plastic lights he works his way toward the steps that lead up to the entrance to the lower areas of the complex. He takes a hold of the rope handrail to his right, fixed into the wall, and climbs the steps with care, his old, aching limbs causing him to grunt with each footstep.

Walking out into the warm night air he takes a deep breath. He is glad that he stayed at the temple. He loves it here. So quiet, peaceful, and whatever had happened to the world seems to have given this place a wide berth, despite what occurred during the Collapse. Behind him, the low vibrating hum of a diesel generator causes him to glance at it. He frowns, looking at the lights that it powers running into the catacombs and off toward the base, and an insect zips around his face, annoying him. He flaps at it, shooing it away then takes a few deep breaths and swings his arms exaggeratedly across his body, something he has come to grow fond of in the latter years as it benefits his circulation, then he makes his way toward a small gazebo where Jerry and the others sit relaxing, playing cards, and reading; an activity Jerry himself is engaged in. Through the course of time, the camp's occupants had grown from four to seven, with some Cambodian people joining Ibi and Jerry's party having found their way to them from the large city to the north called Siem Reap, something Jerry had been grateful for given that two of the men had come with vast knowledge of the city and more importantly where to find fuel.

Reaching the gazebo and upon closer inspection, Ibi spies Jerry's reading material as being one of the Barachiel volumes, and while he is not a confrontational man he is fiercely territorial when it comes to his work, and as best as his peaceful demeanor will allow, he remonstrates with Jerry.

"Jerry Conroy. We have talked about my dislike for the materials to be removed from the chamber. I am quite upset – yes, quite upset indeed."

Jerry rolls his eyes. "Ibi, relax for God's sake. It's one book. One book out of what looks like thousands. Don't get so uptight. Come on, sit down and relax man."

"That is not the point and well you know it. I am trying to discover the meaning behind what may be the most important religious discovery of all time and I have to keep control of everything in there."

"To whom?"

"Excuse me?" Ibi says, frowning.

"The most important discovery of all time, to whom? The fucking world's dead, Ibi."

Pouting, he shakes his head. "No, no, no, that's not right, not right at all. This is important and the world is not dead. There is the girl, the child who is to save us all."

Jerry tosses the book onto the table in front of him and throws his head back. "Oh yeah, the mythical child that everyone talks about, running around with the guy who killed Jesus." He glances toward Ibi. "You don't believe that shit, do you?"

"Oh, and you don't? After all we have seen? All we have been told?"

"Well if she exists, if she had defeated Satan as it has been stated, then why is the world still fucked? Huh? Answer me that? And stop pouting, man, you look like how chicks used to when they took their own fucking photos." He sighs. "Come on, sit down, take a load off, and stop being a grumpy old bastard."

Ibi sighs, and then sits down next to Jerry. He glances back toward the generator. "How long do you think we have?"

Jerry glances at it. "The genny? Few weeks maybe. We hit pay dirt finding that much fuel in Siem Reap with Lee's help, but everyone's luck runs out in the end Ibi... everyone's luck runs out in the end."

He sighs once more. "And what are we to do after that? What about my research?"

Jerry looks at him and smiles, feeling sorry for the man. "Well, the candles are still lit, right?"

Ibi snorts a laugh through his nose and looks down, and Jerry pats him on the shoulder.

"You hungry?" Jerry asks, leaning forward.

"As a matter of fact, I am. Where's the grub?"

Ibi is about to get up when Jerry stops him. "Hey, give over, Lee will get it for you." He signals to the Cambodian man and speaks to him in his native language, causing him to scurry off toward another tent a short way from the one they occupy.

Ibi settles back in his seat. "Thank you, Jerry, you are most kind." He pushes his glasses up his nose once again, the annoyance of them slipping down evident on his face. "So, what were you reading of such importance?" He points at the book.

"Christ, I dunno prof. I have literally no idea how you make head nor tail of this shit." Jerry sits forward, grabs the book, and thumbs through to a page. "Although this caught my eye, especially if we are to believe your Child of Light crapola." He hands the book to Ibi, stabbing a finger on the page as he does. "What do you think that means?"

Ibi's mouth opens wide, a deep concern stretching across his face. Jerry frowns. "Ibi, what is it?"

He glances up at Jerry, once again pushing his glasses up his nose.

"Well, what does it say?" Jerry says, sitting forward, his frown deepening.

Ibi glances back down at the page. On it, a picture depicts two girls, one dressed in white, one dressed in black. Held in the right hand of the child in white, who is on the left of the picture, is a tablet and on it a symbol. In the left hand of the child dressed in black is a book. Ibi looks back up at Jerry. "It says one Child of Light, one Child of Dark." He glances back down at the book, his mouth still open wide. "Where the hell did you get this volume from Jerry?"

Jerry shrugs. "I dunno, erm far right-hand side of the room? I knew you hadn't gotten to them yet so didn't think it would fuck up your cataloguing. I was gonna put it back, prof, I swear!"

Ibi shakes his head. "Never mind that now, it doesn't matter, but this… this is important Jerry. This is really important. I can feel it. I need to research this book right away, plus the volumes that were around it. I feel that there is something crucial contained within them that we must know. We must also speak to Gary at Bagotville.

He needs to know about this."

NINE

She holds her hands over her eyes to shield them from the glare of a sun that doesn't truly exist.

"It's daylight," Charlotte says, as she walks up to the side of Judas who traversed through the portal first.

"It's whatever it wants to be in here," he replies without looking at her. "Other zones may not be as well… lit." This time he does look at her and offers a little smile. "You definitely ready for this? I may not have been here before but I know what it contains, and I have to be honest: this place scares the piss outta me."

She offers him a fake shocked face. "The famous Judas Iscariot, actually afraid? How in the world did this ever happen!" She sticks her tongue out at him.

He grabs her chin between his thumb and forefinger and gives it a wobble. "Since I met you, that's when. I actually have something to lose now." He smiles.

Her playful, sarcastic attitude wanes and she places a hand on the side of his face and rests her forehead against his.

Azazel coughs from behind them.

"As much as I hate to interrupt the tender father–daughter moment, I must act like the responsible guide that I am and remind you that we have a mission to attend to. I think we should get going and not dwell in this horrible desert." He motions around with an outstretched hand.

Charlotte takes in the view, then steps away from Judas. She reflects on how barren the infernal landscape is. In the distance large jutting mountains loom, spewing lava from their summits and at various fissures in their sides. In a few locations she spies large rivers of molten lava bubbling and spitting fiery magma into the air that splatter into the sand, creating dust plumes.

"Is it all like this? Sand and lava?" she says, adjusting her sword harness and walking over to Azazel.

"Not at all, my dear. Other areas offer forestation, albeit twisted, dark, and terrible. Some are covered by vast ancient city structures, while others are nothing more than the blackest of night, where everything horrendous that you could imagine awaits at the edge of your senses." He smiles at her. "One thing though is that you are getting the full and actual Hell treatment."

"What do you mean?" she says, frowning.

Judas joins them at her side. "What he means is that this *is* Hell. Unadulterated, no glamor cover, no wallpapering – this is it. Whatever we see is how it truly is, unlike what others here might be subjected to or the misdirection within Port Dominion." He gives a small laugh. "We should be honored, really."

"Truly," Azazel says, throwing his hands into the air theatrically, "Lucifer has extended you the greatest courtesy."

Charlotte scoffs. "Ha! I'll believe that when I see it."

"You are seeing it, m'lady," Azazel grins at her.

"Okay," Judas says, refocusing the team, "enough chatter and sightseeing, here at least. Let's get going."

"You know where we need to head then?" she asks placing a hand over her brow while squinting at the landscape again. She then removes it as Judas walks to stand in front of where the artificial sun shines brightest, shielding her from its intense glare. Then he looks down at the ground and frowns.

"Err, actually no I don't." He looks at Azazel. "Why don't I know? I should know all that you do."

"As I said, master. Barachiel knew many things, but he also knew nothing of many others. This is *my* world, my land. And you don't know it as I do, because neither did he. That is why I am much more help to you in this form as your guide."

As Judas stares at him, a feeling deep within stirs and he gets the distinct feeling that everything Charlotte has said is correct – that Azazel has an ulterior motive and he is messing with them. Something is not quite right, and the way that the Gatekeeper addressed Azazel has caused cogs to turn within Judas' mind.

"What's your game?" Judas asks, stepping a little closer to the demon.

"My game? Why, to win of course. The same as your game master."

"Yes, but to win what?"

Azazel's mouth twitches, almost forming a smile. "To win freedom for the people of your world, naturally. To see this one rise to her most glorious role as protector of the Kingdom of Man. To win, that is all. I serve you master, no other."

They stare at each other for a few moments until eventually Charlotte breaks the deadlock.

"As much as I hate to agree with the damn thing dad, we have a mission to complete and we ain't gonna get it done it standing here pondering the nature of deceit." She glances at Azazel. "I know he's up to something, and Gabriel tried to warn us such a thing would happen when you first mentioned the sword while we were waiting for him, prior to me returning to the real world. But at the end of the day, we need him more than we have needed anything right now, and only this damn thing will be able to guide us through this God-awful place. So, let's trust it for now, move forward to our goal, and watch each other's backs. Yeah?"

Judas glances at Charlotte and smiles. "Yeah, of course sweetie. You're right. You're always right. Okay then Azazel," he says his name with a touch of petulance, "you lead the way. Where to?"

Azazel smiles and bows, his hand turning in a small circle in front of him, his right leg in front of his left, as though addressing royalty. "The first place we need to go is to the closest down-gate," he looks around, gathering his bearings, "and from the looks of things, I reckon we are closest to Mokwena's gate."

"Mokwena?" Charlotte asks.

"Yeah," Azazel replies, smiling broadly, "she's an absolute darling, as are her children." He now bares his teeth. "But, it is still quite a way's off, so you will need to use that motion-blur skill you seem to be good at. What do you call it, by the way?"

Charlotte glances at Judas and holds her hands out to her sides. "Er, I dunno. I never really thought about it."

Judas shrugs. "Me neither. It just kinda started happening after I met Charley. I think the first time I used it was against Abaddon," he raises his eyebrows and downturns his mouth, "yeah, Abaddon I think. I never thought much about it after that."

"Well," Azazel says, turning toward Charlotte, "all great skills need a name." He ponders for a moment. "How about... shadow-step? Has quite a catchy ring to it, don't you think?"

Judas and Charlotte exchange a look and shrug their shoulders at one another.

"Yeah, sure, why not?" she says, turning back toward Azazel.

Azazel claps his hands together. "Great. Shadow-step it is then. Okay, so you guys are going to have to... shadow-step," he winks and gives the thumbs up with both digits, "and I will guide you to where you need to go."

"Fine," Judas says, preparing to hold out his hand to bring Azazel back into sword form. "But it had better not be far. That skill—"

"Err, shadow-step!" Azazel says, correcting him with a pointed finger.

"Uggh, that shadow-step takes a lot of energy to maintain for long periods of time, and we need to keep it in reserve for fighting."

"Oh, don't you worry master. You will be there before you know it." He smiles.

"Fine. Then Ika, become sword."

Azazel somersaults from a standing position into the air and lands in Judas' hand as the sword Ikazuchi. "Just one other thing," Ikazuchi's hissing voice says, from out of the sword's hilt, "what are you like with spiders?"

Charlotte's agitated attention snaps to it. "What?"

TEN

Three beautiful naked women writhe around on a gothic-looking bed that sports crimson silk drapes hanging from a canopy that floats above of its own accord. They caress one another, running their hands over each other's slender, full-breasted bodies as their jet-black hair dances and sways as though underwater. They run their tongues in and out of each other's mouths, then over their faces that shift from human to demonic at irregular intervals, never the same form twice. Silk blindfolds that match the color of the bed drapes cover their eyes, and their bodies glow a subtle orange from the flames that dance around the perimeter of the otherwise empty darkened circular room. Their clawed fingers explore each other's bodies, in and out of every crevice, gouging flesh and drawing blood as they scrape along the skin, only for it to heal immediately after. Their groans accentuate the horrifying erotic scene as their pleasure reaches heights beyond imagination; they are almost there, almost satisfied, but choose to stop as Lucifer enters the room, removing his suit jacket and tossing it to one side, where it disappears.

He takes a deep breath and runs his fingers through his black slicked-back hair, then sits on the end of the bed, his back to them, and the witches move toward him, then begin caressing his body and licking his neck.

"I'm not in the mood," he says, pushing one of them back, but they ignore him and continue to attempt to please him.

One runs a hand over his chest, then his belly and toward his crotch and he grabs it forcefully and squeezes.

"I said, I am *not* in the fucking mood!" He throws her hand to one side.

The women chuckle and roll away toward the head of the bed and continue to writhe, moan, and groan.

"For fuck's sake, can you just knock it off for a second?" Lucifer commands.

The witches do so, although reluctantly, then each taking a different place on the bed, their gaze focused in his direction, through the material that covers their eyes.

They speak as one, albeit each with a slight delay, making their hissing speech an echo.

"What troubles you, master? Why are you tense?" They chuckle. "Let us relieve you of your worries. Your time has almost come. Your ascendance almost at hand."

Lucifer glances over his shoulder. "That is what troubles me." He returns his gaze to his front. "Are you absolutely sure this time that this will go my way?"

"Yes, YES," they hiss, moving onto their knees and crawling toward him, "the visions were strong, explicit – they showed the Lucifer sitting upon the throne with the sword of power next to him, pleased with himself, happy that he has triumphed. The visions were strong, compelling."

Their last sentence echoes in the chamber multiple times.

Lucifer glances back again while one of them wraps herself around him from behind. "You said that last time and look what happened. And the child's correct time of birth had been shielded from me, something I would have expected you three to know. I was most troubled with that little slip, as it really fucked me over." He reaches up and touches one of the hand print scars on his face.

The witch curled around his body releases him and floats up to the canopy, chuckling. They continue to speak as one. "The visions only tell us what they will. We have no control. They come to us and we repeat them. We know not where they come from, but we listen, we must. We are… bound by them, as you are bound to this world."

Lucifer grins. "Not for long, my witchy friends. Not for fucking long."

They shriek with laughter and the one floating falls back to the bed with a bounce and then moves in between one of the others' legs, her long, forked tongue protruding greedily from her mouth.

Lucifer glances back at them, then takes a deep breath and stands.

He stares at them for a few seconds. "Ahhh, fuck it," he says, unbuttoning his shirt. "I've got time."

He smiles and joins them.

ELEVEN

Careering out of shadow-step, Charlotte crashes to the ground, thrown off course by an explosion of sand erupting to the side of her and she tumbles through the dunes, coming to an unceremonious stop.

Skidding to a halt and moving back to her location, Judas calls her name, and as he races toward her more plumes of sand explode forcing him to maneuver around them.

"What the hell?" Charlotte says, annoyed as she sits upright, spitting sand out of her mouth and then mussing her hair, shaking even more grit loose. She looks toward Judas, weaving in and out of columns of sand, bursting upward around him, and scrambles to her feet and throws her arms out to her sides, her swords snapping into them.

As Judas reaches her the attacks cease, and an eerie silence befalls them. He holds his hand out, and Ikazuchi lands within it as he scans the landscape, barren save for a handful of crumbled structures dotted around that might once have been the arches of a bridge.

"What is that?" she asks, squinting from under a hand held against her forehead, shielding her eyes from the glare of the artificial sun. She takes a few steps forward, her attention fixed upon movement ahead. "Is… is that a person?"

"Yeah, I think it is," Judas replies, moving closer to her, his hand also over his eyes acting as a visor. "Looks like we got company."

"Ugggh," Ikazuchi says, his tone that of exasperation, "this fucking guy!"

"This guy?" Charlotte asks, addressing the sword in Judas' hand. "What guy? Who is he?" She looks back toward the figure as he draws closer at speed, his form bobbing up and down in a lazy zigzag pattern.

"The one with no name. That's who," Ikazuchi replies. "But we call him Sandy."

Judas tosses the sword forward and it transforms into Azazel, and takes a few steps toward the approaching demon.

"Sandy?" a frowning Judas asks. "I thought you said he has no name? So why Sandy?"

"Because… he lives in the sand!" Azazel says, glancing between Judas and Charlotte.

Judas grips the bridge of his nose between his thumb and forefinger and takes an irritated, deep breath.

Turning his attention back upon the figure who has now drawn much closer, Azazel points at him. "Just deal with this one quickly, master," he says while patting down his clothing, dusting himself off. "He's a bit of a dick."

"Hmmm," Judas replies, frowning, stepping forward a little more, "a problem dick or a dick dick?"

Azazel glances back at him. "A dick dick!"

Charlotte offers an angry groan. "Shock horror, a demon in Hell is a dickhead." She rolls her eyes and shakes her head. "We don't have time for this, dad. Let's just kill him and move on."

"She's right," Azazel says, turning back to them, "he was a right pain in the ass for Lucifer, but eventually the big guy relented and told him to go away and be in charge of the sands or some shit. Which he did. I honestly don't class him as anything more than a lesser demon, but he got a 'get-away-from-me-for-a-long-time' type of free pass. I think Lucifer felt sorry for him or something, I dunno. Point is, this is a worthless distraction. Deal with him quickly, as I want to get to our destination sooner rather than later."

"What is he riding?" Judas asks, his frown deepening.

Ahead the demon draws closer, enough for the group to see the mode of transportation he uses to traverse the landscape and why Azazel refers to him as Sandy. He is literally riding the sand, hoisted up by a great moving swell and carried on the wave, snaking his way toward them. And upon reaching their position, he towers above them on the crest of his wave, brandishing a gigantic spear, the wide-bladed head of which emits a dark and mystical energy that crackles and swirls around it. Dressed in dark brown leather armor, he takes a few steps forward and the sand lowers him down to the ground, and then he brushes his jet-black, long, and straggly hair to one side to reveal a brown leather mask that bears a striking similarity to that of Maori sculptures. He speaks, causing Charlotte and Judas to react with surprise as they were not expecting his voice to sound as human as it does, albeit deep and booming, and his words enunciated slowly.

"So... it is true, then. The story the witches tell. That The Light and Iscariot walk these lands with the infamous Azazel as his... tame *pet*."

Judas scoffs and glances to his side, then smirks. "Look, we don't have—"

Before he has a chance to complete his sentence, the demon-lord raises a hand and a maelstrom of sand engulfs Judas and Azazel, lifts them into the air, and hurls them a few hundred feet away, sending them crashing and tumbling across the desert terrain.

"You fucker!" Charlotte says and attacks, slicing at him with her right sword, but connecting with sand only as the desert rises beneath the demon and lifts him back into the air.

Recovering from her over-swing, she follows the move through and spins away from him as he stabs his spear at her, its fierce energy crackling and missing her by the narrowest of margins.

With an angry roar Judas reappears, leaping through the air at the demon having covered the distance in one rage-induced bound, and with Ikazuchi held aloft in both hands he brings the sword down at him.

87

The blade slams into the desert floor, missing the demon as a wave of sand pulls him backward to safety. And Judas must be sharp and alert, forced to drop his left shoulder and lean back as Sandy's spear narrowly misses him, the weapon having extended its shaft into a longer piece and one that covers the full length of the 15-foot distance between them.

Retracting his weapon and quickly focusing his attention on Charlotte once again as she attacks from his left with rapid stabs at him, the sand lifts the demon up and carries him backward with a whoosh, halting him a fair distance away from them.

"I thought you said this guy was a pushover, Ika?" Judas says, not bothering to look at his sword.

"I said he was a dick, master, I never said he was a pushover."

Judas silently mouths a curse. "No, you definitely implied that he would be a pushover."

"Oh I don't think so master, I would have remembered such a thing."

"Look!" Charlotte says, interrupting the bickering. "It doesn't matter! He is in our way and delaying us. We need a strategy. He might not be the best fighter, but he's one of the bloody trickiest we've come across in a while. We need a plan to separate him from that sand, so we can ground the bastard."

"Agreed," Ikazuchi says.

"Something we are in agreement with?" she says, turning her attention on the weapon in surprise, "will this weird day never end?"

Judas stifles a smile. "Ideas?" he says, refocusing the team.

Charlotte glances around for a moment and then points at the ruined, bridge-like structures. "You reckon you can bait him under or close to one of those and I can try to catch him off-guard from above?"

"As good a plan as any," Judas says, nodding.

"Okay," she says, readying herself, "a bit of bait and switch then. I'll attack and draw his attention, then you move in from the side and force him onto you. Try to shadow-step him into retreat, and at the optimal point I'll cut his fuckin' head off."

Without waiting for Judas to respond, Charlotte zooms off toward the demon, who has stuck his spear into the ground awaiting whatever comes next.

Upon seeing her move, he grips his weapon, and rises into the air a couple of feet, drawn along by his strange control over the desert.

The sand slides him to the side as the girl attacks, her blades flashing in the sun and forming almost complete circles of light, such is the speed in which she wields them. Their weapons clatter against each other as he blocks her attacks, and then tries to counter and jab his spear at her. She moves, zipping to his left, and almost catches him off-guard, and so he allows the sand beneath him to move him backward away from her swift strikes. He hears her grunt in frustration and try again, and as before the sand protects him from the threat, taking him out of the reach of danger. However, he must be fast as he feels the presence of Iscariot from behind and spins within the sand, whipping his spear around to block the attack. Aware that they mean to outflank him, he is carried away again on the sand to a new destination a little further away.

As Charlotte screams in frustration he spins the spear around just as Judas throws in repeated overhead strikes, as though he were swinging a mallet down onto a peg. And so Sandy shifts again, allowing his unique method of transportation to drive him even further backward. He becomes aware that the girl hasn't attacked for a few moments and then it hits him, the feeling of being herded toward a destination of their choosing. He has heard many tales of how exceptional Iscariot is with a weapon, that he has defeated almost every demon he has ever encountered, and so knew he must rely on his motion ability to get the better of the angel, but something feels off. It is like Judas isn't giving his all, and as he blocks another attack he glances around to see he has been moved to within the grounds of the old bridge structure that once served a down-gate. He looks up, aware that he is about to pass under a broken arch of the ruined bridge, and can just make out the girl as she speeds up the remains of the bridge's ramp, her swords out by her sides.

With an angry roar, Sandy spins his spear around above his head, calling forth more of its electrical energy and it crackles and fizzes with greater intent, then swings it around 360 degrees obliterating the ruined structure and forcing Judas to evade the attack by jumping back as far as he can.

Above, and caught by surprise, Charlotte feels the ground beneath her explode as something drives through it, and she must leap and somersault to avoid crumpling onto the ground and affording her enemy a much-needed advantage.

She lands but not on top of the demon, which had been her intended target, instead a few feet away from him and she rolls to a stop. Then she spins around on her knees and raises both swords to block an anticipated attack.

The assault does come, but the demon is forced to hold it back at the last moment, his spear tip hanging just above her crossed ones, and through heavy breathing they stare at one another. Charlotte sports a slight grin, at the reason as to why he hasn't followed through. Judas has Ikazuchi pointed into the back of his neck, having shadow-stepped to him when he realized the demon's intentions.

"This was not an attack of aggression," Sandy says, his tone softening and pleading. "This was merely a demonstration. I have no desire to harm you or be harmed by you in turn." He grips his spear tight, and it retracts down into a much smaller rod as he slowly raises his hands above his head.

Both Charlotte and Judas scowl at him as she gets to her feet.

She shakes her head angrily. "A demonstration? What the hell are you talking about?"

Sandy edges into a full standing position, his hands still above his head. "Do you mind?" he says, glancing back at Judas. "I am willing to talk, I would just rather do so without the fear of that thing sticking in the back of my neck."

Judas growls. "Listen, the only reason your head is still attached to your body is because you have intrigued me. And it has been a while since any demon has done that, so I suggest you make this a fucking exceptional story or it's coming off."

90

"I understand," he says, continuing to move slowly, adjusting his position so that he can address them both. "I know defeating you two would be nearly impossible—"

"Damn straight," Charlotte says, her attitude cocky as she reseats her swords in their scabbards.

"…and a change in dynamic down here is on the cards in the very near future. I simply wanted to show my fighting talents so that when the time comes I can prove to be… useful."

Judas lowers his sword. "What in all that is holy are you talking about?"

Sandy opens his eyes wide. "Look, I have no desire to upset you two. The witches told me—"

"YOU LIE!" an irritated Ikazuchi bellows.

Upon hearing the sword, Judas glances to Charlotte, who understands his intentions and keeps her hands poised to draw her blades should the need arise. Judas tosses Ikazuchi in front of him, where he changes into his Azazel form.

"You lie, demon! The witches would never converse with you."

Sandy cocks his head to one side. "I do not lie – they did as I say. They came to me and said the others have been forbidden from getting involved, but that I should wait for you to pass my realm, and when you do I should show you my worth, then leave. That's what they said." He continues to hold his hands in the air, even though no weapon is trained upon him.

Azazel stares at him for a moment, then turns to Judas who has asked him what was going on. "The witches, master, are sages – predictors of futures. And they rarely talk to lowly creatures such as this one here." He looks him up and down. "Although he's made good use of his spare time recently. I remember him being a much poorer fighter."

Sandy glances at Charlotte, then to Judas. "Not all will be allowed to sing in the sun, not all will be able to dance under the stars. Remember Judas, remember what the detective told you. A sacrifice will have to be honored."

"What did you just say?" Charlotte says, stepping toward him, her eyes narrowed and burning with rage.

Sandy glances at her and then rises into the air, the sand carrying him aloft again. "Remember this moment, remember my worth."

He speeds away, back through the desert and then disappears down into the sand as Charlotte, eyes wide, strides over to Judas.

"Seriously," she says, "how did he know that? What I said in the car to Gary and Abi when I spazzed out on the way into New York City? And what the hell does he mean?"

Azazel ambles over to her. "Seems he wasn't lying. Only the witches would know such a thing."

"Right. Fine," she says, shaking her head at him a little. "So he wasn't lying, but what does it all mean?"

Azazel lifts his arms into the air and shrugs, then flaps them down by his sides with a slap, and she exhales in frustration.

Judas sighs, attempting to prevent the inevitable arguing to flare up between them. "Whatever it was sweetie, we will have to wait and find out if it means something. My feeling is that this encounter has been pointless and served no other purpose than to slow us down. I doubt we will ever meet this character again." He holds his hand out to bring Azazel back into sword form, a calling that the demon complies with. "Come on," he says, stowing the sword on his back, "let's be off and get to that down-gate."

She looks at him in surprise and raises her arms to her sides. "Seriously, we ain't gonna talk about thi—"

She cuts her sentence short as Judas shadow-steps away.

"Aaaand he's gone," she says, shadow-stepping after him in a huff.

TWELVE

Uncrossing his hands from behind his body, Gabriel straightens up as the Creator descends the long sweeping staircase. He smiles a little, an involuntary action as the pure warmth of extreme Divinity envelops him, as it always does when in the company of the Prime Being. The divine power that feeds all angelic creatures overjoys him.

He bows as the Creator approaches him, today having opted for the form of a younger man in his mid-thirties. A well-groomed individual, his appearance impeccable, dressed in a dark blue pinstripe suit with highly polished black shoes, and he returns the bow to Gabriel as he clears the last step, adjusting his cuffs.

"Gabe. How are you today?" he says with a smile.

Gabriel nods. "I've been better, my Lord, if I'm being honest." He looks down.

The room in which they stand has no floor or walls, only the dark of space with billions of stars to form the backdrop, and below rotates the Earth, as it has for millions of years.

Gabriel takes a deep breath. "It's funny you know, all of this."

"Oh? How so?" the Creator says, ambling away from him and over to a decanter that has appeared in the center of the room.

"That I overlook the Earth as its protector, as I have always done, and yet I have no clue as to where its fate lies. Until just over two of the human's years ago, I knew everything in all directions, but now how ironic it is that we, the beings of ultimate knowledge, are blind to their future."

The Creator smiles as he removes the square crystal stopper from the decanter. "Oh, I wouldn't say that," he says, picking up the bottle and taking a sniff. He then grabs a glass and pours a drink, the liquid as clear as the container into which it flows and offers it to Gabriel, who shakes his head.

"Not today, my Lord."

"Suit yourself," the Creator says, with a raise of his eyebrows and a shrug. He replaces the stopper and takes a sip from the glass. "Ahh, ambrosia. Wonderful. Just… wonderful."

Gabriel offers the faintest of smiles and glances down again, then returns his gaze to the Creator and takes a step closer to him. "I guess it's pointless saying what I am going to say, since you know what it is already!"

Smiling, the Creator sits in a bland yet functional chair that materializes out of thin air beneath him. "True, my friend, but all the same I like to hear you talk, therefore I'll pretend I don't know."

Gabriel looks down at the planet again. He takes a moment to ponder, admiring the world and its majestic splendor. "I love that place you know," he says, a heartfelt tone to his voice. "All of it. Its construction, its inhabitants, both sentient and those that are merely functional. Its mountains and rivers. Everything the humans have built and what they have destroyed. Their art, their monuments, their… spirit. I love it all." He barks a small laugh and closes his eyes for a moment. "They're on the brink of extinction you know."

The Creator takes another sip of his drink and smiles, while crossing his legs. "Are they? How can you be so sure?"

He looks at his master, irritated with his dismissive tone. "Because you're allowing it to happen."

He smiles and places his drink onto a table that appears beneath his hand. "Oh, Gabriel. You are my first and greatest work, but you can be so bloody melodramatic sometimes. Relax a little. Have a drink. Sit down and chill out."

"Why?"

"Why have a drink? I would think that is fairly obvi—"

"No master, why have you let him rise so far this time? Why are you not doing something about him, like before?"

The Creator frowns while leaning forward a little and placing his left hand on his thigh. "Well, because I'm not sure if I can put him anywhere lower than I already have." He chuckles.

Gabriel sighs, already tired of a conversation that has only just begun.

"Besides, he hasn't taken up against the throne this time," he says, leaning back into his chair, picking his drink up and swigging it down.

Gabriel scoffs and looks down at the Earth once again. "He intends to. That is exactly his aim, exactly what he wants to accomplish and this time he just might do it…" Gabriel grips the bridge of his nose with his thumb and forefinger and sighs once again. "This is pointless, my Lord. I'm not telling you anything you do not already know."

The Creator stands and puts his empty glass onto the table then walks over to Gabriel and places his hands on his shoulders. "Look, my oldest and closest friend. I have done nothing here, this has all been the doing of others. I didn't set Lucifer on his current path… you did when you took the child."

Gabriel snaps his attention to him.

"I didn't make the choices Iscariot made, he did. And for all that is holy, I did not choose Charlotte's destiny for her… she did! They all did. I am merely an observer, as you and the others are to be."

Gabriel shakes his head. "But he will kill them, he will kill them all. I thought they were your favorites?"

"They are. By a mile."

"Then why are you allowing this to happen?" Gabriel's agitation rises.

"Why not?" he replies, flapping his hands by his sides. "Why not! Lucifer is also one of my children. Doesn't he deserve to aspire to something greater than he is? Shouldn't he be allowed the chance to succeed in his hopes and dreams? Why should I pick sides against my children whether I have a favorite or not?"

Gabriel looks at him with confusion that borders on disgust. "Because he is an immortal, God-like entity and they have not been afforded the protection they deserve against such a creature and his charges. That's why." His words border on the petulant.

The Creator's face grows stern. "Careful my friend. Remember who you are talking to."

Gabriel backs down immediately. "I apologize, my Lord, but… I am at great odds with this, and why we are not allowed to get involved."

The Creator turns and walks back to the table with his glass on it. "Oh, I think you've gotten involved a-plenty, Gabe, so don't come that with me."

Gabriel sighs and closes his eyes, then opens them. "True, master. But if you would just unshackle me I would get involved a great deal more."

The Creator throws back his head and laughs. "Oh, I know you would my friend, how I know you would! But that is not your destiny, it is hers."

Gabriel's shoulders sag and he breathes out deeply. He closes his eyes once more and shakes his head a little, then reopens them. "Of course it is. But I don't even know where they are. I know they entered Hell, but I cannot see in there anymore, and again – such a thing bothers me a great deal."

"Well, don't let it Gabe. I see, and I know exactly where they are and what they are doing." The Creator grabs his empty glass from the table and it fills itself with liquid again, then he takes a sip while walking back to Gabriel. He looks down upon the Earth as though he were staring at Charlotte and Judas' exact location. "And let me tell you, they are doing all right – not bad at all."

"They have breached the Gates?" Gabriel says, turning toward him sharply.

The Creator glances at him. "With much aplomb. And taken care of the one they call Sandy."

Gabriel scoffs. "Oh, that guy."

"Hey, don't knock him. He gave a good account of himself this time, bless his little cotton socks."

Gabriel chuckles and shakes his head.

The Creator takes another sip of his drink, then motions to Gabriel with the glass. "You sure you don't want one Gabe?"

With a lazy smile, Gabriel shakes his head once again.

The Creator frowns and flicks his eyebrows up, then drinks again. He points at the Earth once more. "And they are about to meet Mokwena. Should be fun for them, don't ya think?"

Gabriel looks at him with some concern. "Fun? She's gotten much stronger over the centuries. You know that don't you?"

"Of course I do." He turns and walks back to his seat and sits down. "Aggh, I'm not concerned. Not… one… bit." He raises his glass to Gabriel. "You were right about her, y'know, about Charlotte. She is a damn treat to behold. Without doubt my finest work upon the entire planet." He takes another drink. "I'm sure she will make it through, especially if she engages her good 'ole family spirit." He swings a triumphant fist.

"And if she doesn't…?" Gabriel says, glancing back at him, and then returning his gaze to the Earth.

"Then Lucifer wins and they all die." He smiles.

Gabriel blinks at him in surprise.

He laughs. "Oh, stop your fretting Gabe! All is well and they're doing fine. She isn't far off reaching her absolute full potential. Her big moment is close at hand."

Gabriel looks back down. "That's what I'm afraid of."

THIRTEEN

"Call for you, Gary," Jonesy says, as he peers around the door.

"For me?" Gary replies. "Who the hell would be calling me?"

"It's that professor, the one from Cambodia."

He says a quiet, "ahh" then turns toward Daniel, who is struggling to put on his combat body armor. Gary groans and then exhales an irritated breath out through his nose. "You need to pull this bit here—"

"I got it," Daniel says, waving away his hand, "I'm fine, I can do this. I'm freakin' smart you know!"

"Oh, you're freakin' smart all right, a freakin' smartass." Gary beckons over Jonesy. "Get him into his gear for me, will ya, while I take this." He sets off toward the doorway. "Oh, and give him a sidearm and show him how to use it."

Jonesy looks at Gary sharply and raises his eyebrows.

Gary nods. "It's gonna be rough out there, buddy. Everyone goes armed."

He nods and turns around to help Daniel, who sighs and growls from the back of his throat.

"I said I got this!"

Jonesy holds up a finger and gives him a stern look and Daniel says nothing more, instead allowing the experienced Army Sergeant (having gained a field promotion from Colonel Taylor) to continue helping him into his gear.

Gary smirks as he watches Jonesy subjugate the young boy and then walks out of the armory, through a dozen other men and women all prepping their gear for Daniel's portal data-gathering mission.

Following the briefing earlier that morning where the mission plans had been detailed to the team, Daniel had shown surprising speed in preparing his equipment for the operation, speed that could only mean he had been ready for this for much longer than he had let on; but that was his way. Check, check, and check again, and not to give anything away until he was sure – a quality much admired by Colonel Taylor. And so he had presented his plan, discussed its execution, its strategy and chance for success and survival (the odds were not great, he had to concede), and in turn had seen his day go from presentation to action. Nathan had discussed the plan with Dawson, and they both agreed that they needed to do it sooner rather than later, and that evening proved to be the earliest opportunity.

Gary strides down the corridor toward the communications room, greeting various personnel, something he had grown used to such is his iconic status. He rounds a corner at the end of the corridor and then turns right into another, much shorter one with a door at the end with the words 'OPERATIONS' stenciled on it. Turning the handle, he steps into a much cooler environment than what he has just left, the room being full of electronic surveillance equipment, and air conditioning a necessity to keep the hardware at a serviceable temperature.

A Canadian Air Force Corporal waves him over and hands him a headset.

Gary thanks him and takes a seat.

"Professor Yali, this is Gary Cross, good to hear from you, over."

"Ahh, Detective Cross, good evening to you. Might I ask that we dispense with the military speak, all the 'overs and outs' is quite tiresome for me. After all, I am a theologist, not a soldier."

Gary smirks. "Of course, professor. Whatever you say. Are you okay? Is something wrong? Is Jerry all right?"

In the four months that Gary had been communicating with the team in Cambodia (professor Yali having expressed a keen interest in Gary due to his ties with Charlotte and Judas) he had grown quite fond of the old Turkish man and his protector, with Gary and Jerry having talked at great length on many occasions, swapping stories of their encounters and engagements with the creatures, tales that Jerry found fascinating. Despite everything Gary had told him, he still hadn't come around to believing about Charlotte and Judas. But he was a professional and polite man, and as such Gary had gotten on with him a great deal, which is why he is showing concern for him now.

"Yes, yes, detective, he is fine, we are all fine."

Gary didn't bother trying to correct Ibi. He had attempted to on many occasions, but the man positively refused to address him by anything other than his former civic title and so he had given up trying.

"Ah, that's good then professor. That's good. So what can I do for you that's so urgent it has you calling me when you should be sound asleep?" He checks his watch. "By my calculations, it's around 04.30 in the morning your time, isn't it?"

"It is, Detective Cross, it is, but sleep eludes me at present. I have made incredible discoveries and it is keeping me from thinking about anything else. Incredible discoveries, detective. Incredible!"

"Oh, and what discoveries are those professor?"

Out of instinct, and from a life now left far behind him, Gary reaches out for a pad and searches in vain for a pen. He clicks his fingers at one of the Air Force personnel close to him in the room while silently mouthing the word 'sorry', then makes a scribbling sign in the air, to which the woman smiles and walks over to her station. She grabs a pen then walks back and hands it to him and he smiles at her.

"Okay, professor. Shoot. Whaddya got?"

"Oh, it is marvelous, detective, simply incredible."

"Yeah, you said that already, sir. What are the details?"

"Well, detective. A number of months ago, we uncovered a secret area within the ancient catacombs beneath Angkor Wat, and this area, this room, is the archive of an Archangel by the name of Barachiel and it was something I hadn't thought important to mention, until now."

Gary sits upright. "I know that name, professor. That area is not safe. Put Jerry on the line, put him on right now."

"Oh detective, please. I have been studying his work for almost 18 months now. The being is truly long gone."

"You don't know that, professor. That was a rogue Archangel that Charlotte, Judas, and the Hellwatch left to track down before we were separated and…" he takes a moment to reflect, "…bad shit happened to us all. Professor, I'm telling you that area is not safe. Put Jerry on. Put him on right now please!"

"There's two of them, detective," Ibi blurts, interrupting him.

"What? What do you mean, there's two of them? Two of whom?"

"Two of… them. Two girls. A child of light and a child of darkness. There's two of them, Detective Cross. Did you know that?"

Gary looks straight ahead, his mouth wide open, his mind trying to process what the professor is telling him.

"Detective, are you there? Detective Cross? Did you hear me? I said there are two of them."

"Yeah. Yeah. I heard you, professor. I heard you loud and clear."

FOURTEEN

"Stop here," Ikazuchi hisses from his position on Judas' back. "This is close enough."

Both Judas and Charlotte disengage their shadow-step and come to an immediate halt with Charlotte placing her hands on her knees and bending over, breathing in and out hard. "That really does take a lot out of you doing it for that long."

"Yeah," Judas says, taking Ikazuchi from his back and tossing the sword in front of him, transforming it into Azazel. "I thought you said it wasn't far, cos that was far enough for us, not to mention all the time we wasted with Sand-bro back there."

"Ahh, you'll be fine," Azazel says with a dismissive wave. "You're both healthy strong people... well, angels... you get the idea."

Charlotte brings herself to a standing position while still catching her breath. "Seriously though," she says, jabbing her hands onto her hips, "are we not gonna talk about that sand-dude thing?"

Judas shakes his head. "Honestly sweetie, it doesn't seem important to me. The guy was a joke. A couple of seconds later and he wouldn't have been able to plead for his life or tell us about the demonstration he staged." Judas blows air out between his lips. "Absolute joke. Put it out of your mind."

She is about to remonstrate with him when Azazel cuts her short.

"He's right, Charlotte, it is unimportant, and besides…" he turns around and walks ahead of them a few paces, "…I present to you the down-gate of Mokwena." He indicates ahead to a large temple resembling Indian structures that once resided upon the Earth's surface, boxy yet pyramid-like in design, with domed spires that stretch up from many points on its surface, the scene complimented by gigantic carvings on the outside of the large entrance, the nature of which Charlotte and Judas are unable to quite make out at this distance. Around the temple the sky is dark and no longer illuminated by the artificial sun, with a shadow of cloud that lingers at the edge of the area appearing to mark the start of the temple's territory. There is a sense of foreboding that is hard to ignore.

"Gets you right here doesn't it?" Azazel says, taking in a deep breath and slamming a closed fist into his chest. "She really knows how to live in beauty and style. What a woman."

Her interest piqued by this more than her desire to continue probing about the sand-lord, Charlotte glances at Judas and raises her eyebrows, and he does likewise albeit with a small grin.

Stepping forward, she grabs Azazel by the arm and turns him around. "Right, we're here. Where do we go now, and while we're at it you mentioned spiders earlier. What's that all about?"

Azazel smiles, and then his face grows serious. "Mokwena is a Demon Lord – a spider-queen to be more precise."

Charlotte rolls her eyes, and growls softly. "Of course… why wouldn't she be?!"

"Well, yes – quite," Azazel says. "But she is not alone. There are others."

"How many others?" Judas asks.

"Hmmm, well, let me see," he glances up, folds his arms, and taps a finger against his lips, "lots?"

Judas grunts. "Define lots?"

Glancing to the side, Azazel opens his eyes wide. "Fucking... lots?"

Judas looks down and bites his lower lip while groaning. He is running out of patience with his ward.

Azazel holds up his hands, placating the angel who looks like he's ready to snap. "Look, I honestly don't know. It has been an age since I've been here. She had hundreds of... children when I was here last, but now who knows? It could be thousands. Oh... and they're huge. Like, fricking huge." He reinforces his point by using his hands to indicate size, then offers a quick smile. "The point is, within that temple, right at the center at its deepest point is the best down-gate available to get us to Belial. It literally drops us in a stone's throw from the place. I won't lie to you, it is a maze of corridors in there, aaaand I might... just might... possibly get us lost from time to time. So you two best get your A-game on, and we'll get through the place as fast as we can. Capiche?"

Judas takes a deep breath in and out through his nose and turns to face Charlotte. "You got enough energy for a Divinity burst if we get into a tricky situation?"

She smiles at him. "Yeah, I reckon I'll be okay... loads, probably."

She's lying. She doesn't want him to know that The Seal and The Book are draining her of more vital holy energy as each day progresses. Her only hope is to get to the Temple of Belial as fast as possible and end this finally. So, she lied to him. She hated it, but she did it all the same.

"Good," he says. "Then let's get our shit together and race blindly through corridors to the lowest point of a temple we're not sure we can navigate and that is most likely full to the brim with demon spiders ready to murder us."

Charlotte chuckles as she steps passed him. "Oh, when you put it like that I wonder why I was concerned in the first place."

Judas grins at her.

FIFTEEN

Gary traipses back into the armory, where most of the personnel are now fully geared up and ready to go. He looks distant, concerned as Nathan walks over to him.

"What's the matter, buddy? Where have you been?"

He looks up at Nathan. "I just got off the comms with Yali. He told me there's another child, another girl."

Nathan frowns and shakes his head.

"Another Charlotte," Gary says, "only this one's a child of darkness."

Nathan takes a deep and contemplative breath. "Well, there's nothing we can do about that now. We need to complete prep, and you need to get into your gear. Mission go time is 15 minutes from now, so get a shift on will ya?"

As Nathan turns around to walk away, Gary grabs his elbow. "Nathan. What if she is with us?" His eyes are wide. "What if she's been with us all along?" He glances toward Sarah, who is wrapping a scarf around her neck while Isaac fiddles with it, trying to do it for her and she slaps his hands away in annoyance.

Nathan stares at her for a moment, then shakes his head and looks back at Gary. "No! No way. Not a chance."

"Think about it, will ya? Why is she invisible to the demons? Why can't they see her?"

Nathan takes a firm hold of Gary's arm and leads him to the side of the room without anyone noticing what he is doing. "Now you listen to me, Gary Cross. You are one of the smartest people I know, and your radar for detecting wrong folk is literally the best I have ever seen. So you look me square in the eyes right now. You look me square in the eyes and tell me that you suspect her. That your gut-feeling is telling you to suspect her!"

He stares at Nathan for a moment, his eyes darting back and forth and then looks down. "I can't. I… don't think that. Not really."

"That's what I thought. I might have only known that girl for nine months, but there is one thing that I do know for certain – she is pure goodness through and through. If there is another, as Yali says, then I can tell you this much, it ain't her. Now put it from your mind and get your shit together. We got a mission to conduct that we are probably gonna die on." He smiles at Gary, who smiles back while nodding.

"Yeah. Yeah, you're right. I'm sorry I mentioned it."

"Hey. It's what you do, remember? Detective Cross, right?"

"Oh, fuck off with that detective shit," Gary says, playfully pushing Nathan out of the way and grinning.

"Atta boy," Nathan says, grinning back, then moves into the center of the room while Gary goes to his locker to grab his gear. "Right you lot, listen up." His voice is commanding, and the room falls into immediate silence with every man and woman giving him their undivided attention.

"This op is gonna be damn difficult, impossible maybe, but I believe in that young man over there," he points toward Daniel, who offers a nervous smile, "and if he tells me that he can gather sufficient data in order to help construct a defense system against these bastards, then I for one won't argue with him and will do whatever it takes for him to get that information. We are about to bait and hunt the most ferocious fucking prey you have ever seen, and we aim to be right in its goddamn nest, so make sure you watch your quarters, take care of one another, and above all else do your utmost not to get killed." He smiles a little. "Let's bring a win for the home team, yeah, and give the people here who rely upon us some goddam peace and quiet for a change. Because that device will work. Ain't that right, Daniel?"

Daniel straightens up and then glances around the room for a moment. "Yes sir. Yes, it will."

"Good boy." He smiles and nods at him. "Right. Does anybody not understand what it is we are to do here today?" Nathan scans the room knowing full well that none of his team will raise their hand or ask a question, such is their dedication to the task at hand. For the mission. And for one another. Smiling faintly, he nods his head. "All right then. To your vehicles, double check your gear, and prep your minds. We go in 10. Hop to it. And good luck."

There are no cheers, no whoops, and cheesy celebrations, just a fervor of chatter as everyone moves off as ordered to their designated areas.

Daniel lowers his head and whispers to himself, "oh my God, please work please work please work." He jumps when Gary places a hand on his shoulder.

"Hey. Calm yourself. You are one hell of a mathematician, engineer, and probably the smartest fella on the planet right now. This is gonna work. Okay?"

Daniel takes a deep breath and smiles, then puffs out hard, the smile disappearing.

"Good. Now, stick close to Nathan at all times. Do not leave his sight. We know the plan. I'll get to the area to bait the demons and get them to portal in... hopefully, Sarah will then sneak in with the equipment, take the readings, and then we all get the hell out of there. Maybe kill us some bad guys in the process, yeah?" He smiles once again, then takes a deep breath. "You know you don't have to come. If the gear is prepped and ready, Sarah and I can take care of it. You can wait this one out back here if you want. No one will think any less of you."

Daniel ponders him for a moment, then shakes his head. "No. I have to go. How could I possibly come up with a plan that might kill those trying to execute it if I am not prepared to see it through myself?"

Gary smiles, admiring him, then it wanes as an understanding of the internal conflict that must be raging within Daniel right now hits him. The boy is clearly scared, but he is right. How could he send people to their deaths with an insane plan, and then live with that knowing he wasn't courageous enough to go himself? And although Gary doesn't entirely agree with that sentiment, he understands it and why Daniel needs to do this. He smiles again.

Daniel takes a deep breath, then motions toward Sarah with his head. "I know you're concerned about me but are you sure she's up to the task?"

Gary glances toward Sarah. No matter what the outcome of the conversation he just had with Nathan, he cannot help but allow his mind to run scenarios and eventualities – it's just who he is. But for the sake of the mission and more importantly Daniel's confidence, he shakes it from his mind as best he can.

"Don't you worry about Sarah, she's always on point. That girl always comes through."

He considers that for a moment. She does. Always.

SIXTEEN

Charlotte runs her fingers over embossed symbols on the pillars on the outside of the gigantic temple. She looks up, admiring the vast entrance to the structure. "That is one big-ass door," she says, glancing back toward Judas as he approaches her up the stone stairs that lead into Mokwena's lair, then shifts her gaze to Azazel. "How big did you say these spiders are?"

The demon rubs his mouth and then chin with thumb and forefinger. "Well, to say they are spiders is kind of an... approximation."

Azazel grins, and it is not one that Charlotte finds welcoming.

"So, what do all these symbols mean?" She says, returning her attention to the carvings.

"Well," he says sidling up to her, "some tell of Mokwena's reason for imprisonment, as she was not born purebred demon, she was recruited into the higher ranks, a sort of... fast-track promotion scheme by Lucifer for one reason or another." He snorts a laugh. "Others tell the stories of those bound into servitude to her."

Charlotte nods along, her interest piqued. "So, what's her story?"

"Ahh, well you see, it's fascinating – a tale of love, abandonment, treachery, and deceit. A thousand or so years ag—"

Judas passes between them, moving onto the top step, then glances back. "As much as I would like to be regaled by yet another of your stories, Azazel, and by that, I mean I fucking wouldn't…"

Azazel rolls his eyes.

"…we don't have time for this bullshit, assuming that the temple's inhabitants know we are coming?"

Azazel nods his agreement.

"Right, therefore we must get through this place without dying somehow, then get to the Temple of Belial, where we will, without doubt, engage in a fight against Lucifer, War, Death, and whoever the fuck else he feels like throwing into the mix." He looks at them each in turn once more. "So with that in mind I don't think we have time to dally here. Agreed?"

"I don't think we have time to dally here!" Charlotte says, mimicking him, her expression haughty.

Judas turns toward her, slowly, and narrows his eyes, and she smirks at him. He then turns away from her with much the same speed, allowing himself a smirk of his own.

"Well," Azazel says with a clap of his hands, then holding one out to invite them forward, "shall we?"

Judas looks at Charlotte and is about to speak when she cuts him short.

"I know, I know," she says, holding up a placating hand, "no heroics. We stick together. Gotchya." She winks and points at him while making a clicking sound with her mouth. She then turns her attention toward Azazel. "But seriously, how big actually are these spiders?"

Azazel offers a gruff and staggered laugh and then walks toward the entrance.

Taking a deep breath, Judas closes his eyes briefly, shakes his head, then walks past him and into the temple.

Inside, beams of light spread ahead of them for a few feet, plotting a course across gigantic stone slabs, each of which have symbols carved into them. Within the beams dance tiny motes of light in their thousands, glittering against the dark and musky backdrop; the effect is ethereal as they move in unison, as though driven by something that has a master plan.

Charlotte notices, and reaches out to touch the dancing spectacle, only to have it change course, like birds in the dusk light searching for a place to nest.

"Whoa!" she says, as their formation changes once more. "Is everything in Hell freaky and alive?"

Judas glances back at her. "Pretty much, sweetie. C'mon, let's keep moving."

She stares at the anomaly for a few seconds more, then follows him further into the temple.

As they pass the last of the beams, the temperature changes, and it is dramatic, as though they had broached an invisible barrier. Outside it was hot, desert-like, but now it is as if they had walked into a refrigerator, something that Charlotte signifies with a vocalized shiver.

"Holy crap. It's friggin' freezing," she says, wrapping her arms around herself.

Azazel looks at her, unimpressed. "You have talents you know. How about using a few of them from time to time? I thought you'd had a serious awakening when absorbing the Seventh Seal and The Book?"

She curls up one side of her mouth and frowns at him. "How about you shut it… dickhead!" She scowls at him for a couple of seconds and then clicks her fingers. A light sheen of Divinity envelops her, creating a barrier to ward off the cold. "Happy now? Harry-fucking-Nobber!"

Azazel looks at her, confused. "That doesn't even make any sense. I look nothing like Harry Potter."

"I look nothing like Harry Potter!" she says, her tone mimicking and sarcastic.

Judas sighs. "Can we just get on with this, and please sweetie, come on now, ease off on the bad language, yeah? You're really starting to sound more like me every day. It's not a good thing. Clearly I've been a bad influence. Gabe will have a fit."

A voice echoes out of the darkness, female, and elegant sounding. "This... *this* is Heaven's savior? A foul-mouthed unintelligent little girl?" The voice chuckles. "Oh my, it shall be fun as I watch you struggle to make it to the heart of my lair. Hmmm. I'll wager you don't get within 100 yards of the stairs that lead down to the second level, never mind all the way to the fourth."

The voice laughs again.

"Four levels!" Charlotte silently mouths to Judas.

"Yes, my irksome little friend," the female voice replies to her before Judas can respond, "four levels. And here is a just a mere taste of what's to come."

From overhead, a hissing sound causes them to look up. They see nothing, only darkness, vast and foreboding.

Charlotte glances back toward the beams of light they passed upon entering the temple, and one by one they sweep backward, away from them along the floor as though the position of their source had changed, but looking up at where the trail begins, she cannot see anything that might cause such an effect.

A skittering sound above her and to the right causes Charlotte to snap her attention toward it, but still she cannot see anything. The same sound again, only to her left and she whips around, her eyes attempting to penetrate the darkness above. She turns once again, this time toward the entrance as the sound of stone clashing against stone causes her eyes to widen. The entrance closes as giant stone slabs appear from nowhere, slamming into and on top of each other, their appearance rapid, the sound crunching and then as fast as it had begun it is over, and the temple descends into total darkness.

Charlotte grits her teeth. "Enough!" she shouts, and throws her hands into the air causing a blinding white ball of Divinity to erupt that climbs above, illuminating the entire area, revealing not only a huge corridor ahead of them, but also a dozen or so spider demons that dangle above – gigantic and terrifying, with huge bloated sacs making up their bodies, and where a spider's head would be is instead a humanoid torso, faces expressionless, zombie-like, their lifeless jet-black eyes holding no spark of emotion. At the end of each of their eight legs are hands, some curled into fists while the others press against walls palm-down. She takes in a sharp breath as the area under the human torso of one of the creatures opens into a mouth, brimming with razor-sharp teeth, dripping steaming saliva onto the floor, and the sight fills her with revulsion.

Judas holds out his right arm. "Now would be a good time to become sword, I think, Azazel."

Nodding, Azazel takes a step toward him, his gaze never leaving the creatures who hiss and spit above them. "I couldn't agree more, master." He pirouettes clockwise, transforming into Ikazuchi, Judas catching him mid-spin.

Judas glances at Charlotte. "There's something different about these creatures. I can't put my finger on it, but do not underestimate them."

She holds her arms to her sides and her katanas unseat themselves from their scabbards, elegantly releasing and twirling into her hands. She brings the weapons up in front of her. "Yeah, there's definitely something odd about them."

The unseen woman laughs again. "Welcome to you, The Light – the betrayer Iscariot. I am Mokwena and this is the last place you will ever see."

The spiders scream in unison and drop to the ground, then raise their leg-hands into the air as part of a terrifying battle-cheer, and charge.

"Fuck it!" Judas shouts, racing at them with a roar, and Charlotte follows.

One of the creature's chuckles at him as he closes in, Ikazuchi held aloft, and as he swings his sword at it the demon shadow-steps and moves behind him.

"SHIT!" he says, sliding to a halt, and raising Ikazuchi aloft to block an inevitable attack from behind that comes in the form of a clenched fist at the end of the spider's leg, punching down into his sword, and staggering him forward and away. "THEY CAN SHADOW-STEP!" he screams at Charlotte, who is about to engage her first opponent.

"Goddamit!" she mutters, and enables a protective Divinity bubble just in time, as the demon she was about to attack warps behind her and punches into the back of her shield.

The bubble cracks, and she stumbles forward toward another of the demons who punches into her, sending her crashing away in another direction and the shield disintegrates. Charlotte tumbles across the floor, letting go of one of her swords, and it clatters across the stone surface. As she comes to a halt, she holds out her empty hand and the weapon scrapes along, back into her grip, just as another of the creature's attacks, leaping through the air and down onto her, its legs pounding into the ground and its enormous teeth-filled mouth snapping over and over, hissing, snarling, and slavering. She slashes at it while scrambling backward, and it evades by back stepping, the head of its humanoid element floundering from side-to-side with a disturbing grin on its face and its eyes lock onto her.

As it darts forward and snaps at her once again, forcing her to move her head to the side to prevent the teeth ripping into her face, she drives a sword up and into its body, below the section where the human torso branches off, and the demon screeches. It punches its fist-feet into the ground in pain, and black liquid spurts from the wound in thick gluts, threatening to spray into Charlotte's face, something she very much does not want to happen and so she forges another divinity shield to protect herself. Using her holy energy, she pushes herself up and forward into the air driving into the demon and punting it away. Then, dismissing the shield, she drops to the ground, landing on both feet, twirling her swords in front of her, and glances toward Judas who has cleaved his sword around in a clockwise arc, slicing another spider-demon in half. "There are too many of them!" she shouts, motioning around as wave upon wave of demon-spiders now scramble down the walls.

"Okay. Into the corridor!" he shouts back.

Another demon strikes at him, its distance too close for him to swing his sword and so he grabs the blade in two hands and smashes the flat of it against the creature then, driving forward with shadow-step he slams it into the wall and it explodes into a shower of black gore and viscera, as Charlotte zips past to his left, racing into the blackness of the corridor. With a grunt, Judas follows her.

"You're aware we're in a maze, right?" she says, her words hurried, as they navigate the tight space that twists and bends from one route to the next.

"The thought had occurred to me, yes."

A screech above causes them both to look up.

"Look out!" Judas calls, as a spider-demon descends from the blackness on a web-line.

Wasting no time, and not wanting it to hit the ground, he sprints a few feet up the wall to his right, spins around mid-air, and slices the beast in two, then lands ahead of the splash of black blood and demon body parts that flop onto the ground.

"Keep moving!" he urges Charlotte, who had turned to look at him, and she complies, moving forward again at speed.

The corridor's width decreases as they race ahead, and Charlotte bumps her shoulders against each side.

"It's getting too narrow," she says, pinballing between the walls, "we're gonna get trapped!"

"DUCK!" he screams, bringing his sword over his shoulder from back to front.

She does without hesitation, and a crackling dark-energy beam fizzes over her head, from out of Judas' sword and rips into the stone ahead of them causing it to explode and they both leap through the hole and out of the other side, tumbling over the ground, a dust cloud spreading out behind them.

Almost in unison, they skid back up onto their feet, weapons at the ready, a hand scraping along the dirty ground to steady them, the sword held in Charlotte's screeching across the stone.

The creatures that pour through the opening are not prepared for what comes next, as Judas throws his sword forward once again in a wide arc, from right to left, spraying another beam of energy that obliterates every demon it meets, exploding them into thousands of pieces. The attack not finished, he raises Ikazuchi into the air then slams it into the ground with both hands on the hilt, driving it down with furious intent. He looks up toward the gap in the wall at the next wave of attacking creatures.

Behind him, and understanding what is to happen next, Charlotte slams her swords into the ground as anchors and encases herself in a fresh Divinity shield.

Judas screams as he pulls the sword out, causing the ground to shudder with a violent earthquake that undulates the stone floor, rippling it outwards. The area around them, save for a small circular piece of ground that they stand upon, explodes upward into thousands of pieces of shrapnel that spray into the air, shredding the advancing demons. The attack is so powerful, so potent, that it reaches even those that had remained hidden high above, concealed by the darkness, and they rain down onto the ground around Judas and Charlotte, deceased.

As the devastating energy blast engulfs her she tucks her head into her chest and closes her eyes, awaiting what she expects to be an inevitable battle against the kinetic force. It doesn't come, however and so she looks up to see that the event has left both her and Judas untouched. *He's learned to control it,* she thinks to herself. *He can control where it strikes and what effect it has around him.*

A smile twitches on her face. He is an even more incredible warrior than she had ever imagined. Truly Heaven's finest and in that moment with her thoughts calm, she feels that he is even deadlier than Gabriel himself.

Charlotte disengages her protective shield and ahead of her Judas rises to his feet, his head bowed, and shoulders slowly heaving. Around them the area is obliterated, reduced to rubble, the dust settling. She walks toward him, her hand outstretched, ready to place it on his shoulder, to comfort him, when Azazel's voice spikes out from the sword, causing her to stop.

"That won't hold them for long and Mokwena probably has an inexhaustible supply. Might I suggest another strategy?"

"Go on," Judas says, wiping dirt from his cheek.

"Well, I have had time to locate the position of Mokwena's central chamber below and I now know where we need to be in order to drill into it."

"You had time to locate her central chamber?" Judas asks, his gaze fixed down and to his left, his voice inflected with irritation. "At what point did you have time to do this? When we were fleeing for our lives? When we were blasting this place into nothingness?" He holds the sword up to his annoyed face.

"What can I say," Ikazuchi says, his tone sarcastic, "I can multitask. I'm like a chick in that regard."

Judas grunts and sneers. "Yeah. Funny. Keep it up – see where it gets you."

"Look, master, we don't have time to go into it now, suffice to say you need to follow my lead and I shall show you where we need to be."

"To drill, yeah?"

"Yes. To drill."

"Drill?" Charlotte asks.

"Hmmm," Judas says, glancing at her, his voice swimming with suspicion at what Ikazuchi is telling him.

"Well, whatever we are gonna do, we need to do it now. I can hear them coming."

She's right, he can hear them as well. From all around them, regrouping, finding their courage.

"Yeah, agreed, sweetie, let's get out of here." He holds Ikazuchi to his face once again, "but you and I need to have a chat after this, demon. I am getting the distinct impression that you are telling me very little about our encounters in the underworld and it's really starting to piss me off."

"Of course, master. Whatever you want," the sword says, its voice hissing.

With the howls and screams of the spider-demons behind them, they shadow-step away toward another corridor, Azazel's voice calling out directions as they navigate a path through the maze.

SEVENTEEN

She hears something deep within her mind, a voice calling to her, although far away and indistinct. She thinks she recognizes it but cannot be sure, nor can she clearly make out what it is saying as each word echoes over itself, giving it a feeling of multiple voices fighting for clarity within her mind. So strange. And she feels she has talked to this voice before, earlier perhaps? But the memory of that now seems nothing more than a blur scratching at the back of her head, unable to form into something coherent to understand.

This makes no sense, she tells herself. *This makes no sense at all.*

She stops, and looks down at the dirty, dusty temple floor.

Why can't I remember?

The muttering voice echoes out once more.

There it is again. What the hell is that?

Then, a different and whispered voice, closer and more 'in-the-moment' causes her to look up and blink her confusion away.

"Sweetie, you okay?" Judas asks, placing a hand on Charlotte's shoulder, his expression equal to that of her bewilderment.

She frowns. "Er, yeah. Sorry. I don't know what just happened there."

He strokes loose strands of her hair away from her face and back behind her ear. "You kinda zoned out for a second. Are you sure you're okay?"

She looks around, seeing that they are crouched and huddled together at the end of a corridor that opens into a huge cavern, then shakes her head, dispersing the last 30 seconds out of her mind, the action symbolic in cleansing unnecessary information to make way for the more pertinent events that lie ahead. The need to figure out what they must do with the… she glances at Judas again, wondering if they are going to be able to… what was the thing she needed to do before they…

She jabs her hands onto the sides of her head, thrusting her fingers through her hair, feeling herself drifting again, trying to return to the echoing voice within her mind.

Goddamit! What was I just thinking about?

"Well, like I said," Judas continues, looking away from her to the exit of the corridor and whispering, "we ain't getting across here, we need another plan." He gestures toward the bridge ahead that crosses a huge expanse of cavern, broken in two halfway across.

His voice brings her back into the moment again, refocusing her attention on him, easing away her frown, and she smiles. She looks past him and into the cavern. "Wow, this place is gorgeous." She says, glancing around. "Look at the reflections of light dancing across the walls. Look at the beautiful colors, moving from blue, to gold, to green, continually cycling. Another color, violet, then another, over and over, cycling colors. Always cycling colors."

Judas turns his head toward her slowly. "Errr, okay. That's very… precise language you're using. Are you sure you're okay?" He frowns, his eyes darting left and right, searching her face.

"I'm sorry, I don't know why I said that. That was total and utter gibberish." She looks down at the ground, struggling with her thoughts.

Judas is about to respond when Azazel taps him on the arm, and he turns to him.

Charlotte shakes her head. *What am I doing? What the hell am I saying? This isn't important! None of this is.*

She looks at Judas again, conversing with Azazel, plotting on how they are to get across the bridge. Her eyes narrow and she frowns once more at their moving yet silent mouths, and as she continues to stare, her eyes blinking, she sees Judas raise a hand and point toward the way they have just come, suggesting they retrace their steps, his movements in slow motion.

This isn't right, she tells herself again, *Why is he moving so slowly? And we don't need to go back, I could jump us over that bridge.*

She looks around again, as further uncertainty overwhelms her.

No, wait! Can I do that? Have I done such a thing before? No, this isn't right. That doesn't matter. Wait! This isn't right!

CHARLOTTE!

The voice inside her head, that moments earlier was nothing more than a whisper, now shouts so loud she almost stumbles forward and is forced to grab the rocky wall of the corridor to retain her balance.

Can you hear me? Charlotte? Can... you... hear me?

Pestilence? she says to herself.

She is remembering.

The voice. It belongs to the Horseman Pestilence, living inside her mind along with The Seal and The Book.

Yes, that's it.

She blinks her eyes, remembering more.

There was a fight at the Vatican, and now he lives inside her, along with the items she assimilated. And they are draining her.

Charlotte, can you hear me child? Pestilence's voice shouts once again.

She shakes her head and closes her eyes, focusing all her concentration on the space within her mind from where his voice resonates. Her concentration deepens, and she screws up her face, her mouth puckering tight, her cheeks bulging, then realizes she is holding her breath.

Can you hear me child?

I hear you. I hear you, she replies, breathing out hard, *Yes, I can hear you again. What's going on, where have you been?*

Finally. I was getting worried. I couldn't reach you within your mind, despite my power and I was quite concerned. Mokwena really has been busy in perfecting her talents over the centuries. Now listen carefully, Charlotte. You are not where you think you are. You are poisoned. This is not reality. Right now, you are being cocooned, wrapped as a prize for Lucifer.

A prize? What are you talking about? She feels dazed, confused, hearing his words but unable to process their meaning as something in her mind seems to prevent her from understanding them.

Mokwena. She wants to get back into Lucifer's favor and you are her offering. She intends to drag you to the Temple of Belial herself. If you do not wake up now, all will be lost. You will never break the hold she has on you. She has already separated you from Judas. You need to break free and find him. Believe me, she has no such plans for him. She intends to devour him.

What? What are you talking abo—

CHARLOTTE! WAKE UP!

Her mind feels like it has received a bolt of electricity, such is the blinding white flash of light that bursts within her. Her eyes snap open, as if out of the dream. She cannot see anything other than a whitish-gray, and a substance covering her mouth inhibits her ability to speak. Confusion overwhelms her, and she struggles within her bonds, but her arms are wrapped tight to her sides and she cannot free them. She then becomes aware she is on her back and being dragged somewhere.

Shit. Shit. SHIT! she thinks to herself and struggles again.

Calm yourself, young lady, Pestilence says, his tone soothing. *Calm yourself, and your mind. This is not a problem, this is a test. A mere test of your abilities. This will help you grow.*

Are you kidding me? she replies, still conversing with him within her mind, her eyes darting back and forth. *Not a problem? This feels like a really big goddamn problem to me.*

It is only a problem if you make it one. Focus your abilities, connect with my Dark-Divinity and use it to purge the last of the poison from your system, then destroy your bonds. While the venom flows through you, it will dull your powers and make you weak. You must flush it out, regain your composure, break free, and then butcher your enemies. You have been captured by her slaves. Dispatch them, and we can then make our way to her chamber and stop her killing Judas.

He is right. She has no time or right to panic. She has been gifted talents and abilities that she must master and learn to control if she is to become the protector the Earth deserves, and more importantly if she is to rescue her dad. As Pestilence says, this is just another situation she needs to resolve and find a solution to. This *isn't* a problem.

She closes her eyes and steadies her breathing, then reaches down deep within herself, to her core, where her power comes from. The poison working its way through her system has arrested her abilities, but it won't stop her, she won't allow it, she cannot afford for it to. Judas needs her. He needs her to become what he has been training her to be all along.

A spark of energy catches light.

Yes. That's it. And so it begins, Pestilence says, an eagerness in his speech and an air of ecstatic anticipation, and if he could be seen he would be grinning at the knowledge of what is to come. A new evolution in The Light's power. Her next phase.

She feels the venom dispersing from her system, burned away by the Dark-Divinity that whirls inside of her, growing and cyclonic. More of the debilitating substance is purged from her and the development of the dark energy is symbiotic with the poison's decline as it expands within her, surging through and racing over itself, intertwining with veins, her organs, her soul. The reaction increases and erupts, jumping from minimal to full power in a fraction of the time it took to get to where it was before it took hold.

Charlotte explodes with dark-light, evaporating the demonic cocoon that binds her and she rises to her feet as though propelled from behind, her body straight and rigid. Her eyes glow and she thrust's her hands out to her sides, ready to welcome her swords into them, which they do, unseating from their scabbards on her back and twirling into her grip.

The creature that had been dragging her screeches as the back half of its body disintegrates, blasted away by the Dark-Divinity surge that freed her.

And as the creature stabs its remaining legs into the ground, suffering from immense pain, a dozen other spider-demons gather around the glowing woman.

Charlotte eyes each of them and then takes a small step back with one foot, readying herself into a defensive posture, and as the reality of the demons' true sizes is presented to her, she sees that they are nowhere near as large as they were within the dream-state, but much smaller, just a little larger than she is. *Good*, she says to herself, *they will die much faster.*

They scream in unison, and one bursts forward to attack, and as it races toward her, she closes her eyes and takes a deep breath, feeling every ounce of the power that now courses through her. It is like some wonderful narcotic elevating her sensory perception to staggering heights, giving her awareness of everything around her – the sound of the demons' screams manifested into pulse-waves, bouncing into and off her, the changes in air pressure from their bloated bodies as they scramble over the grimy temple floor, the dust that speckles against her skin like snowfall. She feels everything and sees all, more than she ever has as she embraces the new ability. And the glow in her eyes allows her vision to penetrate even the darkest corners of the chamber, the darkness no longer holding her to ransom. She is so alive with energy that her reactions are automatic, as the first of the demons to reach her bares testament to the fact. She turns to her side a fraction, the pouncing creature's movement observed slow in comparison to hers as it passes her by, and she flicks her sword up at it, nothing more than a casual reaction.

The spider-demon skids along the dirty floor toward a wall behind her, its human torso cleaved in half, and the others check their movement, the sight of their deceased comrade instilling a sense of trepidation within them, keen to avoid a similar fate. And so they change their tactic and circle around her, favoring containment.

Twirling her swords, she readies for their advance, a wry smile on her face.

The demons continue to stalk her, moving slowly, waiting for the right moment. Creatures from Hell they may be, but they are not stupid and even they know the woman in front of them possesses a terrifying power that should not be underestimated.

Without warning, the human elements of the spider-demons jerk into life, coughing and spluttering, ejecting black, viscous liquid from their mouths, then they shake their arms while flexing their fingers open and closed several times. And they focus on her, their faces locked in maddening grins.

She twirls her swords in her hands once more. She doesn't have time to waste. She needs to attack, to kill these damned creatures and move on as quickly as possible. She needs to find Judas.

As she prepares to tear into them, each of the human portion of the creature's reach toward their backs and, following their arms and hands, something catches her eye, something she hadn't seen previously – swords, spears, and pikes of varying types protrude out of their bodies. Previously when fighting them in the dream-state, she had dismissed them as nothing more than features of the spider-demons' physical make-up, but now seeing them up close, she understands their nature and what they are to be used for. For the briefest of moments, she wonders at how many of the creatures ahead were hapless, damned souls who had mistakenly wandered into Mokwena's temple, unaware of the fate that awaited them – to be cut down and sliced into pieces by what would later become their brethren and then engage in the same endless cycle of destruction. She dismisses the thought. No time to dwell on backstory. The only thing that mattered was killing them as fast as possible and then moving on.

Gritting her teeth, she attacks.

EIGHTEEN

"What the fuck do you mean, you don't know where she went? She was right there… RIGHT FUCKING THERE! How can she just disappear?"

Judas turns in a circle once again and then takes a step back, his eyes narrowed, and his confusion second only to his anger. He stops moving, frowns, and then looks around once more.

"Wait, what the fuck is going on? This isn't where I just was. Where the hell am I?"

A sultry voice echoes out of the darkness.

"You are my guest until I deem otherwise."

He turns in circles again, trying to pinpoint its location but it is Azazel who ceases his movement.

"Listen to me, Judas. This is very, *very* important. She has something I need. A jewel contained within her. I need that stone and I need it badly. And I must rip it out of her right before the moment of her death. Do you understand me? Do you understand? I must have that stone. Look at me, Judas. Look at me."

Judas focuses his attention on Azazel's hands on his shoulders, as he shakes him and talks erratically, and then returns his gaze to Azazel's face. His entire body feels drained, exhausted by its attempts to decipher just exactly what is going on, and he blinks slowly, his brow furrowing into a deeper frown.

"Are you listening to me, Judas? Tell me you understand."

Azazel clicks his fingers in front of his face.

"Judas. JUDAS! Are you listening to me? I need that stone before we kill her."

Mokwena laughs, walking out of shadow and into the soft, blue glow of the large chamber they are in. "He can't hear you, Architect."

Judas turns to look at her, and Azazel's hands slip off his shoulders. He sees she is naked, her skin brown, with long black hair draping down over and covering her breasts. Her body is sublime, perfect, the most stunning woman he has ever seen, and a deep desire for her grips him. A powerful longing stirs within, one he has not felt for an age. And as her gorgeous, elf-like face smiles at him, her lips full and blood-red, he falls into their beauty and closes his eyes, taking a deep breath. He wants to dive in, to drown in them and he smiles as he opens his eyes once more.

"Concentrate, master," a worried Azazel says. "We are here to kill, not fuck her."

"Kill me?" she says, throwing her head back with an exaggerated laugh.

Her beautiful voice sounds even more serene than it did before, and Judas smiles once again.

"You think you can kill me? Mokwena! Here, in my own lair? My own world." This time her laugh is subtler, nothing more than a slight chuckle from the back of her throat. "Oh, my dear Azazel. Iscariot is nothing more than a fly caught in my web," she chuckles, "pun intended of course, and there is nothing you can do about it."

She strokes the side of Judas' face and he leans into her hand, his smile widening.

Azazel circles around her toward her back.

Mokwena's head turns around to face him, her body still facing Judas whose head continues to nestle in her hand. "And what do you think you will accomplish here, Architect? Do you imagine that you have power over me? That you are somehow able to do something in my world?"

Azazel stares at her for a moment and frowns. *What did she mean by that? In her world? Hell doesn't belong to her, she is a mere pawn, a puppet within its ever-expanding stage show.* He looks down at the ground, his eyes darting left and right. *What did she mean by tha—* He looks up sharply and tries to reach out and grab her, but he cannot. He tries harder and Mokwena grins, her mouth no longer inviting or beautiful, instead her lips cracked and her teeth jagged and crooked. Her tongue snakes out of her mouth and over her lips, licking them and she cackles, her head still facing him, her body still toward Judas, stroking his face, oblivious to what is going on.

"Awwww fuck!" Azazel says, causing Mokwena to burst into laughter. Then, the scowl on his face disappears, replaced instantly with a look of enlightenment, of understanding. He grins at Mokwena, wagging his finger at the same time. "Very clever. Very, very clever. Ousted by my own ruse as this is what I used to do to my victims who entered my realm, before this one freed me." He cocks a thumb toward Judas, still rolling his head around in Mokwena's hand. "In fact, I'm not even mad." He grins, deeper. "Seriously, I'm not. Bravo." He claps his hands. "Bravo my friend. It even looks like something I would have put together. The caverns, the corridors, the mood lighting that creates a dark and foreboding atmos. No, really, I'm not mad – I'm impressed! It's almost as though you have done this just for me, as a sort of… homage." He places a hand on his chest and mimics an overwhelmed face, moving the hand up to wipe away a non-existent tear. He looks around, contemplative, then back to her. "And I thought there was something familiar about the sensation I was feeling, like I have experienced this before." He clucks his tongue, then cocks his head to one side. "Hmmm, no matter. But thank you. Thank you for that, really. I'm touched. I really am. But!" He says, wagging a finger as he walks back to his position next to Judas. "Your problem is you're just not as fucking smart as me. Not even close. Oh, I'll give you your due, this… venom that you have put into us is pretty ingenious stuff, given that Judas and I are tied at soul-level. What works on him also works on me! Very clever."

Mokwena grins.

Azazel smiles a little, then looks up and away, pointing a finger into the air. "The dancing dust in the beams of light that the girl saw when we entered, I take it?"

She smiles again, this time with a chuckle. "My slaves love to spray it around when our little play-things wander into our lair. It makes killing them that much more of an enjoyable experience."

"Hey, I'm not judging," he says, raising his hands into the air, "you do your thing, and fair play to you for doing it. But!"

"There's that word again… but!" Mokwena snarls, her growing irritation at Azazel beginning to show.

"Yes. But. There are two problems."

"Which are?"

"One. You are the custodian of something that belongs to me. And I want it back." His face becomes serious, angry almost, and then returns to playful, smiling. "And two, I only ever allowed one being into my realm at any given time, as letting in more than that always carried the risk of an unwanted interaction between them, and as such, given that I understand how this works I get to enjoy doing this." He glances toward Judas, "Please forgive me, master." His words carry no sincerity, rather deep sarcasm.

Azazel punches Judas square in the face, a blow so powerful, it sends the angel careering over the ground toward the cavern wall, where he crunches into it with severe force.

Mokwena's mouth enlarges unnaturally and she emits a high-pitched scream.

Azazel smirks at her. "Nap time's over. See ya soon, darling." He snaps a half-salute at her.

NINETEEN

Parrying a flurry of duel-wielded sword attacks from the last of the spider-demons, Charlotte activates her Divinity shield as the demon throws one of its legs into attack from her side, its companions lying dead all around.

She had dispatched the others with varying degrees of difficulty, but this one is proving to be the toughest out of all them.

The creature's appendage bounces off the shield, causing electrical arcing to spark at the connection point, which Charlotte then deactivates, favoring swift movement over the armor it provides, and she takes full advantage of a small gap in the creature's defense. Sprinting toward it, her swords down by her sides, and out at a slight angle, she leaps into the air and somersaulting onto the spider-demon's back, then turns and slices at its human head.

Just as the sword is about to connect, the demon rolls onto its back, forcing her to leap off into a controlled tumble across the ground, skidding to a halt a few meters away from it as it wriggles itself back onto its legs.

You don't have time for this child. Kill it so we can move on, Pestilence says from within her mind.

"Don't you think I know that?" she responds out loud, "what the hell do you think I'm trying to do? These things are bloody fast. Now shut up and let me do my job."

"With whom do you speak?" hisses the demon, as it creeps to its left, attempting to circle around her.

Her eyes open wide. "So you can talk."

"Of course I can talk, you fucking idiotic woman."

Unleash a Dark-Divinity beam and let us be done with this Charlotte.

"I can't," she says, through tightened lips. "I'm burning too much energy. And something's wrong inside me. I can feel it."

Pestilence's presence within her feels removed for a moment.

The creature continues to circle around her.

She feels Pestilence return to her. "What the hell was that? What did you just do?" she asks.

I went deep within you. And you are correct, there is something wrong. I don't understand how I missed it before. Not only are The Book and The Seal damaging you, they are killing you by draining you of any energy that you create. So the more you materialize, the quicker the reaction and the deeper they draw on it, depleting it faster. This is most troublesome.

"What, you mean more troublesome than the direct threat ahead of me?"

"Seriously," the creature hisses, "who the fuck are you talking to?"

"Oh, shut up for a second will you ya stupid shit."

The spider-demon screeches, angered, then charges at her.

"Goddamit" she says, reacting in kind.

Their weapons meet, trading blow after blow, blades ringing and chiming around the chamber and Charlotte is surprised at the level of skill that the demon possesses, and she wonders if it were a swordsman in its previous life. She is brought back to her full attention by Pestilence's scolding voice, commanding her to concentrate, a berating that reminds her of the training sessions she had with Judas while in the netherworld, but she pushes the thought out of her mind, aware she has no time to ponder such things.

She parries and attacks again, vocalizing her displeasure with an annoyed scream at having not yet dispatched the creature, and then back-flips away from it, the demon screeching and giving chase, skittering toward her.

Reaching the chamber wall, she leaps and plants her feet on the rocky surface then kicks off. Spinning around, her foot connects square and hard with the human head of the creature and she throws so much force into it she sends it crashing to the side. She then lands cleanly on her feet, and quickly follows up by shadow-stepping toward the flailing demon, stabbing a sword straight through its head. The creature screams and as its body reacts, she brings her other sword up and around, decapitating it, its lifeless form slumping to the ground. She draws her embedded sword from out of the corpse and staggers back, then takes in a deep breath and leans forward, hands on knees, and with her swords pointing out to the sides.

There now, that wasn't so hard was it? Pestilence's mocking voice says.

She heaves a tired laugh. "This is going to be a problem."

Indeed. We must remove those relics from you as soon as we can, or I fear they will consume your energy and in turn you.

"I'll die?"

You'll cease to be. It's not the same as dying. There will be nothing left of you ever again.

"Goddamit!"

Yes, I guess he would if he was overly invested in this affair, which he does not seem to be.

She stands up straight and throws her swords out of her hands, where they fly out and return to their scabbards. Rubbing the base of her back, she offers a contemplative grunt. "Yeah, I intend to ask him about that one day."

Well, quite. But for now we mustn't waste any more time. We must get to Judas.

"Care to help me with directions?"

Child, it is about time you got to grips with your full potential. Your connection with Judas goes way beyond even the normal bond that a parent and child would share. Yours is something that the very essence of the universe itself dictated. Reach out and feel for his presence. You are fated together at a much deeper level than you currently understand.

She stares ahead for a moment, an expression that might have been mistaken for blank and vacant had anyone been around to witness it, then she closes her eyes and concentrates.

Connect with him. Search for him. Latch onto that memory. That one memory.

She knows to what he refers. In the netherworld, as a child, when she fell having performed a particularly daring cartwheel and hurt her knee, and Judas came charging over, the deep concern on his face that of a father who was feeling every ounce of pain his crying child on the ground was experiencing.

Having processed the memory as an adult, it is an event that she recognizes as the most important in hers and Judas' history together. The moment she saw a pure and unfiltered love from him and she knew he had never felt the way he did toward her for anyone else. A love she felt not even God, her Father himself, could ever feel for her. And it was the memory that allowed her to bring him back while he lay dying on the ground at Stonehenge after their fight with The Horsemen, and it is the memory that will bring her to him now. She wraps herself around it and allows it to flow through her very soul. The words she said that day float through her mind.

Then I will become strong and look after you.

She sees herself in his arms as they sit on the ground, her staring into his eyes, accepting her destiny as he lays it out for her.

Then I will become strong and look after you.

The words cycle over and over, repeating within her mind, the emotion ingrained into her and building deep inside. She doesn't even notice the tears spilling from her eyes, rolling down her cheeks or that her hands are clenched so tight her knuckles are white and her fingers blood-red. She doesn't notice, because she sees him within her mind, clear as day, where he is now, hurtling across dusty ground and crashing into a wall.

Her eyes snap open and she inhales deeply. She knows exactly where he is, and shadow-stepping ahead, she moves further into and through the temple at incredible speed toward him. And as she blurs through multitudes of corridors and down flights of stairs, Pestilence converses with her.

Just listen to me, child. Concentrate on getting to him, but listen. I have learned much from investigating the relics contained within you. They were blocking me from learning, but I worked around those barriers and have gained knowledge that I previously had no understanding of. I will keep working and deciphering, but for now I must give you a warning. All is not what it seems and this sword, this demon of power – Azazel – has its own agenda. There is something very wrong with that entity and his motivations. You must be wary of trusting him, for I feel it is his own ends that he seeks to serve and not yours or Judas. Be mindful of him child. Very mindful.

"Oh, I intend to be," she replies, "and I then intend to send his sorry ass back to oblivion."

TWENTY

Judas coughs, drags himself to his feet, and dusts down his black trench coat. He glances toward the ground at Ikazuchi, then bends over to pick the weapon up. "Okay, what just happened?"

"No time to explain, master," Ikazuchi's voice hisses from the sword. "Be on your guard. She is coming, and this time she will not be human."

Judas frowns and is about to answer when the ground around him shakes, forcing him to maintain his balance.

"What the fu—" Judas says, turning around as Mokwena thunders toward him from out of the shadows at the back of the cavern, and, unlike the forms of her slaves, she is vastly bigger, gigantic in fact, even more so than the Gatekeeper, her terrifying appearance exemplified by how her body differs greatly from that of her minions: a humanoid body, arms and legs all situated as would be expected, except in addition to these there are four other limbs, typical of an arachnid, attached to her torso, the ends of which are blackened, sharp spikes. Adorning her face, in fours on either side, sit black, lifeless eyes, that stare at Judas, right into his soul, and as Mokwena approaches him at speed she opens her huge mouth and roars, displaying row upon row of teeth and spraying rancid spittle.

"Not so appealing now is she! I can't believe you let it touch you," Azazel says, his tone mocking.

"All right, enough of that. I guess we kill her!"

"Yes. But remember what I said within the dream. I need that stone from her, the red jewel that you can see on her chest."

Judas frowns. "What is that thing to you?"

"It is a piece of his soul," Mokwena roars, then laughs while coming to a skidding halt a short distance from Judas. "The whole piece having been ripped out of him by his brothers and broken into three, so that they could defeat him and cast him into the abyss."

Judas glances at Ikazuchi and then throws the weapon forward, where the sword transforms into Azazel. "Explain this, Azazel."

The demon adjusts his clothing, straightening it out as he takes a few steps forward. "I think we should deal with this first master," he cocks his head toward Mokwena, "and then discuss the details of my incarceration."

Judas glances at Mokwena who sways in front of them, a large grin spread across her face. "Oh, I dunno, I think she's giving us a moment to catch up here. So explain yourself."

"Master. Please. Let us deal with her, then I will tell all. Please."

Judas stares at him for a moment and is about to call him back when Mokwena interrupts.

"Oh, very well, if the Architect won't spill his guts, then I will – metaphorically and then literally." She bursts into laughter, and taps at the jewel embedded into her skin upon her chest, drawing Azazel's attention.

Judas' patience is wearing thin. He takes an angry step forward. "Get on with it witch, or your demise will come sooner than scheduled."

Azazel smirks at his remark, not least from seeing Mokwena's reaction as her maniacal laughter abates and then ceases altogether.

"That isn't polite, Iscariot," she says with a snarl. "Therefore, I grant you death without knowledge."

Mokwena screeches into the air as she charges at him.

"Shit," Judas says, and holds out his hand. "Ika! Let's go."

"With pleasure, master," he replies, back flipping into sword form and landing in Judas' hands.

Mokwena is upon them in seconds and reaches out to grab him with enormous human arms, the other spiked spider legs stomping into the ground around him.

Judas' trench coat transforms into his wings and he must beat the left one down and forward hard enough to side-step Mokwena's reach and, avoiding her he then shadow-steps forward and under her, raising Ikazuchi into the air, preparing to slice at her exposed belly. He swings the sword, but it slashes at nothing but air, with Mokwena teleporting away from him to the other side of the cavern. She comes to a spinning halt, from back to front, her spiky legs tracing circles in the dirt.

"Fuck's sake," Judas shouts. "She can teleport?"

"I fear she will be able to do many things, master, while she accesses the power of my jewel," Azazel says.

"Goddamit."

Shadow-stepping forward again, he throws greater energy into his ability, aiming for one of Mokwena's legs, intending to take her apart limb by limb.

This time, the spider-queen does not teleport, instead stands her ground and blocks his sword with one of her legs, the force of which shakes her, the level of power that Judas possesses catching her off-guard. She roars her annoyance and stabs her front legs at him, one after the other, attempting to spear him with the massive limbs.

He moves between her fast stabs with shadow-steps, avoiding the lightning attacks until one catches him, spearing into his non-sword arm. He screams as the limb detaches from his body and falls to the ground, blood spurting from it. He steps back, parrying repeated attempts from Mokwena to finish the job, and on the back foot from several of her swipes, he calls out in defiance as he recovers and regains his composure, while bashing another of her legs to one side. As she staggers from being knocked off-balance, he drives his sword into the ground and then pulls it free, unleashing the shockwave.

The force ripples outward causing Mokwena's attacks to cease and instead concentrate on maintaining her balance upon the undulating ground. Just when it seems she might lose her footing, she grunts and teleports to the back of the room once again.

Ikazuchi sees the advantage presented to them. He screams at Judas. "Throw me. Hurl me at her. She needs time to regenerate her teleport energy. Do it NOW!"

An Archangel he may be, but Judas still feels every inch of the pain tearing through the left side of his body from his severed arm; swimming inside his mind, dizzying him, and he must throw everything he has into shutting it out and carrying out Ikazuchi's request. He draws his arm back and hurls the weapon at Mokwena.

To his credit Ikazuchi is correct, and Mokwena neither has the time or the energy, post-teleportation, to repel the attack. The sword slices through one of her legs, raised in some feeble attempt to prevent it from damaging her, and rips into her torso, causing her to scream so loud that it reverberates around the chamber, and she falls to the ground into a clumsy heap.

Judas sinks to one knee, clutching at his wound, blood pouring from it and running down his right hand, onto his arm and to the ground, where it puddles into a red and gray pool. He waits for his regeneration to kick in, wondering if he will have enough time for his arm to grow back before Mokwena regains her composure to attack again. But nothing happens. No familiar tingling sensations signaling the start of regeneration, no knitting together of tissue and bone – nothing. Concern and fear hit him in equal measures and his eyes widen. *Oh God. Have I failed? Have I failed, and Charlotte has been killed? What have I done?*

He begins to panic and attempts to stagger to his feet. And as he takes deep breaths, trying to regain his balance, something inside him stirs, a familiar, warm, and welcoming sensation and he feels Charlotte's presence. He isn't sure how far away she is, but he knows she is still alive and moving toward him. He smiles. But then as quickly as it arrived the feeling disappears, replaced by something more malevolent, darker. He feels the icy grip of Lady Famine rise within, her subdued presence now finding footing sufficient enough to flourish and break forth, while he lolls in his weakened state. He can do nothing to prevent it. He is powerless and she knows it, speaking to him in his mind with a wicked playfulness to her tone.

What's this, Iscariot? Are we in trouble? Oh, that's right – divine beings are not allowed regeneration within Hell's inner walls, the realm's master won't allow it. My, my, that does present you with a little problem now, doesn't it?

She chuckles.

But, I can and am willing to do something about this for you. Out of the goodness of my... heart.

More chuckling.

But in return you must do something for me. You must promise not to lock me away again. I want to play my part in this little opera.

She laughs once more and her chuckling sounds increasingly unsettling.

Judas' eyes are almost closed, his end almost upon him, and he is at the very brink of collapse, something he will never recover from, and then everything will be lost. Through blurred eyes he sees Mokwena stabbing her legs into the ground, attempting to regain her balance following the loss of a leg and having been toppled by Ikazuchi. He knows she will be up soon and upon him.

"What is it I should do Horseman?" Judas croaks, his speech slurred.

The chuckling returns.

Just accept me, Iscariot. Accept me and use my gifts, my ability to walk the line between divine and demonic. Use my ability to regenerate and heal wounds while within this realm, and more importantly allow me access to him – the demon sword. It is the only being to have ever defeated me and it holds power beyond measure. I want its potential to burst forth, and I want to revel in its majestic destruction. It will... amuse me to watch it unleashed.

He has no more strength to argue, no more witty or smart comebacks, and nothing left to bargain with. He is at her mercy, and she knows it.

Across the room, Mokwena is back on her feet and roaring at Judas. She pulls the sword from out of her side and holds it in front of her. "You fucking puppet. Never again will you be the puppeteer, Architect. I will enjoy watching you cast into the abyss for a second time. I will enjoy seeing the look upon your face as you begin eternal imprisonment, and this time I am sure Lucifer will make certain that no-one can find or enter your world again." She tosses the sword to one side where it clanks over the rocky ground.

Time is running out, Iscariot... Lady Famine continues, her words carrying glee and amusement. *Time is running out, but only for you, as you lie here on this dirty ground, bleeding. Upon your death, I will simply return to the Alfather and await the next calling. But you will be gone. Dead. So, what's it to be?*

Mokwena screeches again, and thunders across the ground toward Judas, her face contorted with rage, her intention to rip him apart despite the fact he looks as though he might die at any moment. Upon sliding to a halt and towering over him, she brings two of her gigantic legs up, readying to slam them down into him, to obliterate him. "Now, Iscariot, you die!"

She powers them down.

Judas explodes into a swarm of locusts and engulfs Mokwena, causing her to flail her human arms at them, and within him Lady Famine chuckles again, this time with more verve, their deal now complete.

The locusts change direction and move away from the spider-queen to another side of the chamber, where they flutter back into the form of Judas, his head bowed slightly, standing side on to Mokwena. He raises his arm and Ikazuchi clatters over the ground and then into the air, streaking toward him, where he catches and twirls it around in front of him. Looking down at his reformed left hand, he clenches and unclenches it, then looks back up at Mokwena.

139

"What... what is this?" Mokwena asks, an edginess to her voice and doubt spread across her face. "How are you regenerating within Hell?"

Judas spreads his wings and, glancing at them, sees they are now jet-black, with not a single white feather remaining. And concern hits him. A worry of where his alignment now stands. He beats his wings, attempting to rise, then feels relieved to find that he still has no access to flight, that the Thŭramré is still in effect and therefore his alignment is still to the divine and not the demonic. However, although flight may elude him, his wings feel stronger than ever.

More armor, he says to himself, knowing his wings will now be strong enough to shield him from Mokwena's attacks and, although it is an untested belief, he feels deep inside of himself that it is true.

Only one way to find out. He then takes another deep breath and shadow-steps toward her. *This speed is new,* he tells himself, grinning all the while.

TWENTY-ONE

Charlotte skids to a halt, her arms out at her sides.

"Here," she says, turning in a circle "directly below. I can feel his presence right below me."

Okay. Now how will you get down there? You have no way of knowing how far down he is.

"He's close. I can feel it. No more than 300 feet."

Pestilence scoffs. *That is still some distance to tunnel down. I am sure you can blast your way through with Divinity, but at what cost? Will you be able to fight afterward, or even stand for that matter?*

She's not listening, she doesn't care. Judas is her father, her life, and right now she feels that something terrible is happening and that it might even be too late. It is a feeling she has been forcing herself to shake off, to ignore and tell herself that he is fine, that he is okay, but the closer to him she has travelled, the stronger the concern has grown. And now she cannot shift that notion no matter how hard she tries.

Are you listening to me, child? Pestilence's protestations continue. *Have you thought this through?*

141

"There's nothing to think through. My dad is down there, and that is where I need to be."

She takes a deep breath and closes her eyes to focus her attention. Then, turning her hands over so that her palms face uppermost, she places them on top of one another so that they make a 'W' shape, and with another deep inhale she draws them up against her chest, still palm upward, until they are in line with her breasts then, with a sharp exhale, flips them over, and thrusts them down and forward, creating a fierce beam of Dark-Divinity.

It crunches into the ground, crackling and fizzing, splitting the rock apart, and as the force increases, so does the Dark-Divinity glow within her eyes and her focus and attention is so intense, she doesn't notice the trail of blood seeping from her nose.

TWENTY-TWO

He bursts into a flock of ravens this time, dodging another of Mokwena's massive fists, and fluttering around her he lands on her back, just out of reach, and the spider-queen roars with fury, turning in circles as she attempts to buck him off. Judas then raises his sword into the air, Ikazuchi having been mystically transported within the flock of birds, then drives it down hard toward the back of her neck, but before he can penetrate her skin, it hardens like rock, the effect rippling across her body. The sword clanks as it bounces harmlessly off the armor coating, causing him to stagger.

Seizing the initiative, Mokwena reaches behind and grabs him, squeezing him hard as she pulls him around and into her eye line, and then moves him toward her mouth, intending to rip him in half with razor-sharp teeth. She screeches in frustration as he once again transforms into an explosion of birds that disperse out of her hand and flutters to the ground a few hundred feet away from her.

The fight has been raging for several minutes with neither party able to gain the upper hand. The moment Judas works his way into a position to attack, Mokwena produces yet another new talent or ability to thwart him, and as soon as she gets hold of him, he transforms into either birds or insects and evades her. The only thing on each of their minds now is who will run out of energy first.

"I can keep this up for an eternity, Iscariot. I draw energy from Hell itself, and you would be virtually mortal long before I even feel the first effects of fatigue."

Although she spits her words with venom, there is a touch of vulnerability to them, that not all is as she says, and Lady Famine confirms Judas' suspicions.

She lies. No being except the Creator has endless energy, not least a lowly Demon Lord such as this bitch. Enough with this unproductive fighting Judas, you must use my gifts to much better effect. Remember what it is I do, what it is I am – famine, disease, destruction. Strip away any boon that she might conjure and tear her down to nothingness.

Pursing his lips tight and gritting his teeth beneath them, he shadow-steps toward Mokwena at a greater speed than normal, Lady Famine's energy allowing him access to more power than he's ever had.

Mokwena reacts and teleports away causing Judas to transmogrify into the flock of ravens and pursue her to the other side of the cavern, where he once again lands on her back, and as before, she produces her rock armor. Only this time, Judas plants a firm palm onto the stone-like substance and from his fingers disease spreads, a rippling network of blackened veins over the protective armor, causing it to buckle and splinter into hundreds of pieces that cascade down Mokwena's body.

She screams at the intense pain the spreading sickness causes, and for the first time in the fight she feels truly vulnerable and filled with a deep dread. Never has she imagined that Iscariot would get this far in a battle between them, such was her confidence. She had heard all the stories, the tales of the Iscariot Warrior gaining strength, dispatching countless demons, and that he had even somehow secured the demon sword, but she never thought he would be able to topple her. But this new power that courses through him, the energy of something ancient, is giving him a distinct edge, and she feels danger – real danger – and that he does in fact possess the ability to destroy her. Swallowing her pride, and doing something that she never imagined she would, she screams for aid from her slaves, and the fear carried within the sound penetrates every corner of her temple, causing every spider-demon that it connects with to race to her with terrified immediacy. She then teleports once again to the opposite side of the chamber, her human torso twisting from side to side, attempting to determine the extent of the damage. To her relief, the corrosive spread has seemed to confine itself to the rock armor and has not yet eaten into her skin. But her ability to call forth the protective barrier is compromised, and she wonders if she will ever be able to do so again. She must not allow Iscariot to attack her back, or he will be able to drive the sword in and that will surely be the end.

Lady Famine chuckles within Judas' mind. *You see! You see what I mean? The power I carry within me can break down even the most determined of defenses. And as I have shown, you needn't even concern yourself with which ability to choose, I will do that for you. Her rock skin is no more, so attack now and drive Ikazuchi through her.*

As he prepares to shadow-step toward Mokwena once more, the walls to the chamber erupt with spider-demon slaves clawing their way out. They swarm into the room in their hundreds, then quickly growing to over a thousand, the deafening clacking of their legs echoing as they skitter across the chamber to defend their queen.

Ikazuchi's voice hisses out of the sword. "My, my, she has been busy. Quite the collection of souls. No matter, we will destroy them all."

Judas shifts into a defensive posture, his sword gripped in both hands and raised beside his head, then quickly looks up as a crunching sound spikes out from above, deep within the blackness overhead that prevents him from seeing what it is. Then, his hand moves to shield his eyes as a beam of dark energy bursts downward through the roof of the cavern, illuminating the entire area as it blasts into the ground, obliterating hundreds of spider-demons unfortunate enough to be caught in its path. The ones on the periphery skitter away as fast as they can to avoid disintegration by the energy.

As swiftly as the beam arrived, it disappears, and all eyes remain fixed upon the point where the hole had formed, awaiting further activity. A couple of the demons eye one another, questioning in silence what each thought was going on, then from out of the darkness drops Charlotte, encased in a Dark-Divinity shield, and she hits the ground she does so with such force it buckles and craters beneath her. Deactivating the shield, she slowly rises from bended knee to a standing position.

"This isn't possible," Mokwena screams. "How could you overcome the poison's effects alone?"

Charlotte stares at Mokwena. "I'm not alone." She smirks slightly. "It's a Horseman thing." She glances toward Judas, about 100 feet away from her, and offers a gentle nod to which he smiles and returns the gesture.

"KILL THEM!" Mokwena screams, sending her forces into action.

Charlotte throws her hands to her sides, catching her swords within them and then shadow-steps toward the rampaging horde, moving between them and cutting them down too fast for any to stand a chance against the devastating new heights to her abilities.

With a roar, Judas moves into attack against Mokwena who thunders toward him, her face contorted with demonic fury.

She swipes and stabs at him with human and spider appendages alike, her attacks fast and relentless, accompanied with screams of pure rage.

Judas struggles against several of her infuriated attacks, angling to get the measure of her speed and attack patterns. And so he digs further down within himself, drawing on more of Lady Famine's power, gorging on her intense energy, and embracing the overwhelming nature of it. He doesn't realize, but he is smiling, the same terrifying expression on his face prior to engaging the Gatekeeper, where Famine's power created a maelstrom of energy around him. As he now parries Mokwena's attacks, the same dark energy swirls around him once more, a power that disintegrates any slave-demon that dares to come too close to the diseased, cyclonic force, discouraging further attacks from Mokwena's minions.

Concern hits Charlotte as she glances at Judas and then finishes off a spider-demon foolish enough to attack her, and she moves through the others toward him. However, more and more cut off her path, their numbers continuing to swell beyond measure, and she is forced to deal with those before she can get to him.

Judas is laughing now, cackling at the top of his voice, madness directing the action. The speed of Mokwena's attacks and his parrying of them has reached such speed and flow that no human eye could track them. From deep within his mind, Lady Famine laughs.

This is beautiful. Your sword is beautiful. This creature you fight is not worthy of our attention. She does not deserve to be killed by a warrior as accomplished as us. But die she must. Finish her, Iscariot, break her down and allow your puppet to collect his stone. I can't wait for the next battle, it will be... glorious.

With that, he erupts and shadow-steps so fast around Mokwena that he becomes nothing more than a streak of light that slices through each of her legs, dropping her to the ground with a scream. Then, skidding to a halt, Judas turns and slams into her with the same speed, sending Mokwena crashing onto her back a few feet away from him. He then tosses Ikazuchi ahead, allowing the weapon to transform in to Azazel.

"Yes!" Azazel says, with triumphant raised hands. "Finally, one piece of what was taken from me will be returned."

Mokwena screams, flailing around on her back and Judas strides over to the incapacitated spider-queen. Grabbing hold of huge strands of her hair and wrapping them around his forearm to gain more purchase, he then yanks her toward him and punches into the top of her gigantic head with a devastating blow that dazes and subdues her.

Meanwhile, Azazel leaps onto her belly and makes his way toward the glowing red stone embedded in her chest. Crazed eyes dance with glee within a face that glows red from the stone's radiance, and a maniacal smile spreads wide as he reaches for it. But as he does, a fierce electrical pulse erupts from the stone, blasting him backward and off Mokwena's belly.

Judas glances toward Charlotte at the other side of the room, and satisfied she is holding her own against the horde of demons, he transforms into a flock of ravens, and flies over and lands on Mokwena's chest just above the stone. Taking a few steps away from her head, he then turns around to face Mokwena. "So, Azazel cannot remove this from you! That's a neat little defense mechanism you got there, but I bet there is no such system in place to prevent angelic beings from doing so." He reaches down and grabs the stone, and as he is about to rip it out when Mokwena interrupts him.

"Wait, Iscariot! Wait! Wouldn't you want to know the truth before you kill me?"

He looks around at Azazel unconscious on the ground, then toward Charlotte, and finally back to Mokwena. "Call off your dogs."

Mokwena screeches and at once the spider-demons cease their attack and retreat to the edge of the shadows around the cavern.

Charlotte breathes a small sigh of relief, bowing her head a little, trying not to make it noticeable. She was getting to the edge of her energy reserves, with The Seal and The Book draining her fast, something that would have left her vulnerable. The break in the action is much-needed and very welcome. She wipes her mouth with the back of her hand and makes her way toward Judas, her gaze shifting between packs of the slave demons, motionless yet hissing.

Seeing the attacks cease, Judas lets go of the stone. "Right, speak. Say your piece."

"You have been lied to, Iscariot. You think that the Architect has your best interests at heart? He only cares about himself."

"There's that title again, 'the Architect'. Why do you beings constantly refer to him as that?"

Mokwena attempts to laugh but the pain makes it sound more like a tired cough. "Because, Iscariot, he is the one who built Hell. Everything you see here was forged by his hand from his design."

"You lie!" Judas says, tight-lipped and with a deeply furrowed brow.

"Why would I? It is the truth. The Creator commissioned him and his brothers to make this prison for those whom he knew were going to revolt. The Creator knows all, sees all, and no matter how clever Lucifer thought he was, the Creator was always one step ahead. He wanted the rebellion to happen, welcomed it in fact."

Charlotte moves to within earshot of them, behind Mokwena, and shakes her head in disbelief. "Why would my father welcome a rebellion within Heaven? It makes no sense at all."

Mokwena attempts to laugh again but gives up. She speaks to Charlotte although she cannot see her. "For sport? Pleasure? Who knows! Nothing he ever did or does makes sense. But the point is he won, and those who took up arms against the throne were cast down into a prison Azazel, Beelzebub, and Leviathan created. And believe me when I say this, that creature over there had the biggest hand in everything. He was the most powerful of the three by a long way."

Judas glances toward Azazel, still unconscious on the ground.

"Are you telling me that he knows this place inside out?"

"Of course he does – he is the Architect. And he also knows that Lucifer has closed every down-gate, except the one by the Well of Souls."

Judas' face contorts with rage. "Fucking… fucker!" He closes his eyes, tilts his face up, then opens them and returns his gaze to the stone. "So what is this then? What's this all about?"

"That is a piece of what you would call his heart. It is the source of his power, the stone that sparked life into him by the Alfather. Without it he is still powerful, that is true, but with it… well, let's just say his brothers were keen to relieve him of it when they learned just how powerful he was, given that their own stones combined didn't come close to his power. Seems the Alfather had something of a favorite." Again, she attempts a chuckle but ends up coughing.

"Removed it? Why? And why didn't it kill him?" he asks.

"He cannot be killed. Just as the Creator cannot be killed. Anything gifted life directly by the Alfather cannot be destroyed by anything other than the Alfather himself. The only thing they could do was imprisonment after they removed his seat of power."

"Why? Why did they have to do that?" Charlotte says, her brow furrowed.

"Because after Lucifer fell, and after this place became populated, he became Lucifer's power, his weapon, and he was very good at his job. Lucifer is powerful now with Beelzebub, but when he possessed Azazel

149

he was unstoppable and the sword's lust for dominance far outweighed that of his master's. Lucifer never had any plans to take on the throne again. The defeat he suffered at the hands of the Creator, Gabriel, and his forces removed any desire to do so or to ever challenge the Creator further. But Azazel wanted more, wanted him to have more and so he pecked at him, over the millennia, on and on until Lucifer ceased to be afraid of trying and started to listen to the ramblings of that lunatic. A cunning, deceitful, and highly intelligent lunatic at that. And so Lucifer's lust for the three kingdoms was rekindled and here we are today."

Charlotte's eyes open wide. "Are you telling me the reason all of this is happening – the reason Lucifer is doing this – is because of him?" She stabs an angry finger in the direction of Azazel.

Mokwena cocks her head to one side, still unable to see her, the gesture symbolic. "Yes. That is exactly why."

Judas paces up and down for a moment, then faces Mokwena once again. "Then why did his brothers betray and overthrow him?"

"Why not?" Mokwena says, turning her head toward him once more. "If you thought Azazel was ambitious you should meet Beelzebub. What he lacks in physical power, he certainly makes up for in lust. You take a greedy, jealous sibling, one that exerts influence over the least capable of them and what do you get? An epic power struggle! With his brother Leviathan's help, Beelzebub managed to overcome Azazel, remove his heart, split it into three pieces, and lock him in his prison. With the loss of his power he was unable to escape... until you came along, that is."

Judas looks at Charlotte and then back at Azazel, then furiously rakes his fingers through his hair.

Moving around to the side of Mokwena, who has made no attempt to move from her position, Charlotte addresses Judas.

"We need to deal with him. Now. Before he awakens. He is a problem. He's used you, used us to get here, to get himself back into power. We cannot trust him."

Judas takes a deep breath and closes his eyes. "We are in Hell sweetie, we cannot trust anyone or anything. And besides this one

150

here," he points to Mokwena, "isn't being entirely truthful with us either – are you darling?"

"I have told you much, Iscariot, there is nothing more to say."

"Oh, I think there is. Like how Beelzebub didn't just do this with the assistance of Leviathan. I'm guessing it was with significantly more help. Such as assistance from someone who had developed a particularly powerful neurotoxin over the years. Whaddya think, Charley, that sound about right to you?"

Charlotte licks her lips, contemplating his question. "Yeah. I reckon you're right. I reckon a being such as that would have made an extremely handy ally. I also reckon that such a creature would have been rewarded for their efforts, don't you dad?"

"I do sweetie, I really do, and I think that reward might have come in the form of a powerful crystal, broken into three parts and given to each of those who aided in the betrayal of Azazel."

"Seems legit," she says, her tone dripping with sarcasm.

Mokwena laughs. "Well, I would have expected nothing less from you Iscariot. It takes a betrayer to recognize a betrayer."

The side of his mouth twitches into a smile. "Yeah. Yeah, it does. But I'm still here and you are getting your plug pulled." He reaches down to take the stone.

"Wait, Iscariot, wait!" she shouts. "If you do this, if you take that stone and kill me, and then give it to him, you will regret it – you will regret it deeply."

Judas stares at her for a moment. "Maybe, but I think I'll regret not killing you even more."

He grabs the stone in her chest and pulls. It takes a lot of effort to remove, a process that causes Mokwena immense pain. She is screaming so loud that it causes the cavern to shake, with rocks falling around them.

Charlotte throws her hands up to her ears and looks toward the smaller slave demons as they screech and flail, bound to suffer the fate of their queen, their existence tied to the hive-mind.

Eventually, and with a fierce roar, Judas rips the stone from her chest and she stops screaming and Charlotte removes her hands from over her ears and looks up at him.

Through teary pain, Mokwena laughs. "You have no idea what you have done, Iscariot. No idea whatsoever." She offers another pained laugh. "Believe me, I'll see you again, betrayer."

"No… you won't," he says, and nods toward Charlotte who drives her twin blades into Mokwena's head without a moment's hesitation.

She pours as much Divinity into them as she can muster, and they glow a fierce white and vibrate as the light's intensity grows. The top of Mokwena's head explodes, spraying black blood in an arc to Charlotte's left. She looks toward the other slave demons who scream in unison, the tops of their heads also exploding.

"Huh! Neat!" she says as she removes her swords from Mokwena's head and flicks the dark liquid off them then twirls and reseats them into her scabbards manually for a change.

Judas jumps down from Mokwena's lifeless corpse and walks over to Charlotte, the red stone in his hand. He glances toward Azazel, still unconscious on the ground.

"Are you sure about this, dad? I know she was an untrustworthy bitch, but I believed what she said. And my Horseman has major concerns with that one."

"I know sweetie, but we need him. We have some serious opponents to overcome, and if what she said is true, we are going to need him to navigate through Hell and also defeat them." She starts to protest when he cuts her short. "Look, I have fought Lucifer before, remember, and it is not an experience I wish to repeat unless I bridge the gap between our power. And Azazel getting back some of his will definitely give me more of that advantage. Look. We know that he cannot take the stones himself, so that is something within our control, in our favor. So we'll let him have another one if the opportunity presents itself—"

"Which I'm sure it will, dad, since this has been his goal all along. It sure as shit ain't us hurrying to the Temple of Belial.

"Okay fine, I agree with you, the opportunity will present itself again, but we only allow him two parts of his heart. Once this thing is done and we have defeated Lucifer, then I will put him back in his prison myself."

"*We* will put him back in there. Together."

He smiles at her and touches the side of her face.

She pulls away from him. "Ewww, gross. You got dead spider lady all over your hand."

He laughs and turns away toward Azazel. "Right then, let's wake this fucker up. I have a few questions for him."

He walks over to Azazel, looks at the stone, and then at Charlotte. "Any ideas?"

She shrugs. "I dunno. Just smack it on him, see what happens?"

"Fair enough."

He bends down, glancing at the stone a final time, then slams it into Azazel's chest and it absorbs the gem the instant it touches him.

Azazel sits bolt upright, drawing in a sharp intake of breath while clutching at his chest. He pants, attempting to get his breathing under control, then falls back against the ground, hard, convulsing and fitting for a minute, causing Charlotte and Judas to look at each other with concern.

Finally, the seizure having stopped, he looks up at them, breathes out deeply, and then smiles. "Groovy!"

TWENTY-THREE

Large dust clouds plume into the sky, trailing behind the vehicles speeding across the barren landscape. Although the target destination of their mission will be the most dangerous theatre of operations that they have undertaken to date, this portion of the journey has also given them much cause for concern. They would be easy pickings should anything decide to attack, given the vast open expanse they must cross to reach Saguenay, the last known position of the demonic horde that attacked the scout patrol. Thankfully, however, the journey has gone without complication so far, and nearing their destination, Gary glances over from his position on one of two leading motorcycles, the other ridden by Sarah.

"Nice day for a bike ride, huh? How ya doing over there, kiddo?" he says, speaking into his communication device.

"Say again, over?" she replies, her voice raised over the roar of the bikes, making it difficult to hear him.

Gary snorts a laugh and speaks louder. "'Say again, over!' Wow, Nathan really has done a good job training you." He laughs again.

This time, she hears him and offers a chuckle of her own. "Yeah, well, you have to act like a professional – you're a soldier, dammit," she says, mimicking Colonel Taylor's voice.

Gary laughs again. "He's a strict one all right, but there's no one better at what he does or anyone I would rather have watching my back."

Sarah agrees. Colonel Taylor is an incredible soldier. Every decision he makes ends in a positive result for the team, regardless of any loss of life. "That's war," he tells people. "Losing soldiers is never an option but unfortunately it's a reality in the realms of conflict." Nevertheless, he would constantly remind his teams that he would do everything in his power to bring them home safely from whatever mission they were on, and it was words such as those, plus his resolute determination when saying them, that has everyone who goes into battle with him believing they are true. There are few people left in the world that you can put such unwavering trust in.

Her thoughts once more turn to her sister Abigail.

It seems everything she thinks of these days ends up being about her. She remembers how Colonel Taylor spoke to her and Isaac a couple of days after the event. How he had made sure that people had left them alone to grieve and come to terms with their loss. And then had spoken gently to them, offering his sincerest condolences and heartfelt apologies. She remembered how vulnerable he had seemed in that moment, a side of him she had never even known he possessed. It was then that she understood. A fearless and deadly soldier he may be, but he was still a human being with emotions and feelings, despite the nature of him. From then on, she didn't look at military personnel in the same way. She saw people, families. Caring and warm individuals, not the mindless killing machines that many throughout the world had imagined them to be. Of course, following Abigail's death Isaac hadn't had any such revelation. His hatred and anger still burned fierce, as it does to this day, and it is a good job that he had given those emotions purpose or she feared that he would have succumbed to the darkness.

Aggh, stop it Sarah, she tells herself. Thoughts like this bring on tears, worry, and despair, and today is not a day for her to lose focus.

The plan is simple. Get the demons to spawn from a portal, walk up to the event unseen with Daniel's equipment, take telemetry, amplitude, and data readings, plus other gobbledygook words that she didn't properly understand, and then get out – preferably without being seen and getting killed. What could possibly go wrong? She laughs within her mind at the craziness of the plan and is then brought back into the moment by Gary's voice, albeit unintelligible once more. She shakes her head.

"I'm sorry, say again Gary. The noise, it's making it difficult to read you."

He raises his voice again. "I said, we are nearing the target. The others are peeling away to their holding positions. It's just you and I from here kiddo."

"Okay, copy. Where are we ditching the bikes?"

"First bit of cover we find we'll stow them there, then move further in on foot and see if we can't raise a little hell."

"That's not funny Gary."

He chuckles. "I thought it was a little funny."

His smile then wanes. She was right, it wasn't funny. Nothing about today is going to be funny.

TWENTY-FOUR

"Knock-knock," Jerry says, walking into the chamber where Ibi has his nose planted firmly in yet another volume of text, and plonks a bowl of food down onto the table in front of him, the fork rattling in the process. The noise causes Ibi to glance at it over the rim of his spectacles.

"Thank you Jerry, but I'm not hungry."

"I don't care. You will eat, old man, and you will enjoy it. I made this myself."

Ibi looks up at him. "You made it?"

He nods.

"You've given Lee the night off or something?" Ibi asks, reaching over and grabbing the fork then scooping a portion up. He blows on it and then puts it into his mouth, nods, and makes noises of gratification. It was good, very good in fact. Who knew that Jerry could cook?

Jerry rubs the top of his head. "Lee's gone."

Ibi looks up, his eyes wide, his mouth puckered with another load of food having been shoved into it.

"They all are. Just up and left," Jerry says, with an unconvincing smile.

"What? Why?"

He looks around and then motions with his hands. "This, Ibi. They are terrified of all this. They said that this will bring us death, and if I am being honest I can't say I disagree with them. The more you keep digging, the more worried I get."

"Why Jerry? This is powerful information. Knowledge that we should possess."

"That's just it Ibi. It is powerful information, very powerful." He sighs. "Look, I spent nearly 20 years in the military in a particular line of work, and I can tell you one thing for certain, if information is way above your pay grade then you shouldn't be accessing it. That shit gets you killed plain and simple."

"Nonsense Jerry. I will never be dissuaded from the pursuit of knowledge. It is my life's work and this, this right here, is the most important discovery that I will ever make. It might be the most important discovery humankind has ever made."

Jerry is about to remonstrate with him but stops as he knows it is useless to try. The man is a scholar, and a brilliant one at that. Telling him not to work on this library would be like telling himself not to pick up a brand new, never-before-seen weapon and not fire it. He smiles a little and walks away. "Enjoy the goulash my friend, it's a secret family recipe you know."

Ibi looks up and frowns. "I never knew you were Hungarian, Jerry."

He laughs. "I'm not," and then walks out of the room.

The humor is lost on Ibrahim and he goes back to the book, scanning the pages with his index finger, stopping periodically to eat.

It really was fantastic goulash. He stops for a moment and considers the empty bowl. Where did Jerry get the ingredients for it? And then it hits him. It was just another of the ration packs rehydrated. He drops the fork into the bowl, and sits back, taking off his spectacles and rubbing his eyes. How long has he been down here? Long enough for

Jerry to pull off a 'power of suggestion' prank on him, that's for certain. He looks around. Could Jerry be right? Could this information be too much for any human to bear? He rubs his eyes once more. No. He must keep going, he must find out about the child of the darkness. Who she is, and more importantly, where? One thing is for sure though, having read many of the texts, his life would never be the same again. This Barachiel character was something of an enigma and his descent into madness was fascinating. From what he could decipher, it seems the loss of the Divine Presence affects angelic beings in the most devastating of ways.

But Barachiel was not his focus today.

Finding and learning about the child of darkness was. He was certain the volumes contained information that could help, and that it was here somewhere.

He places his spectacles back on his face and opens his eyes wide, blinks a couple of times then massages his face around them. *Come on, Ibi, only a few hundred more books to read. No problem, sir, no problem at all.* He sighs.

A noise startles him and he looks over to the corner of the room from where it came. He leans back in his chair slowly, peering over his glasses. Lying on the floor where it wasn't before is a book. He knows full well that it wasn't there before, as every text in the room had been housed within the vast shelves running around it. Nothing had been out of place and nothing had been on the floor. He remembers, because not only he had remarked at how tidy the room's owner must have been, and that it had aligned with his own sense of organization, but he had indeed kept it as neat as they day he discovered it.

He slides his chair back, screeching it across the stone floor, then stands and walks over to the volume. Bending down, he picks it up and out of habit wipes the cover, even though it wasn't dirty. The book had no title, no writing of any description on its covers and that felt strange to him. Every text he had researched up to this point had something written on them. Most followed a pattern of volumes, but some just seemed chaotic, as though written in a state of madness, which having learned more about Barachiel he concluded they probably were. But this one was blank, nothing. He turns it over in his hand and runs his fingers over the leather binding. It felt rough to the touch. Then, startling him, the book opens within his hands and its pages leaf over at a rapid rate, stopping on one. Ibi looks around, fear creeping up on him. He has never been a brave man, that was not his calling, but he has never been a stupid one either, and what has just taken place before his eyes scares him. The volume of texts he has been studying did not belong to a benevolent entity and he wonders who was trying to communicate with him. But compelled to do so, he returns his attention to the book in his hand.

About half way down the page, his eyes open wide and he swallows hard. His heart pounds within his chest and at that moment he realizes Jerry was right, that some knowledge should never be known. His eyes water with terror. What he has read has changed him, and for the first time in opening the vault he fears for his life. He wasn't meant to know this. No one was ever meant to know this.

He screams as a hand grabs his shoulder and he sinks to the ground into a protective ball.

"Ibi… IBI, it's me, it's Jerry. We have to go. We have to get out of here NOW! On your feet, man. On your feet, right fucking now!"

Ibi looks up at him through the gap in his arms covering his face. "Oh Jerry. I'm sorry. I'm so, so sorry. You were right. You were absolutely right. But we have to tell them. We have to warn them."

"Who? Warn who, Ibi? Look, it doesn't matter now, we are in danger. We have to go."

Ibrahim Yali gets to his feet and dusts himself down. He has never been a brave man, never in his entire life. But today, that must change as a great deal rides on the information he has just gained.

"No Jerry. We have to tell them. This is too important, too big."

Jerry considers him for a moment. He has been a soldier for most of his time on the planet, and he knows when a mission is more important than his own life, and looking into Ibi's face, into the eyes of a man who in a single instant has understood passing on the knowledge he has just learned is bigger than anything else happening right now, he recognizes he is at mission-critical point. He sighs deeply, and then jabs the butt of his rifle harder into his shoulder, the action symbolic.

"Okay Ibi, okay. But you stick close to me, you got it? And as soon as you transmit your message, we are fucking gone. I don't care in which direction, I don't mind where, but we are gone from this place and never coming back. Understood?"

Ibi nods.

"Okay then." Jerry blows out hard. "Let's get to that comms unit."

He guides Ibi out of the room, the man still clutching the book close to his chest and they make their way through the dank, poorly lit corridors of the catacombs. At no point since they arrived has Jerry felt uncomfortable down here, but at this moment it feels like the pit of Hell itself and every turn he takes raises his anxiety levels. His weapon remains steadfast, raised to his eye line as he moves through the tunnels with haste. He feels Ibi close to his back, bumping into him at times, but he doesn't mind it one bit. The physical contact with the man means his ward is still right behind and following him and it comforts him as it does all soldiers in confined space operations.

Eventually, they reach the foot of the stairs leading up and out of the catacombs and Jerry holds his left arm back to halt Ibi. He turns toward him slightly, enough so that Ibi can see his expression, and raises his finger to his mouth.

Ibi nods. His face awash with fear. This moment is the most important in his entire life, but it does not mean he doesn't fear violence and death. He does. A great deal.

Jerry edges up the stairs, his weapon pointed ahead, and almost at the top, he peers over the edge of the last step. The camp looks clear. He is about to advance when Ibi's voice stops him.

"What do you see?"

Jerry turns back to him, annoyed at Ibi breaking his silence command. But then he remembers that the man isn't a soldier and is terrified, and so relaxes his expression. He whispers. "Nothing. It's clear."

"Then how did you know we were in danger? Why are we leaving?"

161

"Because every single animal and insect in this area stopped making noise at once, Ibi. At fucking once, like the very same instant. For me, that was a blatant message from our animal community to get the fuck out of here." He motions with his head. "C'mon. Let's get this done."

Ibi nods back.

They clear the stairs and skulk through the camp and toward the confined section where the radio equipment sits as dusk's last light makes way for darkness.

The rising panic within Jerry disorientates him a little. He has been in countless similar situations before, but this one feels different. He has fought and killed a lot of enemies and although fear played a part in every single encounter, it had been nothing like this. For the first time since the Collapse he feels genuine terror, and he silently prays to anything that will listen to get them through this situation and grant them a little more time on Earth.

So far, their luck was holding, and they reach the entrance to the communications room, a converted part of the temple that in its day Ibi had said most likely held grain and other foodstuffs. He holds his arm out once more to check Ibi's movement, then advances into the room slowly, ensuring his corners are safe.

As Jerry advances, Ibi looks around. He is at the peak of his terror, waiting for his friend to give the all clear and he does not like it one little bit feeling so exposed with his back against the temple wall and the entire open camp ahead of him. His heart pounds within his chest and ears, and he struggles to control his breathing and Jerry's words are a welcome sound indeed as he clears Ibi into the room. Relieved, he scurries inside.

"Okay, Jerry," Ibi's nervous voice stutters, "one quick call to Bagotville and then we're gone. One quick call indeed, and you better hope the satellite is aligned or you ain't getting a damn thing. And if that's the case we are gone, and we rethink the mission. Got it?"

"Got it," Ibi replies without hesitation while fiddling with the transmitter. He keys the radio microphone, and whispers, feeling the need to do so. "Bagotville, Bagotville this is Angkor Wat, do you read, over?"

Silence.

He sighs. "Bagotville, this is Angkor Wat, do you read, over?" He looks at Jerry, who purses his lips together and raises his eyebrows. Ibrahim repeats the message, this time with more vigor.

Both men jump when the radio squelches into life.

"Angkor Wat, this is Bagotville. State your message, over."

Ibi breathes out deeply and looks at Jerry with a wide smile.

Jerry nods back with a little smile of his own.

"Bagotville, I have an urgent message for detective Gary Cross, is he available, over?"

A small delay and then the radio squelches back into life.

"Negative, Angkor Wat. Detective Cross is in the field on a mission. Relay the message and will ensure he gets it, over."

Ibi looks at Jerry once more and is about to speak when he sees the man edging toward the doorway. "What's the matter, Jerry? What is it?"

Jerry doesn't look back. His voice is slow and monotone. "Give them the message Ibi, as fast as you can. Our time's up."

Ibi's mouth opens but nothing comes out.

"Now Ibi or our deaths will have been in vain."

His eyes open wide.

Jerry inches toward the entrance to the room and raises his weapon. Dotted everywhere within the camp are demons, dozens of them, motionless and grinning. It is the most unnerving and terrifying sight he has ever seen. And at the head of the horde stands their leader – that much is obvious to Jerry as the posture and air of presence that he commands is undeniable.

Lord Asmodeus grins as he points at the armed man standing in the entrance to the temple. "You should be honored. It is not every day mortals end their existence at the behest of a Lord of Hell. This will be a good death."

"Now, Ibi! For God's sake," Jerry says, his voice broken and wavering with a terrified sense of urgency.

Frantic, Ibi speaks. "Bagotville, tell him I was wrong, I got it wrong, tell him—" Jerry's screams stop him mid-message as a demon drops down from the ceiling, tearing into him and his weapon goes off as he grips his rifle and squeezes the trigger, spraying bullets all over the room.

Ibi turns back to the radio handset. "I WAS WRONG, THERE ISN'T TWO, THER—"

A bullet rips through Ibrahim Yali's head, ejecting brain matter onto the radio console.

Asmodeus appears behind the dead man and lifts his head off the table where it had planted with a thud. Turning it around, he sees the wide-open eyes, frozen in their moment of surprise and terror and the Demon Lord's face exudes a mixture of disappointment and disgust.

The radio squelches into life. "Say again, Angkor Wat, message not fully relayed. Say again all after 'wrong', over."

Asmodeus reaches over and clicks the radio off, then turns toward the demon who butchered Jerry, the creature rising to its feet, blood dripping from its jaws onto its brown skin. He nods toward the dead man in his hands. "Really? Fucking gunfire?"

The demon edges back a little and nervously looks at two companions who have now entered the room.

Asmodeus shakes his head and sighs. "I was looking forward to this one. To telling him everything before I destroyed him." He sighs again. "Oh well, not to worry. I'll get another chance with that fucking Gary Cross." He expresses a small laugh. "Eat your fill," he says, walking out of the room, and the demons tear into the corpses of Ibi and Jerry.

***

The radio operator at Bagotville shrugs at his Lieutenant stood behind him, the man's hand placed on the back of his chair. "That's all he said, sir. 'I was wrong, tell him I was wrong. There isn't two.'" He shakes his head. "I got nothing more before the comms went dead."

The Lieutenant sighs, then pats the operators shoulder. "Okay, Frank. Well, there's nothing we can do about it at the moment. There's no satellite alignment for the field team for another four hours. Besides, I'm not sure if Gary will know what the hell any of that was about.

Mark the message, date, and time, and we'll deal with it when they return."

"Yes sir."

The operator turns back to his desk and carries out his superior's request.

TWENTY-FIVE

Gary offers Sarah a piece of chocolate as they sit with their backs to a wall under a small outcrop of stone slab, most likely the former foundations of a house.

"Ooh, chocolate. My word, detective, you are a privileged man." She laughs as she takes it then pops it into her mouth, closing her eyes and humming, the taste flooding her mouth.

Gary laughs. "Yeah well, being the," he makes quotation marks with his fingers, "Chief of Police has its perks I guess."

She smiles. "Nah, it's because people like you. You're a likeable fella. Honest and true, strong and determined. People like that. Father was the same. People liked father too."

He nods a little and gives her a half-smile. "So what was he like, your father? Obviously a good man, but what was he like?"

She smiles. "Wonderful. Loving. Caring. Understanding. Strict. Everything a great father should be. He was a Bishop as well, you know."

His face makes an 'ahh' expression and he smiles.

"Yep, a Bishop and a well-respected man in the community. Funnily enough, though, he embraced a few of the outside ways, even though the way of the Amish was most unyielding. His reasoning was, 'if we cannot understand those outside, how could we possibly expect them to understand us?' Sound logic when you think about it."

Gary smiles again and nods.

"Didn't matter though in the end," she says, looking ahead.

"His understanding?"

She shakes her head. "No. The Amish way. People still fell to Lucifer, just the same as others who did not live our lives. The whole thing was laughable really." She flops her head back against the slab.

Gary looks away from her, out into the nothingness in front of them. "I guess we all found out what we were on that day." He lets out a laugh. "It wasn't for nothing though," he looks back at her and she turns toward him. "Your lives, I mean. It can't have been. Look at the gift you possess. Without it we would have been royally screwed on many occasions."

She laughs, but just a small one. "I don't think it was because of the life we led, Gary. The notion that only the Amish would have been bequeathed an innate ability to not be seen by demons seems illogical to me. I mean, we can't be the only pure people on the planet. There must be others. No – there will be others. People are great and wonderful from all cultures. There are more out there like you and I. There has to be, or this is definitely all for nothing."

He stares at her for a moment. She is right. If there is no one left to fight for, then why are they doing any of this? Sure, the safety of the base is the priority and this mission will hopefully help, but at the end of it all it's just stalling tactics for Charlotte and Judas to do whatever it is they are doing right now, for the good of those left.

His thoughts turn to them, to where they are and what they might be doing. He misses them both a great deal. He almost laughs aloud when Sarah turns the conversation to them, as though she's reading his thoughts, and for a second he asks himself, 'can she read my mind?' then dismisses the thought it as ridiculous.

"Where do you think they are?" she says, looking at him once again. "Charlotte and Judas, I mean."

He presses his lips together and shakes his head.

"Have they abandoned us? Realizing it's pointless and that nothing can be done?"

He snaps his attention to her, his eyes wide. "No! Never. They would never do that. I know them like I know myself. Whatever they are doing, it is for us – for all of us and I have no doubt in my mind that they will succeed." He sighs and looks ahead again. "Whatever it is."

"'Whatever it is!'" she repeats him, snorting a laugh. "No, you're right. I was being silly. Of course they wouldn't abandon us. I felt it when I shook her hand. Her love for all of humanity. It was so powerful. There's no way she would abandon us. No way."

He smiles. "None whatsoever. And let me tell you something – the love that she feels for us is dwarfed in comparison to the love that Judas feels for her. It is actually terrifying. She wouldn't abandon us, and he would never abandon her. So no, whatever it is they are doing, it is for the good of us all – that much you can be sure of." He looks at Sarah as she nods, and in that moment he hates himself for ever doubting her, for even suggesting that she might not be who she is. He screws his face up and thinks, *Goddamit Gary, you can be an asshole at times.*

She smiles and is enjoying their conversation. A welcome distraction from the impending doom that the night may bring as the sun starts its slow descent toward the horizon.

Their radios squelch into life, and Colonel Taylor's voice comes through. "Vanguard, this is Hollow-point. Sitrep, over."

Sarah rolls her eyes. "I don't know who he means, me or you? I can't keep up with all these call-sign changes, seriously I can't." She fiddles with her comms unit, pressing the talk button.

Gary chuckles. "I think he is referring to both of us. It's okay, I got this one." He pushes his talk button. "Hollow-point, this is Vanguard, all quiet, nothing to report, over."

"Okay, understood. Suns setting, darkness soon. You wanna call it a night? Over."

Gary hears Daniel's voice in the background arguing that they can't quit, that he needs the data and he looks at Sarah and laughs.

She laughs also, the comical moment made worse by the fact she can hear Nathan and Daniel wrestling with the microphone of Nathan's comms unit and Nathan berating Daniel with a torrent of foul language. She imagines the Colonel's face trying to push an irritating Daniel away. It doesn't help, and she bursts out laughing.

Nathan's voice grows quieter and distant as he moves the microphone way from his mouth. "Jonesy, will you get hold of this little shit for me and put him somewhere I can't see him. Thank you." His voice becomes clear again. "Goddamit. Using names over comms, so damn unprofessional. Sorry about that Vanguard. Now that we have that little unscheduled interruption out of the way, what do you think, stay or leave? Over."

Gary regains his composure. "Well, I hate to say it, but 'the little shit' is right. We need that data and time is not on our side. We are here now, we should see it through. Plus, demons love darkness, right? Over."

"I don't think they give a shit anymore Vanguard, but it's your call, over."

Gary looks at Sarah who nods at him.

"We stay, we wait. Vanguard out."

Sarah smiles at him. "I wouldn't want to be Daniel right now."

Gary laughs.

TWENTY-SIX

"Have you seen what they are doing, Michael? What in all that is holy are they thinking?"

Michael shakes his head. Archangel Raphael is right, what are Gary and his friends thinking? Having checked in on them from the White Kingdom a few moments earlier, the Commander of Hellwatch feels the same as his Lieutenant – their plan of baiting demons is insane. He raises his hands to his sides. "Well, it would seem young Daniel has a plan to keep Lucifer's team out of the airbase using human technology, and they need to use his equipment at a portal event. That's as much as I know, Raph. We're not great with foresight these days, remember?" he says, cocking his head to one side and half-smiling at him. "And I have only really just begun to tune into this event."

"And He is letting them do this? Putting themselves in the firing line for some strange notion of control? And He is fine with this?"

"Raph! It is not our place to question and I think your involvement with humans in the last few years is making you forget our place."

Raphael looks wounded. "I am not forgetting my place, Mike, nor am I swayed by the humans' actions, I am simply questioning why we are allowing this to happen. What was the point in saving them in the first place if we are just going to let them throw away their lives needlessly?"

Michael struggles to answer. He is finding it hard to provide answers for a lot of things the Creator does recently. The fact that He allowed Charlotte and Judas to walk into Hell, that He has done nothing to instruct Heaven's forces to help take back the Earth. It has all been a mystery to him and the murmurings of disorder among the ranks of angels worries him. Only a handful of celestial beings have ever questioned the Creator in their entire existence, and things have never gone well when they did. But now, at what feels like the end of humankind, the need for answers has surfaced once again, and he is fearful that it may lead to worrisome disturbances among his brethren.

"Look, Raph. Let's just keep our eye on this for the time being, see what happens. We have been issued the command to not get involved in anything they do, and I for one don't intend to upset Him. He's been in a funny mood lately."

Raphael throws his hands up into the air and turns his back on Michael.

"Look, there's no point in getting into a strop with me, I haven't grounded us so just deal with it like the soldier you are meant to be."

Raphael puts his hands onto his hips and turns to face Michael.

"I mean it Raph. I don't need this grief from you of all people. Come on brother, be at my side, not at my throat."

Raphael looks down and takes in a deep breath, exhaling slowly. He looks up again. "Sorry Mike. I'm just frustrated. This makes no sense. None at all."

"I know my friend, I know."

They both spin around at the sound of Gabriel's voice.

"When has He ever made sense, or even had to for that matter!"

Michael nods to Heaven's first in command. "Gabriel! Didn't see you come in."

"Hmmm, so it would seem. I would do your best to keep these… thoughts to yourself, gentlemen, until such time our Lord commands us to do anything differently. Understood?"

Small nods of their heads signal their compliance.

Gabriel considers them both for a moment. "Good. Well, now that we have cleared that up, what's the latest, where are they?"

Michael waves his hand and the floor beneath them changes from pure white to an image from over where Gary and the team are positioned. "They are back at Saguenay, trying to get demons to spawn. And from the looks of the size of the disturbances in the Earth's magnetic fields close to them, I think they are about to get more than they bargained for."

Gabriel muses for a moment, spotting the fluctuations that Michael has pointed out. He emits a low growl from the back of his throat and then waves his hand over the scene, returning the floor to pure white. He ambles over to Michael, his hands clasped behind his back, and leans into his ear. "Be… discreet." Then he walks away.

Michael smiles out of the corner of his mouth, nods, and raises his eyebrows at Raphael.

TWENTY-SEVEN

Gary turns toward Sarah as darkness swallows the last of the day's light, and the yellow of the sand around them turns a murky brown.

"Have you ever seen the movie Predator?"

She shakes her head. "No. Can't say that I have. I'm not much of a movie person. Isaac is though, although he keeps watching movies about war and fighting. I don't understand how people can call that entertainment. Why do you ask?"

He shuffles into a more erect, upright sitting position. "Well, there is this one scene, and I can't believe I'm remembering this as I am usually rubbish with movies," he barks a small laugh, "that's more Judas' thing, but it seems apt now. So, in this scene, Arnold Schwarzenegger is talking with this woman who is describing how the men in her village are taken and skinned alive during the hottest summers."

Sarah screws her face up. "Oh my word, that's horrible. Why would you watch such a thing?"

"Oh, well, you don't see those men getting skinned, well, not those men, you do see some men getting skinned, well not actually watching them get skinned, but you see them after it's happened… and strung up… and one guy gets his spine and skull ripped outta his body—"

She recoils even further. "What? Oh, my Lord above, why would you be telling me this… and now of all times?"

"Wait, no, that's not it, lemme start over."

"I don't think I want you to. That's horrible."

"Okay listen, the point that I am trying to make, albeit very badly I might add, is that in this scene, after she explains what is going on, he gets an idea on how to bring the alien… errr, well, the Predator thing to them."

"Okay… and?" she says, with a raise of her eyebrows.

"Well, in the scene he gets up and walks out into the middle of the traps that they have set up."

Her eyes open wide and she shakes her head. "Oh, you've got to be kidding?"

He smiles out of the corner of his mouth.

"But it won't work with me, they can't see me," she says. "At least I hope they still can't. It feels less of a certainty each time we encounter them."

"I know, sweetie, they can't see you, but they can see me." He goes to stand up.

She grabs his arm. "Gary, that's insane. It's suicide."

"Well, isn't that what I'm here for? And maybe if I get a little further away from you they will sense my presence. Maybe you're blocking me from them. I dunno. Have you got any better ideas? Because we need a result, and we need it now."

She stares at him for a few moments, her breathing racing, and small tears welling at the corner of her eyes. Not from sadness, but fear, borne from an instantaneous knowing that this is it, that everything will most likely begin, and that she might never see him again. She releases his arm and wipes her eyes.

He cups his hands against her face. "Hey, *hey!* It'll be fine. It will all be fine. It won't be the first time I have had to buck from these things."

He offers a small smile. "Just be ready with the equipment. If they appear, I reckon I will be doing the Chattanooga hot-step and you'll need to move fast."

"The what?"

He laughs and shakes his head. "Never mind, it's just an expression. An old, old expression. You ready?"

"No!" she says vehemently.

"Yeah, me neither." He stands up and edges out of their cover into the desert-like terrain and grim open space ahead of them. His heart races and his mouth dries up almost instantly.

The fuck are you doing, Gary Cross? What the fuck are you doing? he tells himself, suddenly realizing that this isn't a movie, he isn't Arnold, and he is probably about to die. Terror hits him as he creeps further forward. But too much rides on the success of this mission, and this isn't the first time he has had to deal with fear of this magnitude. It might not have been against demons, but he's tracked many a monster during his time as a detective, entering homes where the advantage was always with the perp, and he had found ways to push that fear down then. Today is no different.

"Deal with your fear, Cross," he whispers to himself, "deal with and own it."

He flaps his arms in the air. "Well. Here I am Mr. Demons. Come and get me. It's me, Gary Cross, Charlotte and Judas' best friend. Here I am, all tasty-looking and shit."

Nothing. Not a sound.

"Hey! Demons! Didn't you hear me? It's me, Gary Cross… you stupid motherfuckers."

Still nothing.

He glances back at Sarah and shrugs, and she returns the gesture.

A short distance away in their holding position, Nathan watches the event unfold through binoculars as Gary walks out of cover and into the open, waving his hands up and down and looking around.

Jonesy crouches next to him, open-mouthed and his eyes wide. He remains that way for a moment before speaking. "What… the actual… fuck is he doing? Is he mental?"

Nathan laughs a little, although the situation is anything but funny. "You never been hunting before, Jonesy? That my friend is what live bait looks like." He turns around to the gathered military personnel behind him and speaks while keeping his voice subdued. "Okay people, there's a good chance that things will hot up, and soon. Be ready. Not one of you hesitates, screws up, or otherwise jeopardizes this mission, and I'm talking to you too, Daniel."

Daniel nods and takes a deep breath, his eyes glistening with fear, watering at the prospect of what is about to go down, that he will face demons again, something he hasn't had to do since the night of the Collapse. He swallows hard and wets the inside of his mouth, then takes another deep breath.

Nathan nods a few times. "Right, good. Stand to, people. No one dies today. That's an order."

Isaac shuffles forward toward Nathan. "What's going on? What's happening?"

Conrad sidles up next to him, and gets into a kneeling position. "Exactly what needs to happen. Now ready weapon. Do as ordered."

Isaac stares at him for a moment and then also adopts a kneeling position, unslinging his rifle from his back and making it ready.

Gary sighs. He is beginning to feel stupid standing in the middle of a damn desert, flapping his arms around like a chicken. He looks at Sarah once again and screws his mouth up, then shrugs. He glances upward, and closes his eyes, shaking his head a little. He is about to walk back when the night sky explodes with red and portals open around him everywhere with demons pouring out of them. "Oh, fuck. Fuck-fuck-fuck!" he says, turning in a circle, trying to count all of them. "This was a bad idea. This was a very bad idea indeed!"

Sarah grips the data collection device and swallows hard. *Oh God,* she tells herself, *this is too many, there are too many of them. This isn't right.*

A larger portal opens a little further away from the others and two large men stride through. Gary doesn't recognize the first, dressed in an immaculate black suit and with slicked-back hair, but he knows enough about demons to recognize that it is someone very important. The other he does recognize, and his heart sinks.

Demon-Colt, the leader of the cannibals that infested the mall where Gary and his team had been taken prisoner and Abigail lost her life, flexes his muscles, and rolls his head around his neck. Before, as a man he was huge and frightening, but as a demon, he is colossal and terrifying, with a lipless face that exposes all of his teeth, sharpened and black. Clawed hands drape down at his sides, the fingers flexing. His bare torso is charred and blackened with disgusting wounds that pulse as though something means to emerge from them. His presence is daunting. And ahead of him, Lord Asmodeus holds up a hand and smiles.

"Hello. Hello there, Detective Cross. How are you today?" He pauses, placing the tip of his tongue against his top lip and smiling again. "This is a bit odd, isn't it? I mean, finding you here, seemingly calling us forth. Do you intend to accomplish something here today? Or are you merely tired of your frail and pathetic human existence, hmm?"

Asmodeus smiles once more, and it is very unnerving.

"Well? Speak man, dammit," he continues, with a laugh, "I am most intrigued."

But Gary cannot speak – he can barely move. He doesn't feel like there is anywhere he could run without one of these terrible creatures hunting him down. He glances from one to the other – hunter demons, jackal demons, demon knights, fire demons, electric demons, and many that he has never seen before, the list goes on, the variants endless. He looks to his left at the closest portal that has remained open, with stragglers still ambling through. He closes his eyes, clenches and unclenches his fists, then takes a deep breath while saying a silent prayer to himself and walks toward it.

Spotting him, Sarah grips the equipment tightly and also starts to make her way toward the portal. She reasons that he is going to have the demons converge on him and then give chase, and at that moment she needs to be there, to set it down and turn it on. She creeps around the edge of the remains of the building they were hunkered against, her back flush to a wall.

Asmodeus senses movement to his right and snaps his attention to it, frowning. Although he cannot see it, he knows something is moving in that direction, and so he snaps his fingers toward a demon, and then points, and the creature bounds off as directed.

Gary reacts. There's nothing else for it. He raises his weapon and fires at the sprinting demon, hitting it in the torso with holy bullets, causing it to stumble forward and crash to the ground.

The night air erupts into howling and screaming, and the demons attack.

Gary sprints away from the direction he was headed. *Change of plan!* he thinks to himself, hoping to make himself the only target on the battlefield, thus allowing Sarah the opportunity to move to her objective and praying that the portal stays open long enough for her to get a reading.

As Gary attacks the demon, Sarah moves with more intent toward the portal, the foul beast that had begun to make its way toward her now crunching to the ground. As she nears the anomaly, she is forced to stop as the portal closes and the area around it plunges into darkness, with the demons that had exited from it a moment ago hurtling after the fleeing Gary. She screws up her mouth and gently bangs her head against the wall behind her. Then she looks at Gary and the demons in pursuit of him. She closes her eyes, drawing on as much courage as she can and then runs toward him, keeping herself perpendicular to his trajectory.

In both of their earpieces they hear a commanding voice, and the word "DOWN!" followed by the sound of 40mm machine gun fire from one of the Humvees.

Sliding to the ground, Gary covers his head with his hands as the deadly projectiles zip over and into the rampaging demons behind him, their screams audible over the sound of gunfire.

Asmodeus smiles and steps back through his portal.

He rips another one open behind the firing vehicle and punches into the back of it, causing it to buck forward and flip over onto its roof.

Nathan and those around him turn in time to see the vehicle topple toward a group of his team, who are not able to move out of its way quick enough. The Humvee lands on top of them, their terrified screams filling the night air.

Above them, another huge portal opens and out of it emerges a massive winged demon. It swoops down and picks up the upside-down vehicle in its talons and hauls it up high into the air where it then lets it plummet to the ground to crush even more of the ground forces.

Nathan rolls onto his back and opens fire at the suited demon with his rifle and is immediately joined by his other forces.

Smiling, Asmodeus shadow-steps out of the way of each bullet and moves quickly among his enemies, ripping them apart.

"MOVE!" Nathan screams, now up on his feet and grabbing hold of a terrified Daniel, dragging him along toward Gary's position.

Getting to his feet, Gary checks his surroundings and spots a hunter demon closing on him, its claws outstretched and evil face fixed on him. He drops onto his back and unslings his rifle from his back, then unloads it at the beast, the bullets ripping into its hindquarter and damaging it, but not enough to kill.

Smashing into him, the demon knocks Gary off his feet again but in the collision, it somehow becomes entangled with the strap of his weapon, ripping it out of his hands.

Gathering himself and scrambling to his feet, Gary looks toward the beast, struggling to free itself from the weapon's webbing, and he takes full advantage of it being temporarily incapacitated and sprints off in the opposite direction.

Finally untangling itself, the demon screeches and gives chase once again, its speed lightning fast. It is upon him in seconds, and as it closes the distance between them, it leaps.

Feeling the snarling beast almost upon him, Gary slides to the ground and the creature flies overhead, landing in front of him and blocking his path. As it skids to a halt, its claws scrape against the dusty ground trying to gain traction.

Once again Gary gets to his feet and runs back the way he came, only this time he veers to the left then curses at his choice of direction.

Directly in front of him lies an embankment of sand and rubble. It is not a huge hindrance, but an obstacle sufficient enough to warrant scaling on hand and knee. He is running out of time and knows that this game of cat and mouse will end soon with only one winner… and it won't be the mouse. Behind him he can hear the demon drawing closer and to make matters worse more are closing in from the east and the west. He knows that this is looking bad for him, but he won't quit – they are going to have to work hard for their prey. And so he scrambles onto the incline and claws his way up.

The demon leaps into the air, its claws outstretched, its tongue lolling out of its salivating maw, then it slams into the ground and explodes into dust as the Archangel Raguel lands on top of it.

Upon seeing its demise, Gary flops onto his back and skids down the embankment, relieved to see Raguel walk toward him, a hand outstretched to help him to his feet. But before he can accept his assistance, a hunter demon leaps from the top of the embankment and over Gary's head, where the Archangel catches it by the throat.

"Petty creature," He says, before crushing its neck and discarding it to one side like a rag doll, where it too disintegrates.

Flopping his head onto the dirt once again and then sitting up, Gary at last takes Raguel's extended hand and gets to his feet. "It's getting to be a habit with you guys appearing out of the sky to rescue me," he says, while still catching his breath.

"Well, let's not make it a third time Gary, eh?" Raguel says, offering a wink.

Gary nods and smiles, then concern hits him. "Sarah – where's Sarah?"

***

She inches along the low wall to her right under the probing gaze of a jackal demon, its long snout sniffing the air directly above. She does everything she can to make as little sound as possible. Her heart pounds within her chest, and her mouth dries with the feeling of intense terror that courses through her body. She closes her eyes, feeling that she has disturbed a portion of rock that would bring the beast down upon her. But without warning, it grunts and hurtles off to the right and she pokes her head up a little over the edge to see where it has run off to. Her eyes widen as she sees that its intended targets are Isaac and a group of soldiers. Without a second thought for her own safety, she throws the data-gathering device up onto the ground above the wall and hauls herself up, then grabs it and sprints toward Isaac and the others.

"TO THE LEFT!" Isaac screams, as the demon bears down on him and the other team members. He dives to his right and onto his back, opening fire at it and clipping it with a few shots but not enough to stop its momentum. It tears into one of the soldiers who screams as he is taken down.

Although Isaac has done his best to hide it and always played the tough guy, the sound of people dying at the hands of demons still terrifies him, and he hates it with every fiber of his being. But there is nothing at all he can do for the man as he is torn limb from limb, his blood spraying everywhere, his body flopping on the ground as the demon gorges upon him. And so he scrambles to his feet and continues fleeing with the other soldiers doing the same but in a different direction.

Seeing the group scatter, the demon drops the bits of dead man in its mouth and, with a quick glance between them, chooses to pursue the soldiers, grunting with every bound of its massive legs.

It makes him feel bad for the others, but Isaac is very grateful for the fact the creature has chosen to chase them down and not him, and so grabs hold of a concrete pillar to help guide himself around it faster and change direction, then calls out as he thuds into something hard, and rebounds off it and onto his back. He feels liquid flow from his nose and onto his lips, and it fills his mouth with the coppery taste of blood, then pain in his forehead causes him to gently explore it with his fingers, which come away wet, sticky, and red. Whatever he ran into has opened a nasty gash and he looks up, still dazed, at an enormous demon-knight who stares down at him, its huge sword held in both hands and raised to the side of its body. Panic grips him, his eyes opening wide and he scrambles backward on his hands and feet, trying to put as much distance between them as quickly as possible, but unable to find the courage to get to his feet and run.

The demon raises its sword above his head and laughs.

From behind him and to his right, Isaac hears Sarah's voice.

"GET DOWN! FLAT!" she screams, as she fiddles with the automatic rifle of the dead soldier. On her knees, she points the weapon at the demon-knight and pulls the trigger.

"NOOOOOOO!" Isaac screams, an arm stretched out to her as the first bullets race out of the barrel, over his head and into the demon-knight, rocking it from side to side as they tear through him while others zip harmlessly past.

It looks to her and cackles. "Now I see you."

With a terrified gasp, Sarah drops the weapon and looks at Isaac, her eyes flooding with tears.

Isaac screams once again, and pulls his own weapon up, unleashing a hail of bullets at the demon that hit it square in the chest and cause it to raise its hands in front of its face as each holy bullet rips into its armor. The momentary and well-timed distraction provides Isaac with the seconds he needs to get to his feet and run toward his sister, and he grabs hold of her arm, yanks her up, and races away with her.

"What the fuck were you thinking?" he says, his tone angry. "You've attacked them. They can see you now!"

She says nothing, she cannot, she is too numb, realizing that the only advantage she possessed against the forces of Hell was her stealth. And so she runs with Isaac, scrambling over the wreckage of ruined houses, and wondering how they will ever get a reading from a portal and more importantly get out of this. She gasps, realizing that she dropped Daniel's machine on the floor behind them when she picked up the soldier's weapon. But it is too late to go back for it now – the whole mission has failed, she has failed, and they are going to die.

They both skid to a halt as a portal bursts open in front of them and the demon-knight steps through, laughing, its voice guttural. "And where do you think you are going?" it says, advancing toward them.

A series of shotgun blasts startles Sarah and she screams while clamping her hands to her ears. Ahead, she sees the demon rock back with each blast, toward the portal that still rages open. She screams again, flapping her hands at the side of her head as someone else's hands grab her from behind then she stops as she realizes it is Colonel Taylor.

"This way," he shouts, "move!"

The world around her descends into slow motion as she looks to Nathan's side to see Conrad walk past, advancing on the demon, blasting away at it with his combat shotgun, his one good eye focused on the beast, his teeth gritted, his face resolute. And then her attention draws toward Daniel as he races past, and she hears Nathan's slow yet clear voice telling him to come back, screaming at the boy: "what are you doing?" But either Daniel does not hear him or doesn't care as he holds up the data-gathering device, having retrieved it from where Sarah discarded it moments earlier. He turns it on and bowls it toward the portal then turns around and screams, "go, go, we will get it later," and it is at that moment her senses come crashing back and she turns to run. Time seemingly returns to normal, the sound of events speeding up as they flood into her ears and she sprints away, dragged along by Nathan.

More portals rip open in front of them and Nathan screams, "Adjust, move to the left," but it is pointless as they are practically surrounded.

Conrad's weapon ceases firing, the magazine having run out of rounds. His hand quickly paws at his webbing belt, frantic to retrieve another drum, but there are none. "Aw fuck it," he says with an air of defiance, "plan was impossible in first place. We did good, considering."

The demon-knight sprints ahead, powering toward him and Conrad grits his teeth, bracing himself for a fight, for what it's worth, but then takes a small step back in surprise as Michael lands in front of him and slices his sword upward from his right, cleaving the demon in half and sending it flying into the air in two pieces. He then beats his wings hard at the creature as it explodes into a poisonous cloud, and the powerful rush of wind serves to blast the noxious dust up and away from the humans around him.

Michael snaps his attention to Nathan. "Do you have what you need? Has this been worth it?"

Nathan shakes his head, and flaps his mouth open and closed, something significantly unusual for him even in the heat of battle.

Daniel steps forward. "No. I need that. That thing there on the ground." He points to where the portal was a few seconds ago, the data-collection device now lying in its charred footprint.

Michael glances toward it. "Very well," he says, ripping open a portal. "Into it, now. The others are moving the rest of your team."

Daniel steps forward. "No! I need that, I need that devi—"

Michael takes him by the arm and flings him into the portal and then shakes his head. "Is he always this annoying?" he says to Nathan.

"You have no idea," he replies, while bundling the rest of the team through.

Michael smirks at Nathan, then nods after the man as Nathan follows the rest of his team. He then stomps toward the device and scoops it up and turns to face the rampaging horde of demons descending upon him. "Ridiculous pests," he says, his face a mixture of disdain and disgust.

Asmodeus places a hand on demon Colt's shoulder as the hulking man steps forward. "No! Not now. Let them retreat. We will take them at the base and I don't care how many Archangels are with them. We will destroy them all."

Colt grunts and walks backward, slowly, toward the portal that Asmodeus has created.

One of the Lord's lieutenants says, "Master, what of the others on the battlefield with the Archangels?"

"Who cares?" Asmodeus replies, without looking back, then disappears into the portal, followed by Colt.

The lieutenant glances to the demons who are methodically being slain by Michael, then grunts and enters the portal as well.

As he kicks the last demon to the floor to remove it from the end of his sword before it explodes into dust, Raguel and Raphael approach Michael.

Raphael points to the piece of equipment in Michael's hand. "That's what this was all about?"

Michael glances at it. "Apparently so."

"Why? What does it do?" Raguel asks him.

Michael opens a portal. "Well… let's go and ask them, shall we?"

TWENTY-EIGHT

Judas hoists Azazel up by his throat with a grunt, and slams him into the side of Mokwena's corpse, his feet clear off the ground.

"All right, no more bullshit. What the fuck is going on here and just exactly who are you?"

He takes hold of Judas' arm. "Please, master, let go and I will tell you."

Judas regards him for a moment through a thunderous scowl, then drops him.

Azazel lands on his feet and adjusts his clothing, then walks a few feet away from Mokwena and paces up and down. Turning around and glancing at her corpse, he cocks a thumb at her. "Nice work by the way." Upon turning back around, he is forced to lift his chin as Charlotte's sword arrives under it biting at his throat.

"I suggest you start talking, demon," she says, the scowl on her face a clear indication that she is in no mood for his games.

Azazel smiles then edges the sword away with two fingers. "No need to be rude, I will tell all, it will be a weight off my mind if I'm being honest." He glances at Judas and grins.

Judas storms toward him. "Is this funny to you?"

He lowers his head and shakes it, then looks up while pressing his lips together tight.

Charlotte sheaths her sword. "Right then. Well in that case stop being a massive dick and out with it. What's going on?"

Azazel takes a deep breath and glances back toward Mokwena once more. "I take it she spilled her guts?"

Judas nods.

"Hmm," Azazel replies, with a smile. "Well, everything she no doubt said will all be true. That's the long and short of it. And I don't deny it."

Judas scowls. "I said no more bullshit. You love working your mouth, so just talk."

Azazel smiles and then runs his fingers through his hair. "As I said, everything she most probably said will be correct." He looks at Mokwena one final time and smiles, then looks back at Charlotte and Judas. "I was commissioned to build Hell by the Creator and also to do a little… housekeeping. After Lucifer and his lackeys were exiled here, I helped run the place with the aid of my brothers. Prison wardens, so to speak. We provided orientation for the newly Fallen Angels, y'know, show them around their new home." He chuckles. "But then I started to get more heavily involved. You see, the Creator saw great potential in this place, a plane of existence to send those whom He deemed not worthy. To damn them along with the traitorous fallen. And so Hell became home not only to defeated angels, but the worst that humankind had to offer. It was perfect."

Judas frowns. "But this wasn't your intended home. Why did you stay?"

He raises his arms to his side and looks around. "This was my creation. I liked it here. And not only that, once I had helped Lucifer design varying methods of torture for all the foul and nasty souls, I grew proud of it. You see, at first Lucifer wasn't the twisted, murderous creature you know today. He was, in fact, a broken being when he was sent here, parted from the Divine Presence, and yearning for its embrace once more, having realized his mistake and regretting having set the events in motion in the first place." He grins at Judas. "Sound familiar?" he winks.

Judas grits his teeth. "Don't fucking test me, Azazel. Do not." He stabs a finger at him.

Azazel's grin wanes. He knows he pushes Judas often, tests the boundaries of their symbiotic relationship, but looking at the man right now he understands that he may have just crossed one line too many. Despite the power he possesses, he needs Judas. Slowly he backs away with an apologetic smile, then he paces up and down as he talks. "Well, after eons of being down here working with Lucifer and his minions, my brothers and I didn't want to leave. To be fair, the Creator didn't care what we did one way or the other."

Charlotte steps forward a little. "But Gabriel said you were created to keep the balance, this sounds like you picked a side."

Azazel shrugs and then smiles. "I guess we did. And therein lay our problem. The place we created had been too successful and, after a time, even we fell under its corruptive spell and bad influences. I mean, just look at you, at how much foul language you have been using and how you are acting since entering here." He looks around again and smiles. "She really is my greatest work. Alive, breathing, beautiful – and deadly." He ponders for a moment and then looks back at them. "And so began my end of days. I had wormed my way into Lucifer's ear, niggling away, convincing that all power should belong to him, to us, and that I should be the weapon he uses to march on all realities. Oh, in the beginning he dismissed me as a rambling idiot, telling me he had no further desire to take up arms against the Creator ever again, that the pain of the first defeat was too great. But that's the thing about Hell you see, one of its many purposes is to change one's perspective; and change it did. Problem is, another of its important purposes is to nurture deceit and deception, and the power that I craved was also sought after by my brother Beelzebub. He convinced Lucifer that he could serve him better, and convinced my weaker-minded sibling

Leviathan to take up arms against me with the help of this bitch here," he turns around and kicks Mokwena's lifeless corpse, "…and one other. Fucking Cthulhu." He screws his face up at the very mention of the other deceitful Lord. "And together, they jumped me like pussy-assed bitches, pulled out the source of my energy, and threw me into the pit. Funny though, because not long after I arrived there so did Leviathan." He throws his head back with an over-dramatic giggle. "Oh, how I laughed when that happened!" He shakes his head. "Levi. Stupid bastard's own fault for trusting BL. And so there I remained until you came along and got me back in the game."

Judas stares at him for a moment, then stabs a finger at him. "And what is the game? What's your angle? Because if it is to march on the White Kingdom once more, then you and I have a problem. A serious fucking problem."

Azazel scoffs. "Of course not. An endless cycle of millennia out of this place has quelled any notion of wanting any more of that crap. I simply want to be whole again. I want back what is rightfully mine. Is that so terrible?"

Charlotte looks surprised. "Yeah. I can think of a few reasons why it's a bad idea." She turns toward Judas. "You're not buying this shit are you? The I-just-want-my-life-back crap?" She shakes her head.

Judas purses his lips together and shakes his head. "It's not like he can do anything other than obey me, though. I've claimed him. I've named him."

Azazel visibly agrees, pointing a finger at Judas in recognition.

"No," she says, with a dismissive wave of her hand, and shaking her head, "no, no, no, no, no. I don't buy it. There's more to this. Surely if what he says is true my father would have stepped in and done something about it."

Azazel bellows a laugh. "What, like he has done here with this particular uprising? Don't make me laugh."

"Strange," she says, scowling at him, "all you seem to bloody well do is laugh."

Azazel steps toward her. "You just don't get it, do you? Either of you? He doesn't care about humans. Oh sure, he likes them, like a young child who's fond of his toys, but then eventually gets bored of them and doesn't bother playing with them anymore. Sure, he might look at them with happy memories from time to time, but that's about it. Eventually he stops caring and abandons the game completely to let it rot."

"Oh, bullshit," she shouts, throwing her hands into the air, "you are so full of it. He knows we are down here, knows that we intend to stop Lucifer. Why else do you think he has allowed us to have these abilities, my dad and I?"

This time Azazel's laugh is more acute and sharp. "Stop Lucifer? Why would he want you to stop Lucifer! He loves him."

The look of confusion on Charlotte's face is matched only by her disgust for the statement. "You lie. He does not. How can he love the one who intends to destroy him?"

Azazel laughs again and now it is his turn to throw his hands in the air while turning around and walking away. "He loves him because he is one of his children. A naughty, petulant one, but the fruit of his loins all the same, to coin an expression."

She shakes her head.

"Yes my dear. Whether you want to accept it or not, the Creator loves Lucifer regardless of his actions."

"Then why did he imprison him down here?" she shouts, her annoyance increasing.

"Why? The same, 'why' that any parent has for a naughty child… to punish them. Look, I don't expect you to understand the inner machinations of a supreme being and his relationship to his wards, but I can tell you this much. If any of this is by His choice, then the outcome is not the death of one of his favorite children. You need to trust me on that."

Judas steps forward. "Then what the hell is the plan? Huh? Why has He deemed it necessary for us to come down here, for my girl to have absorbed The Book and Seventh Seal if not to destroy Lucifer once and for all? What is this all about?"

Azazel shrugs.

Judas throws a hand up at him. "Awww, bullshit. Charley's right. You know more than you are telling us. Fuck you Azazel." He goes to hold his hand up to call him into his Ikazuchi form.

"Wait!" Azazel says, throwing his hands out in front of him. "Wait. Just wait. There is more. But let's strike a deal. You help me get me the next part of my heart from Cthulhu and I will spill everything else. I promise."

Judas stares for a moment, his mind racing with thoughts of what the demon sword is truly up to. But they are running out of time and options. They need to get to the Temple of Belial and this is an unwanted distraction despite learning more of the nature of Azazel. "You tell me now. I *command* you to tell me now."

Azazel shakes his head. "I cannot do that master."

"I mean it, I command you."

"NO! Strike the deal with me."

"DO AS YOU ARE TOLD, SWORD!"

"NO!"

They stare at each other for a few seconds, Judas with his lips pressed tight together and Azazel with his eyes darting back and forth over the man, trying to figure out what his next move will be.

Judas fumes. "Well, it would seem that giving you a piece of yourself back has created a little more defiance in your character, hasn't it minion!"

Azazel holds up placating hands. "Master, please. My intention is not to defy you. But I do want my pieces back, so please help me get the next one and we will have a chat that will be most... enlightening."

Judas curses aloud and walks away. "Fine. Fuck it. Whatever. But I swear to the almighty himself, Azazel. Do not test me."

He takes a deep breath. "Oh master, I wouldn't dare. And that is the truth. There is so much more to you and testing you is not something on my list of things to do... ever." He continues to hold his hands out in front of him, and for once his demeanor is one of genuine sentiment.

Charlotte lowers her head while shaking it and curses under her breath. Her head then snaps up. "Hang on. Mokwena said you knew that Lucifer closed every down-gate."

Azazel looks at her and takes a deep breath, his eyes opening wide. "Okay, I can see how this looks, but in my defense, I needed to get you here. I needed you to get the first piece from Mokwena."

Judas laughs sarcastically. "That's just great. That's just fucking great. So how much time have we wasted?"

"None, master. Lucifer has to traverse on foot as well."

"Why? How? How do you know this?" Judas asks, walking back to him with a deep frown on his brow.

"Because he carries Seals Five and Six. While carrying them, their very nature will prevent him from moving around down here through portals or even by flight, as their alignment is more toward light than dark. It is a failsafe, so they cannot be used within this realm."

Shaking her head Charlotte moves to Judas' side. "Wait, that cannot be right. Malphas called the Horsemen forward and he had The Seals in here."

"No. He activated them during a ceremony up above. A pretty gruesome one I might add, most of it unnecessary. Simply breaking them was all he needed do. Not sure where 'murder 12 virgin women' came from," he shakes his head in a puzzled manner, "...but that's fucking idiots for you."

Judas closes his eyes. It hits him, an understanding, and he can't believe he didn't see it before, that he'd missed it. He opens his eyes. "It's a trap. This whole thing has been a ruse to get Charlotte down here. He needs her Divine power to activate the last of The Seals."

Azazel sighs and then nods. "I think his plan is to slap them on her, causing her to absorb them, and they will then take their place in their respective slots in the book."

"But how will he use them?" Charlotte asks, confused. "If they are in me, I've won, haven't I?"

Azazel glances toward Judas, then back at her. "Not if he then kills you. The completed Book will disperse from your body and he can take it."

She closes her eyes. Now it's her turn to fully understand. "The Temple of Belial."

Judas looks at her, frowning.

She takes a deep breath. "When I absorbed the Seventh Seal and Book back in the Ark's crypt, I had a vision, a really powerful one. And in that vision a host of information was transmitted to me. A voice said, 'only in the Temple of Belial can The Book be opened by all. It is there that you will be able to banish your problem.'" She sighs. "I knew that message applied to Lucifer as well as me, and somehow I also knew that he knew. So, the logical thing was to go there, defeat him, and then banish him. In fact it was our only option, or this conflict would rage on and on without end. And now I understand. It is the only place, within his own realm, that he can interact with the relics." She looks perplexed. "But why? That bit of information is lost to me for some reason."

Azazel sighs again and lowers his head. "I told you. The Creator loves all his children, even the naughty ones." He takes a moment to consider the next part of his story, walking away a short distance, and then turns back to her. "When He had me build this prison, He asked me to make one special place, a sort of shared custody room if you like, where a father could interact with his child free from the horrors and corruption that this world had to offer. A place where He could come to spend some time with Lucifer to see how he was. And it went on for a while, until either He got bored or Lucifer stopped wanting to see Him, I don't know which. Either way the visits stopped and the Temple went unused. But its importance is that Lucifer will be able to interact with the relics in that place as, like I said, it is free from Hell's rule, and therefore yes, you're right Judas – it is a trap."

Judas begins to remonstrate with him but is silenced by Azazel's erect finger.

"But! If you help me get the second piece that I need you will possess great power. I can and I will help you gain the upper hand. You will be able to utterly destroy any of Lucifer's minions and, most likely, War and Death also, while at the same time she retrieves The Seals, opens The Book, and reads from it. And hey presto! All our problems are solved. Lucifer gets a serious spanking and goes back to an infant in the eyes of the universe, his power diminished, and humankind gets a much-needed respite for what will hopefully be several millennia. You win!"

"Not forever?" she asks, with a shake of her head.

Azazel smiles a little. "Hey, nothing is forever, but it's still a very long time in human history and a damn sight better than how things are now, yeah?"

She nods, although it pains her to do so.

Judas looks upward and takes a deep breath. "Okay. That's a lot to take in. For crying out loud. So now what? Mokwena said that only one other down-gate will be open, the one near The Well of Souls."

Azazel nods and smiles. "Correct."

"Well, how far is that?"

"A long way, master. Too far to use shadow-step energy on. You are gonna need as much of that as possible for Cthulhu and Lucifer himself."

"Great!" Charlotte says, flapping her arms, then slapping them down by her side and walking away.

"But!" Azazel says again with a pointed finger, "there is an alternative. Mazorakors."

Judas raises his arms and shakes his head, looking at Charlotte as he does.

She shakes her head back at him and screws up her face.

Looking back at Azazel, Judas frowns. "The fuck are Mazorakors?"

TWENTY-NINE

"Ahhh, Gabriel," Jesus says from his position perched on the edge of the council bench, and waving the Archangel forward as he enters the council chambers. "Good to see you. Did you get a chance to speak with Father?"

Beautiful and serene music, like melodious wind chimes, plays in the background, a calm and soothing sound as Gabriel approaches the bench. "I did, my Lord."

"How did it go?"

He screws his face up and raises his eyebrows. "As expected," he sighs. "Perhaps He will listen to you... you are His son after all?"

Jesus offers a subtle smile. "I think we both know that if He is to have his mind changed it won't be by me, the hippy of the family." He laughs, and Gabriel joins in.

Gabriel sighs. "Well, I hope Charlotte and Judas manage to find a way to bring this conflict to a close, because I am fresh out of ideas." He glances at Jesus from the corner of his eyes.

"Yes, well, we shouldn't put all our faith into that course of action. They have been in there a long time by an outsider's standards, and that place has a nasty habit of doing funny things to you. Just look at its designer. Terrible creature."

"I agree, but what is it you propose, my Lord?"

Jesus takes a moment to consider his reply. "Where are Michael and the others?"

Gabriel smiles a little. "They are taking care of a little bit of... discreet business, my Lord."

"Hmmm," he says, eyeing Gabriel for a moment, "strange that up until a few moments ago I couldn't sense them."

Gabriel offers a breathy laugh. "If you knew where they were Lord, why did you ask?"

"Oh, I dunno, just to see what you would say. You know we have been given a mandate of non-interference, Gabe!"

Gabriel sighs once again and turns to face him. "I know, my Lord, but this thing, this whole thing feels wrong."

Twitching a smile at the corner of his mouth, Jesus glances down. "It does. And what worries me more is how even I seem to have had my sight limited to what is going on in the world below, as though someone doesn't want other beings to know certain things." He pauses for moment, studying Gabriel. "Tell me, Gabe, do you believe the reason we have been given for the lack of foresight?"

He shakes his head, his brow furrowed. "I'm not sure I follow, Lord."

"The fact we have believed that all sight after Charlotte's awakening had been lost to us, that we have limited access to the future timelines of humankind. To me, it feels like it is being withheld rather than out of reach."

Gabriel shifts awkwardly where he stands, the question making him feel uncomfortable. He hadn't given it any thought as it wasn't his place to. He understood what the Creator had told him, that foresight had been removed from angelic beings prior to Charlotte's compromise, and that information from the Prime Being had been enough for him. He holds up his hands in a gesture of submission. "My Lord, it is not my place to question that which is above my station."

"I know Gabe, really I do, but there aren't many things that are above your station now, are there? Tell me you haven't felt this as well. You just told me that this whole thing feels… off."

Gabriel takes a deep breath, and exhales with a nervous smile, nodding a few times. "Yes. Yes, I did say that, didn't I?"

"Then tell me what you feel."

He shakes his head, trying to find the right words, to find the right way in which to put his feelings, but as hard as he tries, any notion of understanding drifts further away from him, out of reach. He offers a sharp laugh. "I can't my Lord. I just cannot." He shakes his head again.

Smiling, Jesus remains contemplative for a moment, then pushes himself off the bench. "I have an idea, but it is one that will require a significant sacrifice."

Gabriel's head moves back a little and he frowns. "My Lord?"

"If Father will not listen to you or me, then maybe he will listen to one of them – His favorites. One that I know he respects a lot.

Gabriel frowns, looking away for a second before returning his attention to Jesus. "But the Creator hasn't conversed directly with a human in a very, very long time."

With a thin smile, Jesus nods. "I know, Gabe. I know. Which is why I use the term 'significant sacrifice.'"

Gabriel sags. "My Lord. This is too big a thing to ask of anyone with very little guarantee of return. Please. Do not ask this of me."

Walking up to him, Jesus places his hands onto Gabriel's shoulders.

"Gabe. As you said a few moments ago, I too am fresh out of ideas. We must do something if the humans are to survive. I know I ask a lot with this, but it feels like it could be our last roll of the dice. And I know that you – Heaven's finest – would want to say you had tried every possible thing that you could, no matter how great the sacrifice."

Gabriel closes his eyes and lowers his head.

Jesus removes his hands and sighs. "And you know who to ask, don't you?"

He nods, opening his eyes at the same time. "Yes. Yes, my Lord. I do."

THIRTY

Michael and his team step through the portal, which closes immediately behind them, and into an area awash with activity and the screams of the injured and dying as base personnel scurry around, surprised at the sudden return of the team through holy portals.

Nathan turns in circles, as around him medical staff busy themselves treating the wounded and hurrying those with severe injuries to the medical facility. Trying to get a read on the situation to assess how bad the damage and loss of life is, his hard, gritty façade almost fails as Sergeant Jones plants a hand on his shoulder.

"Sir, are you all right?"

He grabs Jonesy by his shoulders and gives him a shake. "Ahh Jonesy, good man. Good man." He stares at him for a second, his happiness at seeing him alive, genuine in his eyes, then takes a deep breath and looks around at the screaming, panic, and chaos raging around them. "Conrad?"

Jonesy holds up a hand while nodding. "He's fine, sir. He is helping carry the critical to the infirmary."

Nathan sighs, closing his eyes for a moment. "Okay. Have the squad leaders that are left do a head count. I want to know how many we've lost and who they were. Then get me a sitrep on the gear we lost."

"Sir!" Jonesy says, his face and combat clothing stained with blood. He turns and sets off toward the nearest crowd of people, his arm already raised, preparing to click his fingers and grab their attention.

"Jonesy!"

Upon hearing his name called, he stops and turns around, to which Nathan nods at him with a half-smile, and so he returns the gesture to his commanding officer then hurries off to carry out his assignment.

"God, I hope it was worth it," Nathan mutters under his breath as he surveys an all too familiar scene, one that he has dealt with many times in his career of violence, and one that he grows increasingly weary of.

No matter how many battles he has fought in, no matter how many missions he has returned from, the sight of those he is responsible for – injured, dying, or dead – always ties him in knots in the pit of his stomach. Today, at the very edge of humanity's survival, feels just about the worse defeat he has ever suffered.

"I really hope this was worth it," he whispers again.

"So do I," Michael says, holding out the data-gathering device as he approaches Nathan, causing the Colonel to turn around and face him.

"Michael! Thank you. For everything. If you guys hadn't come along," he looks around the open area within the heart of the base, "if you hadn't have come along…" his words trail off and he looks down at the ground.

Michael offers the equipment to him. "Let's not think about that now, shall we? Make this count, Nathan."

As the two men stare at one another, contemplating the words, a jittery Daniel runs toward them and grabs the data device from Michael's hand. "Oh my God, you got it, you actually got it. Thank you, thank you, thank you," he continues to say the words again and again, although more to himself as he exasperatedly fiddles with the device, turning it over in his hands.

"Is everybody okay?" Gary asks, as he, Sarah, and Isaac approach them. "How many have we lost Nathan?"

Shaking his head, Nathan glances toward the direction that his Sergeant headed. "I don't know yet. Jonesy's doing the math." His face grows solemn as he turns back to Gary. "But my initial visual assessment is that it doesn't look good."

Gary sighs and lowers his head, then looks at the device in Daniel's hand. "That better be worth it."

"Yeah, so everyone keeps saying," the boy replies without taking his eyes off it. He stops and pushes a button. "Ahhh, you beauty," he says, then kisses the ejected memory card. "More valuable than anti-matter right now."

Gary and Nathan share a look, subtly shaking their head at one another.

Major-General Dawson's voice causes them all to turn toward him as he advances, his pace brisk. "Where do we stand, gents? Was the mission a success?"

Daniel holds up the memory card to show him. "We are about to find out."

Dawson looks at him for a second, then at Gary and Nathan, then back to Daniel. "Well! What the fuck are you still doing here?! Get to the labs and do what you gotta do."

Daniel glances at everyone. "Oh yeah, right – sorry." However, only now does he take in the misery unfolding all around him as his primary thoughts, upon exiting the portal, was for the well-being of the device. Now, as he soaks in the scene, he feels sick, and a sudden pain gnaws away at him. Not a physical pain, but spiritual. His mind processes the fact that this was his idea, his doing, and that so many people have lost their lives because of him. Families torn apart – fathers, mothers, daughters, and sons lost to his plan, to his requested mission. He had tried not to dwell upon the consequences of it before they had set off, nor had he wanted to fully understand them, but now as people lay screaming and dying all around him, it hit him like a freight train, punching into his mind and filling his soul like a devastating disease. And he feels very, very sick.

His eyes fill with tears. And he throws up.

"I'm sorry. Oh my God, I'm so sorry, I'm so, so sorry." He bends over and wipes his mouth with the back of his hand.

To Daniel's surprise, Nathan is the first to comfort him, to put an arm around and bring him back to a standing position. "Hey, hey, it's okay. None of this is your fault. Everyone signed up for this knowing the risks." He places his hands on the sides of Daniel's face and stares right into him. "Just don't let their deaths be for nothing. Okay?"

He nods, tears still rolling down his cheeks.

"Good," Nathan says with a smile. "Now go do your thing. You are the smartest man I have ever known. Go show everyone else just how smart you are."

Daniel smiles. He had called him man. Not boy, not child, but man. He sniffs and wipes the tears away, then breathes out hard. The Colonel is right, it's time to show everyone just how smart he is. This will work. He will be able to save everyone else. It will work.

Sarah places an arm around his shoulder. "Come on Daniel. Let's get to it. I'll help," she smiles at Gary, "for what that'll be worth."

Daniel smiles back at her, and nods as they hurry off to the labs.

"Okay, listen up," Michael says, taking a small step back so that he can see everyone. "They will be coming, and we need to prepare. Asmodeus is a significant threat on his own, and this time he will bring more. Whatever Daniel is doing, I pray to the Creator that he can do it in time before Asmodeus' army pours into this compound, but if he cannot, then you must fight like avengers from God. Your survival depends on it. This is where the future of everything begins. We will fight, or we will fall." He remains silent, saying nothing more to let his words sink in.

Gary takes a step forward. "Michael, where are Charlotte and Judas? Now would be a really good time for them to pitch in, don't ya think?"

Michael stares at him. "They cannot help, Gary. They have more pressing matters to attend to."

Gary exhales a laugh, then places a hand to his forehead and rubs it. "More pressing matters to attend to? Why? What are they doing? Where are they?"

"In Hell," Michael says, his face deadpan and emotionless.

THIRTY-ONE

Hurrying around the laboratory, Daniel directs Sarah as he goes. Grab this. Move that. Get me this he commands, while the girl flits about, equipment in her arms that she has no understanding or comprehension of, her face a mixture of panic and confusion. She dumps the materials onto a workbench and wipes her brow, then puts her hands on her hips.

"Okay. What now?" She stares at Daniel.

He says nothing, his concentration locked, furiously tapping away at a keyboard, entering information and data into the computer that he had cobbled together prior to setting off on the mission. He had used his time wisely before heading out, and the urgency of the situation now at hand has him very grateful that he had made all the necessary connections to a piece of electronic warfare equipment that he had Major-General Dawson's team dismantle and move to the roof of the hastily retro-fitted laboratory that he and Sarah now occupy. His plan is simple, to him at least – enter the collected data into the computer, balance the combinatorial analysis, determine the effective barrage-jamming frequencies, and then enter the coordinates of spread for the area to be covered. *What could go wrong, apart from everything*, he keeps telling himself.

"Daniel!" Sarah says, her tone sharp, bringing him out of his trance-like state.

"What?" he snaps back at her.

She opens her eyes wide. "I said now what? What do you want me to do?"

"Nothing," he says, the response curt. He sighs and readdresses his tone. "Nothing, Sarah. You can do nothing more. I need to align my data and pray to God that I am right on this one, that I haven't gotten this wrong. Or we are all dead."

She stares at him for a moment and then takes a deep breath and walks over to him, placing her forehead against the back of his head. "You won't have gotten this wrong. It will be fine. You will save everybody."

Daniel closes his eyes for a moment and then opens them. "Thank you. I better get to work."

She takes her head away from his and nods. "Okay. Well, I'll be here if you need me." She walks to the side of the room and takes a seat on a tall laboratory stool.

Daniel returns to punching data into his computer, getting up periodically to tamper with various cables and wires protruding out of and into multiple pieces of equipment, and Sarah stares at him, a small, impressed smile upon her face.

THIRTY-TWO

Nathan barks orders at personnel as he walks the perimeter of the base, his pace brisk and his finger pointing.

"I want miniguns here, here, and here. Put extra people there. Reinforce that barricade, for what it's worth. I also want an inventory of how many Claymores we currently have."

The orders roll off his tongue, flowing as easy as he breathes, the most natural thing in the world to him to be commanding, to create defenses, to put soldiers where they need to be, and tell them what they need to do.

And he is very good at it. Always has been. Even from an early point in his career having joined the army as a private (an act designed to annoy his father more than anything else), his fellow squad members would turn to him for advice. Even the higher ranked individuals he reported to would often canvass his opinion, valuing his input and insight. Following a field commission during a particularly arduous tour of Iraq, he had seen himself soar up the ranks and further enhance skills that were already innate to him, which would eventually propel him to the rank of Colonel.

A short distance from Nathan, Major-General Dawson echoes the Colonel's requests, reinforcing them in his own way. He doesn't want to step on Nathan's toes, as the man knows much more than he on how to set up a front-line combat perimeter, but at the same time he doesn't want to be a third wheel and seen as useless by his own people.

Looking toward him, Nathan understands, knowing how important it is for a person who bears the weight and responsibility for so many lives to be respected and trusted to be 'in command.' Not only of their personnel, but more importantly themselves, so that their fear in the build-up to combat is contained. Yes, Nathan understands and respects this, and as he draws closer to Dawson, satisfied that he has done all he can to set up the defenses, he calls to Conrad.

"Sergeant Bzovsky."

"Sir," he replies, in his thick Ukrainian accent.

"Sergeant, please assist the Major-General with his team's preparations in any way he sees fit."

"Of course, sir. It will be done." Conrad moves toward Dawson. "Major-General, how may I be of service to you?"

While Dawson talks to Conrad, pointing at various things around them, Gary sidles up to Nathan. "Nice. That was very sweet of you, dear."

Nathan smirks. "Fuck off, yeah! That man needs purpose, and Conrad will give him that for sure."

Smirking back, Gary refocuses his attention upon the Major and Conrad and nods a couple of times but then his smile wanes and he takes a deep breath. Nathan was right, the man did need purpose. Nathan's arrival can't have been easy for him, what with the man being the clear choice for leader. It was warranted not only for his skill and prowess in combat, given that they live in a perpetual warzone these days, but also his ability to garner respect from just about everyone he encounters. But as Nathan had once put it, it doesn't take men of battle to lead, merely men of courage, and from what Nathan could tell Dawson was such a man. And an honorable one at that.

Gary looks toward the Major-General once again, directing the team around him, fiddling with and adjusting his rifle slung around his body as it keeps drifting into an uncomfortable position. And he smiles a little, knowing that Nathan was right, as he always was in his assessments – Dawson was courageous and honorable, as it is moments like these, with the knowledge of the fight ahead, that would see many 'pencil-pusher' types crumble and fold, realizing that their careers had not been ones designed to contend with the reality of conflict. Not that there would have been anything wrong with that, as not all military personnel are designed or destined to fight, but many would have used it as an excuse to shirk a basic responsibility toward the survival of everyone around them, choosing to use it to retreat once the fighting starts. But that won't be Dawson. Gary sees it. *Damn Nathan and his perception.* He smiles inwardly, knowing that the former Ranger is better at figuring out people than he is.

Nathan points toward the Archangels perched atop antennas and radar dishes dotted around the area of the base to which they have retreated, having done so to widen their visible footprint of observation against the impending threat.

"Only three remain," he says, glancing toward Gary. "Doesn't fill you full of confidence for our chances, does it?"

He takes a deep breath and follows Nathan's gaze toward the Archangels. "No. No, it doesn't." He looks at Nathan. "Kinda' scares the piss outta' me, if I'm being honest! The fact that even these beings they have their limits."

Nathan suppresses a laugh then scans the area. "Yeah, well, it won't matter either way soon. We will be dead or thankful to see one more sunrise. But in the end, if Charlotte and Judas don't do something about all of this, then nothing we do will matter. We simply will not be able to keep going on like this day after day after day."

Gary nods in agreement. "Yeah, well I can tell you one thing for sure – if Judas has gone into Hell, then it is an end-game solution, because trust me he wouldn't have done so if he could have avoided it or it hadn't been necessary," he looks at Nathan. "So let's just do what we need to do, and survive. And who knows, the next sunrise we see might just be the most beautiful that the world has ever known."

Nathan offers a subtle smile and an even subtler nod and Michael's commanding voice causes them both to look up to the antennae he perches upon.

"It's time. They are here. Prepare yourselves."

They shift their gaze from him to the area outside the perimeter, where dozens of portals open, erupting in a straight line on a raised bank of sand a little over 1000 yards from the base.

In front of them, Asmodeus' larger, more intense portal opens, and he strides out, grinning widely, with Demon Colt at his side, then followed by other foot soldiers of various ranks.

"Oh, I am going to enjoy this," Asmodeus says, his grin turning wicked.

Nathan and Gary join Michael at his side as the Archangel lands close to them and Gary looks around, his searching hurried, then sees what he is looking for and calls to him.

"Isaac. On me. I want you on my six at all times."

The boy frowns at him for a moment, not moving.

"NOW!" Gary shouts, his voice commanding, strict, something even Isaac's petulance cannot ignore, and so he traipses toward Gary, the man fixing him with a stern look. "No heroics. You're a handy fighter, but I want you with me. You do not confront anything too fierce and you do not take any unnecessary risks. You watch my back and I'll watch yours. Got it?"

Isaac stares without speaking.

"GOT IT?" Gary demands, his eyes conveying the severity of his emotion.

"Yeah, yeah – I got it," Isaac replies with a small shrug of his shoulders.

"Good. Under no circumstances will I lose another Fisher. No goddamn way."

Isaac's eyes open wide and he stares at him for a moment. Words such as Gary has just said would normally bring his rage to a boil, forcing to think of his little sister Abigail once again. But as he hears the remorseful energy within Gary's statement, an understanding hits him – of Gary's feelings toward the loss of Abigail, about how it had affected him, and the guilt he must continue to conceal regarding her death. He closes his eyes and sighs to himself. Of all the times this could have happened, he's annoyed it had to be now, that this moment couldn't have been a worse time for him to start to come to terms with his sister's death and for the healing process to begin. He feels like shit about it. And he opens his eyes. "Gary?"

"Yeah?" Gary says, turning to face him.

"I… I'm…" His eyes dart back and forth, searching for the right words, the right sentiment and his mouth remains open for them but they fail to come. Instead, he can do nothing more other than offer a small shake of his head.

Gary's mouth twitches. The beginnings of a smile. He understands. He understands it all. And so he says nothing, instead offers Isaac a small nod who then nods back at him, and looks down.

"Arrogant bastard," Michael says, causing them all to turn their attention toward him. "He could easily portal his forces in, but he chooses to pour them out there to mock us." He grits his teeth. "I will take great pleasure in driving my sword through his stupid, grinning face."

"Is he just gonna stand there?" Gary asks, checking his weapon and preparing himself.

"He most certainly will not," Michael replies, and almost as though it were a cue from the Archangel himself, Asmodeus' forces begin a slow march toward them.

Michael draws his sword with a fury to match the aggression on his face. "Get ready!" he shouts as he moves toward the front and center of the positioned forces, with Raphael and Raguel landing on the ground at his side. He looks around at the terrified faces of the soldiers in towers, on top of buildings, within trenches, and resting against sandbag barriers. He closes his eyes, knowing most will not make it through the battle, and prays that he will see them rise. He opens his eyes and turns back to face the enemy, "Fight with everything you have and for everyone and everything you love!"

The demon horde change from an amble, into a trot, and then a sprint, erupting with howls and screams at the height of their charge. Among their vast numbers can be counted all manner of demons, jackal, ape, fire, knight, and hunter but also huge and devastating variants such as the base's inhabitants have never seen before, not even Gary. Fearsome, hulking beasts that tower above their smaller kin, yet nonetheless intimidating and covered in thick, spiky armor and holding weapons ranging from tridents to spiked balls that are attached to chains, to swords. Each unique in design and terrifying to behold.

Nathan looks up toward the minigun operators in towers, crudely erected during the padding out of the base's defenses. "OPEN FIRE. RINSE THEM!" he screams. "PUT SOME FUCKING FIRE IN!"

The miniguns erupt, spitting thousands of holy-converted bullets that rip into the front line of advancing demons with devastating effect, exploding them into dust. And as others race around their dying comrades, portals open and they dive into them, erupting out of the other side, within the perimeter of the base and, skidding to a halt, they turn and charge at the soldiers ahead of them.

The Archangel's shadow-step toward them, their swords aloft, their faces burning with violent intensity, and as they collide with the demons they roar and begin slicing them to pieces.

***

"I think we need to hurry Daniel," Sarah says.

"I know," comes his curt reply.

"The fighting has started."

"I can hear that."

"People will die."

"I fucking get it, Sarah! Now help and stop hindering me."

She stares at him for a moment, stunned, then understanding hits her. He is right, she needs to be part of the solution not part of the problem and she breathes out through puffed cheeks. "Okay. What do I do?"

He points to a panel on a column in the middle of the room, with wires and cables running off it toward and out of a window that lead up to equipment on the roof. "See that dial over there?"

"The gray one?"

"Yeah, that's it. Go over there and turn that dial so that the display next to it reads 10.6 kHz."

She races over and hastily turns the dial to the left, then corrects herself and turns it to the right as the numbers move out of sequence. "Okay. Now what?" she asks, looking at him.

"Okay, the one underneath it, directly underneath it, turn that one to the left until it reads 14.3 kHz, then push the yellow button to the side."

She does as he asks.

He types more data into the computer, his fingers frantic and his eyes darting back and forth.

"What now?" Sarah asks, with a nervous anxiety to her voice.

He doesn't answer.

"Daniel? What now?"

"Just a fuckin' minute," he says, glancing back at her, "I need to enter the co-ordinates and you're distracting me." He closes his eyes and takes a deep breath. He doesn't enjoy being this short with her, but the sounds of battle from outside has his heart pounding and his mind racing.

***

A hunter demon launches itself at Conrad, forcing the big man to drop onto his back and unleash a barrage of shots from his combat shotgun, exploding them into the beast's chest and turning it to dust as it passes overhead. He rolls over, spluttering the foul miasma out of his mouth and wiping at his one good eye. He lifts the eye patch covering his useless one and flaps dust out of it, the coarseness of the grit causing irritation on the area of skin that doesn't suffer from deadened nerve damage. Getting onto bended knee, satisfied he has cleared sufficient offending matter off of his face, he looks ahead as a huge portal opens and out of it strides Colt, a fierce confidence to each step, even more so than when he was a living, breathing human being. Conrad stands, his face tense as he licks his lips and grits his teeth. Then, cocking his weapon, he unclips the drum magazine, pulls another from his belt, and offers it up to the underside of the shotgun, inserting it and not caring about the rounds he may have discarded in the other. He needs to know that he has a full drum attached, as the creature advancing toward him was bad enough in life, but as a demon it may just prove unstoppable, and he will not allow a lack of ammunition to be the deciding factor in whether he is able to take him down or not.

Colt smiles. "Ahhh, the Ukrainian," he says, his voice deep and booming. "I thought I sensed the smell of your failure. At last I get to finish what I started." He looks around. "Doesn't look like you have your friend to save you this time," he guffaws.

"Don't worry," Conrad says, raising his weapon to his cheek, "he is around."

"So fucking what!" Colt says, his mouth curled into a snarl

"Fuck it," Conrad says, then starts blasting.

The shots pummel against Colt, exploding black liquid from out of him, rocking him back with each impact, and Conrad empties the entire 30-round drum into him, the last couple of blasts causing the demon to crash to the ground onto his back with a thud. But he cannot assume the creature's demise. Far from it. And so he wastes no time grabbing another drum from his belt and loading it into his weapon, and his eyes widen as Colt rises into a standing position, his legs straight, his arms at his side and roars with laughter.

"If only I'd had this level of power in life," Colt says, grinning, "that would have been glorious." He offers a sharp laugh and then powers forward into a sprint, his feet thundering into the ground with each footfall.

Conrad unleashes a fresh volley of slugs at him, but it is in vain, and Colt smashes into him, launching him backward by slamming both hands, palms outward, into his chest. Although Conrad's combat body armor absorbs some of the force, it still hurts a great deal and he calls out in agony as he lands and then skids along the ground. His adrenaline levels spike as he comes to a halt against the side of a building, and he screams. Not with the pain, but with fury and anger. Clambering to his feet, he sees Colt bearing down upon him once again and this time, with a duck, he manages to slip the demon's grasp and jab the butt of his shotgun into the side of his head.

It has no effect, save only for Colt to look to his left for a moment, a grin still plastered across his face.

"Pathetic," the demon says, and lashes out at Conrad.

He feels the concussive force of the blow and his nose explodes, showering blood as he lands on the floor around six feet away, with such force that it causes him to grunt the remaining air out of his lungs. *Goddamit, not again,* he tells himself as he reaches up to his nose, broken for what must be the 10th time. He squeezes, resetting it as best he can, provoking a vicious scream from himself and then feels huge hands grab at his webbing, lifting him into the air and he looks down into Colt's maddening demonic eyes.

From out of Colt's mouth snakes a foul foot-long tongue that licks against the side of Conrad's face and he recoils at its touch. Despite his revulsion, his mind comes to terms with his predicament and he knows this is it. That Colt will crush him to death, thus ending the fight.

Colt drops the huge soldier onto the ground as a lump hammer smashes into the side of his head, causing him to rock to the side. He turns toward the source to see the gray-haired man who had defeated him in the mall. "You!" he says, his mouth pressed into a fierce grimace, his eyes burning with intensity.

Nathan glances at the end of the broken hammer, the lump part now missing – all that remains is a pointed shard of stick. "Yeah. Me." he says, returning a defiant gaze toward Colt. He backs off and grabs hold of Conrad's armor. "On your feet soldier. You're not done yet, 'tis but a flesh wound."

Conrad groans a laugh, dragging himself to his feet. "Humor. Good. Need laugh right now." He sways slightly as he takes in a deep breath, willing back his senses, demanding that they return to him for one last fight. And he grits his bloodstained teeth.

A gigantic warrior demon swings its enormous sword at a minigun tower, exploding it into a shower of wood splinters and metal fragments, launching its occupants into the air, their screams trailing as they fall to earth. And a similar story plays out all around as other enormous demons attack the humans, stamping on some, spraying them out from between their feet, blood and guts splashing everywhere, then picking up others and crushing them in their hands, their blood spilling out from in between their fingers, and their pulped bodies then cast aside to skid across the ground, leaving streaky blood trails in the dirt.

Everywhere, gunfire peppers the early morning air, the popping sounds mixed in with not just the screams of humans but demons also, as Michael and his team tear them to pieces, affording them no quarter or mercy.

With fierce determination, Raphael swoops down toward a giant warrior demon and, dodging its enormous ball at the end of the chain weapon that then embeds into the ground with a crunch, he stows his wings and drops onto the chain, then runs up it toward the beast. As he nears its face, he slashes his sword toward it, rippling a shockwave of divine energy from out of his weapon that slices through its head, cleaving it in two. The beast explodes into dust, contaminating the entire area with its noxious cloud.

The dust spreads over the compound, accentuating the screams of humans, and rallying the demonic force that causes a melee of eerie shapes to tear into prey in the half-light, illuminated as shadow from gunfire, like strobe lighting within a hellish nightclub as terrified soldiers blindly attack the enemy.

Severing the head of another of Hell's minions, a demon so far removed from his own skill it is almost an insult that he is forced to dispatch it, Michael turns his attention to the cloud bank drifting across his field of vision, and readies himself for Asmodeus as the Hell Lord steps out from within it.

"Isn't this glorious, brother?" he says, his arms outstretched and a smile upon his face. "Such a beautiful war to end the time of His favorites, so underserving of His love."

Michael spits on the ground. "We haven't been brothers since the day you sided with Lucifer and forced me to cast you and your treacherous kin down into the depths."

Asmodeus laughs. "Yes, yes you did do that, Michael. My, my you were a sight to behold that day. Nothing could stand in yours and Gabriel's way. You cut through our numbers like a hot knife through butter and Lucifer certainly felt the bitter sting of Gabe's abilities, I can tell you!" He smiles. "But things are different now. The old bastard wouldn't last five seconds against my master and you will last even less than that against me." He shadow-steps to the side, attempting to outflank Michael, and so the Archangel follows, matching his trajectory.

They meet each other some distance ahead of where each was standing, their swords hammering as they jostle for the upper hand with flawless and fluid swordplay, with each swipe blocked, each thrust side-stepped, and each overhead swing parried and riposted. To anyone that might bear witness to the event, they would be enthralled – captivated by the fight's harmonic beauty as two expert swordsmen battle to the death.

Out of character and unlike himself due to his rising frustration, Michael overreaches with a lunge and is fortunate that Asmodeus was leaning in to attack at the same time, as he ends up on the inside of his opponent with his head exposed and unprotected, and Asmodeus takes advantage of the rare lapse in defense. Although unable to cut Michael down due to his proximity, he instead stabs the hilt of his sword hard into the side of Michael's face, causing the Archangel to tumble away.

Rolling across the floor, out of instinct Michael folds his wings around himself for protection, coming to a halt on his back as his opponent leaps at him and rains down blow upon blow with his sword. Gritting his teeth, thankful that his wings deflect the brunt of Asmodeus' attack, he waits for a gap in the barrage, knowing he will have but a fraction of a second to react. However, to an angel capable of moving at incomprehensible speeds, a fraction of a second can be an eternity and his patience pays off as he spots an opportunity. Unfurling his wings, he kicks out at Asmodeus with both feet, launching him high into the air where he smashes through a building and out of the other side.

Asmodeus roars with rage as he clears the building, rubble and dirt exploding and cascading off him, and he assumes his full demonic form while spreading his wings to halt his flight. But he takes his eye off the fight for a moment and in doing so he can't repel Michael's follow-up attack, as the Archangel powers through the hole in the building toward him, spearing into his midriff and causing him to exhale with a grunt and propel backward.

Michael roars as he forces Asmodeus ahead, his arms wrapped around his waist, moving him through the air at a supersonic speed, coming to a halt only after they smash into metal and concrete, and explode through the remains of a superstructure that was once a power station. Tumbling out of the fall, they skid to a halt on the dusty ground, their hands acting as steadying oars so that they remain on their feet, and Michael then stands, his face like thunder, his teeth gritted with Asmodeus following suit, his expression much the same.

With furious roars, they charge at one another again.

***

Unleashing a long burst of gunfire at the jackal demon bounding toward him, Gary scrambles backward, partly on his back, partly on his haunches, kicking his feet into the dirt to increase his momentum. The holy bullets rip through the beast's face, and causing it to tumble forwards where it bursts into dust, causing Gary and Isaac to raise their hands to shield from the residue as it peppers them. They cough and turn onto their fronts, spluttering in the dirt.

Behind them another demon screams as it skids to the side, its claws raking at the ground as it tries to gain traction enough to move forward and charge at its prey laid out on the floor.

Gary screams at Isaac, "Open fire! I need to reload."

"So do I!" comes his frantic reply.

"What? You're supposed to stagger your fire so that…"

He tails off as the demon's screams and grunts are almost on top of them.

The beast explodes into dust as bullets rip through its body, the foul matter once again showering Gary and Isaac who are then forced into further coughing and spluttering fits.

"For fuck's sake," Gary screams, "I'm sick of this shit." He wipes his eyes and looks to the side from where the gunfire came to see Jonesy wave and nod. He is about to signal back when a portal opens behind the sergeant and a winged demon tears out of it, grabs him by his body armor, and hoists him into the air causing Gary to scream after him.

Jonesy calls out in surprise as the creature lifts him into the air and then powers away, out of Gary and Isaac's sight line. Instinctively, Jonesy raises his weapon and opens fire, rippling bullets into the beast and destroying it, causing it to explode into dust and drop him. He lands on a rooftop and rolls across it, out of control, coming to an abrupt halt against a wall at the roof's edge. He sits up, wincing from the painful landing, but has no time to lick his wounds as a screech from another winged demon dives toward him. With a grunt, he gets to his feet, fires a volley at a skylight ahead of him that shatters the glass, and then jumps through, the demon's swooping talons missing him by a fraction of an inch as he falls to the ground with another painful thump and rolls onto his back, groaning with pain.

"Fuck my life," he says, as he turns over and gets up, staggering forward.

Gary and Isaac hurry to their feet and run to their left and around a building, attempting to get a fix on Jonesy's position. Scanning the sky, they see nothing but then focus their attention on the sound of another screech from a rooftop a little further away, followed by gunfire and the shattering of glass, and Gary grabs hold of Isaac's body armor.

"Come on," he screams, "let's go."

He drags Isaac toward a door in the building from where the gunfire erupted.

"Okay," Daniel says, as he stabs a finger at the 'enter' button on his keyboard, "cross absolutely everything."

He looks to a panel on the column of equipment in the center of the room and the first of four lights illuminates with a beep, then the second, the third, and finally the fourth. He looks at Sarah, his eyes wide, and holds his breath.

The machine emits a high-pitched squeal, not unlike that of a recharging flash on an old-fashioned camera, the sound lasting nearly 30 seconds as it builds in intensity, causing Daniel and Sarah to exchange glances. Realizing he is holding his breath, Daniel exhales hard just as the machine clunks and fierce electrical arcing shoots out from it to a corner of the room where a purple cyclonic portal bursts open.

"Er, that's not supposed to happen," a gravely concerned Daniel says. "Seriously, that's not supposed to be happening at all."

"Shut it off," Sarah screams, "shut it off right now!"

"That's not supposed to happen," he screams back at her, as he turns around to trawl through the readings on the computer. "That's not supposed to fucking happen!"

"I get it," Sarah shouts back, "it's not supposed to happen! But you need to shut it off. You need to shut it off right now!"

***

An unexpected portal event to its side startles a lone hunter demon. It sniffs the air at the anomaly, the scent of it unrecognizable, and the color is all wrong. It has never seen one such as this and it growls, baring its teeth. Edging forward, it inspects it with its snout, working around the crackling and fizzing energy and growling again it sticks its head in.

Jonesy calls out in fright as he rounds a corner in the darkened building, bumping into Gary and Isaac. "Holy fucking shit," he says, lowering his weapon, then leaning forward and breathing out hard, "you scared the living piss outta' me."

He starts to laugh, and Gary joins in while planting a firm hand on his shoulder. Isaac looks back and forth at the pair. He doesn't find the situation funny, nor does he understand why they do.

"I thought you were done for when that damn thing grabbed you and took off!" Gary says, taking a small step back and surveying the area.

"Not as much as I did. I just starting blasting away at it and got lucky, I guess."

Gary smiles. "Well, you need to stay with us then, keep that luck thing rolling."

All three of them spin toward the direction of a female scream from further down the corridor, and they raise their weapons.

"Sarah?" Isaac says, his voice trembling.

***

Nathan ducks under a fierce right hook from Colt and then counters with an uppercut, driving it into the chin of the demon. It has little effect and serves only to increase the pain in his fist that has been building since he started hand to hand combat with the creature a minute or so earlier. He dodges another wild and overreaching swing, attempting to work himself into a position to throw a punch of his own, but Colt is too fast, spinning around and slamming his forearm into Nathan's face, launching him into the air and onto his back a few feet away with a painful thud and next to his weapon that had been punched out his grasp by Colt at the start of the fight.

Conrad leaps at and drives his fist down at the monster with as much force as he can, slamming it into the side of its head and to his surprise he rocks Colt, staggering him to the side a little. Recovering, the demon turns to look at him in disgust.

Colt rages as he raises a huge leg and kicks at the man's chest, his pained scream causing him to grin widely as the man hurtles back through the air, landing some feet away, where he skids along the ground and into the wall of a building, smashing his head against it and knocking him unconscious.

Nathan rolls over, grabs his weapon, and fires a volley into his adversary's back and the bullets ripple into the demon, spurting black blood out from each wound, causing him to stagger with the impact. Nathan then glances at his weapon as it stops firing, the chamber open signaling an empty magazine, and so he reaches to a pocket on his armor, but it is empty. His head flops back with a sigh, resting on the ground, then, with a grunt and gritting his teeth, he throws his momentum forward and drags himself to his feet in time to see Colt turning toward him, his eyes burning with rage, a viciousness to them that pierces even Nathan's tough exterior. The man truly terrifies him, and he knows that he has pretty much run out of options, that running would be futile. His only hope is that someone or something will intervene to prevent this monster from beating him into a bleeding pulp and he doesn't hold out much hope for it having seen the Archangels being kept busy with their own problems.

Colt advances toward him and then stops as another volley of gunfire ripples into his back. With a snarl he turns around to see one of the soldiers firing at him and rages at the man, then leaps toward him and punches into the ground in front of him, knocking him down. He roars as he reaches down and stabs fingers into the screaming man's chest and rips him apart, blood erupting from his torso. Turning back toward the gray-haired man he had been fighting, he hurls one half of the corpse at his enemy.

Nathan dives out of the way, narrowly avoiding being hit by half of the butchered soldier. He rolls over onto his back just as Colt's enormous hand grips him by the throat and hoists him into the air, causing him to claw at it while struggling for breath, and his eyes widen. Not only at the painful throttling he is now experiencing, but also at the speed in which the demon covered the distance between them.

Colt growls as he relaxes his grip a bit, allowing the man to suck in as much air as he can to fill his lungs. He then pulls him closer to his eye line and chuckles. "I think I will make an example of you, soldier boy." He bellows a laugh once again.

***

Sarah screams as the snout of the hunter demon appears from the portal. "Oh my God Daniel, shut it off, shut it off now!"

"I'm trying," he says, while frantically stabbing at the keyboard. "This isn't supposed to happen, I must have—"

He stops midsentence, his eyes wide and glazed as he stares ahead. "That's it… that's what I did wrong."

"Do something!" she screams, as the demon stalks into the room and then leaps onto one of the benches, causing equipment and paperwork to scatter, the glass items smashing on the ground. She scrambles backward as the demon sees her and then charges, causing more paperwork to explode into the air.

The door to the lab bursts open and Gary races in, firing at the creature and hitting it in the torso, sending it careering off the bench and tumbling to the ground.

"I only hit it with normal rounds," he screams, "I have no holy bullets left. Heads up – it'll be back."

Behind him, Isaac, and Jonesy charge in, their weapons raised and scanning the room.

"Sarah?" Isaac screams.

"Over here, I'm okay, I'm over here."

He moves toward her, his weapon still up and tracking from left to right as he creeps toward her while searching for signs of the creature, trying to pinpoint its position. Upon reaching Sarah, as quietly as he can he bends down on one knee, hooks his left arm around her and helps her to her feet. "Are you okay?" he whispers.

"I'm fine," she says back at the same volume. "Where is it?"

He shakes his head, and his eyes dart all around.

A shuffling to their right causes everyone to snap their attention in that direction, but they see nothing.

222

Screwing up his face in fear, Daniel taps on the keyboard as softly as he can and then eases himself off his chair and tiptoes toward the column in the center of the room.

"What the fuck are you doing?" Gary asks, his voice hushed but forceful.

Daniel raises a finger to his mouth and opens his eyes wide while edging toward the center mass of electronic equipment, his frame illuminated purple by the portal that continues to crackle and fizz.

A beaker rolls off a surface and smashes onto the floor and the others spin around at the sound while Daniel continues to creep across the room.

Gary motions for Sarah to get behind him and she does, eagerly grabbing hold of and tucking herself into his back. He nods at Isaac to take up position on his left and he complies, his weapon never leaving the direction from where the sound came from.

Manipulating the two dials that he had Sarah work on earlier, Daniel then flicks three other switches, their clicks causing him to wince each time as they sound like just about the loudest thing on the planet right now. Then, completing the sequence, he moves back toward the computer with the same speed and care, musing at how ridiculous he must look to the others as he tiptoes along like a pantomime villain, but then glances toward them and realizes that their attention is on the corner of the room and not him.

Reaching his desk, he sighs with relief as he types on the keyboard, again trying to make as little noise as possible while moving as quickly as he can. He looks at Gary and the others and jerks his mouth downward while keeping his teeth together as though to say, 'here goes nothing' then stabs the enter key and, as before, the machine beeps as the first of the four light sequences powers up.

A loud noise erupts from the opposite corner of the room to which Gary and the others have their weapons trained. The sound of scrambling claws is loud in the confined space.

The hunter demon clambers onto a bench around 20 feet away from Daniel.

Beep. The second light burns.

The demon streaks across the surface toward him.

Beep. The third light.

Gary, Isaac, and Jonesy open fire, their aim off at having to adjust at such short notice and one or two of Gary's bullets hit it, but not enough to alter its trajectory. Isaac misses completely, and Jonesy looks down at his weapon in horror as it clicks open after firing only a couple of times, its magazine now empty.

Beep. The fourth and final light illuminates, and the machine cycles its power up again, the same camera flash charging sound increases in pitch, only much faster this time, reaching its peak a second or two after it starts.

The demon leaps at Daniel and he screams, raising his arms in front of his face and closing his eyes, his only thought being *I hope this works. I hope I save people.*

The machine clunks and electrical arcing sparks from it again and the portal instantly closes with a sucking sound. Then, the demon explodes mid-leap, showering Daniel in black blood.

Opening his eyes and blinking a few times, while still holding his breath, he slowly turns toward a stunned Gary and Sarah, his face locked in shock and terror, dripping with demon blood and he splutters some of the foul liquid out of his mouth.

***

Colt is about to squeeze closed the throat of the man who bested him during their fight in the mall, the one he holds the most contempt for within this pathetic band of humans, and then tear into and devour him, when all around his brethren scream and screech, the smaller of which explode without warning. Letting go of the man, he goes into an uncontrollable fit, unable to move as he vibrates at a frantic rate, his skin bubbling as though boiling and streams of pain race through his body. One of his eyes bursts, spraying black liquid onto the ground. But he is locked in place, unable to move or reach up to the wound, and as his body reaches the peak of vibration, he screams, demonic and full, as though a thousand voices dwell within it.

Colt explodes with massive detonation, causing Nathan to roll over onto his front and wrap his arms around his head.

Across the area demons do the same, bursting into pieces, and not one into the typical clouds of dust – all erupting with gore and viscera in every direction where they stand, Daniel's machine having more than one unexpected effect on them. The larger warrior demons shower entire areas with their putrid entrails, and the fire demons explode lava across a wide radius, spraying over unfortunate souls who happen to be near them, their screams accompanying the demons' as the molten fire consumes them.

A startled Raguel looks down at the soggy mess at his feet, the opponent he was wrestling with having dropped to the ground and then burst, and he wipes away part of its body from his face in disgust. He glances toward Raphael who looks back at him, a similar gory mess bubbling away at his feet.

"What in the name of the Creator just happened Raph?" he says, his eyes wide.

Raphael surveys the area, shaking his head. "I have no idea, brother. I have no idea at all."

***

Gary edges toward the remains of the hunter and stares at it in disbelief. He then looks at Daniel who is still in the process of wiping bits of demon from his face while making gagging noises.

Daniel spits into the ground, "Agggh," he says, poking his tongue in and out of his mouth, "well, that was unexpected."

A battered and bruised Michael punches Asmodeus in the face hard, then grabs his head and launches him across the ruins of the building, smashing him through metal and concrete posts as he soars through the air.

The demon rolls across the floor of the abandoned power station that has been further demolished by the warring pair, then steadies himself and gets back onto his feet where he charges at his enemy again.

225

Then, while in the process of attacking and without warning he feels a sudden and strange energy radiating from the direction of the base behind him but doesn't have time to consider what it means as he bears down upon the Archangel.

Michael roars. "Who do you think you are?" Holding his hand out, his sword rattles across the ground and into his grip, the weapon having been knocked out of it moments before. He then flicks it down and to his right, charging it with holy light, and then he spins to his right with the same speed as he would in shadow-step. Catching Asmodeus off-guard, he slices the weapon around, straight through the demon's sword arm causing his weapon to fall to the floor and roll across it with a clank. He then grabs Asmodeus' head before he has even had time to pass him, digs his fingers into his flesh and with another roar, slams him down onto the ground.

Michael has had enough of games, and enough of the creature beneath him.

As fierce, terrifying, and tough as Asmodeus is, and as much power that has been granted to him by Lucifer, he is no match for the Archangel Michael, and now as he lays at his feet, a knee jabbed into his throat, he knows that.

"Your time is over demon," Michael says, his lips curled into a snarl. "We are done with you. I am done with you. We will find a way to convince the Creator to unshackle us and enter all of our kind into the war, and then your pitiful breed will die screaming at our feet while we watch The Light tear Lucifer to pieces."

Asmodeus chuckles. "Are you sure, Michael?" He laughs again. "There might be something you wish to know abo—"

Michael stabs his sword straight into Asmodeus' face and he explodes into dust beneath him.

"Enough talk, demon. As I said, I am done with you."

***

Walking out of the laboratory building and into the main area where the battle took place, Gary scans the area, stained with the remains of demons. He doesn't know how or what Daniel has just done, but he knows that it has saved his life and the lives of those that remain. He turns toward Jonesy as concern hits him. "Jonesy, take a few of the guys and check on the civilians holed up below."

Through a deep breath, Jonesy nods and calls a couple of the remaining personnel over to assist him, then trots off toward the direction of the main facility.

Nathan ambles forward, clutching his side and breathing heavy. "Medic!" he calls.

Gary hastens over to and puts a steadying arm around him.

"Not me, buddy," Nathan says, then motioning back with his head, "Conrad, over there, he took a real beating into the wall at the hands of that big bastard. He's either unconscious or dead, and I would prefer it not to be the latter."

A young woman races to Nathan, a medical pouch hanging from her side. She attempts to take Gary's place, but he waves her away, ushering her off into Conrad's direction to which she acknowledges and hurries toward the downed man.

With a thud, Michael lands in the middle of them, the scars and lacerations on his face and arms in the process of healing and is joined seconds later by his two lieutenants. "What happened here Gary? What turned the course of battle?" he asks, his arms raised by his side.

Gary glances back toward Daniel, still trying to wipe bits of demon off his body. "The smartest man I know, that's what Michael. That's what."

Daniel looks up at the enquiring faces staring at him.

Shuffling to him, Nathan puts his arm around his shoulders and then pulls him close into his side. "Well done, son. You did a fantastic job. A goddamn fantastic job."

"THAT WAS NOT DISCREET!" Gabriel's booming voice calls as he marches toward the crowd.

"Oh, hey Gabe," Michael says, his eyes wandering while he scratches the side of his head.

Gabriel stabs a finger at Michael, his face like thunder as he stomps toward him.

THIRTY-THREE

Charlotte drops out of shadow-step, sliding to a halt, her breathing heavy. Ahead of her, Judas senses her stopping and disengages his speed travel, bringing himself to a halt then races back toward her.

"What's the matter? Are you okay?"

She bends over, her hands on her knees and takes a few deep breaths. "I'm fine, just a little fatigue is all – give me a minute."

He considers her for a second, his eyes blinking, then he takes her arm and sits her down on a rocky outcrop while Azazel ambles over to them, his outstretched arms questioning.

Judas ignores him and instead kneels in front of Charlotte and strokes her hair. "You remember when you were nine and you woke me up from a nap, as you were doing your best to secretly hoover up the hundreds of candy sprinkles that had somehow made their way onto our carpet?"

She laughs a little. She does remember the event and more importantly what caused it.

"Remember how I came into the living room, all cranky, asking why you had woken me up? And I saw the sprinkles all over the floor and I looked at you, and you said—"

"—it wasn't me, my friend Phyllis did it," she says, interrupting him and smiling.

"Your friend Phyllis did it. Your imaginary friend Phyllis." He smiles also. "And you proceeded to tell me this wonderful story about how Phyllis went into the kitchen, took out the tub of sprinkles and was dancing around the room, shaking them like a maraca, when the bottom of the tub burst and sprayed them everywhere."

This time she laughs hard and looks down at the ground.

"Although your story was intriguing, you were about as convincing as you are now with your 'I'm fine' tale." He raises his eyebrows.

She offers a small, conceding laugh and smiles, then looks up and strokes the side of his face. "Lying to you never was my forte, somehow you always knew."

He chuckles. "I'm an angel sweetie, I always know." He winks.

"Yeah, I know," she says, shifting onto her knees and placing both hands at the side of his face, "but you never pulled that crap with me, you just acted like my dad, no 'angely' stuff – just us as humans, a father and daughter against the world." She smiles again, removes her hands, and then sits back down on the rock. She sighs. "The Book and Seal, they're killing me."

He takes a deep breath, and his eyes darken. "What? What do you mean, they're killing you?"

"Every time I use Divinity, be it dark or light, they absorb a portion of it and I never get it back. Pestilence says if I don't get them out of me and soon, I'll most likely die."

"Goddammit," he says, standing quickly, "GODDAMMIT!" he shouts into the air. He puts a hand onto his forehead and then runs it down his face. "Right, we need to get you to that damn Temple, kill every one of those bastards, and get those things out of you. And sooner rather than later." He spins angrily toward Azazel. "Did you fucking know about this? If I find out you knew about this—"

229

"Dad… dad!" she says, causing him to turn and face her forlorn look. "We need to get to Belial fast, I couldn't agree more, but I am scared that it won't matter. I'm worried that The Seals operate on Earth's time and the longer we stay in here, the faster they will degrade me. We have been through the gate a half-day now, and that must be at least a month and a half up top."

Azazel raises a finger and bends down slightly. "Ahhhh, I wouldn't worry about that too much."

She rolls her eyes then focuses her attention upon him with a sigh. "Why not?"

"Because, once we got through the gate, I put Hell on our time… y'know, so that you would actually have something to go back to." He smiles, and although in shifting the timelines to help them could be considered an act of civility, he still comes across as deceitful.

Charlotte gets to her feet. "Are you kidding me? Is he kidding me?" she says, finishing her words looking at Judas. "Dad, don't you think that is a little too convenient, that this whole thing is a little too… convenient? I mean, he *just* happened to put Hell on *our* time so that we would have something to go back to." She shakes her head. "This thing, this whole damn thing is about him and him alone. He's not doing this for us. Whatever he's planning he's doing it for himself." She shakes her head again and walks away. "Just happened to put Hell on Earth's time my ass. Fucking liar." She turns back to Azazel and glares at him.

Judas sighs. "Y'know, one way or another he has done us, Gary, Nathan, and all the others up there a big favor. And right now I don't care to dwell upon it any further. I just want to get this mission over and get those damn relics out of you, then we can all go home and get what we want. Right?" He raises his eyebrows at her.

"But—"

"Right?" He raises his eyebrows a little further.

"Yes!" she blurts, her tone one of irritation.

Judas is about to turn away to speak with Azazel when Charlotte interrupts him.

"Yes, I want things to go back to normal. I want my dad back for one. Don't think I haven't noticed the difference in you since we have been in here, the influence over you that this…" she looks at Azazel in disgust, "…thing has. And let's not forget about your wings. Your jet-black wings that are looking more demonic as time goes by." She shakes her head and glances down. "Whatever's happening to you, I want it to stop. I want the normal you back. Not the demonic-influenced you, not the Horseman-driven you, the you you, that's what I want. So yeah, let's get this mission over and done with so it can all go back to normal."

Azazel chuckles. "That's a bit rich, isn't it? Especially from someone who has a Horseman in them as well." He grins at her.

She steps up to him, her face almost touching his. "Yeah, but the difference with me is that my Horseman offers me his gifts out of respect, his Horseman gives them in exchange for a piece of real estate, an equal footing in his life. That is *not* the same thing."

Azazel steps back and looks down his nose at her. "How could you possibly know these things? You're not privy to the inner workings of his mind, no matter how strong your bond."

She walks away from him toward Judas. "I don't have to be. Like I said, my Horseman offers me things without the need for something in return. In this case, information about his sister's motives. What can I say, it was a long run and I enjoyed the chat!"

Azazel chuckles again. "Oh really? Fond of talking to you, is he? I wonder what other delights he would have to offer, should you ask?" A grin spreads across his face.

"That's enough," Judas says, moving in between them but facing him. "That's… enough. You're treading the thinnest of thin lines, demon." He stares intently at Azazel who, after a few seconds, smiles, bows graciously, then backs away. Judas continues to stare for a further few seconds before speaking. "How far have we got to go to find these Mazorakor's?"

Walking to the cliff edge of the path they had been following, Azazel waves a hand in front of himself. "Well, whether it's luck or fate that is the place down there."

Judas and Charlotte walk to the edge and peer down. Below them is a dense forest, ripe with vegetation, albeit varying shades of red in color. Charlotte shakes her head.

"It's hard to believe a place like that exists in a world like this."

"You wouldn't believe the kinds of things that exist in a place like this," Azazel replies without turning back to look at her. "But when I made it, I didn't see any reason not to fill it with wondrous things, irrespective of its intended purpose. Strange though, I don't remember coloring this bit red."

Judas glances at him. "Life finds a way 'n all that."

Azazel looks at him and grins. "Quite."

"Okay then," Charlotte says, moving away from the edge, "let's get down there and bag us one of these Mazorkadorks."

"Mazorakors," Azazel says, "Ma-zor-a-kors. Mazorakors."

She rolls her eyes. "Whatever, Mister Rogers. Let's go."

Azazel looks at Judas. "This is you, ya know – she gets this from you."

THIRTY-FOUR

"Michael!" Gabriel says, turning around to face the leader of Hellwatch as they enter the conference room within the air base, the lights flickering on above him to reveal a sparse room except for a few desks, chairs, and a whiteboard at one end, with red and green text written on it. He stabs a finger at him. "I thought I made it pretty clear not to draw attention to yourselves?"

Michael struggles to find the right words. Behind him, Raphael, Raguel, Gary, and Nathan file in, their attention flitting between the two angelic superpowers.

"We have a mandate, Michael. We are not supposed to get directly involved, it has been broken too many tim—"

"Oh, save it Gabriel will you? Just save it." He stares at the shocked Archangel for a few seconds. "What would you have me do, hmm? Leave these people to die? To be wiped out entirely? And how many times have you intervened in the past? How many times have you gotten involved, had *us* get involved? Save the sermon for another day."

"Yes, *yes!* I have gotten involved in the past. I did send your team. But we have to be careful. We have been disobeying the mandate a little too often recently, and that kind of behavior can lead to a one-way trip. We are not the first to think we can circumnavigate the rules, and their fate did not end so well – you'd do well to remember that."

"Are you kidding me Gabe, are you *actually* kidding me?"

The two Archangels argue, their voices raised, pointing at one another, waving their arms, and pacing the room, and after several minutes of them at each other's throats, Gary has had enough.

"STOP IT! Just fucking STOP IT!" he says, glaring at them, a fire in his eyes, his annoyance peaked. He is annoyed at the way the world is now. At being forced to the brink of extinction. Of feeling powerless. But most of all, he is sick of the arguing. He takes a deep breath and looks down before returning his attention on the Archangels. "Seriously, how is this helping? There are people dying out there. There are children, wives, and husbands who will never see their loved ones again, and here you are bickering like kids over whether you should get involved in a war that your kind has perpetrated."

His heart races, and he breathes in and out as though he had just run a mile. He wiggles his fingers, clenching and unclenching his fists, his palms sweaty. A few years ago he didn't believe in God or angels and here is he now, chastising two of the most powerful beings in existence. He licks his lips, and they sting, cracked and broken from the environment they have endured for so long, then he breathes out hard and looks down again and rubs his forehead with a hand. He looks back up. "This world – our home – was fucked up before, but now it's gone. No matter what happens going forward, it will never be the same. People will never be the same. We have been shown things that most of us thought only existed in fairy tales, and the ones that did believe now probably wish they didn't, that everything was, in fact, just fantasy and myth." His eyes narrow, furrowing his brow, his expression pleading. "We're out on a limb here, and at the end of it all. We have no capabilities to continue this fight and I am sure there are others around the world as equally ill-equipped as us." He moves toward them. "This is it, the end, and no matter what time Daniel has just afforded us, we will not be able to sustain any more of these attacks without help. No matter which way you cut it, this is a war between Heaven and Hell, a war that my kind has been thrust into. Lucifer doesn't care about us, about destroying us – that's just something to piss off God. His issue is with Him and you guys. It's an argument – hell, a damn fight – that has been raging throughout time for longer than our minds can deal with. But here we are, at the raggedy edge, dealing with the consequences and there you are, arguing about whether you should get involved." He shakes his head and screws up his mouth, taking a step back. "So please, Gabriel, continue. Tell me how that is right, how it's fair, because we are tired, we are broken," he motions around, "and we are almost done. And then it won't matter, because all it will be is you and Lucifer waging war against each other for all eternity – the exact same thing that you are saying you shouldn't be doing now." He stares at them both for a number seconds, the silence in the air tangible, then scoffs and waves a dismissive hand and walks out of the room.

Nathan stares at the Archangels for a moment, and then follows him.

Looking down at the floor, Michael sighs. "Gabe, Gary's correct – this isn't right."

Gabriel offers a subtle smile. "No, no it's not. But we are not afforded the same luxuries as them. We are not allowed a will of our own. That is not what He created us for."

"No, you're right, He didn't. He created us to watch over them, to nurture them, to move them along the path so that they might enjoy paradise. So why should it follow that now, at the end of days, we are to abandon them to judgment? What has this all been for? What has been the purpose?"

Gabriel slowly shakes his head. "I don't know, Mike, really I don't."

Michael steps toward him, his arms raised. "But you are the first of us. The very first. There is no being that can stand against you other than the Creator himself. If you don't know, then what hope is there?"

Gabriel places a hand on his shoulder and smiles. "There is always hope, Michael. And that is the message. They are not alone. They never have been. Believe in her, believe that she will get it done."

He sighs, continuing to stare into Gabriel's eyes. "And if she cannot?"

"She must. Because there is no one else."

THIRTY-FIVE

"I present to you... the Mazorakor," Azazel says, with dramatic flair, his arm outstretched toward the red valley a short distance below, lush with vegetation and a stone's throw from a forest the same color. "Strange. There is normally more of them."

Charlotte edges her gaze toward him, her wide eyes leading her head, her mouth open. She points at the beast. "Yeah, well, we call it something different on Earth. In our stories, it's called Cerberus."

"Oh, I know," Azazel says, turning toward her with a smile, "but you will find that a lot of what man has named from our world isn't the true name of things. But there you are, a Mazorakor." He frowns. "Seriously though, there are normally more of them."

Judas pushes past him. "Well let's take it as a blessing, shall we? That is one big-ass puppy." He looks at Charlotte. "How do you want to play this?"

Azazel holds up a finger. "Well—"

"I asked her, not you," Judas says, glaring at him.

"I understand that, master, but – and hear me out – there has to be a certain order to things here. She has a power that she is yet to understand, but has it she does." He smiles while holding up a placating hand, eager for Judas to hear him out and to understand his plan.

Judas stares at him for a second and then sighs. "Fine. Let's do it your way."

"Okay, well, first off we need bait." He raises his eyebrows.

Judas rolls his eyes. "Figures."

"Well, quite," Azazel says, releasing a laugh. "Then, my dear, you must somehow get onto the creature and, umm, influence it."

She shakes her head a little, her mouth open. "Influence it? Can you be a little more specific?"

"Er, give it all you got. Get right in there, work its mind, y'know… influence it." He offers a cheesy grin.

"Er, no, I don't know. I need you to define 'influence it.'"

Azazel sighs. "You have a power to control things. The beasts of your world will bend to your will, so to speak, and down here," he glances at Judas with his eyes alone, "you can do the same."

She turns away, her hands on her hips.

"Look! I know it sounds whacky—"

Her eyes open wide. "Whacky? That's what you're calling it? Whacky!"

"But when you arrive at the moment, I am sure you will understand and it will all fall into place." He smiles. An unconvincing one.

"And if it doesn't?" she says, turning back to face him.

"Then we all die, horribly, horribly?" He raises his eyebrows.

She stares at him and then exhales a sharp laugh. "Fine, FINE! Let's get on with it then."

Judas grins a little at her, then surveys the landscape. "Okay then. Well, I guess without the ability to portal, getting the big bastard somewhere that you can jump onto it is our only chance at nailing this thing." He points ahead. "Hmm. This ridge runs along the entire perimeter of the forest… marsh… swamp – whatever – so I will get down there and draw its attention." He glances a look of 'let's see how that goes' at her and says, "then lead it into the forest, drawing it up against the side of the ridge. You track us from above and at the opportune moment…" he takes a second and then breathes out hard, "at the opportune moment, you take a leap of faith." He looks at her and smiles.

She nods. "Okay. Okay, sounds like a plan. A plan to get us both murdered, horribly, horribly," she shoots a mocking glance at Azazel, "but a plan nonetheless."

Judas laughs.

"Excellent," Azazel declares, clapping his hands together. "Then let us get the hunt underway."

Judas holds out his hand. "You! Back in your box."

Azazel spreads his arms out to his sides and begins to remonstrate, but then capitulates, slapping them down against his thighs. "Fine! But don't fuck this up. We have a long way to go, and we need that damn thing." He leaps into the air, assuming his Ikazuchi form and landing in Judas' hand where the angel immediately stows the weapon on his back, the tiny arms once again protruding from the sword and wrapping themselves around him.

"Okay, baby girl. It's game time."

She nods.

"This is a bad idea," Judas mutters to himself, stalking up to the rear of the enormous three-headed beast as it lies sleeping. "A fucking bad idea."

The Mazorakor hasn't seen him yet, something he is most thankful for, as he isn't quite in the right position, that he is a little to its left and not in the optimum place to begin his run. The gigantic beast must be fast, or they wouldn't be doing this, but just how fast he has no idea, or whether his shadow-step will enable him to out run it.

"This is a very fucking bad idea!"

He crouches lower, his arms outstretched, balancing himself as he creeps through the red undergrowth that almost covers him, the hell weed prickling his face, and it takes all his focus not to reach up and scratch it, his gaze instead focused ahead. He stops as the beast's heads snap up, almost in unison, with all three sniffing at the air.

They growl. And it is loud. Very loud. And so Judas takes full advantage of the masking sound to move with haste to his right and into the position he has been edging toward. The growling intensifies, and the Mazorakor stands and shuffles around. It knows he is there, and he knows that it knows he's there. He needs just one more moment to get into his ideal position, just one more second so that he will be best placed to begin his run. But he doesn't get it, as the creature rounds on him at a frightening speed and all three heads roar, raining saliva down on him.

"Fuck!" he says, and then runs.

The Mazorakor is on him in seconds, forcing him into shadow-step to avoid it.

"Holy shit, it's fast," he says, as he tears into the forest, the beast hot on his heels.

From above, on the ridge, Charlotte sees Judas break into a run, and then enter his shadow-step. "Shit!" she says and then follows suit, bursting along the rocky pathway in parallel to them, tracking the Mazorakor that obliterates everything in its path. Red trees explode, vegetation sprays into the air and she must put all she can into her shadow-step to keep up.

Hold on, dad. Not far now and then it's my turn.

Zigzagging through the forest, Judas remarks to himself that he has never met a creature with so much pace and ferocity, and he wonders if he will indeed make it to the drop-point where Charlotte is to engage the beast. Although it is not a time to worry about the plan, his mind cannot help but wander onto the next phase, and what it means for her. Azazel better be right. She had better be able to control the thing, or his only option will be to put it down. And if it tries to hurt her, he will slaughter it.

The Mazorakor closes in on him.

240

Inside, he feels an energy swirl, a darkness no longer brooding but taking control, moving through him at an electric pace. He growls and his eyes narrow.

Hello, Judas, Lady Famine's voice calls from within him, *how about a little pick-me-up? Seems you could use a speed injection. My, my, that thing is fast.* She chuckles.

Judas grunts within his mind. *Do it.*

She laughs again. *Are you sure? You seem to be offering much of yourself up to me recently. And I like it. I might want to stay when all of this is done.* She cackles again, her laughter maddening.

Just fucking do it will ya and stop talking about it!

Very well.

Ikazuchi's voice sounds aloud, cutting through. "I don't like the fact that you are giving this witch so much Judas. I am not a sharing type of guy."

Lady Famine laughs harder. *Well then, my erstwhile friend, it's a good job that you are not in charge, isn't it?*

A massive surge of power courses through Judas and he roars. His shadow-step increases, moving him further ahead of the Mazorakor, gaining more precious ground. The event happens not a moment too soon, as from his left another Mazorakor lunges at him.

"FUCK!" he shouts and moves further to his right toward the edge of the ridge that Charlotte tracks them from above.

"I knew there should be more!" Ikazuchi declares with laugh.

"NOT HELPING!" Judas shouts as the beast snaps at him, but misses, causing the one behind to slam into the side of it and both to tumble to the ground.

He needed that, the small respite that it provided, although it is only a brief one as both creatures race to their feet at a shocking speed and regain their momentum. He looks up and sees Charlotte slightly ahead of him. *Whatever you are gonna do, Charley, do it now!* He doesn't want to fight them both. He knows fighting one is inevitable, but both might be a stretch before she can get down here. And they need one of the damned things. He glances up again, and prays to everything he can think of that she understands what she must do when she gets on one of them.

Seeing the second Mazorakor charge toward Judas, she throws more force into her shadow-step. She has no more time to gamble for the optimum jump point, she knows that he will have to deal with one of the beasts and must call on whatever power it is within her to bring the other under control. She shakes her head, hoping that the revelation of what that action is to be will hit her immediately, or she is going to have serious problems. As Judas said, that is one big-ass puppy.

Below, Judas has brought himself and the demons closer to the side of the ridge.

Good, she thinks to herself, *it's now or never.*

Looking up again as he nears the wall of the ridge, Judas sees Charlotte leaping through the air, down toward him, a warrior's cry erupting from her.

She throws her arms to her sides and the Katanas of Destiny unseat from their scabbards and fly into them, then she lands on the lead Mazorakor and drives her swords into its back so that she doesn't get thrown off.

The Mazorakor goes wild, bucking and spinning in all directions, moving off to the side and away from Judas.

He grits his teeth. Now it's his turn. He throws his arm to the side and Ikazuchi lands in it, then, turning around, getting low, and unfolding and throwing his wings forward, he slides backward and slashes at the front legs of the demon-dog that is almost upon him, sending it crashing to the dirt and skidding away, roaring in frustration. Coming to a halt in a defensive stance, Judas prepares himself for the inevitable onslaught of the beast.

Time seems to slow for Charlotte as the Mazorakor intensifies its desire to repel the invader. It crashes to the ground and rolls over onto its back and her eyes open wide in alarm, understanding its intentions. She lets go of her swords and leaps into the air, her arms close to her body, somersaulting above the beast in the same direction that it travels.

The Mazorakor completes its roll back onto its feet and roars once more as it feels the human land on its back once again.

She grips hold of the one sword that remained lodged in the demon, the other having spiraled out into the forest during the maneuver, and then thrusts her empty hand to the side where she holds it for a couple of seconds, her face locked in concentration. From within the forest, the sword whistles through the air and lands in her hand and she plunges it into the creature's back once again, then closes her eyes as Pestilence's voice eases through her mind.

The foul demon sword is right, you know. You can control the beasts of the earth and indeed the denizens of this world. Perhaps more.

What do you mean?

Empty your thoughts, child. Allow yourself to see your potential. Pour your energy into this creature and enforce your will upon it. Use what I have offered already. Find the balance between light and dark and move into it, between it, over and around it. So many things are yours to command, you need only believe and listen to yourself. Concentrate your mind. Exert your will.

"Exert my will," she says, slowly opening her eyes.

The Mazorakor continues to thrash, attempting to shake her from its enormous back as though sensing it is about to lose control of its mind and come under the control of the holy being that stands upon it. The Mazorakor has never been in this situation before, where it hasn't given itself freely to a rider, and the notion incenses it, enraging it further.

Clearing her mind, Charlotte closes her eyes once again.

"I exert my will," she says, and energy encircles her, traveling down from her shoulders, over her arms, her hands, and into the swords.

The Mazorakor's eyes turn the color of the energy flowing from Charlotte and into its body, then it screeches, stops bucking and bursts away, heading for the entrance to the Hell forest at a breathtaking speed.

Control. Control, she repeats, attempting to force commands of direction into the demon.

Although she has completed the first part of asserting her dominance over it, the most crucial factor – steering the Mazorakor – eludes her and she wrestles with it in her mind, attempting to work her commands through the demon's consciousness to calm its beastly nature and erratic movement, to exert her will.

Judas grabs the mouth of the central head of his Mazorakor as it roars down on him, the other two snapping from each side.

More power? Lady Famine asks within his mind. *You only need to ask and I will grant it.*

"More!" he says aloud and then cries out as she pushes her darkness further into him.

His eyes turn jet-black, his face contorts, and he grits his teeth then throws the beast to one side where it crashes into the wall of the ridge with a fierce and angered roar.

In the blink of an eye, it is back on its feet and powering toward him again, its tongues lolling from side-to-side within its mouths, its multitude of giant, deadly teeth bared ready to tear into him. The ground shakes with each footfall as it thunders toward him, destroying foliage, ripping up the forest and spraying it behind.

Judas closes his eyes, crosses his arms in front of him, Ikazuchi pointing straight up and then throws them wide open. Black wings that now look almost fully demonic spread from his back and he rockets upward, high above the Mazorakor that attempts to skid to a halt beneath him, its heads fixed upon him, causing it to crash into a large tree, uprooting it and knocking it over. Losing its balance, it crashes to the ground.

"Careful, Iscariot," Ikazuchi's voice calls from within the sword, concerned that the Thŭramré temporarily no longer holds sway over him, "this isn't a power you wish to call the norm. Get down there and be done with the creature, then push her back into the pit of your soul and leave her there. You don't need her, and you do not need this demonic energy."

Whether he was listening or not it didn't matter. Judas loops in Hell's sky, and powers down toward the Mazorakor below, which is now back on its feet and looking up at him again. His speed is insane, and his face contorts into a demonic-looking grimace as he begins to laugh, low and guttural.

The Mazorakor doesn't stand a chance as Judas crashes down onto it, slicing his sword into its back and landing on the ground, having traveled through the demon-dog, and burying Ikazuchi into the dirt up to the hilt. Then, he grunts while pulling it out, and the ground around him erupts, obliterating the Mazorakor into thousands of pieces and spraying it over a large area, leaving a circular pattern of black blood and guts around him.

Standing, Judas screams and drops Ikazuchi to the ground, where the sword rolls and transforms into Azazel. He claws at his face as he continues to cry out, his eyes changing from black to white, his features morphing from demonic to human. Someone grabs the sides of his face, and screams into it, the man's eyes fixed on him, his mouth opening and closing, but no words come forth, not a sound. The only thing inside him now is pain, a screaming, cackling, whirling pain that prevents him from seeing himself, his own form, his soul. He doesn't know who or where he is. He doesn't know why this is happening or who the man in front of him is. All he knows is the pain, the terrible, horrifying, beautiful pain, and he smiles, which turns into a grin, and he utters a strangled laugh.

Azazel thrusts his head against his, and concentrates, gritting his teeth. "Remember who you are. Remember. Who. You. Are. Push her down. Force her back. You are not hers to have. She cannot command you. This is not the form that you are to become. She will not have you. She will not have you." He presses into Judas' forehead harder, pushing against it with all his might, all the while repeating that she will not have him, that she cannot control him.

At last, something makes it through. A semblance of order is restored. A recognition of the world outside the madness. And Judas sees Azazel, sees the demon sword, *his* demon sword, working his way through his mind, forcing the darkness out of it, shoving the pain back down, away from where it has been relishing its position, its dominance. And light filters into his mind as the darkness clears and travels away, and he hears Lady Famine screaming, her voice growing distant. And then as quickly as he had lost himself, he comes back, his mind once again his own and clear, and he sinks to his knees, Azazel dropping down with him.

"Are you all right, master? Can you hear me?"

Judas takes a deep breath and waves Azazel away, placing a hand on his knee and pushing himself up to his feet. "I'm fine, I'm fine."

Azazel sighs. "You need to be careful about her, you know. If you take too much from her, she will never want to leave, and you will never be the same again."

Judas breathes out hard again and nods. "I said I'm fine!"

But he's not fine. And Azazel is right, he must be careful at how much control he allows her again. But what he experienced, the power, the energy that she gave him – it was incredible. A feeling hard to shake, a desire almost impossible not to want again. He shakes it from his mind and looks around. "Charlotte?"

"She went that way," Azazel points. "I think we should get over there if we can. Are you fit to travel?"

He looks down at himself. He is. And he's surprised at the fact, given all he had to do force Lady Famine from his mind. He holds out his hand and Azazel somersaults into it as Ikazuchi and he speeds off in shadow-step.

Charlotte loses concentration for a moment and grunts as the Mazorakor slams into the ridge wall and scrapes along the side of it. She furrows her brow deeper, forcing more energy into the beast, attempting to bring it under control and it peels off of the wall, then gallops to the right, its speed increasing with every bounding step. She looks down at its heads snapping and growling at one another, almost as though each contains its own identity and is fighting against the control exerted over the other. She digs deeper and pours in even more energy, closing her eyes, trying to find the space in its minds where she can finally exert her dominance over it in entirety.

There. She has it. The place within, where all its thoughts converge from each of the beast's heads, and she dives in, penetrating the energy that surrounds the space and filling the control center with her own force. She is in. With full control assumed.

She snaps her eyes open and not a moment too soon as they near the edge of a cliff, a drop to another level of Hell that sits at the perimeter of the forest. She grips her swords, using them as reins and drives the Mazorakor to the right.

It turns, slow at first, Charlotte still getting to grips with controlling it, then faster as she exerts more of her will into its nerve center.

The Mazorakor's legs skim along the edge of the cliff, dislodging small rocks and dirt over it that cascade down hundreds of feet, and it digs its claws into the ground, grabbing more traction, powering away from the precipice and back toward the forest.

She smiles, riding atop the huge and magnificent beast. It belongs to her now.

Judas skids to a halt at the forest's edge to see Charlotte approach, jockeying the Mazorakor, the demon-dog now under her full control. He punches the air, exclaiming his amazement out loud, a wide smile on his face.

He sees her hold out a hand, signaling for him to get ready to come aboard, and so he begins his run, adjusting his timing to hers, and then enters shadow-step, catching up to them and leaping into the air.

She grabs his hand and yanks him onto the beast's back behind her and he wraps his arms around her waist.

He beams a smile as she screams her delight, driving more energy into their steed, rocketing it into the forest ahead.

Ikazuchi's voice cuts through the rush of wind, whistling past them. "Right. Fantastic. Good job everyone. Now, follow my lead. Next stop, the Nine Circles."

"What?" Judas calls out, a deep frown on his face. "I thought you said we need to head to the Well of Souls?"

"We do. But it sits at the heart of the nine, and we need to jump through them if we are to get to it."

Charlotte glances back. "Jump? What the hell do you mean by jump?"

THIRTY-SIX

Gary rests against a table, arms folded, his mood solemn as air base staff work in pairs to bring bodies into the hangar, his eyes wet with tears, and his mouth tight-lipped. How long must this go on for? How long can they endure? He closes his eyes and a tear tracks down his face as the staff set the body of Major-General Dawson down on the floor with great care and then cover him with a tarpaulin. The hangar is filling up with bodies and Gary wonders how many people in the base are now left. He looks over to the opposite side at a woman and child sharing a teary embrace on bended knee above the body of what must be the husband, the father, then on seeing Gabriel approach, he wipes his face with the palm of his hand, stands, then adjusts his clothing as though driven by a need to straighten up in front of the Archangel. Not that he needed to, but he does nonetheless.

"Gary, might we talk for a moment?"

"Look, Gabe. I'm sorry I lost my temper back there, but I meant every word I said."

"I know. I know. And you're right, something must be done about this," Gabriel looks back to the bodies littering the hangar floor. "This must stop. We have to stop this." He returns his attention to Gary. "But my hands are tied. I just do not possess the power nor authority to do something – anything – about this."

Gary half-laughs, although nothing about the situation is funny. "Then where do we go from here, Gabe? Huh? What's to be done?"

Considering Gary for a moment, Gabriel licks his lips and then purses them together with a sigh and, taking him by the arm, leads him away in a gentle stroll. "We angels are bound by laws and rules. It is what has kept order since the beginning, and even more so since a certain someone once took it upon himself to challenge the way of things."

"Lucifer," Gary says, glancing at Gabriel.

He nods a few times. "Yes. And due to that, it really is not in our power to question the Creator."

"God, you mean, why not call him who he is, or she, or whatever?" he shakes his head, "you mean God so why not just say that?"

Gabriel smiles. "Because to us, He is more than God, He is our father, our alpha and omega, our Creator. He is everything to us, and like good children we do as we are told," he smiles a little once more, "well, for the most part."

Gary offers the faintest of smiles back.

"But the same cannot be said for you, for humankind. He shares a deeper affinity with you, a totally different dynamic of respect."

Gary brings their stroll to a halt. "Then why is he allowing us to die in our millions? Why has he abandoned us to forces beyond our capabilities, huh? Why?"

Gabriel stares at him for a second. "That's a very good question. And I think you should ask Him."

Gary's eyes open wide, and he is taken aback a little. With a deep breath, he glances around. "Right. Great. Well, yeah, good – let's do this. How does it work then?" he looks up, "Is he gonna just… appear or will only I hear him, or something?"

Gabriel closes his eyes, takes a deep breath and exhales, then opens them. "You need to ask him in person."

Gary stares at him for a moment, unsure of what it is Gabriel is saying. Then it hits him. And a sinking, sickening feeling embeds itself in the pit of his stomach, causing him to swallow hard. Finally, he takes a deep breath and exhales.

"Oh!" he says, taking a step back.

"Oh," Gabriel repeats, moving around to the side of him. "He respects you Gary, of that I can assure you, and Jesus thinks tha—"

Gary laughs, a sharp and loud sound, and runs his hands over his head and down his face. "Of course, why not – Jesus. Makes sense."

Gabriel offers a small, sympathetic smile. "Look, I know this is a significant thing to ask of you and believe me, I wouldn't if it wasn't important. This is something I didn't want to do, but hearing you earlier, seeing the devastation here today, well… this is a decision that only you can agree to. And if you would rather not, then I wouldn't think any less of you whatsoever and that will be the last time we ever discuss it."

Gary closes his eyes and looks down, then opens them and shakes his head, just a tiny amount. He knows that Gabriel means it, despite being an angel and bound to tell the truth, he sees the sincerity in his eyes. Saying something because you must and meaning it can be two different things, but looking into Gabe's pleading face, he knows that if he should choose not to do this, then nothing more will be said about it ever again.

A million and one thoughts race through Gary's mind. He closes his eyes to try to focus them, to understand what they mean. He thinks about Charlotte and Judas, wonders what they would do in his situation, then a notion occurs to him that he wouldn't see her again for a long time. Hopefully, if she was successful in her mission he would have to wait until he could embrace her, congratulate her, and tell her she did a fantastic job. But then another thought grips him and takes over, a powerful one that ends his deliberation. He might see Jacob again, his long dead son. Opening his eyes, he smiles at Gabriel.

"All right. Let's go and talk to God," Gary says, taking a few deep breaths and moving closer to the Archangel. Shaking out his hands and arms, he gently bounces on his tiptoes like a boxer preparing for a fight, and then breathes out hard again. Staring at Gabriel, he nods a few times.

Gabriel offers a doleful smile, then places a hand upon Gary's chest. Closing his eyes, the Archangel pushes, and Gary takes a sharp intake of breath, his own eyes closing, and is then eased down by Gabriel who rests his head against Gary's forehead.

"See you in a moment, my friend."

THIRTY-SEVEN

"Whoa! Whoa!" Charlotte says, bringing the Mazorakor to sliding halt at the entrance to a cave set at the foot of a wall of rock that stretches far beyond the zenith of vision. She looks to her left and right, seeing that it continues in each direction and that she cannot make out an end to its vastness. "The cave, I take it?" she asks, pulling her swords out of the demon-dog and jumping to the ground, followed by Judas who tosses Ikazuchi out in front of him, materializing Azazel.

"Yup, the cave," Azazel says, dusting himself down. "I'm bloody filthy," he mutters, while taking a few steps forward.

Charlotte shakes her head at him and then turns toward the Mazorakor. She pets the side of one of its legs, and it emits a low groan of pleasure, the right-hand head bowing toward her. "Well, we don't need you anymore fella so off you pop."

The Mazorakor's eyes change from white to its normal piercing blood red, and it shakes his heads at different speeds.

Six eyes stare at Charlotte for a moment, and Judas holds his breath, his hand twitching, ready to call Azazel back to his sword form at the first sign that the demon-dog will attack.

It doesn't. One of its heads sneezes and then the beast turns and speeds off in the direction from which they came.

Charlotte raises a hand. "Bye dog dude. And thank you."

Judas smiles to himself, and then walks to her, placing an arm around her shoulder. "You're something else, ya know that?" he says, giving her a little squeeze.

"Course I do. I'm a damn delight." She laughs, and they walk to the entrance of the cave, entwined in a father-daughter embrace.

Azazel turns to face them both and their merriment ceases. He holds up his hands and pats the air. "Okay, listen up. Everything that has come before has been child's play." He cocks a thumb at the cave entrance. "In there are the Nine Circles, each housing a certain type of punishment for a certain type of character, and it has produced some significantly dangerous individuals. Believe me, no one likes going through there."

Charlotte slips out from under Judas' comforting arm and advances toward the cave entrance, talking to Azazel, although her attention is focused on the black hole ahead. "Why, what's its deal?"

"It's deal, young lady, is that the tortured creatures within are ferocious, fierce, frightful and feral, umm..." he peers upward, his head shaking a little as though struggling to find a word, "...fuckers. And all other manner of words beginning with F. I dunno, the point is we must be careful. And furthermore," he moves toward the cave so that he is in front of them, "nothing stays dead in there. If you strike something down, it will rise again and be significantly more pissed off than it was before you killed it. We have to move with haste and purpose and not miss our jump points."

Charlotte frowns at him. "You mentioned jumping before, what do you mean?"

"You'll see," he says, half-smiling and walking into the cave entrance.

Judas taps Charlotte on her back. "Come on Charley. We ain't got far to go now."

She smiles and nods at him, and then they follow Azazel into the never-ending blackness, so dark in fact that Charlotte throws a pulsating ball of Divinity up above their heads to illuminate their path.

Judas flashes his eyes, and his Divinity vision that allows him to see in the dark turns off. "Thanks," he says, looking at her. "I keep forgetting you don't have this ability."

"Oh, I'm workin' on it," she replies with a smile.

They follow Azazel through the narrow and winding cave path, the walls scraping against their shoulders as they squeeze through. The journey may be modest, but it excels at being uncomfortable and Charlotte visibly displays her relief when they exit the passageway and walk into a vast cavern. An area so large, it could easily contain an entire city.

"Oh... my... God," she says, wide-eyed and ambling forward to the edge of the rocky precipice that overlooks the Nine Circles.

Judas shakes his head. "I have never seen anything like this in my entire life."

Azazel holds out a hand. "My friends, welcome to the Nine Circles of Hell."

Ahead, nine gigantic circular platforms gyroscope around each other, their speed slow at the outer edge due to their enormity, and faster toward the center, and Charlotte jumps backward in alarm, as the outer rim whooshes upward, past her.

Judas steps forward to catch hold of her.

"Holy shit," she says, then takes a deep breath. "Exactly how are we meant to get over there?"

"I keep telling you," Azazel says, with a sigh, "we need to jump." He walks to the cliff's edge and sits on a rock that juts out of the ground. "Get comfortable for a while, as sadly we just missed our first jump point. The opportunities will come quicker once we move down the circles, and we must be ready for them. We really cannot afford to miss a single one and be then forced to wait for the next opportunity. Not with what will undoubtedly follow us."

Judas looks around and then signals to Charlotte to take a seat on another jutting rock. "Might as well get comfy."

She smiles and sits down, then shifts up a little so that he can sit next to her, which he does.

"Hmm," she says, looking around, "how long has it been since we ate? Feels like forever, and I'm still not hungry," she chuckles. "This place is insane." She shakes her head.

"It's Hell, sweetie," Judas says with a smile. "What did you expect?"

She laughs and then nudges his shoulder with her forehead. "No wonder you didn't want to come down here," she mimics him, "under any circumstances." She laughs once again.

"Oh, so you're brave enough to do my voice in front of me now, are you?" He laughs and gently returns her nudge.

She takes a deep breath and sighs, then looks ahead again. "Seems so long ago, doesn't it?"

"What does?" he says, looking at her.

"The day after you saved me at the orphanage, when we sat against the giant tree in Bohemia State Park, waiting for Abaddon to find us." She breathes out a small laugh. "God, that seems like a lifetime ago."

He says nothing, just smiles and nods.

"I was such a wimp back then," she says, shaking her head.

Judas laughs. "You were six, and friggin' terrified. And I didn't blame you either. I was friggin' terrified too."

She looks at him and smiles, then returns her gaze ahead. "You know, despite everything that happened during those three days, they are still the best of my life and some of my fondest memories."

He looks at her with a deep frown. "Getting chased by demons, falling off skyscrapers, and being captured by Lucifer! Those are some of your fondest memories?" He looks ahead again. "Strange girl." He smiles.

She nudges him again. "No, silly. Meeting you. Gary and Abi. Sitting under the tree and getting to know you. That feeling I got when you walked back into Father Keel's church. Father Keel himself. They are some of my fondest memories ever. Despite what happened around them."

He looks at her and smiles. "Yeah, kiddo, me too. I couldn't imagine a world where I hadn't met you. You changed everything for me during those three days."

She smiles, resting her head against his shoulder and closes her eyes.

Azazel claps his hands startling Charlotte out of sleep.

"All right campers. Our jump point approaches."

She smacks her tongue around inside her mouth and then wipes her lips with the back of her hands. "How long have I been asleep?" she asks Judas.

"Not long, sweetie – 10 minutes or so."

"Uggh, feels longer."

"It always does," he says, laughing. "Okay, let's get to it."

Azazel moves to the edge of the rocky platform overlooking the gyroscope. He rocks back and forth, measuring up the timing of the jump.

"Okay," he says, without looking back at them, "get ready."

Charlotte and Judas rush to their feet and move to the side of him.

"I don't know about this," she says, as she focuses on the gigantic ring speeding its way toward them.

Judas grabs hold of her hand. "It'll be fine Charley."

"Yeah, it'll be fine," Azazel repeats, grinning, his attention still focused ahead and below, "just do not hesitate, jump when I jump. Okay. Here we go. NOW!" He leaps into the air and Judas follows him, tugging at Charlotte's hand.

He glances around, his hand slipping from hers, as she hesitates. "NOOOO!" he shouts as he moves away from her.

She leaps, and although it is a fraction of a second behind them, she peels away a great distance.

She screams as the ground races up to her, and wraps her hands around her head and tucks herself up, expecting to crash into the floor. She does not, instead landing softly, as though deposited onto the ground from only inches above. Somewhere in the distance, she hears Judas call her name.

"Here, dad. I'm over here," she shouts back, looking around. "Oh, Charley, Charley, Charley, you stupid girl. What have gone and done?"

she says, angry with herself as she walks ahead. "Goddamit. You had one job. All you had to do was jump at the same time, that's all you had to do you stupid, stupid girl. He told you, jump at the same time, but ohhhh noooo, you had to hesitate."

She stops and cocks her head to one side as muted chatter drifts toward her. She thrusts her arms to her sides and her swords fly into them. "Well, thank you very much Azazel, thanks for the spooky pep talk earlier. I might be the daughter of God, but I am now currently shitting my panties." She stops, straightening up a little. "Aaaand I'm talking to myself." She shakes her head.

Judas grabs hold of Azazel. "We have to go back for her right now."

"Master, if we miss the next jump point, we will have to wait for another cycle and that just allows the inhabitants to converge on us in greater numbers. She knows the plan Judas, trust that she has the sense to make the right choices."

"NO! We go back for her right now!"

"Look, our next jump point is a couple of minutes away, we won't make it to her in time. You know how smart she is, she will make a jump when she realizes what to do next and we will have wasted time getting to her location, just for her to have moved on. And trust me, this first level – Limbo – is the least of our worries. If she gets to say, Anger, without us, then you do the math. Understood?"

Judas looks at him for a moment, his face thundering with scorn, and then jerks away from Azazel. "Goddammit. GODDAMMIT!"

"She'll be fine, Judas. She is smart and tough as old boots. Look, we have a couple of minutes. Let's move back toward her as far as we can and then make the jump. If she's smart and lucky, she will remain relatively close to where she landed, and we can converge on one another closer to the center. Agreed?"

He jabs a finger into his chest. "You had best be right."

"Hey! Don't blame me! I told her to jump, you know."

LIMBO

"Oookaay, Charley. What would be the smart thing to do here?" she says, trotting ahead, her eyes searching.

She starts a conversation with herself.

"Well, the smart thing would be to make the first available jump to the next ring and move into the center and toward dad and that damn sword."

"Yeah, but what if you make the jump and they don't?"

"No, they will – they know that's the smart thing to do!"

"But they could make a jump, move toward you, make another jump, and then be behind you, and we would miss one another."

"Yeah, but at some point we would get to the middle and meet up."

She stops and sighs, shaking her head. "What the hell am I doing? I think the best thing would be to stop talking to myself and make the next jump."

A sly voice echoes from her right-hand side.

"You can't. You can't. You won't. You won't."

259

Ahhhh, shit! she tells herself, adopting a defensive stance and looking all around.

The ring is not in total darkness, nor is it well lit, there is just enough light to make eerie shadows out of everything.

Another voice causes her to spin to her left, where a ramshackle hut now stands, one that she was sure wasn't there before.

The voice speaks again.

"It's only me. Only me. And him. But he's not there. Only her. Alone. Alone forever. Limbo. Limbo. Limbo."

It repeats the word 'limbo' over and over, the sound wispy and drawn out.

Charlotte squats down and squints into the half-light to try to spot who or what is talking and to consider her next move. A hand grabbing at her leg causes her to jump and fall onto the floor, where she scrambles away.

A humanoid creature crawls along the ground toward her.

"Can you help me? Can you save me? I am here! Where am I?"

She shakes her head. "I'm sorry, I don't know who you are. And you are in limbo."

It stops and looks around.

"Limbo? Who is limbo? Where is me?"

"No. Here…" she motions to the ground, "this is limbo, this circle." She looks up. She knows she needs to get moving, back toward the edge, so that she doesn't miss another jump opportunity, and so stands up and begins to walk away.

The creature rises, like a marionette pulled up by its puppeteer.

Charlotte readies her swords.

"You must save me. You must save us."

It moves toward her, its body movement jagged, jerky.

"We can't be here. Don't want to be here."

It creaks and groans as it draws closer, the sound sickening, and around her she sees other creatures, their bodies dark and ephemeral as though they exist only as shadow. They stand motionless, their bodies at strange angles, with long clawed hands hanging down by their sides and their eyes shining a pale white, accentuated in the darkness against

260

the contrast of their darkened forms. They whisper to her from all around.

"Don't go. Don't go. Don't stay. Can't stay. Can't leave. Don't want to be saved. Don't want to go."

"Oh my word," she says as she turns in circles, the creatures' numbers increasing with each cycle. Still, she doesn't see where they come from, only that they are greater in number each time she looks. She turns to face the creature that had been creeping toward her and she startles as the thing stands right in front of her face, its silver and sharp teeth shining within its shadow form, locked in a permanent grin.

"Are you the light? Are you our light?"

She tries to push it out of her way, to move it back and give her more room, but instead she falls through, its shadowy form having no solidity to it, and she struggles to regain her footing. Turning around, she sees the creature's face push through to the back of its head, its body still facing the other way. She blinks and its whole body now faces her, not just its head. She edges back, glancing behind to make sure her way is clear. The whole scene has her creeped out, as the shades do nothing other than stare at her with their piercing white eyes. In the distance and behind her, she hears the familiar sound of the next circle approaching and so, thankful that she has landed close to the edge of the massive ring, she sheathes her swords and races toward it, preparing to jump.

As she approaches the edge, a shade warps into view in front of her.

"NOOO! DON'T LEAVE US!" it begs.

Startling her, she loses her concentration and jumps a little too soon, tumbling through the air and toward the next and slightly smaller ring as it approaches fast. And as she enters its airspace, a fierce wind blasts into her, slamming her backward across the ring. This time, she hits the ground hard, causing her to exhale sharply as she bounces off and back into the air.

She hurtles toward the ground once more and again hits it, this time skidding as the wind tears into her, thrusting her across its dusty surface toward the ring's edge. Another strong blast brings her airborne once more and, clawing at thin air while screaming, aware that she can do nothing to prevent spiraling out of control, she flies over the edge of the ring, about 100 feet in the air and screams once more. As she clears the edge the wind disappears, and she falls – fast. Below, the third ring spins away, and in the distance on its surface she can just make out what she thinks are the shapes of bloated creatures, but cannot be sure. She looks ahead toward another ring racing toward her, and she raises her hands to her face, awaiting the inevitable impact. As she approaches it she wonders where she will land, having been thrown massively off course.

LUST

Fierce winds buffet Judas and Azazel as they land on the next circle and Judas has a hard time maintaining his balance. Pieces of debris whizz past his head forcing him to lift an arm to shield his face while Azazel walks toward him, unaffected by the winds that grow in intensity.

Raising his voice to be heard over the noise, Azazel motions around them. "The force of Lust, Judas. How fierce its energy flows, for those consumed by it of course." He laughs. "And now, the living has disturbed its grounds – this should be interesting."

"Define interesting!" Judas shouts, pulling himself across the ground toward a lone parking meter in the middle of the area.

Azazel smiles. "Look."

He points to an area ahead where several buildings sprout from the ground, concrete crunching against concrete, spewing dust and dirt in all directions, accompanying the noise of the wind. At the same time, more parking meters rise out of the ground in a line moving away from him, and cars rain down from the sky, smashing onto the ground yet remaining in pristine condition. The wind's ferocity intensifies as more buildings rise up, followed by billboards and trees, while paving slabs unfold over one another, clunking into place to form a sidewalk.

As the large street nears completion, the force of the wind increases until it reaches hurricane strength, and it lifts Judas' legs off the ground while he clings to the parking meter.

Azazel looks at him and sighs, then walks over to him and grabs his arm.

Judas drops to the ground with a thud, exhaling an 'ooft'. He stares at the ground for a moment before pushing himself up onto his feet, then looks at the finished street that has debris and trash hurtling along it from the fierce winds. Looking all around, he sees more evidence of the atmospheric effect on the environment but frowns at not feeling it on himself. He looks at Azazel.

"It was getting in the way," the demon says, then smiles.

Judas looks down at his hands, then his body, and back to Azazel. "Why do I get the feeling that you have more control over this place than you've been letting on?"

He waves a dismissive hand. "A simple parlor trick Judas, nothing to get excited about. I have just prevented the winds of passion from affecting you."

"Just like that, eh?"

"Yeah. Just like that!" he replies, with a brief smile.

Staring at him for a few moments more, Judas then turns his attention back toward the street. "I know this place," he says, taking a few steps forward. "It's Hollywood Boulevard."

Azazel smiles once again. "Yes it is. And I gather you once enjoyed the delights of its strip bars then?"

He expresses a short laugh. "The fuck do you mean, once?" he says, glancing back at Azazel, then returns his gaze to the street, taking a few more paces forward. "Had some of the best days of my life here with some of the greatest women ever."

"I think some of them are wanting to return the favor, Judas," Azazel says, pointing.

From out of the ground, human female forms take shape as though gliding up through water, their bodies stunning and voluptuous, naked save only for wearing heels. Upon completing their arrival, they stride into exaggerated walks, their hands against their hips, the action sensual and sexy. The first of them, a blonde, reaches Judas and brushes her hand across his face.

"Hello there handsome. How honored we are."

He glances toward Azazel with a mischievous smile upon his face and before he has chance to answer, another dark-haired beauty approaches from behind and copies the first's action of stroking his face.

"Play with us, Judas. Come and play. You always loved it when you played with us, as we did playing with you."

He frowns. "Candice?"

She laughs, then pirouettes into the air, dust swirling beneath her creating a mini-tornado. Her laugh turns into a cackle and her features contort. Her legs fuse together, forming one solid mass that bends and warps as scales ripple along its surface.

"Come play with us, Iscariot," she says, her voice now demonic, "we will enjoy feeding on you over and over." She laughs again as she completes her transformation into an enormous, half-woman half-serpent.

"Giant snake-ladies!" Judas says, then rolls his eyes and sighs. He holds out his hand, and Ikazuchi lands into it. "Of course. Why the hell not!" He leaps into the air and slices the creature in half, exploding it into dust that covers the ground. Landing on both feet, he is about to walk away when the blonde's cackling behind him turns into a scream joined by others, and then even more, culminating in a cacophony, all coiling around one another. He turns toward the screaming to see hundreds of snake-women sliding up out of the ground and with them the creature he has just destroyed, reforming from the dust. "Shit!" he says and starts running.

Ahead, more buildings spring up, forcing him to change his direction and he recognizes many of them from cities he has been in all over the world – London, Bangkok, Amsterdam, building upon building, city upon city. Beneath him, the ground rumbles and a large building explodes upward, carrying him along with it, which in turn causes him to sprint across the skylines of the world, leaping from building to building with thousands of demon serpent-women chasing him down.

"Holy shit Judas, how many did you sleep with?" Ikazuchi's sarcastic voice calls out.

"Not this fucking many," he responds while scrambling up and over a huge air conditioning unit that has clunked into place directly in front of him. He grunts as he tumbles off the other side of it and continues to flee and, almost catching him off-guard, he is forced to lean back and slide under a clawed hand that reaches for him as a serpent-woman slides up out of the ground in front of him. Skidding to a halt, he quickly turns, and slices her head off with his sword then returns to his original trajectory as serpents cascade over the air conditioning unit behind him and up the sides of the building. Ahead, he sees another loom into view, a skyscraper rocketing up, and he throws all his might into sprinting toward it, the overwhelming screams of the demon's spiking all around him as they close in. He considers calling on Lady Famine, on borrowing some of her talent for demonic flight, but dismisses it. Azazel was right, he should be careful at how much of himself he offers to her and so upon reaching the edge of the building he jumps, his arms and legs circling in the air as he leaps, with the skyscraper racing up beneath him. Behind, he hears the screams of demons tumbling over the edge of the building he just left, unable to leap and follow him.

He lands onto the new roof with a viscous thud and tumbles out of control, his sword releasing from his grasp and clanking away under more of the rooftop's structure.

"Goddamit," he moans, as he painfully slams into the side of more air conditioners, then focuses his attention to the side of the building as more serpent-women stream over its edge, screaming, hissing, and snarling. Holding out his hand, Ikazuchi slides along the structure and into it, just as the closest one lunges at him and he slashes at her, cutting her in two, bursting her into dust a fraction of a second before she claws into him.

He is running out of time and doesn't know how much longer he can keep this up until the tens of thousands swarm and overwhelm him. Again, he considers using Lady Famine and as before dismisses it. He scrambles to his feet and starts to run again.

"Look up!" Ikazuchi shouts and he sees what his sword refers to. The next ring.

With a grunt, he clambers up the side of the largest of the air conditioning units on the roof and sprints across it as serpent-women swarm up its side to within touching distance of him. He leaps into the air and one of them grabs his leg, but instead of pulling him back and preventing him from rising, the ring's bizarre gravity takes him and the creature up toward the next circle.

Judas lands on both feet, as though he had jumped off and down, not up, and the creature tumbles away from him, screaming and writhing around on the ground in agony, and then explodes showering dust everywhere.

He raises his arms in front of his eyes, then as the dust clears he throws Ikazuchi out in front of him while looking back at the ring he has just leapt from, with the screams of serpent-women fading into the distance.

Ikazuchi lands on the ground as Azazel, walking forward and pointing to where the serpent died. "This isn't its ring. Not its sin. They can't exist away from their own plane."

Judas turns his attention to Azazel, nods, then dusts himself down. "Okay, understood. We need to find Charley, and now."

VIOLENCE

She lands on dirty and dusty ground, knees bent, her gaze searching. Her hands twitch, ready to call her swords into them at the first sign of trouble. But nothing happens. From the way she left Limbo's ring, assaulted by the terrible winds, she was certain that she was going to crash into the ground and suffer catastrophic injury; but no, she landed safe and surefooted, and so she assesses her surroundings. Nothing. Barren. A vast, dusty surface stretching out into the blackness and she comes to understand how lucky she had been on the previous ring for the erratic and unpredictable cycles of spin to have come her way at the appropriate moment to allow her to land on this one and not disappear into the nothingness of the cavern. She wonders how long it will be before the next ring approaches, at how much time she has to grab her bearings. One thing is for sure – she must abandon any notion of the laws of gravity and trust that jumping to the next ring will yield the desired result. She looks around again, unsure of what to do or where to go. She calls out to Judas into the darkness in the hope that he is close enough to hear her or indeed she is lucky enough for him to be on the same ring as her. Nothing, not a sound, not even the echo of her own voice.

She sighs. *Worth a shot,* she tells herself, once again looking around. *Okay Charley, just sit tight and wait for the next ring. The plan is to get to the center and rendezvous there. That's what dad would do.* She nods a couple of times. *Yeah. That's what he would do.*

A solid plan, child, Pestilence's voice says within her mind.

Oh, hello, she replies, *and where have you been?*

I have been accessing archives. Information buried deep within your psyche and I am quite surprised that it has taken this long for me to gain access to it. Yes, quite surprised indeed.

Oh? Care to share?

Forgive me young Charlotte but not now, I would rather you concentrated on your current predicament than worry about some other thing.

So it's something I should be concerned about?

Well, that depends.

On what?

On your definition of a problem.

Oh, for crying out loud. You're starting to sound like Gabriel now. Quit it.

Pestilence chuckles.

Charlotte rubs her hands together and blows into them. She hadn't noticed before, but the place feels cold, or maybe it has always been that temperature and only now is she feeling the effects of the loss of adrenaline.

Gettin' a little chilly in here or is it just me?

I am afraid I do not feel the cold, or the warmth for that matter. Nor will I ever.

You don't feel anything?

No. I just… exist. At the right time.

When you're called?

Correct. When we hear the call, we obey. As it has always been.

She frowns. *You've been called before?*

Indeed. But not by your Creator, or any in his dimension. There is more to the existence of space and time than you could possibly imagine. For now at least. But in time, more corridors of information will open to you and you will see. You will know.

She sighs. *Oh great. Just what I need – more pressure.*

She looks around once more. Still nothing, black, empty.

So, this… problem you've found. Can we play charades for clues or something? I'm kinda bored.

Let us focus on the task at hand, child. There will be time for revelation later.

Oooo, revelation – you make it sound so mysterious.

Yes, well, be on your guard, things change quickly in here.

What do you mean, things change quickly in here?

Hell is designed to provide a tailor-made experience to those who come into it. And no more so than these rings. From the moment you touched the surface, it has been reading you, preparing to present you with the most suitable version of Hell. Some who come here experience the same environment as others, depending on how strong their bond was in the previous life. Most, however, go it alone, tormented for eternity, lonely, frightened, and in great pain.

Huh! Okay. It's taking its sweet time though. I've been here a few minutes and nothing.

It is getting a read on you. You're not dead, you see, and you are a powerful being, probably one of the most powerful it has ever encountered. It is studying you. Give it a few moments, however, and it will respond.

Well, I'm not sure I wanna wait for it to do so. How long till the next ring swings by? And which one are we on now for that matter?

Not long I would say, although the rings' movement are hard to predict.

I'm surprised you don't know, being the all-seeing-eye that you are!

Sarcasm doesn't become you, Charlotte.

You sure? I reckon it's one of my best traits. She smiles to herself.

Very funny, he tuts. *Too much like your father, and I don't mean the one above.*

She laughs.

But anyway, I am sure it will be quite soon. The cycle will be much swifter, given your proximity to the center—

I'm close to the center? she says, interrupting him before he has a chance to tell her which ring she has landed on.

Yes. And as for where you are, I believe you are on the Seventh Circle: violence.

Shit! she says, glancing around again. *That sounds like a bad one.*

There's good ones? Pestilence replies.

Oh har-de-har. Now who doesn't suit sarcasm? Charlotte grins and lets out a quiet laugh. She rubs the upper parts of her arms, exposed by the black vest she wears.

She really is getting colder.

She sees her breath billow out in front of her.

Something isn't right.

The temperature is dropping, and it is getting colder by the second.

She looks around again.

It's getting colder, definitely much colder now, she says within the confines of her mind.

Yes. It is happening. Your event seems to have been prepared. But I also sense the next ring will pass soon.

Oh? How soon?

Difficult to assess. Best to keep your senses alert, even though the cold works to numb them.

She looks around, trying to sense a direction in which to travel, to see if any structures exist so that she may seek shelter from the rapidly plunging temperature. Her eyes narrow, and she frowns while holding out a hand. A snowflake drops into it, melting instantly upon touch. She looks around to see thousands more floating downward, sparkling, a light source from somewhere illuminating them. She then realizes what that is as lights blink on one by one, travelling away from her in tandem as though lighting a street. *Yes, a street, that's exactly what they are,* she tells herself – streetlights. She takes a step forward and a familiar crunching sound makes her look down to see the ground covered in snow a couple of inches deep, and looking up she sees that the tiny snowflakes are now much bigger in size, and even more constant. In the distance, she makes out more lights that arc up and away from her, and her frown deepens as she moves toward them. As she draws closer, a hint of familiarity strikes her, but she is unsure of where she is. She stops and looks around. Then recognition hits.

"Brooklyn Bridge," she says, this time aloud, her head cocked to one side. She shakes it slightly. "Wha… why Brooklyn Bridge? What does this mean to me?" She looks back to where she has come from and sees nothing but heavy snowfall and beyond it the solid darkness. She returns her gaze ahead once more.

Be on your guard, child. Something comes.

What? What is coming? What's going on?

Hold it off as best you can and then jump when I tell you. The next ring approaches.

Wait! Hold what off? What's coming?

Rage. Pure, unadulterated rage.

A sound causes her to cease concentrating on the conversation within her mind and focus upon it as she peers into the snowfall ahead that has worsened into a blizzard. The sound is familiar to her, metal scraping against a hard surface. Something being dragged across the floor.

The scrapes connect in threes each time, followed by a very brief pause, and then continue, and after another series a different sound joins them, a low, gurgling noise, human-like, that then turns into moaning, and then the scraping continues.

Charlotte holds her hands out to her sides and her swords fly into them as a blurred shape appears at the edge of her vision in the chaotic swirling snowstorm. As though sensing or hearing the action of her swords releasing, the scraping and moaning ceases and Charlotte takes a deep breath while moving into a defensive stance.

The shape does not move. It stands, motionless save for a slight swaying.

Taking a deep breath, she presses her lips together tight, and then breathes out through her nose hard. Closing her eyes, she thinks for a few seconds and then shakes her head, unsure if she should do what she is about to. And so she calls to it.

"Hello? Who's there?"

She shakes her head once more, and whispers to herself. "For crying out loud, Charley that was dumb. Dumb, dumb, dumb."

The shape doesn't move. It continues to sway, although the action has gained a little more purpose to it.

Unsure of what to do next, she takes a single step forward and attempts to peer into the snowstorm, to make out more of the shape, when, without warning, it bursts into life with a shrill and piercing scream and sprints toward her, something held above its head. "Fuck!" she says and grits her teeth. The tension within her rises as the creature approaches at high speed, its screams filling the cold, snow-filled air. It has around 100 yards to cover before it gets to her and she prepares herself, squatting into her defensive stance a little more.

Then, teleporting the distance in the blink of an eye, the creature is upon her, and Pestilence was right – it is pure, unadulterated rage.

It continues to scream as it rains down blow after blow with the short sword it carries, over and over, the swings coming from above its head but lightning fast, forcing Charlotte to defend and not allow her any opening for attack. With all the demons she has encountered, this is the most ferocious and the insane velocity at which it attacks has her on the back foot, unable to bring the fight under her control.

She grunts as the creature forces her back, her feet shuffling through the snow, the demon continuous in bringing the fight to her. Long, black, matted hair straggles in front of its eyes that sit within a charred and decomposing face. Sections of missing flesh and skin around the mouth give it the appearance of grinning, mocking her.

She's had enough, and calls upon a blast of Dark-Divinity, expelling it from her in a radius around her body. The energy wave hits the creature and launches it backward, almost somersaulting it into the air.

Charlotte takes a moment to catch her breath, bending over, her hands on her knees, but as soon as the demon hits the ground, it scrambles toward her on all fours, continuing to scream.

"Shit!" she says, as it stands and resumes its attack, relentless in its strikes. This time, however, she does get a moment to counter, and parries one of the blows causing the demon to stagger, then rams a sword through its chest. It looks down at the weapon and then back up at her and screams into her face while pulling itself off of her sword and raising its own in readiness to attack. Not giving it the time to do so, Charlotte spin kicks the creature sending it careering away to her left. But, once again it is back up and attacking her within seconds.

She grunts hard and before it has a chance to connect with a strike, she shadow-steps forward and plants a fist square in its face, sending it sprawling backward. "Two can play at that game," she says, defiantly. And it screams again as it raises itself onto its feet, its back arching. This time, however, it speaks, and she realizes that it is in fact female.

"Kill, kill, kill," it screams, slicing the air in front of it with its sword, attacking a seemingly invisible enemy and for the briefest of moments, Charlotte wonders if it is her the thing sees, or if it is attacking an entity within its own Hell.

"Kill, kill, kill," it screams once again.

When's the next ring due, Pesti? she says to herself, her gaze never leaving the creature ahead as it slices at thin air.

It's coming, soon, he replies. *And... Pesti?*

Yeah. Pesti. My new nickname for ya. And it had best be soon, as I would very much like to get outta here. This thing is a freakin' maniac.

The creature continues to hack at nothing at a rapid pace, but as Charlotte watches it she cannot help but feel some sort of recognition, as though the creature is familiar to her.

"I feel like I know this one!" she says to Pestilence, only this time out loud.

Without warning, the demon ceases its attacks and snaps its attention to her, to which Charlotte again moves into a defensive stance.

The demon charges, screaming once again.

"STOP!" Charlotte screams and to her surprise it does.

As though sensing something, it studies her, its head slowly moving from side to side, one eye visible among the strands of hair hanging in front of its face. The demon shakes her head a little, her deformed and decrepit mouth still locked in a grin, and then holds out a hand and moves toward Charlotte a little. A whimper escapes from her mouth and she then pulls the hand back, and a croaking sound rises from the back of her throat. She shakes her head again, this time more vicious, and places her hands at the side of her head, banging the hilt of her sword against her temple. "No, no, no, no, no," she says, shaking her head. "You are not supposed to be here, that wasn't supposed to happen!" she screams into the air. "THAT WASN'T THE DEAL!"

The demon's attention snaps toward Charlotte and it then scampers toward her, causing Charlotte to raise her swords, having lowered them at the fascination of watching the creature go through some sort of meltdown.

"That wasn't the deal. That wasn't the deal," it repeats, wagging a finger, then scampers away, appearing to talk into the ground, and then scurries back and reaches up to Charlotte's face. "Why? Why have you come? That wasn't the deal. You are not supposed to be here."

Charlotte backs away from the blackened fingers, and frowns. "Do... do I know you?"

"Know me? Yes... no. You don't know me! I know you. I... knew you."

"Who are you? What's going on here?"

The demon's face scrunches up as though it means to cry and then snaps its attention to a series of screeches and howls from the direction in which it had arrived. She screams toward them and then turns back to Charlotte.

"Go now. You have to go... now. They are looking. Always looking. But they never found you," she chuckles, "they never found you," she laughs again, "but now they have, and you must go." She turns away, back toward the sound of other approaching creatures and once more screams in their direction. She looks back at Charlotte, sees her swords edging down to her sides, her mouth agape, and she groans at the sight, a high-pitched squeal rising from the back of her throat. "Go. Look." She points up. "The circle. It comes. Go. Go!"

Okay, Charlotte, it's time to go. You must jump. Now! Pestilence urges.

Charlotte stares at the creature as it shrieks and races off toward a large group of shadows emerging from the blizzard ahead. "Mom?" she says, as her eyes bead and a small tear tracks down her face.

Now Charlotte, you must jump now!

She runs as the gigantic ring looms up to her side and above her. "It's too far, I won't make it."

You will make it. You don't belong here, you can move between them. You need to learn that Hell's laws cannot ground you. Now JUMP!

Sheathing her swords, she leaps into the air and leaves the ground far below her. Looking up, she sees the next ring approaching fast, a loud whooshing sound following it, and she places her arms in front of her face, this time convinced that she will indeed crash into the ground.

FRAUD

Slowly lowering her arms, Charlotte peeks over them. Once again, she has landed feet first and steady upon the next ring, only this time as she takes in her surroundings, it has already begun to populate itself with furniture and structures. As she edges forward, a deep frown on her face, she recognizes the place. She has been here before.

"The bus station," she says, "this is the bus station where my mom left me, where the police officer found me and then took me to the precinct before child services came for me. Why would this place be here? What Circle is this, Pesti?"

This, my child, is the Circle of Fraud, where the malicious and deceptive dwell. Those who would deceive and profit from such actions and hold no remorse from doing so.

"Then why are my memories here?"

Pestilence says nothing.

"Why are my memories here presented to me like this? And... that creature, that... woman. Was she my mother?"

More silence.

She is about to repeat herself, when he interrupts her.

Yes. She was your mother. Once.

She looks down at the ground and takes a deep breath. She doesn't know how to process the information or how to feel. Many times she had condemned her mother for her actions, for *this* action – abandoning her, aged five, in a rundown and terrifying bus station in whatever God-awful town it was, where anything could have happened to her while her mother sauntered off with the latest drug-fueled love-of-her-life. She had hated her for that, hoped that her mother's life had been terrible without her, that the decision to abandon her had led to the realization she had made the most terrible of mistakes that she had paid for them for the rest of her life. But now, with her mother's fate having been revealed, she feels anything but hatred. She feels something deeper. Pity and sorrow. She wipes her face, another tear cascading down it, and sniffs.

Looking around, she searches deep within her memories trying to remember the place where she had sat, patiently waiting for her mom to return, having been told that she would be back in a moment – one that never came.

As she glances toward a familiar set of benches, she sees a young girl sat on one of them, her back to her and she walks over, knowing full well who it is. As she moves alongside and in front of her, she stares into the innocent face of her five-year-old self and more tears bead in her eyes.

Young Charlotte looks up and smiles, a small and anxious one. "She's not coming back, is she?"

Older Charlotte places her hand over her mouth, attempting to stifle the sorrow that threatens to cascade from her lips. Her eyes glisten with tears as they fill. She shakes her head, causing them to spill down her face, then takes her hand away from her mouth. "I'm sorry. I'm so, so sorry. No, she isn't. But it gets better. Someone does eventually come for you, and it gets better, he is so much better." She smiles and wipes the tears from her own face.

Young Charlotte smiles back. "It always has been better. This never happened."

At once the scene disappears, leaving a teary and confused Charlotte staring at the dusty ground. She looks from side to side and then turns around as a voice catches her attention.

"Hey kiddo," a bearded man says, as he hands her a brown teddy bear, "this is Mr. Tumbles and he's gonna keep you company while your mom keeps me company." He laughs and walks away from her, and she realizes she is sat on a dirty couch in a dirty flat.

She looks down at the bear and runs her hands across its fur. "Mr. Tumbles? What... what's going on?" She looks around, and next to her sits her younger self. She smiles again.

"This never happened."

Again, the scene disappears as quickly as it had arrived, and she sees that she isn't sat on a couch anymore, nor is she holding her old teddy bear. Instead she is stood, confused and alone. She turns again, the sound of yelling and screaming from behind drawing her attention, and she finds herself in a motel bathroom, one that she knows she has been in before, like the one she and Judas holed up in when they first met. She looks down at the sound of scuffling feet. Sitting in the empty bath is her younger self.

"Shhhh," her younger self says, placing a finger to her lips. "This never happened."

And the scene disappears.

Once again, Charlotte is alone.

"Pestilence, what's going on?"

The next ring is here, child. We must leave. And you will be able to jump to the center from the edge of that one. Let us get there and signal the others.

She looks up and leaps into the air. "Fine. But I want answers, dammit."

You shall have them, child. I just hope you are ready for them.

279

WRATH

The air is thick with deep and booming screams as Judas swings Ikazuchi once more at an enormous bloated demon and slices it in half. Ahead, dozens more fattened creatures charge at him, their motion exaggerated by their size, their arms down by their sides and swinging from front to back. They lean backward, their gaze skyward as though it is impossible for them to look ahead due to the way their heads rest upon their huge bodies, and between their demonic cries they groan and moan with each footfall, waddling at high speed toward him as he tears through them with ease and upon dispatching them, they explode, showering coins and various treasures over the ground.

"There, master. The next ring. Jump to it now."

"Is there no way of skipping a few?"

"Too risky. You may miss entirely and end up where you have just come from, plus we need to try to pinpoint her position."

Judas frowns and shakes his head. "You were right earlier. She does think like me, so she will head for the center. It will be the easiest place to find each other."

"Assuming she makes it there."

Judas grunts. "She can more than take care of herself, and stop talking like a dick, okay? She'll be fine. Let's just get out of here and head for the center, I'm tired of killing these things and I swear to God one of them looked like my cousin Macario, the piece of shit."

He leaps into the air, toward the next ring as it approaches, and lands on it, then takes a moment to orient himself.

"Well, that must have been Greed, so this is Wrath I assume?"

"You assume correctly, master."

Judas hurls Ikazuchi into the air, away from him and Azazel lands on the ground, a spring in his step.

"Ahhh, good old Wrath. The favorite noun of the Gods." He chuckles. "Well, shall we make ourselves comfortable while we await the next ring master?"

Judas turns in circles, looking over the vast emptiness. "Whatever. Just knock off the 'master' shit will ya. We both know you are being facetious when you say it."

Azazel smirks. "Okay, what would you prefer that I call you?"

"I dunno, anything other than master," he glances at him, "but nothing like dickhead or other insults either.

Azazel chuckles. "How about... Judas?"

He nods, while looking around some more. "Yeah, sounds about right." Turning his attention back to Azazel, he walks over to him, as the demon sword waves a hand over the ground and a pair of dirt-rock chunks rise to provide seating. With a frown, Judas stares at him for a few seconds, then points to the small structures. "The fuck is that?"

"What?" Azazel says, his eyes wide.

"Don't fucking 'what' me. That... manipulation of the terrain. THAT!"

Azazel looks down at the seats while in mid-hover, his backside a couple of inches from his rock. "Oh, that! Well... y'know, as the Architect, I still have some control over, y'know... stuff."

"No, y'know, I don't know, you need to, y'know, explain it."

Azazel slowly sits, while considering his words carefully. "Well... I can create some things."

281

"Right, that's enough. Cut the horseshit, Azazel, how much control do you have here?"

He smiles, a nervous one. "A fair bit? It's hard to quantify." He scrunches his mouth up and raises his eyebrows, then stands bolt upright as Judas stomps toward him.

"Wait, wait," he says, holding up his hands, "genuinely, I had virtually no control when we arrived, but being in here for this long and getting a part of my crystal back, well, it would appear that I am refueling, y'know – powering back up." He staggers backward as Judas bears down on him. "I'm serious, Judas. It's been happening in the last half hour or so. I have felt a shift in my abilities." He takes a deep breath. "Look, you will need me to be at my best, or at least as much of it as I can achieve with only one third of my power cell."

Judas grabs him with one hand, scrunching up his clothing. "Get us to the center… NOW!"

Azazel pulls away from him, wrestling out of his grip. "ENOUGH OF THIS! Enough! You need me as much as I need you. This… arrangement we have, that I have been playing along with all this time, is a mutual benefit thing. The door definitely swings both ways on this one, Judas."

His face curls into a snarl as he circles around Azazel. "Is that so? And what is it you wish to gain from this 'mutual benefit' thing? I thought that me naming and taking control of you, of releasing you from your prison was payment enough. What could *you* possibly want?"

Azazel barks a laugh at him. "You think that being released from the Nether was my only goal?" He laughs again. "This is my goal… all of this, it belongs to me," he slams angry palms onto his chest. "It was taken from me by betrayers, thieves, dirty rotten cheats. And I want it back!"

Judas frowns. "You want to control Hell? But that's not possible for you. You are an Ancient. A being like you cannot own this place."

Azazel chuckles. "No, I cannot, but I can run it at its master's side."

Judas' anger rises, and he bears down on Azazel once more. "You wish to aid Lucifer, not help me defeat him."

"DEFEAT HIM!" Azazel erupts into laughter. "Oh, my dear boy – you cannot defeat Lucifer. Even if you were to take his head. You cannot win."

"I will take his head, and I will win."

"No, you will lose. You cannot remove that which must not be removed."

Judas eyes him with a mixture of contempt and confusion.

"You just don't get it, do you? The balance, my good man. The balance must be maintained at all times."

Judas frowns and shakes his head.

Azazel releases a laugh. "There must always be a Lucifer, an evil, to the Creator's good. If you were to defeat Lucifer in battle, then you would take his place. There must always be good, and there must always be evil. The balance *must* be maintained."

Judas stares at him for a moment breathing heavily, then looks down, shaking his head. "Bullshit."

"It is not!"

"YOU LIE!"

"I DO NOT! The balance must be maintained Judas, so I ask you now: with what you know, what do you intend to do? Hmmm, what is your mighty plan?"

He snaps his attention to him. "Oh, and I suppose you have it all figured out. Hmm? Had a scheme cooking up from the beginning no doubt?"

Azazel's angry and defiant posture diminishes, and he smiles. "Well, as a matter of fact I do. The plan is simple. You keep Lucifer busy in a brawl while I dispatch Beelzebub and lord knows you are more than capable of going toe-to-toe with Lucifer this time. He won't have it easy with you like he did a couple of years back. And once I defeat my brother, I will offer my services to Lucifer in exchange for him leaving the kingdom of man alone for a millennium or two."

Judas scoffs. "Oh, and I suppose you reckon he'll love that idea, fall over himself for it – give up everything he has been working toward for the last God knows how long."

"He will, because even he knows that without a sword of power, he will have no chance against the Creator. Taking over the kingdom of man is one thing, but going up against the big guy? Well, that is something altogether different."

"And 2000 years? Well, thanks for that," he says, turning away from Azazel.

"Hey! It might be nothing to us, but it's a damn long time for the humans. And for her."

Judas snaps his attention back to him but says nothing. He runs the thought through his mind. Lucifer's cycle may very well repeat itself, but at least Charlotte would be in a better position, even more so than she is now. By that time she will have ascended, and may even be powerful enough to prevent Lucifer from even trying again. It has to be better than the alternative. Much better, as he very much doesn't fancy an eternity as the next Lucifer.

Azazel's face softens. "The next ring approaches, Judas. Let us discuss the finer details later. Besides, we need to get to her. The rings have a way of presenting information based on the individual, of drawing things and entities from their lives toward them and we wouldn't want her to learn the little secret now, would we?"

His attention snaps to the demon sword once again and he is about to speak when Azazel stops him. "We have company approaching, Judas. Game-face time."

Judas holds out his hand and Azazel returns to it as Ikazuchi.

Chuckling creeps out from the darkness followed by the sound of shuffling, and a voice.

"Judas, Judas, Judas, my old boy. We always knew you would end up here eventually. So black is your heart, so dark is your soul." It chuckles once again.

From out of shadow ambles a stooped form, a hood covering its face, ragged clothing draped over its body, and scraps of cloth swinging from the arms near the wrists. In its hand it carries a dagger.

Judas recognizes the creature, even before it pulls back its hood to reveal burnt and blackened skin. "Hello uncle," he says, disdain dripping from each word.

Judas' uncle chuckles again. "How long has it been since I let you see the fruits of your labor? Let you see your Christ bound and gagged upon the floor." He laughs again. "I received a hero's welcome in here when I arrived," he looks toward the ground and ceases shuffling toward Judas, "but those things never last, not in here... no, not in here if you are not on Lucifer's A-list list and among his favorites. So here I am. And I get to kill you this time. And I will be a hero again. And he will welcome me back, and I will leave this accursed ring." He laughs hard at the thought.

"This isn't a shade, is it? He's real, yeah?" Judas asks Ikazuchi.

"Yup!" comes the swords reply.

Judas' demonic uncle continues to laugh as he stumbles forward toward him, the dagger raised high.

"Good," Judas says, then shadow-steps behind him and plunges Ikazuchi deep into the back of his head. "Fuck. You." He says, as he pulls the sword out and the demon crumbles into dust.

Judas breathes out hard. "Now that... that is the best thing to have happened all day, and well worth the trip."

Ikazuchi chuckles.

Above and catching Judas' attention, a sharp and high-pitched chime pierces the dark followed by a brilliant white light that stretches out from the center and to one side of the gyroscope and he smiles. "Good girl." He holds Ikazuchi out in front of him. "No more fucking around, Ika. With your power now much stronger, can you take me straight to the center? I don't want to mess about visiting anymore rings."

Ikazuchi pauses for a moment.

Judas holds the sword up to his face and is about to speak when it interrupts him.

"Yes Judas. I think I can. Especially now that we know where she is."

"Right then. Good. Take me to her."

"Understood," Ikazuchi says.

And Judas jumps, the sword ahead of him.

THE WELL OF SOULS

Charlotte advances toward the gigantic circular pool of glowing light, in awe at the spouts of energy, like water from dozens of drinking fountains rising with hisses and then dropping back into it. The light radiates a strange, warm glow that feels odd against her skin as she draws closer, and although its brilliance is intense, she feels no need to shield her eyes from it.

So this is the Well of Souls, Pesti?

It is, my dear. This is the southern well, to coin a phrase, where every creature bound to this realm's essence resides. The White Kingdom has one also, the northern one I guess you could say.

Interesting, she says, approaching it, *every creature, you say?'*

Every creature, without fail. Every being that has been committed to this prison has their soul stored in here, swimming for eternity, connected to their physical form, and aware of all the horror and torments they are subjected to. It is a much different experience in the White Kingdom, however, where their souls rest peacefully, equally aware of the ambrosia the physical forms enjoy.

So if I wanted to get someone out of here, what would I do?

Pestilence emits a sympathetic grunt. *You wish to free the woman!*

She nods. *I wish to free the woman, yeah. So what do I do?*

He laughs. *Being honest, I couldn't say this has never happened before. But what do they say in your world? 'Learn by doing?' Yes, I think that would be appropriate. Learn by doing.*

She nods again a couple of times, then climbs the small steps leading up to the pool of light and stares into it. *You think I'll make it back with her?*

You are The Light, are you not? You can accomplish much, greatness even. But remember, you are The Light, so why not be that to the woman and guide her to you?

She smiles out of the corner of her mouth and raises a hand into the air. A beam of brilliant white light explodes from it and shoots upward, and with it a high-pitched chime rings out.

Done, she says, then stares into the Well again.

Good. Pestilence says, *Now do it.*

She takes a deep breath and closes her eyes. "Oh, Charley, Charley, Charley. You really are out of your freakin' mind," she says.

Charlotte dives into the Well of Souls.

***

Judas lands in the center of the gyroscope, marking the 10th Ring of Hell. He looks around. "Charley? Charley, are you there?" He hears nothing and so stands still for a moment, opening his ears to the possibility of any sound and repeats her name.

He grunts, breathing out deeply while at the same time striding toward the Well of Souls, then stops to look around again. He throws Ikazuchi out in front of him. "You said she was here, that this was the place."

"It was," Azazel says, landing on the ground and commencing a search of his own. He walks around the circumference of the Well and then back to Judas. "I swear this is where the beacon originated. I am not mistaken on this."

Judas growls, and turns in a circle, furious. "Then where is she? She wouldn't leave, not if she signaled. Could something have happened to her?"

"Come on, Judas. There would be bodies here if something had but hers wouldn't be among them. You know how powerful she has become. Maybe she went through the down-gate over there." He points to red-glowing portal at the other side of the large chamber on the opposite side of the Well, rotating within a decorative casing depicting giant, demonic figures.

Judas grows angrier. "She wouldn't have left. Not without me. She would've waited here."

Azazel glances around once more. "Look, all I'm saying is that I cannot sense her nearby, and I built the damn place. She must've moved somewh—"

Both jump in surprise and stagger away from the Well as the pool behind them erupts, spraying energy everywhere, and from out of the white liquid a figure is tossed onto the ground and rolls across it toward Judas, halting at his feet.

From the center of the pool, Charlotte floats forward, her arms outstretched, the white energy draining off her and she eases onto the ground in front of the Well.

Judas looks down at his feet to see Abi Colter staring up at him.

"S'up!" she says, shaking and naked.

FORTY-FOUR

"Well, you must be someone very special indeed. Not everyone is lucky enough to have the Archangel Gabriel escort them here personally," the voice chuckles.

"Wha... what?" Gary says, blinking open his eyes, and pure white light bombards his senses.

"Hush now, Peter," Gabriel says, "allow him to orient himself."

"Oh, sure, okay, what do I know?" Peter replies, his tone sarcastic, "I've only been welcoming people into the fold for thousands of years. No, of course Gabriel, let's do it your way."

Gabriel smiles a little. "Be off with you now, I'll look after this one."

Peter shakes his head, sighs, and begrudgingly wanders off.

Gary sits up but stops halfway through, feeling light headed.

"Easy now my friend," Gabriel's soothing voice insists, "take your time, get used to your surroundings."

Easing himself up, he moves into a sitting position and takes a deep breath, rubbing his mouth and chin. Glancing around, he sees that he is in a room of pure white with empty walls and devoid of any furniture. A quiet sound, much like the chiming of crystals, can be heard, complementing the ambience. He looks at Gabriel and offers a small, crooked smile. "It's a bit minimalistic don't ya think, Gabe?"

Gabriel smiles and helps Gary to his feet. "In time it will be whatever you want it to be."

Gary nods. "So, the other guy – Saint Peter I take it?"

Gabriel looks to the direction in which Peter grumped off into. "Oh yes, he's a Saint all right, Saint pain-in-my-ass," he smiles, "but he's a good guy, of course."

Gary's eyebrows rise sharply. "Gabriel, I do believe that is the first time that I have ever heard you curse."

He smiles. "Well, my friend, we are having to do a lot of firsts today."

Gary barks a laugh and glances in Peter's direction. "Wow! Saint Peter, eh? I guess it wasn't a crock after all." He smiles.

"No, Gary, it wasn't, and you will find a great many things are not either. Everything comes from some measure of truth, regardless of how bizarre. It's all a matter of perception. Come now. Let us see if we can grant you an audience with who you came to see."

"He doesn't know I'm coming?"

"Oh, he will know. I just didn't ask his permission first."

"Oh!"

"Yes. Oh indeed."

"Is that going to be a problem?"

"It depends."

"On what?"

"His mood." Gabriel enforces his hopefulness with a raise of his eyebrows.

Gary groans, closes his eyes, and shakes his head. "Bosses who don't want to be disturbed. That never ends well."

He follows Gabriel out of the room and into a corridor much of the same design, except this area has décor – gold leaf patterns spreading out across the walls, with beautiful carvings of animals, humans, and buildings dotted around. The music has changed into a more orchestrated piece although still subdued, and Gary likes it.

As they continue along the corridor they pass other people dressed in various outfits befitting their time periods, yet in every case the clothing is immaculate, pristine and each person nods to Gabriel and then in turn to Gary and he returns the gesture while at the same time bouncing his attention from one sight to the other, him looking very much the new guy amazed at everything around him.

Eventually, Gabriel comes to a halt in the center of a large room with branching pathways leading off in all directions. At the edge of one of the paths Gary spies a beautiful garden, and down another a glorious waterfall with people sitting around it, chatting and laughing and it causes him to smile. But that wanes when his mind comes back to the reason for him being here, for the pain and suffering that others continue to endure on the planet below, if it even is below or on another plane of existence. Whichever it is, he needs to be on his A-game today if he is to convince God to get involved and help those remaining and indeed to ensure that Lucifer's plan to continue his march to these fine halls fails. He feels dizzy again as the notion hits him, and he understands what it is he is about to do – petition God Himself for help in defeating the Devil and he must steady himself with an arm against the wall and take a deep breath. "This is turning out to be the craziest of days," he says aloud.

"Can you stand for it to get a little crazier?" a familiar female voice says from behind him.

Fighting back tears, he turns to see his ex-wife Emily standing before him. He places his hands over his mouth, his eyes glistening, and then reaches out to her and pulls her in close. His relationship with Emily ended a long time before the Collapse but he still cared for her a great deal, and his embrace echoes that feeling of dear friends who haven't seen one another in a long time.

They remain that way for a few moments and then allow themselves to separate, Gary wiping his cheeks and sniffing while clearing his throat and looking to his side a little.

"So, how long have you bee—"

"Pretty much from the first moments, Gary," she says, cutting him short. "Tony and I were enjoying a lovely dinner in town, when… well, you know what happened."

He lowers his head. "Yeah. And Tony?"

She smiles. "He's here too. He's fine."

Gary smiles back at her. "I'm glad. Really, I am. And I'm happy you found peace with him."

She nods, pursing her lips and lowering her gaze. She looks up again. "I hear you've become quite the celebrity?"

He frowns for a moment, then nods, offering a small, breathy laugh. "Ahh, yeah, you mean with Charlotte and Judas and stuff?"

She smiles and nods.

"Yeah, it's been crazy down there, y'know. The whole last two years. I wouldn't even know where to begin. The day I met them," he suppresses a laugh, "now that's a day I'll never forget."

She laughs also. "We do get to hear one or two things up here. It sounds like you have had a heck of a ride."

He laughs again. "Oh Em, you don't know the half of it."

She smiles. "Well, perhaps you'll have some cool stories to tell Jacob." She motions back with her eyes.

Several yards away, behind Emily, holding Tony's hand is Jacob and he waves at Gary.

This time, he cannot contain the tears. He rushes over to his son, grabs him, and scoops him into a tight embrace, telling him over and over how much he has missed him while tears continue to roll down his face. He holds him close, smiling at his familiar smell and tiny form and he closes his eyes. He doesn't want to let him go. He must though as Jacob grunts at the restrictive embrace and, moving his son's head away from his chest, Gary runs his hands over the boy's head a few times, ruffling his hair and causing Jacob to protest further. Gary laughs, then hugs him tight once again, the gesture reciprocated by Jacob.

"Are you here to stay daddy?"

"You bet, champ, you ain't getting rid of me."

From behind, Gabriel's gentle cough draws his attention.

"I'm sorry to interrupt this emotional moment, Gary, but He will see you now."

Gary nods and wipes the tears from his face. "Yeah. Okay. Yeah." He turns toward Jacob and places his hands gently on the side of his face. "Hey champ, daddy's gotta go speak with the big guy now to see if he will help everyone else down there. But I'll be right back, and you can tell me all about your adventures since I last saw you, okay?"

"Sure. But I want to hear yours with Charlotte and Judas more."

Jacob smiles, and Gary emits a sharp laugh.

"Absolutely kiddo, I'll tell you everything. It's pretty cool stuff."

"Gary," Gabriel says, prompting that keeping the Creator waiting might not be a wise thing to do.

Gary turns toward him and nods, then gets to his feet and rubs a hand over Jacobs's head to which the boy pouts and once again puts his hair straight. He walks up to Gabriel, then turns toward Emily and smiles and she smiles back. "Okay, Gabe, lead on."

Gabriel takes a deep breath and leads Gary to a large set of gold leaf double doors.

The deep sigh didn't go unnoticed by Gary, and a small amount of dread rises within him and he starts to question whether this had been a good idea.

Gabriel places a hand in the center of the door and they effortlessly slide open. "Good luck, my friend," he says, as he walks away, his eyes wide.

"Good luck?" a nervous Gary responds, "What do you mean? Why did you say it like that?"

From within the chamber, a male voice echoes. "Detective Gary Cross. As I live and breathe. Please come in."

Gary takes a deep breath, closes his eyes, and steps inside.

FORTY-FIVE

"It really is good to see you again, Abi. Really good," Judas says with a warm and sincere smile. He looks toward Charlotte. "Well kiddo, you said you were gonna do it and you did."

She nods, a small smile on her face. Looking down at Abi sat on the floor, she then turns toward Azazel. "Hey, can you do something about that?" She motions toward her nakedness, her vulnerability.

Azazel nods. "Sure thing. So, young lady, what's it to be?"

Abi looks up at him. "Jeans, T-shirt and sneakers still a thing?"

Azazel smirks. "Sister, you ain't been gone *that* long." He clicks his fingers, instantly clothing her.

"Cool," she says, getting to her feet with Judas' help, then looks at him and offers a nervous smile, then looks away, unable to maintain eye contact.

"Hey, hey!" he says. "It's fine. It is fine."

She begins to cry. "I'm sorry. I'm so sorry, it was all my fault. And I couldn't help attacking you, I wasn't in control."

"Hey, stop that," Judas says, taking her head in his hands. "I should be the one apologizing to you. You did everything right, *everything*. I'm so sorry I failed you and condemned you to this. But you have her to thank." He motions toward Charlotte. "She said she would get you back. She bloody said she would." He smiles.

Abi looks turns toward the girl and stares for a moment, then opens her mouth wide. "Charlotte?"

Charlotte smiles and nods, small tears beading down her face.

Abi opens her arms and runs to Charlotte, embracing her, and both women sob. Tears at being reunited. Eventually, Abi pulls away from her.

"How long have I been down here?"

Charlotte laughs, wiping her eyes. "Would you believe only two years?"

Her smile wanes. "No. No I wouldn't. Every day in here, if you can call them days, felt like an eternity. But then you came." She looks to her left. "Somewhere, out there, my tormented body wandered, subjected to horror beyond imagining. It felt like a lifetime's worth and then, all of a sudden, an angel was above me and my body turned to dust, and then, a second later, I was here at your feet." She smiles and motions toward Judas.

He smiles back. "Well, at age seven she said she would put things right, that she would set you free. She's a persistent little bugger that one, you know."

"Oi!" Charlotte says, grinning back at him.

With a clap of his hands, Azazel steps toward them, his stride over-exaggerated. "Okie-dokie. This has been wonderful. I'm feeling all emotional about it, touched in fact. I very nearly cried. Seriously, I did – I nearly cried for the first time in, oh, for*ever*. But if you please, we have a mission to finish. So… yep. Scootles pip." He shoos them with his hands.

Abi frowns, turns back toward Charlotte, and cocks a thumb at Azazel. "Who's he?"

Before she can answer, Judas interrupts. "Why, he's the man who built Hell."

Azazel smirks and bows his head.

Abi opens her mouth and points at him, but then closes it, puffing out her cheeks.

FORTY-SIX

"Drink?" the Creator says from behind the bar as Gary walks into the room.

He frowns while looking around. "I don't understand. This is… Flanagan's. I used to drink here back in the day, before… everything." He snorts a laugh. The bar is the same as he remembers it to the letter: the walls adorned with tatty Irish memorabilia, the pool table in the corner, the old Wurlitzer at the side of the room which he'd asked Mel Flanagan if he would sell it to him, and then reeled at the price, it being worth tens of thousands of dollars. Everything looks the same.

"Bourbon, isn't it Gary?" the Creator asks with a smile, holding up a bottle and then motioning for him to take a seat.

"I'm sorry?"

"Your preferred tipple, a nice bourbon. We have the finest here, anything that you could ever want, the best bar in town." He laughs, and again motions at Gary to take a seat.

"Yeah, yeah – bourbon will be fine, thanks," he says, walking over to the counter and then taking a seat on one of its stools, still admiring the place.

The Creator hands him the drink, which Gary takes with thanks, then the Creator grabs a glass and pours himself one.

Gary looks at it for a second then raises it to him, and they each take a taste from their glasses.

"Hmmm, that is so sooooo good," the Creator says, closing his eyes.

Gary nods and smiles in agreement. Taking a moment to let the whiskey sit in his mouth, he then swallows it and shakes his head. "Y'know, I thought you would be older. Look older, I mean."

He smiles. "White hair, beard, and all that jazz? Not a 40-something nondescript fella?"

"Yeah, something like that," Gary replies with a small laugh through his nose.

"Would this suit better?" The Creator changes his form.

Gary shakes his head, partway through taking a drink, closing his eyes briefly in the process. He swallows. "No. No, that would not be better at all. Please go back to the other one. As much as I would love to, I can't have a serious conversation with Morgan Freeman. I just… I just can't. Not today. I'm sorry."

The Creator laughs and reassumes his original form of the 40-something nobody.

"So Detective Cross, what is it you hope to accomplish here today, hmm? Pretty ballsy move I have to say." He leans against the bar and takes another sip of his whiskey.

"Please, just call me Gary – I haven't been a detective in a long time."

He nods and smiles.

"Well," he pauses, realizing he is unsure of how to address him. Should he call him your highness or goodness, or something? It has him stumped.

"Bud!"

"What?" Gary replies, somewhat surprised.

"You're struggling for what to call me and the obvious just doesn't seem right, does it? So just call me Bud." He smiles.

Gary shakes his head slowly. "This is too weird!"

'Bud' lets out a laugh. "Ya got that right Gary. Ya sure got that right. So come on, spill. What are you hoping to achieve here today?"

Again, Gary pauses, only this time he takes time to consider his answer, then takes a deep breath, scrunches up his mouth, and closes his eyes. "Well, I'm sure you already know, but I have asked for you to hear me out today so that I might convince you to get involved in protecting the people down below, or at least order your forces to help them. You see, we are getting slaughtered by the minu—"

"Agggh, nope, sorry Gary. No can do!"

Taken aback by the sudden interruption, he stares at him, eyes wide, and open-mouthed. After a couple of seconds, he shakes his head. "I'm sorry. What?"

"Can't get involved. Sorry my friend but it ain't gonna happen." He smiles.

"You're joking, right? You are actually fucking joking?"

Bud lets out another sharp laugh and sits forward. "See, that's what I like about you Gary, you don't go for all this 'cannot swear in holy places or when in the presence of… Bud,'" he taps the side of his nose, as though signaling a secret between them. "You're always content and confident to be yourself, no matter what. I like that." He smiles. "But it is weird, I'll give ya that."

"Again. I'm sorry – what?"

"You said earlier, just a few moments ago, that it was weird. I agree. I mean, two years ago you flat out denied my existence and now here you are, swearing in front of me and shit. That's some pretty messed up stuff right there, don't-cha-think?"

"No," Gary says, shaking his head, "it being weird is not what I'm apologizing for, I am actually in physical shock that you won't get involved. What the hell are you do—"

Bud interrupts him with a finger. "Oh, wait, I love this song." Then he beats it in time to the music drifting from the jukebox in the corner and sings along. "Sometimes it's hard to be a woman, dum… dum… dum-be-dum-be-dum. Giving all your love to just one ma—"

Gary stands, sharply, the stool he was sitting on toppling to the ground. "HELLO! BUD! Why are you not taking this seriously? And why the hell are you singing Stand by Your Man?" He jabs his hands onto his head and then runs them through his hair with force while growling. "This is insane, utterly insane."

Bud sighs. "You need to lighten up Gary, that's your trouble. You're too tense. Things have a way of working themselves out. Always have, always will."

He frowns and shakes his head a little, his arms flopping down by his sides. "What? Things have a way of working themselves out? People are dying down there at the hands of one of your supernatural creations. Their means of fighting those damn creatures dwindle by the day and you say things will work themselves out? What the hell! Do you even care?"

"Of course I care," He says, pushing himself off the bar and standing up straight. He swirls his drink around. "Why do you think I set Charlotte and Judas on their path? Didn't you listen to a single word Judas said to you in the police cruiser, as you all drove into New York City on your way to my dear old friend Father Keel?"

Gary looks at him, frowning, his mouth open.

"He told you outright that asking for my help, asking me to get involved, would never be an option, never an answer. Humans would expect it from me absolutely every time. It would remove purpose for them."

"You think this is purpose? You think this is something they need to figure out for themselves? To see their loved ones, their friends, murdered, no, slaughtered in front of their eyes? To live like cowering rats awaiting the inevitable? You think this is how people want it? Huh? All it would take from you would be to put Lucifer back in his box and let people get back to normality. They wouldn't even have to know that you did it, they would just wake up one morning and it would all be over. Please. I am begging you to put an end to this."

"Gary. I would if I could, but I can't."

"Y… you can't. *You* can't?"

"Nope. Sorry. Another drink?" He grabs the bottle and pours a generous measure into his own glass.

"*No*… no I don't want another fucking drink," Gary replies, his eyes wide. He then sighs, rubs his forehead, and looks down.

Bud sighs as well. "You seem upset, Gary."

He looks up at him, slowly, disbelief spread across his face.

"But don't fret. I can offer you some cheery news. Charlotte and Judas are alive and well and doing great. In fact, they have just found Abi again, y'know – the hooker."

"Yes, I understand who you meant, you didn't have to tag on her old profession."

"Oh, okay – sorry, thought I best spell it out for you in case you thought I meant the little girl."

"No, I got it, the little girl liked to be called Abigail, you would know that, and therefore you would have used that name."

He smiles. "You've always been a sharp one, you." He makes a clicking sound with his mouth and points a finger at him. "Strange that two important people in your life would have the same name. Weird odds, huh! She's here too, y'know, brightens the place up as well, the little tyke. I'm really quite fond of her." He smiles, looking away from Gary and into thin air.

Staring at him for a few seconds, Gary's frown furrows deeper. "Grown quite fond of her? She was murdered at the hands of a demon… one of *your* former Archangels. She was terrified. I WATCHED HER DIE!" Tears well up in his eyes as he is forced to relive the memory of Abigail's passing.

Bud stares at him for a few moments and then clicks his fingers, refilling Gary's drink. "Look, I can see you're having difficulty, but your idea of what you cling to down there is not shared by those who eventually end up here. This is the life they have always wanted. Everything down there has been a test, of sorts, to determine the next stage of their journey. People are happy here. You will be too Gary, one day."

He looks up again. "One day? What do you mean, one day?"

Bud stands and looks at a non-existent watch on his wrist. "Oooo, would you look at the time. Lots to do, Gary. Busy-busy-busy. I have to continue weaving the timelines together and this has put me a bit behind schedule." He draws air over his teeth. "And they are not far from making their discovery. It's all coming together nicely."

"What?" Gary asks, his face almost hurting from the amount of confused frowning he has had to do in the last few minutes. "Weaving timelines? What timelines? What discovery?"

Bud lifts the bar hatch and steps through to Gary's side, then ushers him toward the door. "Well, it's all very technical and I haven't the time to explain, but it has been a pleasure to meet you finally, Gary. A real treat. And I genuinely mean that."

"Wait, wait. At least just tell me where Charlotte and Judas are."

"I already did. They are in Hell and have just rescued Abi." He smiles and clicks his fingers.

About to say something, and still holding his breath, Gary looks around to find he is no longer in the room, but stood outside in front of the door. He turns around toward Gabriel who is stood waiting patiently, then cocks a thumb back to the door. "That man right there is bat-shit crazy."

Gabriel purses his lips together to prevent himself from laughing.

FORTY-SEVEN

"Hey guys, have any of you seen Gary?" Nathan says, poking his head into the laboratory occupied by Daniel, Sarah, and Isaac. Each shake their heads at him and he taps the doorframe, sighing in the process. "Okay, well if you do see him tell him I'm looking for him."

"Errr, yeah, sure thing Colonel," Daniel replies with a nervous grin.

Nathan stares at them for a moment and then frowns. "What are you kids up to?"

Daniel acts surprised, an unconvincing act at that. "Erm, us? Nothing, just, er, cleaning up the lab after our little unwanted visitor." He motions around to the devastation caused by the demon that had appeared through the initial portal.

Suspicious, Nathan is about to enter the room when Jonesy walks up to him and catches his attention.

"I can't find him anywhere, sir. You want me to gear up a team and see if he's gone outside or something?"

303

Nathan looks back into the room, eyeing them, then turns back toward Jonesy. "Yeah. Yeah, let's grab some gear and widen the search in the base, will ya? Something don't feel right."

"Yes sir," Jonesy says, then jogs off down the corridor.

Nathan stares at the kids again for a moment, squints, then turns and follows Jonesy.

Daniel breathes out, deeply. "He's onto us, I know he's onto us."

"Would you relax?" Isaac says, grabbing him by the arm. "He's not onto us, but he will be if you keep behaving like such a weird dick."

"*Isaac!*" Sarah shouts, her eyes wide. "Honestly, I despise this behavior of yours. What has gotten into you?"

He looks at her for a few seconds then sighs and lowers his gaze. Looking back up, he places his hands on her shoulders. "Look, I'm sorry, okay?"

"Not to me... to Daniel."

He smiles and huffs. "Fine. Daniel, I'm sorry but this is important, we need to do this."

Daniel shakes his head slightly. "I dunno about this."

"What's not to know? Today you gave the Colonel a weapon against these bastards, tomorrow we could be presenting a means of portalling in behind them, without them even knowing. This is a powerful win-win, one that puts us in the driving seat where we can catch these fuckers off-guard for once. Imagine how impressed with you Colonel Taylor is gonna be."

Daniel smiles a little as he runs the thought through his mind.

"Excuse me!" Sarah interrupts. "I can't believe you are even considering this! That you would actually *want* to lock onto the signal of a demon or group of them by replicating what you did wrong the first time and create a portal so that will bring them in here? Are you actually nuts?"

Daniel holds up his hands and shakes his head. "Oh, no, no, no. I wouldn't do anything as dumb as that. I would offset the entry point to the signals vector by quite some distance, allowing us to be close enough to observe but not close enough for them to see us. Well... in theory at least."

"In theory?" she says, her eyes wide.

"Well, everything is theory until you put it into practice," he says, releasing a laugh through his nose then looking at Isaac.

"Exactly," Isaac says in agreement and pointing a finger at him. "And later we will put it into practice and be the goddamn heroes in all this."

"Heroes, hmm?" Sarah says, putting her hands onto her hips and briefly turning away from him. "Heroes!" She glances back at him while raising her eyebrows and biting her bottom lip. "Are you sure the word you're looking for isn't martyrs, dear brother?"

Isaac screws up his face. "Don't be ridiculous, Sarah. I want to win this war, not die in it."

"Uh-huh!" she says, still unconvinced.

He frowns. "Besides, you won't be going with us – I don't want you getting into danger."

She scowls at him. "Are you deliberately, reverse psychology'ing me?"

"What? No. I'm just saying you can't come. I won't allow it."

"Oh... you won't allow it, huh? *You?* Like I'm your chattel?"

"Oh, for crying out loud!" he replies, throwing his arms into the air and flapping them down to his sides while turning away from her.

Pointing to a bench on the other side of the laboratory, Daniel moves toward it. "Errr... I'm... just gonna, go, ummm, fix this... yeah."

Isaac pays Daniel no heed, either by not hearing or not caring, the latter being the more likely of the two. Instead, he turns back to Sarah and stomps over to her. "No sister, I don't think that you're my property – you're my responsibility. There's a fucking difference."

"I ceased being your responsibility six months ago, *brother*. And don't you *dare* talk to me like that. You might get away with swearing at the guys, but not me mister man!"

Entering a full-blown and noisy argument, they continue to row with each other as Daniel unnecessarily moves equipment around the lab with a nervous and tuneless whistle.

FORTY-EIGHT

Dismounting from a Mazorakor, Lucifer lands on the ground smiling and with a slight spring in his step. He stretches while looking around then turns back to the gigantic beast and pats it. The Mazorakor responds by bowing its head and then bolts off. Lucifer looks at Samael, who is climbing off his mount.

"You know, you spend an eternity flitting in and out of portals, spiraling through down-gates, and end up missing the pleasant and lovely journeys that you wouldn't have otherwise had." He glances toward the direction his Mazorakor sped off in. "It has been a long time since I took a ride on one of those majestic beasts." He smiles. "I love this, y'know, all the little things."

"The little things?" Samael replies, somewhat sarcastically, and glancing back toward the others in the group. "No wonder you keep certain things around you!"

Lucifer laughs and wags a finger at him. "That's why I like you Sammy, you got the comedic fire in ya belly." He smiles and turns toward the entrance to the Circles of Hell.

Malphas eyes Samael with contempt, irritated at the quip and that the former Archangel seems to be the new favorite of the Lord of Hell. He brushes past him as the rest of the entourage dismount from their mounts and send them on their way. "My Lord, should we not just await Judas and the bitch here, defeat them and drag them to the Temple, then take what we need?"

Lucifer sighs and turns toward Malphas, who takes the tiniest of steps backward. "What have I just finished saying? Hmm?" He glances around at the congregating demons. "Anyone?"

"The details are in the journey," Samael responds from behind Malphas.

Malphas glances over his shoulder at him, not all the way, but enough for the action to be noticed.

"Exactly, Sammy, that's the correct answer – 10 points to Gryffindor. The details are in the journey. Let Charlotte and Judas come through here, let them experience what they will within the Circles. Let them free the whore. It matters not. The outcome will be the same, but they may just learn a thing or two on the way." He moves closer to Malphas and taps a finger on his forehead. "Head fucks, Malphy. Isn't that what we're all about? Head fucks! Seriously my old mate, I'm a little surprised and tired to be reminding you of these things lately. You used to be so reliable." He glances toward Samael, the action almost secretive but still noticeable by Malphas, which serves to further incense his burning hatred for him.

Samael moves to Lucifer's side. "You think they will actually go by the way of Mokwena?"

Lucifer glances at him, then turns back toward the entrance to the cave. "Yeah, course they will. Azazel will be calling the shots by now, whether they know it or not. He will want the pieces of himself back." He smiles at Samael. "I'm quite aware of what his game will be. But if I'm being honest, we need to ensure it doesn't come to fruition as I may need to take him up on any... offer he might wish to make." He enforces the word 'offer' with his fingers as quotation marks in the air.

To his side a figure appears, morphing into view from within a dark gray cloud, and dressed in darkly colored spiky battle armor, complemented by a swept-back horned helmet. His enormous and heavy footfalls crunch into the dirt and his armor clanks with each step.

"You need not worry about my brother, my Lord," Beelzebub says as he approaches Lucifer. "His incarceration has made him weak and his attempts will be futile. I will destroy him and your march on the humans and the White Kingdom will go undeterred."

Lucifer smiles. "He and Judas made short work of Barachiel and Leviathan, did you think about that?"

"It is of no consequence. My lesser brother was exactly that – not worthy to stand in battle against Azazel. Our fight will be glorious. His death even more so."

Lucifer laughs. "Well, cool ya heels there fella. I don't intend to waste you on that trash. No. War, Death, and the boys will take care of those two." His eyes narrow and a darkness floats across them. "Your destiny lies in me driving you into my father's cold black heart, and me looking him in the eyes, all the while grinning as his life force ebbs into you. Then we will plan what we have in store for the other realms." He looks at the entourage once again, his face playful and mischievous, and then winks. "It'll be fun."

Lucifer walks into the cave and his team follows him.

After a brief journey, they arrive at the edge of the Nine Circles and Lucifer holds up his hands, causing the Circles to slow their movement and then come to a complete stop. Then, they start up again, slowly at first then gathering more speed as they travel into alignment with one another, creating a flat disc with a complete and unbroken pathway to the center.

"How far behind us do you think they are?" Lord Astaroth asks, sidling up to Lucifer.

"An hour or so, tops," he replies, glancing upward. "And I think Father is also having fun. I sense the timelines connecting. It seems that all three kingdom's time frames are being brought together." His mouth twitches as he whispers to himself. "What are you up to, old man? What's your game?"

Samael moves to Lucifer's side once more and points ahead. "It's a long way."

Lucifer smiles. "Then it's a good job we don't get tired and can run fast."

Shadow-stepping away, the others follow him.

FORTY-NINE

"Sir," Jonesy says, jogging up to Nathan. "We've found Gary."

"Is he okay?" Nathan says, sensing concern in his tone.

Jonesy stares at him for a moment, wets his mouth, and then cocks a thumb to his rear. "He's, errr…"

"Where?" Nathan says.

"Motor pool, behind one of the vehicles."

Nathan pushes past Jonesy, who lowers his head with a sigh, then looks up and follows his superior officer.

Sprinting into the hangar, Nathan spies a crowd of people gathered around something or someone in the far corner and so he races toward it. Sliding to a halt, he moves through the crowd, who part to allow him access, and throwing his hands into the air and turning away from the sight, he offers a loud groan of despair. Turning back to Gary's outstretched corpse, he closes his eyes, then lowers his head and breathes out deeply. "How long?" he asks, looking back up, addressing the attending medic who is putting his instruments back into his satchel.

The medic stands and shakes his head. "I dunno, sir. Maybe 20 minutes, a half-hour tops."

"How?"

The young man opens his mouth and raises his eyebrows, and all he can do is shrug and shake his head.

Nathan looks at him. "So you're telling me that one of the smartest, courageous, and strongest willed men I have ever met simply walked over here and died? That it, soldier?"

"No sir, I am merely indicating that without a proper examination, which incidentally is something beyond my skill, I cannot tell you how he died. I'm sorry, sir." He looks around at the others and breathes out hard.

"FUUUUUUCK!" Nathan screams, so loud that it makes most people jump, then grabs a jerry can lying on the ground and launches it far across the hangar, causing everyone to take a few steps back and allow him some space as nobody wants to be on the receiving end of his ire.

Without warning, the hangar shakes, a solid and tangible thud, and Nathan glances at the vehicle that Gary's body had been lying behind, the squeal of its tires causing him to notice it has moved sideways a few feet, evident also by small black streaks of rubber.

"The fuck was that?" he says, glancing at Jonesy, who shakes his head and attempts to find the words to explain something he cannot.

It happens again, only with more force, and this time the sound of the vehicle moving is much more audible.

A notion hits Nathan, a suspicion he had earlier now awarded meaning within his mind, and his teeth grind together in anger. He sets off walking back the way he came. "What the fuck are those kids up to?" he says, then clicks his fingers. "Jonesy, on me."

Nathan sprints away and out of the hangar with Jonesy in tow.

"What the hell was that?" Isaac asks, frowning at Daniel.

"I don't know. It should've worked."

"Well, it didn't did it? Where's the fucking portal?"

311

"I don't know, it should've worked. I put the co-ordinates in, there was a significantly large energy source that it was keyed to – and by that I mean huge – but it disappeared and, well... nothing."

"Try again."

Daniel shrugs and shakes his head, struggling to find the words, his mouth opening and closing at the same time.

"I SAID, TRY AGAIN!"

"Isaac!" Sarah shouts at him, having seen Daniel jump at his outburst. "Enough of this."

He looks at her and then back at Daniel. "Try... it... again," he says, his words forceful.

Daniel puffs hard and then glances toward Sarah, whose eyes narrow at him, her face pleading for him not to. He lowers his head and pushes the button once more. Another powerful thud that again shakes the entire building, causing more equipment to topple off their surfaces and fall to the ground, some smashing.

"See. Nothing," Daniel says.

Isaac growls and begins pacing the room. He rakes his fingers through his hair and furiously rubs his head, his movements tracked by Daniel and Sarah who shift their gaze from him to each other, their eyes wide.

After a minute of uncomfortable silence and without warning, causing all three of them to snap their attention toward it, the machine fires into life with a loud squeal, emitting an energy pulse with a thud, and in the corner of the room a portal rips open with so much force it causes Sarah's hair to push backward as though blown by a sudden powerful gust of wind.

"Yes!" Isaac shouts and leaps into the air, punching it as he does. "You did it buddy, you fucking did it! Well done!"

"Look," Daniel says, grabbing both of their attention.

Sarah and Isaac turn toward him and follow his line of sight. A glass cylinder that had rolled off the desk, disturbed by the portal opening hovers in the air in suspended animation. They look around the room to see other items in a similar state.

"What the hell is this?" Isaac says, glancing around further.

"Holy shit!" Daniel says, his eyes wide, and edging toward the doorway.

Sarah and Isaac spin around to try to get a glimpse of what he is looking at, then move to their sides to get a better view, and, peering around and through the door, they see Nathan, his face contorted with anger, and closely behind him Jonesy, both frozen in time.

Sarah frowns, staring at them for a few moments, then looks down at herself. "Why are we not affected?" She looks back up and at Daniel. "Why are we okay?"

He shakes his head and again has no words to offer.

"Who cares?" Isaac says, "Let's have a look through this portal."

"I care!" Sarah says, grabbing his arm and pulling him back. "I care why. What if we have broken something fundamentally important in the universe? Did you stop to think about that? What if this is permanent? We need to figure this out and shut it down."

"She's right," Daniel says, moving to her side, "we have to figure it out." He looks down at the ground. "What did I do wrong?" He looks back and then walks over to the machine.

Isaac regards him for a moment, his lips tightened, and then moves toward the portal.

"Wait!" Daniel shouts, thrusting an arm at Isaac. "I didn't do this."

Isaac frowns. "Yeah you did. You flicked the machine on, and then... this happened." He motions toward the portal.

"No, I did turn on the machine, but as nothing happened the first time, it then went into reset, meaning I would have had to re-sequence it, which clearly I forgot to do because you was shouting at me." He looks back at them both. "The machine did this on its own."

Isaac scoffs at him and walks over to the portal.

Daniel gently places his hands on Sarah's shoulders. "I am telling you Sarah, I did not do this."

She nods. "I believe you, but we need to stop him and figure this out."

He nods back at her then looks up at Isaac who has now reached the swirling and crackling event on the other side of the room.

He looks back at them and smiles, then sticks his face through.

Immediately he withdraws his head, coughing and spluttering in severe distress, and then bends over, retching, saliva falling from his mouth in a thick rope, and he grips hold of his throat, his tongue poking out of his mouth as the violent action continues.

Racing to his side, Sarah and Daniel try to aid him, but he bats their hands away and stumbles around the room, his respiratory system working against him.

After a few moments, he manages to gather himself and the spasms and coughing ease and then cease altogether. He bends over, his hands on his knees and takes deep breaths, saliva continuing to drool from his mouth. Spitting a few times, he then stands up straight and wipes his mouth with the back of his hand.

Daniel moves to and in front of him, his arms out. "What the hell was that?"

Isaac winces as he rubs his throat, his breathing not quite back to normal. He swallows hard then points toward the portal. "The air. Unbreathable. Bad. Really, really bad," he says, his voice gruff and broken.

Daniels nods a few times. "Right. Well, that settles it then. We figure out how to shut that down and hopefully it will reverse the effect and we can all take a kicking from Colonel Taylor and that will be that." He breathes out deeply then looks up at Sarah. "Right?"

She nods, but then turns toward Isaac as he pushes past her. "Isaac, where are you going?"

He doesn't answer, instead he opens the door at the opposite end of the room to where Nathan and Jonesy remain frozen in space and time.

Daniel and Sarah exchange a look as they hear lockers being opened and rummaged through from within the corridor Isaac has stomped into. A clanking follows and then footsteps, and Isaac returns, finishing off putting firefighter breathing apparatus onto his back.

"There's more in lockers back there. The hangar firefighting team's stuff. Grab one each."

Daniel takes a deep breath and turns left and right on the spot. "Oh, you are out of your fucking mind." He runs his fingers through his hair and walks away, and then back again. "Have you considered why you cannot breathe the air in there?"

Isaac looks at him, his expression a clear indication that he has not.

Sarah nods, looks at Daniel and then back to her brother. "Isaac, where do demons come from?"

He stares at her for a second, then clips the waist belt of the apparatus together while shrugging the breathing gear on his back into a more comfortable position and pulling his shoulder straps tighter.

"Isaac," Daniel says forcefully, "are you listening to her?"

He says nothing and instead walks over to the portal, the breathing apparatus mask in his hand and then pulls at its rubber straps, readying to slip it over his head. He stops for a moment, contemplating while looking down, and then looks up at them again.

"So you coming or what?"

FIFTY

Lucifer halts his party at the head of a long stone bridge that crosses a vast lake of lava. At the end of it and in the distance stands the enormous Temple of Belial, a circular structure, much like the coliseums on Earth where gladiators would battle against one another to the death. He glances back at Samael, who offers him a thumbs-up, and then turns back to face his front with a grin.

"All right, Cthulhu," Lucifer shouts across the bridge, "let's get this over with."

Nothing happens.

He glances back toward the party, and then back to his front and his about to repeat the statement when the lava lake explodes and from out of it rises Cthulhu, a gigantic demon with a squid-like head and scaly body. Huge wings flap open from his back, and he throws his arms out to his sides, spraying lava in a wide arc, and then screeches into the air.

Lucifer turns back to the party. "Look, no one get him talking about Lovecraft, right! He will bore you to tears about how wrong the man

316

got it and we ain't got time for that shit, not today." He turns back to face the massive demon as it wades through the lava toward them.

A few of the lesser demons at the rear take one or two steps backward but then stop as Lord Astaroth's unimpressed gaze fixes upon them, and they edge back to their original positions.

"Human form, if you please Cthulhu," Lucifer shouts.

The demon pays him no heed.

"I said, human form if you… oh shit, he's pissed," Lucifer says, rolling out of the way as Cthulhu swings a massive clawed hand at him, and raking up huge mounds of dirt in the process.

"Fine!" Lucifer shouts, defiantly getting back to his feet. "Then so be it." He jerks his shoulders forward and demonic wings sprout from his back, then holds out his hand. "Makarus, to me."

The demon sword Beelzebub's dark fog explodes above Lucifer and he somersaults out of it, transforming into the sword Makarus, its conquered name, and into Lucifer's hand.

Lucifer's body covers itself in his bone-plated armor, and he roars, thrusting his wings downward and powering himself up into the air and into attack.

FIFTY-ONE

The sound of breathing apparatus cuts through the cold and misty air as Isaac steps through the portal and into Hell. He glances around and sees nothing so then sticks his head back through and beckons to Sarah and Daniel. Walking forward he takes in his surroundings and it isn't what he thought it would be like. Ahead lies a huge stone bridge that cuts through the middle of a frozen lake, and he looks up at the snow drifting down all around him. He stares at it, a deep frown upon his face then looks to the edge of the lake, where the frozen body of a gigantic, squid-like demon lies half-in and half-out of the ice, the top of its head cleaved open. He looks back toward Sarah and Daniel and shrugs.

"Is this Hell? It's... snowing?" she asks, looking around, the same notions of disbelief hitting her that had gripped Isaac a moment ago.

"I don't know," her brother replies, walking over to the corpse of the demon.

"Careful Isaac," she says, raising a hand to him.

"It's dead, Sarah, that much is certain," he says, approaching it.

"What happened here?" Daniel asks, siding up to Sarah.

"The Lord only knows," she says, walking toward Isaac who is poking his foot into the side of the enormous demon head. "What's that over there?" she says, pointing at a huge circular structure.

"It looks like the Colosseum," Daniel says, squinting a little as he joins them.

"Are we in Rome?" she asks.

"Absolutely not," Daniel replies. "This is no geography that I have ever encountered in my studies. Believe me, I would remember something like this."

"Then let's go see what's in there," Isaac says, walking ahead, not waiting for them to agree or disagree.

FIFTY-TWO

"How are you?" Charlotte asks Abi as they sit on the steps of the Well, waiting for Judas and Azazel to finish assessing the down-gate to ensure it is programmed to go to where they want it to take them.

Abi half-smiles and looks to her front. "Oh, y'know – tired, terrified, confused, all the usual stuff when we're together." She laughs.

Charlotte laughs with her and bumps her shoulder with her own. She looks down and then back up. "I missed you a lot you know."

Abi smiles again. "I missed you too. I think." She laughs.

"It was that bad, huh?"

"Yeah. It was *that* bad."

Charlotte purses her lips a little.

"I'm so sorry I got you captured," Abi says without looking at her.

"You have nothing to be sorry for. It wasn't your fault. Besides it all worked out in the end." She looks at Abi. "Well, kinda." She offers an apologetic smile.

Abi laughs. "I got what I deserved. People get sent here for a reason you know."

"No, that's not right. You allowed your beliefs to imprison you. You should never have come here. Judas said that if you would've had the chance for an interview, as he puts it, with Peter before your judgment he is certain that you would have been sent up and not down. It was Lucifer who unfairly claimed you, and for that he is gonna pay. And for so much more, believe me. The piece of shit." She looks forward again, a seriousness in her stare.

Abi regards her for a few moments and is about to say something when Judas and Azazel return.

"Okay," Judas says, "on your feet guys. The gate is taking us to the bridge just outside the Temple. But we might be walking into a trap. Azazel says it has already been used, obviously by Lucifer and his cronies."

"Obviously," Abi says, mimicking him and shrugging.

Judas wags a finger at her. "Genuinely, I've missed this. I really have."

He smiles and Abi grins back, then sticks out her tongue.

"One other thing," Azazel says, "we may have... someone else to deal with. Honestly, it could go either way."

"Cthulhu!" Charlotte says, standing up.

"Yeah," Azazel replies, frowning at her. "How'd you know that?"

"I dunno," she says, a look of discomfort on her face, "I just do." Suddenly, she feels very ill and grabs her stomach while doubling over and groaning.

Judas grabs her and eases her to the ground. "What's the matter, sweetie? Are you okay?"

She takes a moment and then gets back to her feet with a grunt. "I'm fine, I'm fine. I guess it is getting late and I need to get these things out of me."

Judas nods. "Yeah. It is getting kinda late. We're almost there, kiddo. You still got the fight in you?"

She snaps her attention to him and raises her eyebrows.

He smiles broadly and squeezes the top of her arm.

"Get what out of you?" Abi asks, stepping forward.

Charlotte smiles and shakes her head a little. "It's a long story, honey, and I will tell you but not now, we don't have time."

Abi glances to Azazel and then Judas and then back to Charlotte. "Kinda feeling a little left out here, but whatever."

Charlotte smiles. "I promise."

Abi looks at her for a few seconds, then nods.

"Okay team," Judas says, turning toward the gate. "Let's go end an Apocalypse."

The group makes their way to the down-gate and step through, a sucking noise following each of them as they enter. On the other side, the same sound marks their arrival and they are in an alcove of rock, with huge uneven walls stretching up each side, continuing forward for around 100 feet that then give way to a vast open space with a long stone bridge that crosses a huge lake of lava. On the other side, they see the Temple of Belial and at the head of the walkway stands a smartly dressed man in a blue and white pinstriped suit, a hand held up to them.

"Hello," he shouts, in a chirpy and aristocratic sounding British accent. "How are you? Please, come forward, let us discuss the terms of your surrender." His smiles is wide and toothy.

"Confident little prick, isn't he?" Charlotte says, glancing toward Judas, who smirks at her.

"Be careful," Azazel says, "Cthulhu is anything but little. I advise taking care of him quickly while he's in this form."

"Well then," Judas says, stepping forward, "let's get it over with."

The others follow as he walks toward Cthulhu who has, in turn, started toward them.

Cthulhu smiles once again. "Well, it's a pleasure to meet you all finally." He acknowledges the others behind Judas. "And Azazel, my word, how long has it been my old friend? Centuries? Millennia? And look at you, you haven't aged a day." He chuckles.

"He's anything if not smooth," Azazel says, winking at Charlotte.

"And of course you must be Charlotte." Cthulhu smiles once again. "My dear, what an honor this is. To finally capture The Light and present her to my lord, Lucifer."

Charlotte snorts and shuffles on the spot, unimpressed.

"Your lord?" Azazel says. "And here was me thinking you still wanted to depose him and take your rightful place at the head of the table," his tone darkens, "with a little piece of me fueling you." He glares at him.

Cthulhu smiles, a darkness to his gesture. "Well, let's just say we had a little chat earlier, and it was in our mutual interest to… work together." This time, his smile isn't so confident.

Azazel guffaws. "Roughly translated, he kicked your ass."

Cthulhu screws up his mouth. "Look—"

"No, you fucking look Cthulhu," Azazel barks, "give me my stone, allow these fine people past, and we won't destroy you. And by that I mean fucking end you… forever."

There is no craftiness to Azazel's tone, no sneering or sarcasm, this is Azazel as he really is. A demonic entity whose power is beyond measure and a creature who wants what is rightfully his back.

Cthulhu sneers. "Very well. So be it."

"STOP HIM!" Azazel roars.

But it is too late. Cthulhu is too fast. He rises into the air and moves backward over the lava before Charlotte or Judas have time to react.

Judas holds out his hand and Ikazuchi lands within it.

Charlotte throws her hands to her side and her swords fly into them.

Slamming a fist into his chest, a storm-like cloud erupts around Cthulhu, transforming him into his gigantic demonic self and the lava beneath him explodes and tsunamis outward, upon him landing in it. He roars while running a hand through the lava, and scooping it up he launches it at Judas and Abi.

Judas turns to and grabs hold of Abi, then shadow-steps away out of the path and splash zone of the molten liquid.

"I just need her!" Cthulhu roars, pointing at Charlotte, who has rolled out of the way of the lava and is back on her feet. He strides forward and drives a huge fist down at her.

Judas drops Abi onto the ground and turns back toward them. "CHARLEY!" he screams, getting ready to shadow-step toward her.

Cthulhu's massive arm whistles through the air, rocketing its way toward her, then crunches to a stop, and he grunts in disbelief as the tiny woman halts it with a single horizontal-held sword. He stares into her one visible eye, the rest of her face covered by matted hair that worked itself loose in her evasive maneuver.

Judas takes a few steps forward and, open-mouthed, admires how she holds one of the largest demons he has ever seen at bay with one hand. And then grins.

With almost no effort, she pushes back into Cthulhu's fist, launching him away and onto his back, the lava parting in waves as he slides through it. She spins her swords in her hands and adopts her defensive stance, awaiting his inevitable retaliatory attack.

"Shall we do something, Judas?" Ikazuchi's voice says from within the sword.

"Why?" He says, grinning.

Cthulhu pounds his arms into the lake, splashing lava everywhere as he attempts to right himself back onto his feet. After a few seconds, he succeeds and roars as he charges at her once again, and lava erupts under each of his gigantic footfalls. Within seconds, he is launching himself at her.

Charlotte leaps into the air, avoiding his overreaching fist and then shadow-steps toward his head, punching into the side of it and knocking him down again, where he crashes into the ground on the other side of the lake and skids across it, causing the area to shake and shudder. Landing on top of him, she throws in repeated punches, each strike rocking his head backward and opening wounds, causing black blood to spurt out. She leaps into the air once more and then powers down, driving a knee into his face, and bone crunches.

Within a matter of seconds, Charlotte has incapacitated one of the most powerful demonic entities that have ever existed.

"Holy fucking shit," Ikazuchi says.

"You got that right," Judas replies.

Charlotte stabs a sword into Cthulhu, who screams in response, then looks toward Judas and holds out a hand.

Ikazuchi flies out of his and toward her, causing Judas to look at his hand and then her. "How did you do that?" he says to himself.

Abi can do little more than look on, blinking and open-mouthed at everything playing out in front of her. She looks around and realizes there is no one there to talk to and discuss the incredible things she is seeing, and so she turns back to the scene, her mouth downturned.

Charlotte tosses Ikazuchi in front of her and onto Cthulhu's head where he transforms back into Azazel. "You. Find what you need. I'm allowing you another piece only to help my dad defeat Lucifer, but take a look at this one beneath me, take a good long look. Do not cross me, demon."

Azazel does, glancing at Cthulhu, immobilized with such little effort by her, then back to her, nodding slightly. He smiles, looking down at the defeated demon-lord. "You punched into your chest," he says to Cthulhu, "so I assume that's where it is." He walks over to Cthulhu's face and looks down at his chest. He runs a hand over a large area. "Yes. Here. It's here." He signals toward his master. "Judas. Would you be so kind as to come and take this for me?" He grins.

"Wait, WAIT! I am supposed to give you a message," Cthulhu says, turning to Charlotte.

She sneers at him. "Message? What message?"

Judas' face grows stern, and he trots over to them.

"An important message. One that will reveal your true identity."

Judas shifts into a run, and then into shadow-step. "IKA!" he shouts, leaping into the air, calling Azazel back into sword form.

Cthulhu bellows a laugh. "Your father Lucifer is looking forward to seeing you again in the Temple of Belial."

Cthulhu's raucous laughter is cut short as Judas grips Ikazuchi mid-air, and cleaves the top of his skull open.

Charlotte takes a step back, open-mouthed, shock taking effect, her eyes wide, her breathing shallow. She offers a sharp and heavy breath as she looks at Judas. "What is he talking about? What did he just say?"

Judas drops the sword that returns back to Azazel with a roll across the ground, and he rushes to her, his hands held out in front of him.

"Sweetie… sweetie, look at me, listen to me, just listen to me."

She leaps down from the dead demon's face and staggers toward him, her gaze fixed on the ground. "Wha-what did he just say?"

"Charley! CHARLEY! Look at me, look at me."

Tears form in Judas' eyes and roll down his face, and that action alone is enough for Charlotte. She looks up at him.

"You knew?" she says, her mouth remaining open and her eyes narrowing, a shadow casting over them. Her brow furrows and she looks down again. "It's true, and you knew it. You knew and you didn't tell me." She looks up at him as he tries to get her to listen to him. "You knew. How long have you known?"

"I didn't, I… I… I didn't, it was when we killed Barachiel, I got all this information, and… I didn't know – I didn't know." The tears come faster now.

She takes a step back from him. "You lied to me."

He shakes his head. "No! Never!"

"You lied to me."

"I didn't lie… I kept it from you… to protect you."

"It's the same thing. It's the exact same thing. How could you not tell me this?" She begins to cry. "You of all people. You kept this from *me!*"

Judas grows angrier although still he's visibly upset. "How could I tell you such a thing, huh? How? What would I say?" He holds his hands up to place them at the side of her face, but she steps away from him, an action that wounds him. He offers a deep sigh and then shakes his head. "But it doesn't matter—"

"IT DOESN'T MATTER?" she screams. "It doesn't matter that I find out I'm not the daughter of God, but the daughter of Satan? And you say it doesn't fuckin' matter?"

Tears flow down her face at a greater rate and she drops her swords and turns in circles, unsure of what to do or where to go. Once again, Judas tries to put a hand on her to calm her, but she bats it away.

"Don't touch me. Do not fucking touch me!" she sobs. "Why did you not tell me?"

"Because it does not matter what you were meant for, it only matters what you have become, who you decided to be. That is all that matters. You are still the instrument of God and no amount of extra information will change that." His eyes plead with her to listen, to understand.

She sniffs and wipes her eyes with the back of her hand, then holds both out and calls her swords into them, sheathing them upon her back. Anger blazes in her eyes.

"You're a fucking asshole!" she says, walking away from Judas without looking at him.

They have argued before, raged and screamed at one another, but what she just said in the context of the moment hurts him, cuts him deep and he can do nothing but stare into space, his lips trembling.

Abi hurries over to Charlotte. "Sweetie. Sweetie, are you okay?"

"I'm fine," she says, continuing to walk away. "Let's just end this then be done with it all."

"CHARLOTTE HOPE!" Judas shouts at her with conviction, causing her to stop in her tracks although she doesn't turn to face him. "You're right. I should have told you. I should have told you that your mother once made a mistake by getting in with the wrong people, and that your purpose had been to be the instrument of evil, not good. I should have. But I didn't because that's what fathers do. They protect their children until it's the right time to tell them what they need to know. I would have told you eventually, when you could process the information, but that time and that place was not here." He stares at her for a moment, struggling to find the words, then looks up, pursing his lips. Then he looks down and back at her. "Everything that has happened, everything we have ever been through, it has all been for you. Everything I have ever done has been for you, for your own good. You changed me, changed me into the man, the being that I am today, and no agent of evil could have accomplished that." He pauses for a moment, his shoulders heaving from anxious breathing. "That is what fathers do. They protect their children. This has never been about me. This has always been about you."

Her head moves to the side in his direction, just a fraction. "But you're not my father, are you! He's in there. And I'm gonna fucking kill him."

Judas moves toward her. "Charley. CHARLEY, WAIT!"

But she isn't listening, she has already shadow-stepped ahead with furious speed and intent.

FIFTY-THREE

"I wonder what happened here?" Sarah says, her voice muted from having the breathing mask on. She wraps her arms around herself and rubs them, the cold becoming too much. "Look, I don't want to be here anymore. Can we go please Isaac?" she says as her, Isaac, and Daniel draw close to the end of the bridge. "Isaac!" she repeats with more force.

"What?" he says, snapping at her and turning around.

"I don't want to be here anymore! I'm scared. Neither of us can hide from the demons anymore and Daniel never could anyway. What if they swarm over the bridge behind us, huh?"

Daniel looks back and then slowly returns his gaze to her. "Yeah, I'm like, with her on this one. I am freakin' the fuck out right now."

Isaac stares at them for a moment and then sighs. "Look, I can't explain it, I just know we have to go on, we have to go inside that place over there." He motions to the structure that is now within a few hundred yards. "There is something important in there. Something is telling me that there is something important in there and we must go on."

Sarah glances at Daniel who draws in a deep breath and shrugs.

"Come on," Isaac says. "Whatever has happened here has happened and it's moved on. Look." He points to a set of enormous black gates, one of which is broken, dangling on its side, resting against the outer wall of the structure as though something had punched through it. "Nothing seems to be alive around here. It's cold. Cold, frozen, and dead. Let's just take a peek inside and then be on our way if there's nothing in there."

"That's what I'm hoping for," Daniel says, glancing around and shivering, "nothing in there."

Isaac smiles a little.

"One thing to consider," Daniel says, halting Isaac as he steps away, "is that this breathing apparatus has a normal working time of around 50 minutes. However, I've been hyperventilating for about 10 of those, so that time could easily be down to 30 minutes. So let's not dick around in here, yeah?"

Isaac nods. That piece of information he does understand to be important. "I hear ya Daniel. I hear ya." He looks at Sarah. "You okay?"

She looks at him in surprise. "No! But I'm with you. Always."

He smiles and she smiles back at him. He holds out his hand to her and she takes it, then walks toward the gates, guiding her over the rubble littered around the area. Once or twice she loses her footing and he is forced to steady her and be certain she is surefooted again before moving on, while Daniel sarcastically complains to them to 'not worry about him, he is just fine.'

As they pass through the ruined gates, a brilliant white light illuminates the other side of the area, revealing it to be a frozen warzone with statues and structures that are obliterated and lying in pieces everywhere. The walls of the huge amphitheater also look as though huge objects have smashed into them, with varying sizes of craters dotted around the perimeter.

"What the hell?" Daniel says with a frown and stumbling over more rubble, his concentration fixed ahead of him. "What is that over there in that light? Are those... people?"

FIFTY-FOUR

"What about me?" Abi screams as Judas prepares to shadow-step after Charlotte, his hand held out toward Azazel.

He looks back at her. "You'll be fine. Just… just wait here while we end this."

Her mouth opens wide and she flaps her hands in the air while turning away.

"Judas," Azazel says, "I need that stone. I really need it and you should want me to have it."

"Fine," he says, leaping onto Cthulhu's corpse and moving quickly to the area that Azazel had indicated to a few moments earlier, and punches into the demon's chest with a grunt, reaching in deep and retrieving the blood-red stone. "Got it," he says, presenting it to Azazel.

"Good," he replies, gesturing to his own chest.

Judas shakes his head. "There's no time for you to be incapacitated, we need to go."

Azazel is in the process of telling him to wait when the call-to-sword prevents him, and he flips into Judas' hand.

He looks toward the sound of something large breaking, and he sees Charlotte smash through the huge gates that form the entrance to the temple. Gritting his teeth, he shadow-steps to her with furious intent.

Punching through the gate, smashing them to the sides, Charlotte comes to a sliding halt within the temple grounds, taking in her surroundings.

She is within an ancient and peaceful-looking area with statues and monuments dotted all around amid greenery and beautiful flowers. In the center sits a fountain with water trickling from it and the place looks more like a serene garden than the temple of evil she had imagined it to be.

Behind her, Judas slides to a halt also and she glances over her shoulder without looking at him. She says nothing.

"No matter what your beef is with me right now Charley, we need to stick together, okay?"

She nods and turns her attention to the mass of demons on the far side of the area.

Lucifer claps his hands and looks around at his subordinates. "Well, it seems that today was simply horrible for Cthulhu. One of those 'I wish I had stayed in bed' kinda days." He laughs, and the others all join in except The Horsemen, Samael, and Malphas who edge themselves into position at his sides. "I take it from the looks on both your faces that Cthulhu spilled the beans as well as his brains?" He laughs again and once more his sycophantic cohorts join in.

Charlotte ambles toward Lucifer and his group, and Judas follows her.

This causes War to unsheathe his massive battle sword and Death to drop his hands to his sides where his scythes then slide into view.

Lucifer holds up a hand. "Fellas, fellas." He offers a mocking, shivering gesture. "So intense! Let's take a moment before we engage in needless bloodshed, shall we? This place is too beautiful for such ugly violence." He smiles again.

Judas comes to a halt behind Charlotte. "Ugly violence?" he says, his attention flitting between the numerous groups of demons who have started to surround them. "That's an interesting turn of phrase.

Especially since that is the only reason you have gotten us down here in the first place."

Lucifer opens his mouth wide, and glances around while placing a hand to his chest. "Me? I got you down here? You think I did that?" He laughs. "Oh no, no, no, dear Iscariot, that wasn't my doing, although I will agree that it was my desired outcome. No, that honor lies with your trusty friend there. The one in your hand." He smiles. "Come now, let us all be who we really are. Let him have form so that he may speak and then I might reveal a thing or two." He grins again.

Judas snarls and his nostrils flare as he takes an angry breath. "Fine!" he says, through gritted teeth and tosses Ikazuchi forward, allowing Azazel to transform himself.

"Ahhhh, Lucifer. Nice to see you again," Azazel says while adjusting his clothing and taking a few steps forward.

"Azazel," Lucifer says, with a slight nod and a dry smile.

"And look who we have here," the demon sword says, glancing around, "a veritable who's-who of Hell's finest." He smiles. "Here's Lord Astaroth," he winks and points to him, "always nice to see the man who sent in his sneaky fucks to spy on me." He looks to Lucifer's right. "Oh, and Malphas, the errr..." he screws up his mouth and frowns, while wagging his finger, trying to find the right words to describe him, "...prick," he concludes simply, settling on the only word that he thinks suits. "And let's not forget Sama—"

"Oh, will you please shut up!" Charlotte shouts, her patience having worn thin. She pushes past him, taking a few steps toward the group of demons around 50 feet away, an action that causes Azazel to screw his face up in annoyance. She points a sword at Lucifer. "Give me the other Seals, send your lackeys home, and be done with this pointless crusade of yours and I won't fuck you up."

Lucifer looks around at his forces, his eyes wide, the action taking several seconds, and then he bursts into uproarious laughter, again accompanied by the lesser demons. He turns back to face her. "You... you promise you won't 'fuck me up'? Oh well, with such an offer how can one refuse?" He laughs again. "But you do realize, as I was about to say, that you can have those things inside you removed at any time? You do know that, right?"

She looks at Judas, who looks at her with the same amount of confusion she is offering him, and he shrugs.

Lucifer laughs once more. "Oh my word, this is perfect." He claps his hands and turns away, then back to them. "The Book and Seventh Seal that reside within your body were put there by none other than your Mr. Azazel. No one else. No cosmic force, no divine intervention. Only by the demon sword of fucking mischief himself." He laughs again, his enjoyment and delight evident while delivering his revelations.

Charlotte's face reddens, and she breathes in deep, her lips tightening.

"You've been conned, my dear. Both of you. You have never been in control! This has all been an elaborate scheme by Azazel to get himself back down here and claim what he thinks is rightfully his. He has conned us all, the clever bastard. Even I thought everything relied upon us being under the sign of Belial, until the witches put me straight before I came here."

Judas steps forward. "This is old information. This I know. He told me."

Charlotte slowly turns her gaze on him. "More secrets dad?"

"Oh, did he now?" Lucifer says, "and I suppose he also told you that he was the one who set Barachiel on his path, hmmm? Working his little mystical magic from within the Nether, once he had gained enough power to influence the outside world. Right?"

This bit of information Judas doesn't know. "Bullshit!" he says, screwing up his face.

"Oh no it isn't. He used my new friend Samael here to weave his influence with Barachiel, and then in turn you."

Samael says nothing, but the look on his face suggests that this information is new even to him.

Lucifer continues. "Hey, don't get me wrong, I have been plotting ever since your little bitch laid her hands on me, then drained and deported me back here." His overconfident attitude wanes for a moment. "I definitely owe you one for that, girlie."

She sneers at him. "It was my pleasure. But if you like that, best get ready for what's coming next."

Lucifer grins. "Oh, I am my dear." His gaze lingers on her for a moment and then he returns it to Judas. "You see, Judas, it's amazing what knowledge you gain when you have Lord Astaroth's spies follow people everywhere." He glances to Astaroth and nods, who returns the gesture. "And so now you know. Your sword, your minion – your so-called *friend* has been using you all along. In fact not only you, but many, many other folks. And his final act, so he could move his pieces on the board to where he wanted them, was to place The Book and Seventh Seal within her the very moment she opened the Ark. And as such he guaranteed that you would have to come down here looking for me, with the false understanding that this place is the only location where I can interact with the relics." He mocks Charlotte's voice. "I am the relic and there is only one place I can go now to stop what is happening." Lucifer laughs hard once again. "Oh man, those witches. When they get it right, they get it so right!" He lets out a small laugh this time. "You're only here, my dear, so that he could get to Cthulhu, whose realm lies outside the temple." He points to Azazel, who is looking down at the ground to hide his smirk.

Charlotte turns her head to the side a little and looks down while screwing up her lips and cursing under her breath.

"Oh man, that is priceless," Lucifer says through his laughter, "the looks on your faces as this all starts to make sense." He glances around at his demons again. "Didn't I say this would be worth it? Eh? Didn't I promise you that it would be a hoot, telling them everything!" He nods at them all. "It's *awe*some, isn't it?"

A few of the demons laugh.

"Listen, fuck-face," Charlotte says, "I don't give a rat's ass as to what or why things happened the way they have. My only concern now is with removing your stupid fucking head and mounting it on one of these statues here. That's all that matters to me."

"Really?" Lucifer says, his face awash with intrigue. "Well, I'm guessing that's another part of the story you don't know. Honestly, I thought you would have had more knowledge by now, but it seems you only know what Azazel wanted you to know."

She looks back at the demon sword, anger etched into her face, her head shaking, but he avoids her intense stare.

Lucifer walks over to the fountain, admiring it. He takes a deep breath. "This is where we would often sit, you know, father and I," he returns his gaze to Charlotte, "you know, after the…" he dives his hand downward through the air with a whistle, then smiles. "He just couldn't stay away. Kept saying that, even though I had done bad things he still loves each and every one of his children. And so he had Azazel build this place, a haven outside the laws of Hell and where he could come and visit me. Poetic, really, that it will play a part in his demise." He smiles. "Maybe you and I will come here someday, as father and daughter, y'know, when I allow you a break from eternal torture every now and then, just to get nostalgic about the good old days."

She snarls and starts toward him.

Judas catches her by the arm. "Stop. Just… stop."

"Let go of me," she says, struggling against his grip.

"Charley, just listen to me."

"Yeah Charley, listen to daddy Judas," Lucifer says with a laugh.

"You cannot kill him," Judas tells her.

"What?" she says, her face screwed up, her eyebrows furrowed together. "Just fucking watch me."

"No. I know you probably could, but you cannot. If you do, then the balance will need to be maintained, and whoever kills him will become the next Lucifer. The balance, Charley – the balance must be maintained."

"Horseshit!" she says, her face even more steeped in aggression.

"Oh no," Lucifer says, rubbing his hands together, "it's true. For once, the betrayer doesn't lie. I mean, he's lied to you for a while now about your origins et cetera, and let's not forget his lack of detailing that you are in fact my daughter. But – and it's a big but – he's not lying about this. You cannot kill me." He grins.

She shakes Judas' hand free, gritting her teeth at him. "So what do you suggest then?"

"Nothing," Lucifer says, laughing, "because there is nothing you can do." He offers a weary sigh and glances to his minions. "Fellas, get me my Book and Seal please."

Judas holds out his hand. "IKA!"

"Why has he not called forth Beelzebub?" Azazel says as he somersaults backward into weapon form and lands in Judas' hand.

"Because he's not a fucking idiot and won't risk him," Judas says in response.

The lesser demons scream and shriek as they race forward into attack.

Raising Ikazuchi into the air, Judas plunges it into the ground and detonates it, launching each demon up into the air and causing Lucifer and the other higher demons to shadow-step away. As soon as each creature is airborne, Charlotte shadow-steps between them all and slices them to pieces – heads, arms, legs all clinically removed. Nothing is safe from her swift and devastating attacks.

Skidding to a halt a short distance away from Judas who now moves against another group of demons, she senses an incoming attack and raises her swords to block it. War's mighty battle sword smashes against hers, crossed above her head, quivering against the might of the Horseman's power.

He pushes down further against her, causing her feet to scrape along the ground. "This is nothing personal, my child," he says, his red eyes burning into her, "this is... the calling."

"Good," she says, between grunts, "then you won't mind me taking your fucking head." Summoning her Dark-Divinity she pushes against him, exploding him backward and skidding him through the dirt.

From his position on the other side of the temple, Lucifer takes a few steps back, admiring the fight. "A Horseman's power resides within her. Unexpected," he says, his hand twitching, considering whether to call upon Beelzebub and engage him in the fight. With a low growl he decides against it, indicating with his fingers for Malphas, Astaroth, and the others to move in.

Samael starts forward, but Lucifer halts him.

"Not you, Sammy. You hang back with me."

Decapitating three demons at once, Judas then turns to a fourth, slicing through its arm and sending it splashing to the ground in a huge puddle of black blood. It screams at him and he punches into its face, exploding its head into a smear of gore. His face contorts with anger as he turns to see Malphas and the other Demon Lords bearing down on Charlotte, the closest of which is Astaroth, whose silver metal armor clanks into place upon his body and he swings an enormous sword at Charlotte. With a grunt, Judas shadow-steps toward her.

Metal clashes against metal as Judas arrives behind Charlotte just in time to block Astaroth's attack, him having snuck up on her. Then, using the hilt of the sword, he jabs it into Astaroth's face before he can react, sending him sprawling backward across the battlefield. Following up, Judas reaches him and rains in a series of strikes, each of which are avoided by the Demon Lord.

Malphas is the next to attack Charlotte, swinging his staff at her.

She blocks and pushes against it, then swings both her swords down from overhead with a twirl, splitting the staff clean in half.

He looks at her in astonishment and then attempts to attack her with both halves gripped in each hand.

Meeting each strike with ease, she counters and slices at him.

Although Malphas is quick, he is not quick enough, and the strike slices across his chest. He screams and takes a step back, seeing that she is preparing to move in to finish him off, and so he looks toward Lucifer and then back to the battleground, considering running for it. Preventing him from performing his cowardly action, Charlotte shadow-steps and punches him square in the chest, launching him across the arena and into a wall that splinters and crumbles around him.

With Malphas dealt with, she then turns her attention back to War, who has regained his composure and is now stampeding toward her.

She sprints at him, sliding onto her back and slices at his legs just before they meet. He anticipates the move and leaps into the air and over the blades, landing surefooted, then turns back to face her with surprising speed and agility despite his enormity.

Completing the slide and back on her feet, she spins around to meet his powerful swing that connects with her swords, and grunts as he breaks her guard, her arms thrown outward. Realizing he has exposed her to a follow-up attack, she activates her Divinity shield, and with not a moment to spare War's sword crashes into it, causing the shield to crack and splinter.

Thankfully, this has provided her sufficient time to recover, and she spins to her right, plants her swords into the ground, deactivates her shield, and kicks out at War, a burst of Dark-Divinity exuding from her foot, one that explodes energy in all directions as it connects with him. It sends him flying toward the outer wall of the Temple where he smashes into it, cratering within the structure in the same way Malphas had. However, unlike the hapless General who is now nowhere to be seen, War erupts back out, spraying rubble everywhere and charges at her once again.

Judas drops to one knee as Astaroth over-reaches his swing, and Ikazuchi slices through the Demon Lord's leg, severing it just above the knee. Wasting none of his advantage against the screaming Astaroth who is falling backward, Judas drives forward and slams his sword into the helmeted face of the Demon Lord and screams, as fearsome energy travels up the blade and into him, Ikazuchi now absorbing every ounce of Astaroth's being. Feeling the massive swell of power course through him, he knows that he has no time to dwell or catch his breath following these events. He must get used to defeating demons in this way, and get back into the fight even as he absorbs their energy, which is why he cries out aloud with fury and raises Ikazuchi, still vibrating from Astaroth, and slams it straight into the heart of Lord Oriens who had believed he had the drop on an incapacitated Judas. He did not. And now Judas must contend with even more, as Oriens' dark essence transfers from Ikazuchi's violent vibrations and into him. He grits his teeth, throwing all his concentration into containing the power. Then, from within his mind, Lady Famine speaks with a soft chuckle.

My dear, why not allow me to aid you in this little skirmish? This is exactly what I was meant for and now that I do not feel the pull of the calling, I am free to help you to lay waste to your enemies. She chuckles again.

"No," Judas grunts, through gritted teeth, his speech croaky. "I don't need you."

Are you sure, Iscariot? I have only the best inside information on my brothers, you know.

He grunts even further as he continues to wrestle with the enormity of the energy coursing through him. "Leave me be, witch. I can take care of this on my own. Ika and I can do this."

Judas stumbles forward, breathing heavily, and then shuffles to regain his footing as the absorption process ceases and an understanding hits him – Ikazuchi has been choosing which souls to absorb and which to leave, him having had no interest in the lesser demons, but he doesn't know how much more of absorbing higher beings he can take without it leaving him vulnerable. And he dreads the thought of dispatching a Horseman. Unfortunately for him, the decision is taken out of his hands as Death drops down into attack from a portal above his head, forcing Judas to evade by rolling out of the way, the Horseman's scythes narrowly missing him and embedding themselves into the ground.

Death is agile and nimble, and he handsprings forward, chasing down Judas as he rolls away from him.

Wind-milling on his back on the ground, Judas kicks out catching Death off-guard, and although he causes the Horseman no damage his action allows him time to spin onto his knees and get to his feet. The very moment he does, Death is back on the offensive, his attacks fast and powerful, swinging and spinning his scythes until their movements are a blur.

Judas moves and blocks, repeating the process, trying to create an advantage so he can move in for an attack of his own. But Death is too fast and relentless and therefore realizes he must force an opening, even at the risk of exposing himself to injury. He is about to shadow-step and shoulder charge into Death when Lady Famine speaks again.

My brother is fast, too fast for you Iscariot, so you must be smart. Something I think you once said to you darling little girl. She chuckles languidly. *My, my, she is a vicious little fighter isn't she? I think she is giving my brother War a hard time.*

"I said shut up."

He charges into Death with shadow-step, certain he will connect, and braces himself to do so when Death suddenly disappears and reappears further away, his version of the speed movement allowing him to move in between realities, and, having been baited into attack, Judas misses him and smashes into the outer wall, screaming his annoyance as he does.

Lady Famine bursts into laughter within his mind. *Oh my. Priceless, utterly priceless! I told you Iscariot, you must be wily if you are to cheat Death.*

"And I told you, witch, be silent," he says, pulling himself out of the ruined wall.

Ahead, Death crouches into a defensive posture, his head cocked to one side, his scythes held under his forearms and sweeping upward toward his back. His expressionless face is unnerving, even to Judas who takes a deep breath and holds a sword out to him.

Charlotte launches both of her blades and they spin through the air in a wide arc, perpendicular to and moving toward each other. As they travel, they decapitate dozens of enemies, including some of the lesser Lords, thus trimming the battlefield to a mere handful, leaving only them, herself, Judas, and the Horsemen, with Lucifer and Samael looking on from further afield. "Coward," she says staring at Lucifer who harbors an unconvincing grin upon his face as her swords land back in her outstretched hands. She takes a moment to glare at Hell's ruler, having yet again deflected one of War's attacks and sent him crashing to the ground a moment earlier. Now, however, the Horseman is back on his feet and racing toward her.

Calm your mind, Charlotte, Pestilence's voice says. *My brother is awash with rage and that is to your advantage. Calm your mind and free him from the calling so he might return home to the Alfather.*

She does as he instructs, bringing her erratic breathing under control and focusing her attention upon War as he thunders toward her.

The Horseman swings at her, wide and sweeping, and she blocks, then steps inside the attack and head-butts him. It hurt her clearly more than it did him, and she staggers.

Well. That was unwise, Pestilence says.

Yeah, thank you, I got the memo, she replies in her mind, holding her hand against her forehead.

War attacks once again, forcing her to regain her composure and block. However, she wasn't ready, and the brute force of his side swing sends her sprawling to her side, where she skids across the ground and crunches into the base of a statue.

Lucifer draws air into his mouth through puckered lips, then points at her and turns toward Samael. "Now that looked like it hurt," he says, to which Samael nods with a smile.

Charlotte cries out from the intense pain, having not had time to engage her Divinity shield and as such her back took the full brunt of the impact. It is broken in many places and the pain is electrifying.

Heal yourself, Charlotte. Do it now. Do it quickly.

She screams again as she tries to twist her body, then eases herself back. "How?" she says, tears streaming down her face. "I... I don't—"

You do. Like the time you healed Judas at Stonehenge. Only this time, channel the energy inward.

Struggling with her breathing, she attempts to shut the pain out of her mind and focus as much Divinity as she can into the wounds at her back. She pours all she can into her concentration, and although painful, to her great relief her back starts to crack and knit itself back together. She puffs and pants as the process nears completion but is still yet unable to raise her sword due to the necessary back muscles having not yet repaired.

War stomps toward her, sensing she is there for the taking and raises his sword. He is ready to bring it crashing down upon her.

At last, and through more tears and grunts the final strands of muscle and sinew weave back together and she regains mobility. Taking advantage of War's exposed midriff, she powers herself up with shadow-step and slices him open, cutting deep and sending him crashing to the ground. Skidding to a halt on the opposite side of his body, she regains her composure and moves back toward him with haste.

War is on bended knee, holding his stomach. He attempts to get back to his feet, but Charlotte is too fast and shadow-steps a knee into the side of his head, careering him across the ground and into a statue, where he comes to a halt. She is upon him in an instant and raises her swords into the air.

"Nothing personal," she says.

Judas and Death trade blows, with Judas once again on the defensive. He shadow-steps to one side and Death follows. He does it again with the same outcome and each time Judas thinks he has the upper hand, Death is there to meet him, and the fight is growing tiresome as he has never engaged an enemy so frustrating.

Remember, my dear friend, sometimes you have to sacrifice a pawn to get into the position you want. Don't be afraid to sustain a little damage to get that which you desire. Lady Famine chuckles once more.

"All right," Judas says, breathing heavy, "perhaps I will listen to you. Guess it is time to cheat Death a little." He blurs backward and away from The Horseman and adopts a similar stance to the one he had when he first shoulder charged him, and then rockets forward. As predicted, Death waits until the last second and then blurs away from him, but this time Judas anticipates the change and skews his path to the left, chasing down Death. As the Horseman skids to a halt, Judas shadow-steps and slices at him.

"NOOOOO," Ikazuchi screams as the weapon connects with nothing but thin air, Death's form evaporating into a wisp. "DECOY."

Judas' mind races and a fierce panic sets in. It erupts and gnaws away at the pit of his stomach, and he looks up toward Charlotte who stands over War, her swords raised. "CHARLEY!" he screams, as Lucifer's maddening demonic laughter drifts across the battlefield.

"Nothing personal," War repeats, as he looks up at her, his brother Death in midair leap behind her, his hands outstretched.

Charlotte feels something land on her back and plant firm hands on the sides of her temples, and she gasps.

A single thought enters her mind before everything fades into nothingness. An image of her, as a child, looking up into Judas' eyes and saying, "Then I will become strong, and look after you."

Oh dear, Pestilence says within her mind as blackness engulfs him.

Judas screams harder than he ever has before as Death tosses Charlotte's body to the ground and walks away holding The Book and Seventh Seal.

War gets to his feet and follows his brother, having received the call from Lucifer to return.

Ignoring his enemies, and skidding to a halt at her corpse, Judas discards Ikazuchi and scoops Charlotte into his arms. "No, no, no, no, no. Wake up baby girl, wake up. Come back to me. Come back, do you hear me? Come back." He strokes her hair furiously and shakes her. "You're not gone, stay with me, you're not gone, you're not gone." Tears stream down his face, and his head snaps upward. "GABRIEL!" he screams. "GABRIEL, HEAR ME!" He rocks back and forth, continuing to stroke Charlotte's hair to try to will life back into her body.

Samael turns toward Lucifer. "Shall I end him?"

Lucifer laughs. "What, are you kidding? This is a most satisfactory conclusion to today's events. Look at him. I couldn't have broken him more if I had done so myself. No, this is perfect, too perfect in fact. Leave him to weep and scream and call to those who cannot hear or help him."

"And if he comes back?"

"Then it will be too late, and you can do whatever you wish to him. Besides, without her fueling his spirit he will be nothing."

"Or he will become something with nothing to lose." Samael glances at Lucifer once again.

Lucifer says nothing, instead walks away, and raises his hand, creating a portal. "Ah, now that I control The Book as well as The Seals it would seem everything is as it should be." He laughs and glances upward. "How convenient" he says, then steps through, followed by Samael and the Horsemen.

War takes one look back at Charlotte and Judas, then lowers his head, sighs, and steps through.

"Oh my God, oh my God, oh God, no!" Abi cries, gingerly stepping over rubble at the broken gates. She places her hands over her mouth and bursts into tears. "This isn't possible, this cannot be."

Having assumed his human form, Azazel lowers his head. Even he finds the scene discomforting. He walks away and sits down upon the shattered remains of a broken statue.

Judas continues to rock back and forth with Charlotte in his arms. His eyes burn, bloodshot and red, and his face is dirty and streaky from the tracks of his tears. He places his face against her hair and squeezes her tight. And he cries again.

After what seems like the longest time staring at them, Abi gets to her feet, having slid her back down against the outer wall, lost within her own grief and mourning. She wipes her face and ambles over to them. Speaking softly, she reaches out and lays a gentle hand on Judas' shoulder.

"Hey. I'm so sorry. I'm so, so sorry. But this isn't over yet."

"It is for me. I'm done."

Abi fights back further tears, her lips scrunching together. "But so many more are relying upon you. Everyone will die."

"Then everyone dies." He buries his face into her hair and closes his eyes.

Abi wipes the tears away with the back of her hand. "You don't mean that."

"WHY NOT!" he screams at her, lifting his head up and making her jump.

She bursts into fresh tears. "Because she wouldn't want you to give up! She would want you to fight, to see this through to the end! She wouldn't want you to be like this!"

"Without her, there is no point, there is no, to the end," he says, returning his face to Charlotte's hair.

Azazel joins Abi at her side. "Judas, please listen to her."

He grunts and moves his head from side to side. "Ohhh, you had fucking best get away from me right now. You better leave, so help me God."

"Judas. Please. Think about thi—"

"GET THE FUCK AWAY FROM ME, NOW!"

Azazel screws up his face into one of defiance. "No, I will not. Think this through. She has passed and it is terrible."

Judas squirms, not wanting to hear what Azazel is saying. He grits his teeth and closes his eyes.

"But she will without doubt have gone to the White Kingdom, and if Lucifer wins he will get to kill her all over again. That's what he meant earlier about pulling her out of her torment. He will be unstoppable and will not leave it with just conquering the kingdom of man, you know this. You need to stop him. We need to stop him. Right now, before he has a chance to end everything. He will not expect you to come for him, and trust me he will not be able to deal with you."

Judas says nothing, instead keeps his face buried in Charlotte's hair. After a while, he looks up at him slowly, his red eyes burning into him.

"Forget what I said earlier, Judas. Use her. Use Famine's power. Unleash the Horseman. Use what she offers and break the Thŭramré. My plan still stands, and it will work. We can end this and allow your fine and beautiful young woman the peace in the next life that she deserves."

Judas stares at him for a few moments, and then shifts his gaze to Abi who nods at him through her tears. Looking down at Charlotte once again, he leans over and kisses her forehead, then lays her on the floor as gently as he can. He looks up at Abi. "You take good care of her. I will be back."

Abi continues to try to fight back her tears and nods her head, then kneels beside Charlotte and strokes her hair.

Judas looks at Azazel. "Do not fail me, Ikazuchi. Do not." He holds out his hand as Azazel nods at him, and then lands into it in his sword form. He then throws it onto his back.

Abi looks up at him one final time and smiles. He doesn't smile back.

"Come to me Horseman," he says.

As you command, Iscariot, Lady Famine replies.

His eyes glow a fierce orange, like the heart of a fire, and he tenses violently, clenching his hands into fists, and then shakes while gritting his teeth hard. He trembles and grunts, breath escaping between them and from out of his back his blackened, charred, and now demonic-looking wings unfurl outward. A low growl escapes from the back of his throat, one that escalates into a roar as he fights against the Thŭramré all around him. Bending his knees and gritting his teeth even harder, he screams one last time and launches himself into the air, powering away, leaving a stunned Abi beneath him with Charlotte's body cradled in her lap.

TALIA

She blinks her eyes open, only to be greeted with a sea of pure white and she turns her head left and then right. Nothing but white everywhere.

She looks up, the awareness that she is lying on her back hitting her, and sighs. Then a muted cough draws her attention and she sits up, propping herself on one elbow.

A little way from her stands Pestilence, his hands behind his back, his eyebrows raised. "Well, that could've gone better."

Her head flops forward and she sighs. "Ya think?" Sitting fully up, she places her elbows on her knees and breathes out deeply. "Goddamn Death and his sucker punches no doubt?"

Pestilence closes his eyes for a second and nods.

"Thanks for the warning Pesti!"

"What my brothers do is their business. I am no more able to predict their behavior as I am yours or Judas'."

She raises her head slightly. "You sure about that? He's fairly predictable, you know."

Pestilence manages a small smile. "All the same, you know what I mean."

She nods while looking around again. "Yeah. Yeah I do," she agrees.

Standing, she places her hands into the small of her back and pushes her hips forward with a grunt, then rolls her head around her neck. Taking a deep breath, she looks around once more.

Still nothing but white.

She huffs. "This Heaven?" she asks, turning her attention back to Pestilence.

He shakes his head.

"Purgatory?" she says, with a raise of her eyebrows.

He scrunches up his nose and raises his hand, flipping it left and right a little.

"Great," she says. "Now what?"

He shrugs. "Well... you tell me!"

"Ummm, okay then. I go back and get another shot at the title?"

Pestilence's laugh causes her to breathe out hard again, her body deflating in the process.

She flaps her arms. "Well, I'm all out of ideas. Don't suppose you have a deck of cards?" she says, while miming the process of dealing them.

Pestilence smiles at her.

"Nope? Figures." She sighs once again.

Pestilence walks toward her.

"So, is it true?" she asks.

"Is what true?"

She cocks her head to the side and takes a deep breath, exhaling slowly.

"Ahhh, the 'is Lucifer really my father', thing. Yes. It is true. He is your father."

She closes her eyes and shakes her head a little. "How could Judas keep that from me? From me of all people?"

Pestilence laughs a little. "You're still annoyed at that? As he said to you earlier, how does someone break such a thing to another person? Especially given the environment you were in. 'Oh, hey there, just

350

thought I would let you know, your father isn't the Creator as you first thought, it is actually the man who rules this land.'" He smirks. "Not an easy thing to put into words, is it?"

Pursing her lips, she frowns and shakes her head. "I was harsh, wasn't I?"

"Oh, I'd say."

"Fuck," she says, closing her eyes and letting her head flop forward again, then shakes it and opens her eyes. "How?"

"How did it come to be?"

"Yeah, how did it come to be? And I don't mean the gross stuff, I mean, y'know, how did my mom get herself in such a mess?"

He laughs. "Well... that mess produced you, so it wasn't all bad now, was it?"

"You know what I mean."

He pauses for a moment, then walks closer to her. "Shall I show you?"

"Show me?"

"Yes. Show you."

"Awww, are you gonna do one of those weird Scrooge things? The visions?"

His eyes dart left and right and he frowns. "Well... yeah!"

She sighs. "Fine. But no gross stuff."

He pouts at her. "Believe me, no one wants to see that."

A wind whips up behind Charlotte and she raises her hand to control her hair as it flails wildly, then places the other to her eyes to shield from the dust that blusters around. Surveying her surroundings, she sees buildings and structures suited to a Middle Eastern environment and a sudden burst of gunfire makes her jump. She turns toward Pestilence at her side, his hands still behind his back.

"Where are we?" She says.

"Gaza, 2007. A fierce conflict rages here between Fatah and Hamas factions for control of the region."

"And, what, exactly, are we doing here?"

"Give it a moment, you'll see."

She stares at Pestilence for a few seconds before her attention is drawn to a doorway bursting open and two people who bundle through it, locked in combat. One, a woman in her mid-twenties, the other a man who looks a little older. They wrestle on the ground for a few moments before the woman knees him in the face, takes a knife from her belt, and stabs it straight into his skull, then flinches and covers her face as rapid gunfire peppers the ground around her, forcing her to flee on foot.

As the woman does so, Pestilence freezes the memory, allowing Charlotte a chance to study her.

She is dressed in dirty, desert combat fatigues and a green sweat-stained vest, and has long brown hair, sweat-matted to her face. And even though she is in the throes of panic, attempting to escape the life-threatening situation, Charlotte can see she is very beautiful and strong.

Pestilence draws closer to Charlotte and points at the woman. "Talia Vaez, 28 years old, former Israeli Special Forces operative-turned mercenary, currently employed by Hamas in this timeframe."

Charlotte looks at him and frowns. "Israeli Special Forces? A woman?"

"Yes, Charlotte, a woman. The Israelis were very progressive when it came to such things. Well, warfare at least. But she grew tired of the male-dominated environment and their chauvinistic attitudes and so she left and plied her trade wherever she could. Believe me, she was *very* good at what she did. Charlotte Hope, or should I say Charlotte Vaez, I would like you to meet your mother."

A swell of emotion overwhelms her as she peers into Talia's eyes. It isn't the image she had become accustomed to. That women had been drug and drink-fueled, pale skinned, and blonde haired. She shakes her head. "No. That isn't my mother. My mother didn't look like her."

"She is your mother Charlotte. Stick with the history lesson. All will become clear."

The environment changes as quickly as it had arrived, and they are sat in a booth in a bar somewhere in America, evident from the chatter around them and the way in which it is decorated and the sports showing on various television screens.

"New York City, mid-2008," Pestilence begins. "A seemingly chance encounter that will forever change the world. Watch." He motions toward the doorway as Talia enters, removing a scarf from around her neck while chatting and smiling to a young man who has entered with her. She looks happy and the scene causes Charlotte to smile a little.

At the bar, a heavy-set man stands. Clearly he has had too much to drink, and as he staggers toward the door he bumps into the young man with Talia, sending him crashing to the ground.

"Watch where you're going, you fuckin' asshole," the drunk man says with a thick Brooklyn accent.

Enraged, Talia makes short work of the drunk with three quick jabs to his face, and a snapping kick into his knee. The assault causes him to scream with pain and drop down onto the floor. She then knocks him clean out with right cross to the temple.

The bar erupts into cheers and laughter, but the young man on the floor stands and, feeling humiliated at having a woman fight his battles, looks around then leaves the bar in a hurry. Talia tries to call after him, but he is gone, and she shakes her head, sighing. A couple of men lift the beaten man to his feet and carry him outside and the bartender comes over to her to apologize.

"See that," Pestilence says, pointing to her. "That is one of her gifts, looking like she is just a small, frail, and beautiful woman, while hiding her ability to take care herself in almost any situation. The bartender is practically falling over himself to apologize. Look, he's even offering to pay for a couple of her drinks. A remarkable woman. She really was."

"Yeah. *Was*," Charlotte says, forlornly. "So how come she ended up down below?"

"Shhh," Pestilence says. "All in good time. Keep watching the show. No spoilers."

She eyes him and smirks.

Talia sits at the bar with another sigh, then looks at and smiles at a guy sitting next to her as the bartender places a drink down in front of her and puts his hands together into a praying gesture, then walks away. Talia chuckles and then smiles again at the man next to her as he mimics the bartender.

"Everybody was kung-fu fighting," the man sings, chuckles, and then imitates chops with his hands.

Talia bursts into laughter and looks behind her at the spot where she just laid the drunk out. "Yeah, something like that." She smiles again and holds out a hand. "Talia."

"Patrick," he says, taking her hand and shaking it.

Each grab their drinks and then take a swig.

"Say, Talia," Patrick says while still swallowing the liquid, "you look like you just got ditched. Fancy getting wasted and acting like a pair of dicks?"

She bursts into laughter again and raises her glass to him. "Sounds like a fine plan, Patrick, a fine plan indeed."

The scene changes, and Charlotte and Pestilence are stood in the corner of a room, the living room of a flat, with Talia sitting on a couch over on the other side of it. Patrick light-heartedly dances into the room from the open-plan kitchen carrying two glasses filled with alcohol.

She laughs at him. "You're quite the mover, honey, quite the mover indeed."

He winks, hands her a drink, and sits down next to her, then leans in and kisses her.

Charlotte turns toward Pestilence. "Hey. I said no funny business!"

He holds up his hands and laughs. "Trust me, that is as far as they go."

"Ugggh," she says, rolling her eyes.

Talia laughs once more, causing their canoodling to cease.

"What's so funny?" Patrick asks with a smile.

"This," she says, motioning around with her eyes. "This is just too weird. I mean, I came out on a date, could handle myself better than him and he ran away, then I ended up with you. As far as days go... it's pretty strange."

He laughs. "Yeah. Yeah – I guess it is. So, do you like study karate or something?"

She laughs. "Finally, Patrick. You have plucked up the courage to ask me how come I know how to fight."

"Well, I didn't think that it was suitable conversation for a bar." He smirks.

She laughs. "No. No karate lessons, at least not in the way you think. I was in the military, but that was a long time ago." She leans in to kiss him, but he halts her.

"The military? Seriously?"

She smiles. "Yeah, seriously. Why?"

He laughs. "Wanna job?"

She sits up and takes a deep breath. "Doing what?"

"Oh, this and that. Mostly that."

"Mostly that, huh?"

He smiles.

"Hmm," she says, with a deep breath. "And just like that you're gonna pick me up and I'm gonna fit into your neat little plan, huh?" She smiles and leans forward, placing her drink on the table. "Okay. Who?"

Patrick smirks, leans his head back and dances his tongue behind his lips. He suppresses a laugh through his nose. "That obvious, huh?"

"Yeah, Patrick. That obvious. To be honest, I kinda made you a few hours ago, but thought… what the hell and went with it, whatever *it* is."

Patrick Laughs. "He said you were a smart one."

"Who said I was a smart one?"

"Barney."

Talia raises her eyebrows. "Barney? Barney from Brooklyn?"

He smiles and nods.

Talia offers a laugh and moves to grab Patrick who pulls a handgun out from under his cushion on the couch, pointing it at her.

"Nice, nice," she says, calming herself and moving away a little, then leaning back and crossing her legs. "And the big dumb motherfucker whose ass I kicked?"

"He'll be well paid. Enough to cover his hospital bill and much more." Patrick smiles again.

Charlotte turns toward Pestilence, then looks back at the pair. "What the hell is going on?"

Pestilence freezes the timeline. "Well, you see, your mother used to work for a man called Barney Gumble."

"Fuck off!" Charlotte says, snapping her attention back to him.

"No, I'm serious," he shakes his head a little. "Well, in truth his name was Trevor Gumble, but everyone called him Barney."

"Ahh," she says, cocking her head back a little.

"And while in the employment of Barney, she had taken a few things that didn't really belong to her."

"Like what?"

"Like a half-million dollars."

"Holy shit!" she says, her eyes wide.

"Well yes, quite. And Barney was keen to retrieve it."

"I bet he was."

"Oh no, don't misunderstand me. To Barney, a half-million dollars was a few days' work, small change really. No, it was the fact that someone, a woman no less, could walk into his vault and lift it without so much as raising an ounce of suspicion. It was quite the caper, I can tell you," he shakes his head, "but that is a story for another day. So, Barney sent a few of his men, Patrick here included, out to find her, and find her he did."

"So what happened next?"

The scene shifts to a warehouse, where Talia, Patrick, and three other men stand facing one another, with Patrick and Talia on one side, him holding a gun to her head, and the other three men across from her.

Talia throws a medium-sized brown bag to one of the three, who kneels down, opens it, and looks inside.

"And I'm supposed to trust you that it's all there then, am I?" he says.

"It is, and I have no reason to lie to you since I'm gonna be dead soon and you can count it at your leisure," she responds.

The man laughs and looks around at the others. "You always did have a great sense of humor, Talia. I really liked you ya know. This breaks my heart."

"Yeah, well," she says, smiling, "I'm sure you'll get over it Barney."

Barney shakes his head. "Such a fucking waste." He glances toward Patrick.

Before Patrick has a chance to pull the trigger, Talia disarms him, puts a bullet through his head, and has the weapon pointed at Barney's face before the other two men can react and draw their guns.

Barney raises his hands. "Whoa, whoa, whoa Talia. Let's just all calm down here and talk about this like rational adults, okay?"

Talia smiles and licks her lips. "You need better men, Barney. Much better men." She shoots the other two behind him in their heads, then looks back at Barney, pointing the gun at him. "What if I had been one of Caglione's guys, huh? What then?" She lowers the weapon to her side.

Barney slowly lowers his hands and turns toward the two dead men on the ground. "That was Pete Francis," he says, pointing at one of them, "we go way back. I liked Pete."

"I liked Pete too, Barney. But the man would've gotten you killed." She sighs. "Do you honestly think I wanted to steal a half-million dollars from you?" She shakes her head and grimaces. "Barney, for fuck's sakes, I earned four million on the Benson hit alone. The fuck would I want a poultry half-mill for?"

He shakes his head. "What are you saying?"

"I want in, Barney. To run your personal security detail. You're a man going places and I want to go along for the ride."

Barney's eyes open wide and he takes a deep breath. "You could've just fucking asked. You didn't have to murder Pete!"

"I didn't murder him Barney. I provided you with a practical demonstration on how your chief of security would have eventually gotten you killed. Barney, if I had been working for Caglione you would be dead right now, lying on the ground next to Pete, fucking, Francis with your brains all over the floor. Do you understand what I'm saying?"

Barney takes one last look at Pete and then back to Talia. "Yeah. Yeah, I understand." He holds out his hand to her.

Eyeing him for a couple of seconds, Talia tucks the weapon into the back of her trousers, takes hold of his hand, and shakes it.

"Welcome to the fucking team," he says with a smile.

Charlotte looks at Pestilence who raises an eyebrow to her and the scene changes again.

Talia walks past them, looking drop-dead gorgeous in a blue and sparkling tight fitting dinner gown that clings to her perfect form. She busies herself around the room, greeting people and smiling.

Charlotte walks forward a little and looks around, frowning. She turns to Pestilence. "I know this place. This is familiar to me."

He raises an eyebrow and nods. "It should be. It's pretty much ground zero to every event in your life." He motions toward Talia, now talking to a couple of Japanese gentlemen. "New York City, December 2009. A group of business associates," he rolls his eyes at her, "have been taking serious control over the city in the last 18 months and this event is supposed to bring concerned parties together to show that there are to be no hard feelings, that the city can still be divided equally. You'll notice a few men dotted around the room who don't look like they are having fun?"

Charlotte scans the room and nods.

"Well, they are some of the most powerful mobsters in New York. Your mother is now Barney's right-hand man, so to speak, and nothing goes on within his organization that she doesn't know about. Over the last year and a half, she has gained his implicit trust and he pays her what she is worth, which is a lot. Barney now holds quite the seat of power within New York since a certain Mr. Caglione passed away under mysterious circumstances." He looks at Charlotte and raises his eyebrows again. "And Barney looks after her very well, and not once has he drunkenly forced himself on her or asked her to do anything that she would find uncomfortable, unless it was for the benefit of the business and that she agreed to it in full. It was a match made in mob Heaven."

Still frowning, Charlotte holds up a finger. "I know this place. This is the Tonada building."

Pestilence smiles and nods. "And there… is your destiny." He points to a corner of the room.

Lucifer saunters through, chatting and being charming with many of the well-dressed women present. He exchanges handshakes and laughter with various people, all of whom are drinking Champagne from delicate crystal flutes. He glances across the room and stares at Talia, who is mid-laugh and charming the Japanese men. Charlotte points at two of them. "Kento and Masakai." She shakes her head and then looks around. Her eyes chase around the room for a few moments and settle on what she has been searching for. "Yep, and there's Zenaku Hotoke. The piece of shit."

Pestilence places a gentle hand on the top of her head and guides it around. "Look. It's happening."

Lucifer approaches Talia, and Kento and Masakai bow their heads and walk away. The action doesn't go unnoticed by Talia.

"My, my," she says, with a charming smile, "you must be man of great importance to command such obedience without speaking."

"Oh, I have my moments," he says, smiling back at her. He holds out a hand. "Nick. Nick Foster." He smiles once more, and it is even more charming than hers.

She takes his proffered hand and shakes it gently. "Talia. Talia Vaez."

"Ahhh, such a beautiful name. Israeli?"

She looks surprised. "Yeah. Very good Mr. Foster. Most impressive. Most people do not associate it with the region despite its Jewish origins."

"Oh please. Call me Nick."

"Okay then, Nick. Would you be charming enough to get a lady a drink?"

He smiles. "Why of course." He clicks his fingers without taking his eyes off her and a waiter shuffles over to him. He smiles at Talia once again. "Hmmm, let me guess." He crosses his arms in front of him and places a finger to his lips, tapping it against them. "Hmmm."

She smiles, while looking away slightly, then back to him.

Lucifer smiles and nods. "I'm gonna say you are a Scotch on the rocks type of woman."

Talia laughs and looks away again. "Jesus Nick, you should take that shtick on the road." She looks back at him.

He turns toward the waiter. "Scotch on the rocks for the lady and the same for me please."

Nodding, the waiter then hurries away.

Pestilence halts the scene. "Okay, so they chat for a while and let me tell you, Lucifer is very taken with your mother. Up to now he has had his people searching for the perfect mate. A woman who would bear him the most viable solution to put on Earth and serve his best interests. Your mother is, or should I say *was*, clearly it."

The scene changes, moving ahead a few hours and Lucifer grabs the guest's attention with a few taps of his glass with a small silver spoon.

"Ladies and gentlemen. Thank you so very much for coming tonight. I look around this room and I see very powerful people who I have the utmost respect for, especially for some of the things you have done. Truly wonderful human beings in my eyes. But all good things must come to an end I am afraid. But fear not, there will be substantial work for some of you in my other organization down below. I am sure you are going to love it there." Lucifer turns toward Zenaku and smiles. "Would you be so kind?" He motions forward with his hand.

Zenaku, Kento, Masakai, and a few of the waiters transform into their demon jackal forms and tear the room to pieces.

From out of thin air, Lucifer appears next to a startled and wide-eyed Talia, who draws a small pistol tucked inside her garter at the top of her thigh.

He places his hand on it. "Oh no no. You won't be needing that my dear. You have a new employer now and your position is to be one of the highest importance."

Trembling, Talia looks to her side to see Barney being savaged by a demon, and as she stares at the scene Lucifer leans in and kisses her and she is powerless to stop him or, more to the point she doesn't want him to stop.

Charlotte turns away from the carnage in front of her. "Okay, that's enough. I get the picture."

The scene changes once more, and she is stood on a dingy-looking backstreet covered in snow. She looks up at the streetlight providing meager illumination and then at Pestilence.

"Brooklyn, November 13, 2010," he says, looking down at her and then back to a door in front of them. "Two days after your birth."

The door bursts open, and from out of it runs Talia and a young man, breathless and panicked. The man clutches at his ribs and appears to be in pain. He falls back against the wall.

"Talia. Talia, I'm fucking struggling here!"

She looks at him and her face sinks with despair. "You're bleeding. A lot."

"I know," he says, looking at her, "I need a doctor."

She shakes her head, tears glistening in her eyes. "No, Billy, you need to get the fuck away from me."

His eyes narrow and he frowns. "Talia. Please. I need your help."

She shakes her head. "No, Billy, she needs my help." She motions to a bundle of blankets in her arms.

Charlotte looks at Pestilence with her eyes wide.

He shushes her, although she hasn't said anything and indicates for her to continue watching.

"Talia, please," Billy says, his eyes filling with tears and him grunting while trying to push himself away from the wall but unable to do so.

A tear trickles down Talia's face. "I'm sorry Billy. Even if I could carry you, which I can't, your blood would lead them right to us. It's fucking snowing, Billy. Red and white make bull's-eyes. I'm so sorry. Really I am. Thank you. Thank you for getting us out. I will never forget you Billy. And I will never forget what you have done for us."

Billy thuds his head back against the wall and he fights back the tears.

Charlotte steps forward. "Help him, mom. Don't just leave him."

"She can't hear you," Pestilence says. "This is just a memory, remember."

Charlotte turns back toward him. "She doesn't... I mean she didn't just leave him here, did she?"

Pestilence's eyes plead with her. "Charlotte, she had more important things to worry about." He nods toward Talia as a baby's muffled cries drift out from within the blankets.

Charlotte takes a deep breath and her eyes flood with tears. "That's, that's me?"

Pestilence nods.

From further down the alleyway, a group of voices call out.

"She's over here," a male voice shouts. "She's over here, I've found her. Over here!"

Flashlights sweep back and forth, their movement erratic from running and Talia grunts and races away.

The scene changes again as Talia passes Charlotte and Pestilence.

Another change, and she runs past again.

Another.

And another.

Eventually, and after yet another change, Talia ceases running and bends over, trying to drag as much air into her lungs as possible, but the biting cold hurts her throat and her face reflects that. She looks up to the sky as snow blizzards down, landing on her warm and steaming skin, disappearing the moment they touch it. Tears roll down her face. "Please. Please don't let them take her. Please. I'm begging you."

The snow stops falling. No more flakes hit her face. She slowly lowers her tear-filled gaze and looks around her to see the snow hanging in suspended animation, and she frowns. A male voice then causes her to turn around.

"There is indeed another way, Talia. She needn't be lost to these creatures."

"Who's there?" she calls, peering into the blackness, "who are you?"

The man steps forward into the light. "My name is Gabriel, the Archangel Gabriel to be precise. And I come to you tonight with a proposition."

"Gabe!" Charlotte says, stepping forward.

With a frown, Gabriel glances toward her direction, and stares for moment, then turns his attention back to Talia.

"He sees me," Charlotte says, looking at Pestilence.

"Impossible," the Horseman replies, "this is merely a memory. He can't see you."

She stares at Pestilence for a few seconds and then returns her gaze back to the scene.

Talia utters a brief laugh. "You know, 12 months ago if you had introduced yourself as the Archangel Gabriel, I would've kicked your ass for being a weird creep, but after the things I have seen over the last year, not so much tonight."

Gabriel stifles a smile.

Talia sniffs. "So about this proposition?"

He breathes out slowly. "Give Charlotte to me. I take her, and they never find her. We will endow her with many… gifts and watch over her until she is age seven, where she will begin to do great things upon the Earth. Quite literally the exact opposite of what she was destined for."

Talia laughs and closes her eyes, a small tear escaping from them. "And if I refuse?"

"Then you refuse. And they will find you. And they will kill you and take her. And I will be forced to deal with her later in life and I would very much rather that didn't happen. She is a unique soul, one who can and will bring immense joy to the world. But… I cannot make you give her to me. That choice has to be yours alone."

Talia laughs lightly, one that is closer to crying than merriment. "Some choice!" She looks up into the sky and closes her eyes.

She remains that way for a short while, breathing deeply, then opening them, she lowers her gaze to Gabriel. "You promise you will take good care of her?"

Gabriel steps forward. "Oh, Talia. The very best. As though she were my own."

She looks down at the infant Charlotte and bursts into tears. "I'm sorry. I'm so, so sorry." She leans in and kisses her. "You were the only thing in my life that was good. The only thing that I ever loved," she says as more tears stream down her face. Closing her eyes for a moment, and laying her head against her daughter, she then hands Charlotte to Gabriel, the action one of reluctance.

Adult Charlotte sobs. "Mom. Mom."

Wiping her eyes, Talia asks, "So, how will this work then? I mean, y'know – everything?"

Gabriel offers a sympathetic smile. "Well, first – and this is something that fills me with great pain – is to give her false memories. Of you, of her younger years, everything. We will make it appear her mother cruelly abandoned her so that she shouldn't feel the need to want to find you, at least not in her earlier years that is. I will take her to a place outside of the time of man where she will be safe and able to grow to the age at which we need her to have her awakening, and then we will simply let it happen and place her among humankind."

Talia wipes her eyes and looks away, nodding. "Okay. Sounds good. But what will stop them searching for her when they don't find her tonight?"

Gabriel closes his eyes, then, with a deep breath, opens them. "Because they will think she perished with you."

She knew this was coming. She knew how it was to work. The life she has led has made her understand. She nods and tries to manage a smile. "They're not fucking stupid you know, they will figure out that I am not holding a child."

"This should suffice," Gabriel says.

Feeling something appear in them, Talia looks down into her arms, and sees she holds a blanket with what appears to be a baby wrapped in it.

Gabriel smiles. "An illusion. Nothing but a prop. But it is snowing and cold, and you will have jumped before they get chance to see clearly."

Talia looks behind her, toward the Brooklyn Bridge, then turns back with a sigh and nods.

Gabriel looks up, the snow having started to fall once more. Slowly, but definite movement. "I'm not allowed to keep this up for very long you know. It messes with things." He offers a thin smile.

Talia nods, walks away, then stops and turns back. "Thank you."

Gabriel nods.

She pauses for a moment. "Will this make it right?"

He pursues his lips and shakes his head and Talia can see genuine sadness in the gesture.

She smiles. "The things I've done, huh?"

Gabriel nods. "The things you've done. I'm so sorry."

She smiles once again, shakes her head, and then sets off running. Glancing back over her shoulder, she sees the snow falling as normal, and flashlights dance from side to side once again. Gabriel and her child are gone.

Charlotte wipes her eyes, her mouth downturned, and she fights against further tears.

The scene changes, and Talia is on the other side of the guardrail on Brooklyn Bridge. A dozen men and women surround her and are attempting to talk her out of jumping.

"Don't come any closer!" she yells at them. "I mean it!"

A man steps forward.

"Talia. Talia. You don't want to do this. You don't want to hurt your beautiful baby girl."

"You have no idea what I want, you fucker," she snarls at him, "so stay the fuck back. I fucking mean it."

Pestilence looks at Charlotte. "You don't have to see this. We have seen enough."

She shakes her head. "No. I do. She deserves to have her sacrifice witnessed by more than these animals."

Pestilence lowers his head and then returns his attention to the scene as it play out.

The same man holds his hands out to placate Talia. "Please. Come back to this side. We can talk about this. Everything he promised you will still be there. Look. You got scared, you didn't know what you were doing. It's natural for a new mother to feel these things. Come back now and I am certain all will be forgiven."

Talia looks down at the icy depths below then back up at the man and smiles. "He will never have her." She pushes off.

The man screams while turning in a circle, then shape shifts into Malphas and savagely attacks other members of the small crowd. A few of them also turn into demons and start to devour the humans along with Malphas.

Charlotte sinks to her knees, sobbing, and Pestilence ends the scene.

They are back in the white.

"Everything I am is a lie," she says, her tears dropping onto the floor.

Pestilence frowns. "How do you figure so?"

She looks up at him, mouth agape, her eyes red. "EVERYTHING I AM IS A LIE. I was destined to destroy the world, not save it."

Pestilence nods and screws up his mouth. "True. But you didn't, and you haven't, nor will you." He squats down next to her. "Look. You had no more control of where you came from than a child born to a poor farmer in a drought-ridden land. But even that child can control their own destiny, and many have. The history books are littered with those born into abject poverty but who rise above it and push on to greatness, even inspiring it in others and they didn't let their preconceived destinies determine their fate. No. They took control of their lives and did what they felt was right. So I ask you, Charlotte Hope, what do *you* think is right? Who do *you* think you should be? Hmmm? Destruction… or salvation?" He stands and holds out a hand to her.

She wipes her eyes and looks up at him, pondering the question. He is right, her destiny has not been decided upon by any person other than herself. Of course Gabriel had a hand in altering its path, but in the end she was the one to decide what she wanted to be, not Lucifer, not Gabriel, and not even Judas. She did. Her.

She was, of course, lucky to have been rescued by Gabriel and to have received the amazing level of guidance and support that she had from Judas, but even he had stated on many occasions that her destiny was her own, that she could either save people or she couldn't, that they either wanted to be saved or they didn't.

She smiles. Judas had been giving her the best lessons, even when he didn't know her history. She closes her eyes. *Just like a good father should,* she tells herself.

"Yes," Pestilence says, with a smile. "Just like a good father should."

She looks up at him, nods, then takes his hand and stands. She sniffs. "You're a pretty good motivational speaker for an instrument of the Apocalypse, ya know."

He smiles. "And you're a pretty good savior… for an instrument of destruction, that is."

He winks, and she laughs.

Taking a deep and calming breath, she looks around. "Well. I feel like I've made a powerful leap forward on an incredible journey of self-discovery that would have really benefitted the world. Too bad I'm bloody dead."

Pestilence offers a sharp laugh. "Who said anything about you being dead?" he says, an air of mischief about him.

She snaps her attention to him. "But… earlier, you said…"

He smiles. "Every savior needs a resurrection, don't ya think? In fact, I'm pretty sure it's an actual requirement for the role." He laughs, then considers her for a moment and takes a deep breath. "This is it for me, Charlotte. This is the last leg of our journey together." He smiles at her, a warm and caring one. "You are going to do wonderful things. Wonderful things."

She smiles. She understands.

"Use what I taught you to be the world's good health, not its disease." He cocks his head to one side a little. "After you kick Lucifer's ass that is."

She laughs sharply.

"You are a fascinating one, Charlotte Hope."

"Vaez," she says, smiling. "My name is Charlotte Vaez."

Pestilence nods. "Yes, it is." He smiles. "Fascinating indeed." He takes another deep breath. "Goodbye, Charlotte Vaez."

He places a finger on her forehead and pushes.

Abi screams as Charlotte rises from her lap, the woman's body straight and stiff as though someone was under her, lifting her up.

Charlotte takes a deep breath, her eyes wide, then smiles while looking around. She then turns toward Abi. "Hey, hey. It's me, it's okay. It's me."

Abi continues to hyperventilate. "Oh my God, that scared the shit outta me. Scared the absolute shit outta me. And we're in Hell!" She places a hand to her forehead. "Holy shit!"

Looking around again, Charlotte's eyes narrow at how the landscape has changed, become frozen, with snow drifting down. She ponders whether this could have been a result of Pestilence showing her the past but dismisses it. Something else is happening, and it is something bad. She looks at her hands. She feels different, as though a fundamental change has occurred within her. She closes her eyes and takes a deep breath, feeling the cold air rush in through her nose and down her throat. Azazel's trickery with planting The Book and Seventh Seal within her had given her a false sense of eternal knowledge, but now she feels different. *This* feels different. Pestilence may have left, but he has left her gifts – talents, and significant ones at that. And not only that, she feels well again, the best she has ever felt in-fact. She turns back to Abi, the woman still talking about how much her resurrection had scared her.

"What happened here, Abi? Where's my dad?"

Abi composes herself and then shakes her head. "He left a little while ago. I think he's gone to finish this. And then not too long after he set off everything went nuts, the ground shaking and shit and then the land froze. It just... froze." She takes a deep breath. "But he said he would be back for you."

To the side of them one of the statues splinters and crumbles. Nothing more than a simple act of expanding ice exposing its structural weakness, but it makes Abi jump.

"Goddamit, I hate it here," she says, close to tears. "I fucking hate it here, I can't take this anymore."

Charlotte regards her for a moment and then offers a sympathetic smile. "You know what, you're right. You shouldn't be here. And you don't deserve this. You never have." She walks over to Abi and places her hands on either side of her face. "It's time you went to where you belong."

Abi looks at her, eyes glistening with tears. "What? I don't understand."

Charlotte smiles. "You will." She leans forward and kisses her forehead, then embraces her.

Charlotte emits a huge amount of Light-Divinity that swirls around them both, encircling them, bringing them off the ground and slowly rotating them in the air.

Abi closes her eyes and a sense of serenity washes over her. She feels the warmth of Charlotte's divinity enter her body, swim through, around, and inside it, and she takes in a sharp breath. The holy light enriches her soul, filling her mind with every wonderful thought from her life. Nothing ugly or violent remains, not a single bad memory and she smiles.

Gently pushing her, Charlotte releases Abi to float away, the Divinity continuing to flood over the woman and, opening her eyes, Abi smiles, then mouths the words, 'thank you.' And although they were silent, Charlotte hears them as if she had said them out loud.

Holding her arms straight out to her sides and laying back her head, Abi gently explodes into a thousand motes of light, calm and serene, and each bead swirls around within a beam that stretches up high.

And with that Abi Colter ascends into Heaven.

Touching down with grace, Charlotte smiles while continuing to look up at the last flecks of light as they disappear. Then, a voice behind her, calling her name causes her to spin around, eyes wide with surprise. Her mouth drops open. "Sarah, Isaac. What the hell are you doing here?"

FIFTY-SIX

He powers through another up-gate with furious intent, guided to his destination by the voice of Ikazuchi held out in front of him. His face epitomizes aggression. A solid fixed point of death and retribution and in his entire existence he has never had so much rage burning within him, irrespective of Lady Famine's assimilation. He cares not for his fate; the destruction of Lucifer is all that matters. She is gone, taken from him, her physical existence erased. The prophecies have stated that she would heal the world in human form not her ascended one, and now that she is gone nothing will ever be the same again.

He feels cheated, robbed. This wasn't supposed to happen. He was supposed to take care of her, to look after her until she took her rightful place as humankind's savior. She was to become strong and look after him – all of them.

Azazel was right. Lucifer will never leave her alone. He will dominate the kingdom of man and then march on the White Kingdom and make her his prize. And there is no way he will allow that to happen. His face contorts further as his rage burns with a greater intensity. He won't just kill Lucifer. He will utterly remove any trace of his existence. And he will crush The Horseman. He will destroy them all.

Yes, Iscariot. Everything will come from your rage, your desire for revenge. Forget what you have ever been told, this is how the universe works. Exact your vengeance, feel its positivity, revel in its glory. You are the instrument of death for my brothers and their leash-holder. You will do great things here today, Iscariot. Great things indeed, she cackles.

He doesn't care. He isn't listening to her anymore. He wants her strength, her gifts, and nothing more. Everything will die. Everything must die.

He rockets over the Hellscape, past the horrors that lie below, creatures in torment in their millions, oblivious, uncaring, and he enters another gate then explodes out of the other side. Ahead, the Red Keep looms, and its design is familiar to him.

"Have you been preparing me for this moment all along, Azazel?" he says to his sword.

"You have referred to me by my true name and not my conquered designation. This surprises me, Judas."

"It doesn't matter anymore. Nothing matters. Answer me. Is this why you showed me this place during my time within your realm?"

He is referring to when Azazel tormented him during his time trying to claim the weapon within the Nether. How he had chased him toward this very same gigantic tower that stretched far up into Hell's sky, its huge, black, spiked gates protecting a courtyard and littered with demented, screaming, and writing bodies attached to them. Lucifer's fortress.

"Everything happens for a reason, Judas. I am sure you have come to understand this now."

"Everything happens for a reason," Judas repeats, his words dripping with scorn. "And her dying, that was for a reason?"

"Perhaps. Perhaps. But focus on the task at hand. You will see her again. She surely must have ascended."

"It's not the same. It wasn't supposed to be that way. She was supposed to save humanity as one of them. And I shouldn't have left

371

her alone in Hell. Her brother took days before he ascended. What if that never happens? What if she is to be confined to that place? What if it will not let her go? This is a mistake. I have to go back."

"Judas, no! Remain focused. Complete this and I personally guarantee you that she will be released should Hell remain wrapped around her. You have my word."

Judas scoffs once more. "Your word? After all that has happened, I am to trust your word?"

"Whether you want to or not, we must now fully trust one another Judas. What comes next will be like nothing you have ever faced before."

Judas says nothing. He throws more force into his black wings and races ahead.

FIFTY-SEVEN

Holding up her hands, Charlotte halts the incessant bickering between Isaac, Sarah, and Daniel. "Look, I don't care whose fault it was. I just want to know how you got here."

"We told you," Isaac says, sighing. "Daniel thought he had created a shield, but it turned out to be a weapon but not before we realized it could also be a portal. We then deliberately created a portal so that it could be used with the weapon, because it wasn't a shield." He breathes in deep, the explanation having exhaled all his lungs' capacity.

Charlotte stares at him for a few seconds. "Are you shitting me with that?"

His mouth flaps open and closed and he looks round at Sarah and Daniel.

Sarah steps forward a little. "We... we have the portal back there, just across the bridge near the big dead thing." She smiles. "Isaac has explained what happened, although not very well." She glances at him.

"And you all walked through a portal with no clue as to what was on the other side?" Charlotte says, shifting her gaze between them incredulously.

They look at one another.

Daniel nervously points to his breathing equipment. "We… we put on masks!"

Charlotte opens her eyes wide, then shakes her head and blows out hard.

Isaac shoots Daniel a look, silently remonstrating with him as though to say, 'you're making us look stupid.'

Charlotte waves a hand. "Fine, whatever. It's time you guys went home. We have things to do. All of us." She holds her hand up and snaps it into a fist.

Nothing happens.

"Hmm," she says. "Well then. It would appear that you are here for a reason." She looks upward. "I wonder what forces are manipulating this situation." She sighs. "Okay, I can't create portals. Looks like we're using your elevator."

Daniel smiles a little, feeling a sense of pride. He gingerly approaches Charlotte and holds out a hand. "Hi, I'm Daniel…"

"…Holtz," she says, taking and shaking it. "Yeah I know." She muses for a second. "I do know." She nods. "Huh! Thank you, Pesti." She smiles.

Daniel looks at the others and they each shake their heads a little.

Exiting the portal and arriving back in the laboratory, Charlotte looks around while the others follow behind her. She frowns and her head moves back a little. "Time freeze? Why is time frozen?"

As though triggered by her words, time returns to its normal state with Nathan and Jonesy bursting into the room.

"What the fuck are you kids doing?!" Nathan shouts while stumbling through. Then looking around in confusion, he takes a few deep breaths. "What just happened? I feel like something just happened." Seeing Charlotte, his face lights up. "Charlotte. Oh God, it's good to see you." He moves quickly to her holding out a hand, which she shakes. He looks around. "Judas?"

She shakes her head. "No. But he will need our help. I need you to gather everybody that's able to fight." She offers a solemn look. "Everybody Nathan." Reaching out, she places a hand on his shoulder. "This isn't over, and we will need to work together to finish it."

Pursing his lips, he nods. "We won't let you down." He places a hand over hers.

She smiles. "I know."

With a brief smile, he then removes his hand and clicks his fingers at the others. "You three. Come with me. Seems you won't be getting an ass-kicking today after all." He then smiles and winks at Charlotte who lowers her head and presses her lips together tight to suppress a laugh.

Removing his mask, the last one to do so, Daniel breathes out hard. "Oh, thank God."

FIFTY-EIGHT

Judas lands with a thud at the spiked gates and hurls Ikazuchi out in front of him, bringing Azazel into his human form. Striding over to the demon, who turns toward him and is about to speak, he slams the gem into Azazel's chest, blasting him backward and onto the ground where he enters the same seizure state he did within Mokwena's lair upon receiving the first stone.

Azazel writhes around for a couple of minutes, bucking and jerking, and then finally regains his composure, the event having completed. Getting to his feet, he takes a deep breath and closes his eyes for a second before opening them. "You might have warned me, Judas," he says, contempt in his words.

"Yeah, well everything happens for a reason doesn't it?"

He walks past Azazel, who offers a crooked smile, feeling hoisted by his own petard. "Do something about this," he says, pointing at the gates.

Within the throne room of the Red Keep, Lucifer rips off his shirt and stands close to his seat, his arms outstretched. He sniffs and rolls his head around his neck as Death approaches him, The Book held in one hand and The Seventh Seal in the other.

Placing The Seal into its slot on The Book's cover, Death's lifeless masked face, devoid of any emotion, looks up at Lucifer, and the Lord of Hell nods, prompting Death to turn The Seal and clicking it into place. The Book shakes within The Horseman's hand, emitting a glow, first around the three embedded Seals, all in their rightful places, and then spreading over the entire object. And as powerful as Death is, even he struggles to contain the relic as it vibrates within his grasp and he looks up at Lucifer one final time. He nods again, his face determined.

Death slams The Book into Lucifer's chest and fierce Dark-Divinity explodes outward from the point of impact, knocking every creature over within the throne room.

Lucifer growls, his hands clenched into fists, his teeth gritted tight. His eyes flood with Dark-Divinity, replacing the blood-red that they were. He opens his mouth and cries out as the reaction intensifies and a further energy pulse blasts out of him.

Judas looks up to an area high up in the Red Keep as an energy pulse radiates outward. His attention snaps to the ground, as ice crunches over and spreads through Hell.

"NOW, AZAZEL – DO IT NOW."

Lucifer sinks to the floor, breathing heavily, and then starts to laugh hysterically that borders on the insane. "Yes. YES!" he shouts, slamming his fists against the ground. "It is time." He stands, still breathing hard, and looks to his demons who are getting to their feet.

"He is here," War says, indicating behind himself with a slight nod of his head.

A low growl rises from the back of Lucifer's throat. "It doesn't matter. He is too late."

"Our sister aids him," War continues.

Lucifer takes a deep breath and exhales through his nose. "Then I suggest you deal with it," he says, his words rich with annoyance. He then turns, opens a portal, and steps through.

Within the main hall of the Red Keep, hundreds of demons stand guard awaiting the arrival of Iscariot, all eager to kill him, desperate to be the one to win the Lord of Hell's favor by saying, 'I did that, I killed the great prize that Lucifer has sought for centuries.' They snarl and hiss, hopping from one foot to the other, keen to get the fight underway, unaware that the rage that is about to burst through the door will spell their doom.

The ground shakes and they glance at one another. Then it rumbles, and they shift in their positions. A Demon-Knight roars and the others join in, the hall filling with the battle cries of demonic entities.

The giant doors to the keep explode, forcing the demons to raise their arms to shield their faces.

Riding atop Azazel, now in gigantic serpent form, stands Judas and he screams at them. Leaping down, he holds out his hand and calls Azazel into Ikazuchi. He is going to enjoy ripping them to pieces with the sword. Azazel's serpent form is not to have that privilege.

A portal bursts open into the dusk twilight of New York City, a few yards in front of the ruins of the Tonada Corporation building and Lucifer exits, a wry smile upon his face. Closing the portal with a flick of his closed fist, he turns around to face the remains of the building and smiles. "Now. My time has finally come." Closing his eyes, he takes a deep breath and, with his palms facing upward, raises his hands into the air.

The ground beneath Tonada shakes and vibrates, and the structure creaks and cracks, with pieces of it breaking off and falling to the ground. As the intensity rises, the area around Lucifer tremble, causing other buildings to shake and crumble, broken by the magnitude of the quake. Dust clouds plume across the area as the ground buckles and warps, and above, the sky fills with an unnatural crimson cloud, obstructing the moon and stars from view, bathing the scene in an eerie red glow.

Suddenly, the ground explodes, and the top of the Red Keep rises under and into the Tonada building, obliterating it.

Lucifer grins as he brings Hell to Earth.

FIFTY-NINE

Startled by the sudden opening of a portal next to him, Gary steps back and looks at Gabriel, who is equally surprised.

Out of it walks Charlotte, resolute and determined. She frowns at Gary, and then raises a finger to him. "Why are you here?" Before he can respond she walks away. "Never mind, I'll deal with that in a minute." She strides toward the Creator's chamber and as she passes Gabriel, she acknowledges him with a nod.

Gabriel nods back automatically, albeit still confused and he looks at Gary who shrugs and shakes his head.

Approaching the chamber doors, she raises a foot and kicks them off their hinges and as she passes through, one of them falls off leaving the other dangling. "Hey!" she shouts through gritted teeth. "Get down here. I wanna talk to you."

Behind her the doors repair, and she looks back to them just in time to catch a glimpse of a surprised Gabriel who had been approaching them before they close shut. She turns back around at the sound of the Creator's voice.

"My, my, you have come a long way, child. Let me get a look at you." He smiles and puts his hands on his hips.

She looks around as the room changes into what appears to be a cozy log cabin, complete with bearskin rug and rocking chairs. She glances at the rug. "Nice," she says, her tone dripping with sarcasm.

He smiles. "Oh… it's not real, it's just for show." He approaches a globe-shaped drinks decanter and starts to pour a drink.

"Yeah, right!" she says, looking around more, not sure if she believes him or not.

He looks hurt by the flippant comment, stopping what he is doing and turning to look at her. "Hey! I created all these things you know. One way or another. And I wouldn't harm a single one."

"Oh, that's rich," she replies, unimpressed, "but you'll let Lucifer murder millions of people, right? But that's cool, as long as the bears are okay. Good job, man. Good job." She gives him a sarcastic, two thumbs up.

He screws up his mouth into a smile, then nods toward the globe. "Drink?"

She frowns. "No, I don't want a fucking drink. Are you kidding me?"

He raises his hands to his sides. "Hey, every great conversation in history has involved booze."

"I highly doubt that," she says, stomping toward him. "Shut this down," she says, stabbing a finger at him.

"Shut what down?" he says.

"This," she says, her annoyance piquing, and waves a hand and the room changes to the view from space, looking down at the planet, a dark-red veil covering it. "Shut this down right now."

"Wow!" He says, taken aback. "You are really accelerating your gifts. I am impressed. Very impressed indeed." He takes a sip of his drink.

"I don't care if you are impressed or not. I only care about what is happening to those people down there, and it may come as a surprise to you but by that I mean what little remains of the ENTIRE FUCKING PLANET." Her anger reaches new heights as she examines the face of the most powerful being in existence and his annoying, flippant attitude.

He sighs and smiles again. "You know, I think you will find there are more of you left than you realize."

She stares at him for a few moments and then coughs a surprised laugh. Running her hands over her head she turns around, facing the way she came in, and then back to him. "You cannot be serious with this shit surely?"

He frowns.

"Do you care at all what is happening down there? That Lucifer is bringing Hell to Earth and is about to murder every living thing? Does none of that mean anything to you?"

It is now his turn to be angry. "Of course it does. This is not what I had in mind for any of you." He takes another sip of his drink. "This whole situation just got a little out of hand."

She strides closer to him, her eyes wide. "A little out of hand? A LITTLE OUT OF HAND? Look at it. LOOK… AT… IT."

She waves her hand again and the picture beneath them changes to the view above where the Tonada building once stood, now replaced by Lucifer's Red Keep with hundreds of demons pouring out from every available opening, the ground surrounding it broken and cracked with puddles of lava everywhere, Hell truly having come to Earth.

"You call that a little out of hand? I call that the end of days and I want you to shut it down. Right… fucking… now!"

The Creator waves a hand, changing the scenery back to the log cabin.

Charlotte growls with frustration and her head flops forward. She ambles to one of the chairs and collapses into it, her elbows on her knees, her head drooped forward, and her hair dangling between her legs. She shakes her head. "You know, all this time I thought I was your child, your daughter, and that one day you would visit me. Come down to Earth and talk to me. You would scoop me up into your arms and tell me exactly what my higher purpose was, what I was meant for. But it never happened. You never came. And today? Well, today I learned that I am not your daughter after all. That I am the daughter of evil. And to make matters worse, I poured scorn and derision onto the only person who ever loved me like a father should, because I thought he had kept the information from me when he should have told me." She screws her mouth up, and breathes in deep through her nose, then runs her fingers through her hair. "I'm such a friggin' idiot!"

Pursing his lips, the Creator moves to a chair opposite her and takes a seat. He takes a drink from his glass, closes his eyes, swirls the remaining liquid around within it, and then swallows and offers a deep sigh. "I'm sorry."

The sudden change in his attitude causes her to raise her head and look at him in surprise, her hands still atop her head.

He smiles. "But you're wrong. I am your father. I'm everyone's father. I feel it all. Everything. Their pain, their sorrow, anger, rage, and joy... and their deep, meaningful love. I feel everything from everyone. Even now. I also feel Lucifer's pain. The pain he feels from the absence of the divine. Believe me, Charlotte, I never meant it to go this far. His punishment was supposed to be nothing more than a petulant child sent to his room for a bit."

She scoffs. "You call an eternity a bit?"

He smiles. "In our world, time means nothing. It's just a concept. Just another thing we use as we choose." He sighs. "But I will concede I didn't handle the situation well."

She laughs and leans back in her chair, resting her head against the top of it.

"Look Charley, at that time I was new to most things. I had been created by the Alfather to look after my realms, but I had not been given any instruction. I was new to it all."

She looks at him, her mouth open, her eyebrows raised a little.

He cocks his head to one side. "Yes my dear, even I have a Creator." He smiles and then takes another sip of his drink and looks away from her. "A God I may be, but it still took me a long time to get to grips with my role. And despite everything, y'know, a few lunatics or so running around down there, I don't think I've been doing a bad job of it, especially the last 50 years or so of your time." He glances back at her. "Y'know, in the grand scheme of things..."

She sits forward a little, then looks down into her lap, considering what he has just said. And as much as she hates to admit it, he is right. Despite a war or two here and there, and sporadic terrorism, humankind had it good, certainly better than it had in its earlier formative years. With huge advancements in technology and medicine, the general attitude of most human beings had improved and become mostly civilized – the removal of public executions, draconic laws, and barbaric practices from most developed cultures. Yes, He was right – He hadn't been doing *that* bad a job of it. However, it was far from perfect. The way things are now are far from perfect, in fact they are downright unacceptable.

"I liked the dinosaurs though," He says, staring into empty space, and nodding. "I had fun with them."

She smiles and looks back down at her hands, fiddling with them, then sits back with a sigh. "But why haven't you gotten involved? I mean, this time around? You could so easily take Lucifer out. Why haven't you? Why did you allow him to call forth The Horsemen, lay waste to the planet? I don't understand."

He looks back at her, his eyebrows raised. "Oh, the Horsemen are way beyond my control, Charley. No. They belong to the Alfather. And if they receive the call, they come and there isn't a damn thing I can do about it." He takes another drink and looks away from her again. "And as for Lucifer, well… how does one kill his own child?"

She shakes her head. "But we are all your children, remember? And he certainly has no problem with killing us. Don't you care about that?"

He looks back at her and smiles. "Yes, of course I care. But… he's my second born, one of two that I would truly class as my actual sons. The first being Gabriel, of course."

She closes her eyes briefly. "Of course." She smiles. "But what about the other son? Jesus?"

He chuckles. "You mean this guy?" He transforms himself into Jesus Christ.

She closes her eyes for a second, and then shakes her head and utters a laugh. "You've got to be kidding me," she scoffs. "Nice disguise."

He laughs. "Yeah. I thought so too. Gabe would go off his rocker if he knew." He laughs again. "I love Gabe to bits. Honest to a fault. He's never been a fan of me taking human form and living among them, seeing if I could influence them into living good, honest, and better lives." He smiles at her. "And if he knew I was actually Christ, well, I think he would be a bit upset. Especially considering the grief that it caused."

Charlotte frowns. "But... surely he must have guessed? I mean, you are supposed to be the holy trinity, yeah? That Christ was you and all that? He must have an inkling, surely?"

The Creator frowns and raises his eyebrows. "I'd like to think he does and just plays along with me, but I know that not to be true." He laughs. "Everyone's got their secrets, my dear. Besides, I kinda liked it for a bit y'know? Being a child, a human child with loving and doting parents. They were all right they were, Mary and Joseph. He was a good guy. Especially considering his missus had effectively been knocked up by another guy. I thought he took it well."

She laughs, looking up. Although none of the situation she is in is funny, she can't help but chuckle at that remark, even as twisted as it is.

"Yeah. He was all right that Joseph. A good guy. A good bloke." He takes another drink. "Got bored with it after a while though. Needed a break. Kinda gained a new respect for humans after that, how they trudge through their lives, the things they had to endure." He nods. "So, at age 12 I took a break, a sabbatical if you will. Came back at age 30 to see the whole martyrdom thing through."

She nods. "Did it hurt?"

He frowns. "The crucifixion?"

She nods.

He shakes his head. "Nah. I don't feel physical pain. What did hurt was the pain it caused my mother, well... his mother." He glances at her and smiles. "And Judas. I have to admit, I regret the pain I caused him. Most of that was uncalled for. He's another of life's good guys." He nods.

She admires him for a moment, his change in demeanor, reminiscing about the past. And she wonders how many opportunities he gets to engage in conversation like this.

"Very few," He says.

The remark startles her, then she realizes he knows what she had been thinking. She breathes out through her nose at him. "Please don't do that. It's rude."

He shrugs and smiles. "Sorry, man, it's ma' thing. My blessing and my curse."

"I think I'll take that drink now," she says.

He smiles and stands, walks to the decanter, pours her a drink, walks back and hands it to her and then retakes his seat.

She stares into the glass for a few seconds, swirling the liquid around and then takes a sip. She coughs a couple of times and puts it down on a table to her right. "Oh my God, I've changed my mind. That is shit."

He bursts into laughter. "Sorry, I should've made that a cola."

"Yeah," she says, still coughing, "you should've."

He watches her for a few moments, amused at her coughing into a clenched fist. Eventually, her spasms subside and she clears her throat, and he takes another sip of his drink.

She takes a deep breath and coughs once more. "So. Are you gonna do something about this or what?"

He shifts in his seat and shakes his head. "Ugggh. And we were having such a nice conversation, really connecting." He places his drink down on his table with a thud. "You're gonna persist with this, aren't you?"

"Of course I bloody am! Why the hell d'you think I came here?"

"Look, I've done enough, it's up to others now to see thi—"

"Done enough?!" she says, interrupting him, "done enough? You've done nothing. Jack shit." She stares at him, her eyes wide.

He leans forward, his posture one of anger. "Oh haven't I? Hmm? Who went down and walked the planet as Jesus to help these people? Hmm? Who sent Gabe down to offer you a different path? Who kept Judas on the straight and narrow, leading him to his destiny? Who stopped time and opened a portal for Daniel and the others so that you would have a way back? Eh? Me, that's who. Although to be fair, that Daniel's a smart kid, I reckon he would've figured out it in the end. Point is, I do a hell of a lot and no one ever gives me credit for it or thinks it's me. And I have done something even greater than that. A gift that I gave to every creature I created. Free will." He nods at her. "Free will. It is what has gotten humanity as far as they have come, it is what has started wars and more importantly settled them. It is the thing that drives every hope, dream, and ambition that they have ever had and the thing that has damned many of them. So don't you dare try to tell me I haven't done anything!" He stands, angry, and paces to the fireplace where a welcoming fire burns. He leans against the mantle, tapping a finger against it.

"Everything you have created?" she asks, standing also.

"Yes. Every single thing."

She glances to her side. "Well, Gabe and the others don't seem to think so. They seem to be bound by a lack of free will. How am I supposed to believe you if that fact isn't true?"

His head flops forward and he runs his hand over his head. "Okay, that one is probably my fault. Seriously, I mean it when I say everything I have created has free will of some variety or another. All creatures and plants on the planet have a form of it, subtle for most, but it is still free will. But with Gabe and the others, well…" he pushes himself off the mantle with a sigh and turns toward her. "Look. I'd had a few drinks one time, and one thing led to another and I kinda intimated to Gabe and the others that they had no free will, that it was something I had only created for humans. Gabe and most of the others took it well enough, y'know, didn't question it, but a certain few… kinda didn't."

"Oh, my God!" she says, turning away from him, then walking to the other side of the room, her hands planted on the sides of her face.

He ambles toward her. "Look… I know, I know. I should have put a stop to it, but quite frankly… well… look, I didn't mean for it to get this out of hand." He shakes his head and sighs.

She rounds on him. "Are you fucking trying to tell me that everything down there, all of the people who have lost their lives to your lunatic son, is because of a drunken joke? Because you didn't have the stones to tell them that they did, in fact, have free will and were not bound to the amount of servitude you led them to believe?"

He holds out a hand to her. "Look, when you put it like that, sure, it sounds bad but it wasn't like that—"

"WASN'T LIKE THAT!? Are you fucking kidding me? Wasn't like that? Oh God, oh my God." She places a hand to her forehead and turns back and forth. "This is madness, this is completely insane."

He shakes his head. "Look. This is getting us nowhere. In time, you'll come to understand when you're running things."

Her attention snaps to him. "What?"

He looks confused. "Well, yeah. That's where your destiny lies. As my successor." He shakes his head. "You haven't figured that one out yet? In time you'll be my replacement."

She stomps toward him and holds up a finger. "I don't wanna hear it. I don't care. Sort this out."

"I can't," He says, holding up his hands.

"Sort this out," she repeats.

"I can't," He says, with more force.

"Give the command to Gabe and Michael. Get them involved."

"I can't," He says, this time even more forcefully.

Her anger peaks. "GIVE THE FUCKING COMMAND!"

"I CAN'T!" He replies, with equal venom.

She stares at him, rage burning in her eyes. She breathes out hard. "Why not?"

His face softens, and He smiles.

Walking backward, the Creator moves away from her and the room changes to pure white, with a long spiral staircase that stretches up into clouds. Turning to face the stairs, He then glances back at her. "Because. It isn't my command to give." He then walks up the stairs and disappears.

Charlotte stares at the space he just occupied, wide eyed, then looks down and her eyes dart left and right. She then snaps her head up and marches toward the door, and it opens for her without her interaction.

388

Outside, Gabriel and Gary have been joined by Michael, Raphael, and Raguel who eagerly eye her as she approaches them.

Gabriel walks toward her, frowning, his hands held out to his sides and palms up.

"Gabe, Michael, gather everybody," she says, striding toward them.

"Why? What's going on?" Gabriel asks.

"We're going to war."

Raguel punches the air. "It's about goddamn time."

SIXTY

He is a force of unmetered rage and uncontrollable violence. He cannot be reasoned with and hears no pleas for mercy, bringing swift and decisive vengeance to anything that gets in his way.

The lower hall of the Red Keep is awash with the blood of demons as Judas Iscariot whirlwinds through it, carving the denizens of Hell into pieces regardless of their size or standing within the kingdom. He cares not. He is a reckoning.

Throwing Ikazuchi out and to his side, it spins through the air like a disc, arcing its way around and through a crowd of demons, exploding them into a mass of body parts and spraying black blood everywhere. Before, the hall was filled with the battle screams of demons, now it is filled with their pain and acute terror as Heaven's maniac ploughs through them without stopping or taking a single faltering step.

Catching Ikazuchi, the sword having boomeranged around, he leaps into the air and performs a plunging attack, splitting a Demon-Knight in half, and he is oblivious to the noxious and toxic cloud that bursts up from its gory remains, immunity from it being another of Lady Famine's gifts.

Ahead, another large group races forward, attempting to block entry to the elevator leading up to Lucifer's throne room and he is about to sprint toward them when the Keep shudders and jolts, the ground beneath him shaking with violent tremors. As fast as it arrived, the quake ceases but he senses another force acting upon the structure. Upward momentum. The Keep is rising, and that can only mean one thing. He charges at the remaining demons, sword raised high, and they retaliate, howling and screaming as they sprint at him. Upon drawing close, he transforms into an engulfing mass of rotting and diseased ravens, ripping through and tearing them to pieces, sending them into the air and spraying their foul blood everywhere.

Then, changing back into human form, Judas strides onto the elevator and turns around so that he faces the carnage.

Littered with bodies, the room echoes with the moans and groans of the obliterated, and in the center a demon stands, perfectly still, eyeing him with wide and strained eyes. It then splits in two, the top half of its body sliding off at a diagonal angle and wetly thudding onto the ground.

Stabbing Ikazuchi into the floor of the elevator, it rises, and Judas takes a deep and contemplative breath.

Side by side within the throne room, War and Death stand patiently awaiting his arrival. War holding his massive battle sword out to the side, the tip of the blade embedded in the floor, and Death with his scythes down by his sides, swinging gently. And at last the elevator comes into view, sliding Judas up into place and facing them.

Lifting his sword out of the ground, War walks toward him. "You have fought admirably, Iscariot, a man truly worthy of our respe—"

Judas shadow-steps to him as fast as lightning and punches him square in the chest, launching War across the room into Lucifer's throne and then turns his attention to Death, who attacks with his scythes, spinning them in front of him. Judas blocks each of the swings then shadow-steps to his right and then left in quick succession and swings Ikazuchi, catching Death off-guard.

Death reacts quickly and spins out of the way, but the tip of the blade catches his mask, tearing it off and he comes to a halt with a raised hand to his face. He grins, his face a rotted skeleton, his eyes black and lifeless, then he leaps into the air and launches a scythe that spins toward Judas.

Raising Ikazuchi up horizontally, the flat of the blade outward and the tip held in his other hand, he blocks it, and the weapon rattles against his, the metal chiming as the scythe batters against it in rotation. Glancing between the weapon's blur, he sees Death shift to his right, attempting to outflank him, and so he lets go of Ikazuchi and moves to intercept.

His sword immediately transforms into a giant hulking beast and grips the spinning scythe in a huge clawed hand then crushes the weapon into splinters.

Judas holds out his hand and Ikazuchi flies back into it, shifting from beast to steel in the blink of an eye, then he throws the sword forward and meets Death's follow-up attack, blocking his remaining scythe.

Death no longer looks to be grinning. Within his black eyes there flickers a trace of concern, and well there should be as Judas pushes against him, sliding him across the room, where he scrabbles his feet against the floor trying to maintain his footing.

With an angry grunt, the Horseman breaks the hold and shadow-steps away but is met by Judas as he exits the move, the angel equal to if not faster than his speed. He moves again with the same outcome. Again and again, each time stopping only to have Judas appear in front of him, his face emotionless, relentless.

Pulling himself out of the obliterated throne, War roars and bursts forward to join his brother in the fight, and upon seeing the other Horseman advance, Judas disengages from attacking Death and shadow-steps toward him and strikes, forcing War to defend.

They trade blows, each attempting to work themselves into an opening, their swings and strikes moving at a speed that is invisible to the naked eye.

Springing around the room cat-like, Death clambers up a wall and, using it to propel himself up and forward, launches at Judas. But before he can get near him, Judas drops and leg sweeps War's feet from under him, then rises quickly and punches Death mid-air, careering him to the other side of the room where he crashes into a wall.

Taking advantage of Judas' focus on Death, War lashes out with one of his massive legs, sending Judas skidding backward, but the angel doesn't lose his balance. He remains upright, causing War to scream with anger and streak toward him, his sword to his side trailing down at an angle. And, leaping into the air, War then brings it over his head and crashing down toward Judas who uses his new heightened power to its fullest advantage and shadow-steps backward, causing the weapon to slam into the ground and miss, thus staggering War due to overreaching his attack.

Blazing forward to him in shadow-step, Judas slams Ikazuchi into War's chest and The Horseman's eyes open wide. A crunching sound erupts, and War looks down at his chest and then back up and into Judas' face, who regards him with a blank stare. Then, another crunch, and the sword begins to draw him in and absorbs him. His armor cracks and buckles as his body ebbs, him trying to fight against it, to pull himself free, but it is of no use as Ikazuchi has him now and he will not let go. War screams as the weapon consumes his body bit by bit, creaking and crunching it into Ikazuchi, and within seconds only his head remains. He smiles. "Well done, Iscariot," he says, as the final part of him disappears.

Death pounces across the room in a zigzag, attempting to catch Judas off-guard as the angel struggles with the energy coursing through the sword and in turn into him. And so, moving around him fast and cat-like once again he attempts to use his agility to confuse Judas.

Knowing he has no time to allow War's energy to compromise him, Judas throws everything into burying the Horseman deep within him for a short time while he deals with his brother. But he doesn't know how long he will be able to keep the ferocious power that rallies inside him at bay, so he must do all he can to hang on until he is able to defeat Death. Anticipating the remaining Horseman's next move, he steps toward him and lashes out with Ikazuchi, but connects with nothing as Death disappears. He turns in circles, attempting to pinpoint his position, but to no avail. Then he receives a heavy blow to the side of his face that spins him around and staggers him, and he swings his sword in the direction from where it came. But there is nothing there.

"Okay, you tricky little bastard," Judas says, "so you're slipping in and out of this reality, moving through the room and then striking at me? Yeah. You are a tricky bastard, ain'tcha?"

With a grunt, Judas then drops to one knee as Death's scythe cuts through the top of his leg forcing him to hold up his sword in defense, expecting the next strike to be at his face. But nothing comes.

Lady Famine chuckles. *Here, let me get that for you.*

Dark liquid spreads over the wound, quickly healing his leg and he stands again.

"Any ideas?" he asks her.

My brother is toying with you. He enjoys this. But it will be his undoing.

Death materializes behind Judas again out of the reality time-stream, and punches him in the back, knocking him to the ground.

Judas scrambles back to his feet and slashes behind himself with Ikazuchi.

Stop that, Iscariot. It is pointless. He is between our worlds. But he will have had enough fun now and will want to finish this so that we can all go home. Do you trust me, Judas?

"Er, no, not really."

Lady Famine laughs once more. *Fair enough.* She chuckles again. *Let me rephrase that. Will you trust me this one time?*

He groans and grits his teeth. "Aggh, fine! I don't really give a shit at this point."

More laughter. *Very well. Then let his next attack succeed. He will approach you from behind and life-drain you.*

"What? You're kidding, right?"

No Judas. Please, just trust me. You must let this happen. Quickly now, get ready, here it comes, I can feel his presence approaching. Let his attack complete and I will do the rest.

Dropping his guard, Judas takes a deep breath and exhales.

Exactly as Lady Famine predicted, from behind him Death appears out of the time-stream, leaping at him in mid-air and lands on his back, wrapping his hands around his face.

Judas does not panic, nor does he scream. He simply closes his eyes. "Okay. Do it," he says to Famine.

She cackles as she transfers her disease and despair into Death and the Horseman lets go of Judas immediately and drops to the ground, where he claws at his head and face as though a million parasites crawl over it.

He is feeling something he never felt before. In all their existence, the Horsemen have never once fought against one another, and it has become clear they are not immune to each other's powers. Death writhes on the floor, clutching at his throat, forced to experience Lady Famine's carnage firsthand.

Ambling toward him, Judas grits his teeth as the Horseman rolls onto his back and faces him while still tearing at his throat, face, and body, Famine's disease overpowering him.

Death grins through a pained smile as Judas slams Ikazuchi into his face and fires up the absorption process once again. And as soon as it completes, Judas screams – one terrifying, fierce, and piercing howl. He raises Ikazuchi into the air, both hands around the hilt as he violently shudders and shakes, struggling to maintain a standing position against the terrible energy flooding through him. At the apex of his rage, he slams Ikazuchi into the ground, releasing both Horseman's energies at once and the upper half of the Red Keep explodes.

SIXTY-ONE

Michael, Raphael, and Raguel walk away, eager to gather Heaven's forces and march them into war.

Charlotte stops Gabriel by the arm as he is about to follow them. "Hey. Got a minute?"

He smiles. "For you? I have all of them."

Returning his smile, she looks down at the ground for a moment then back up at him. "Thank you," she says, while leaning in and kissing his cheek.

"For what?" he says, taken aback.

"For everything. Saving me, offering me a different life."

He closes his eyes and sighs. Opening them he smiles again, briefly. "So you know then."

"Yeah, I know."

"And you're okay with it?"

She releases a small laugh. "It took some getting used to, but a friend showed me how it all went down. So yeah, I'm okay with knowing."

He frowns, his eyes moving to the side a little as though searching a memory within his mind. "So... you were there, that was you!"

She takes a step back. A wide smile on her face. "I knew you could see me. I told Pestilence that you saw me, and I was right. He said it was impossible, but I knew it."

"Well, seeing you is a bit of a stretch. I sensed something there, something familiar but I couldn't put my finger on it."

"Pestilence said it was a memory and that there was no way you could have known I was there."

Gabriel glances to the doors leading to the Creator's chamber. "Hmmm, maybe other forces were at work."

She glances into the same direction and her mouth curls up into a half-smile. "Yeah. When this is all over remind me that you and I need to have a serious chat about a few things."

He chuckles. "Deal. And you're welcome."

She shakes her head and with a small smile admires him. "You've been there for me for so long and I never even realized. How long did you look after me?"

"Until you were four and a half. I had placed you in the orphanage around 18 months before the day you met Judas, but you had in truth only been six months old at that time... Earth's time of course. We'd cooked the books, so to speak, including altering the perception of what time you were born for the memories planted into the minds of those who thought they had been present. We needed as many insurance policies as possible, you see."

She nods. "Yeah, makes sense. You rescued me, took me into the alternate reality where I grew to age four and a half, fabricated my birth, then hid me in the orphanage with Sister Marie." She looks puzzled for a moment. "But why? Why take me from the alternate reality and put me somewhere I could have been in danger... where I *had* been in danger?"

Gabriel rolls his eyes and cocks a thumb back to the chamber doors behind him. "You would have to ask, He who works in mysterious ways. He said it was time for you to go to Earth and learn about being a child with real people. He wanted to put you in a foster home but I insisted on the orphanage, stating it would be the safer option with people with whom we had... connections." He shakes his head and sighs. "Some plan of mine that turned out to be. Damn that Father Mallory."

She places a hand on his shoulder. "You couldn't have known Gabe, it wasn't your fault." She glances back toward the doors, "but I suspect someone did."

He looks at the doors again. "Well, it's not my place to question." He pauses for a moment and then smiles and looks back at her.

"Oh Gabe, please do remind me that we need to have that chat when we are done." She laughs.

Walking up to her, Gary breaks the moment. "Hey you. It's really great to see you again."

"Heeeeey!" she says, flinging her arms around him and squeezing tight. "I have missed you."

They remain that way, each enjoying the familial bond between them, of her enjoying a hug from her uncle Gary, and him for the girl he has come to consider as his niece. After a few moments, she breaks the embrace and gently punches his arm. "But what the hell are you doing up here? I thought I was pretty specific when I said do not get killed!"

He makes a playful, hurt face while rubbing his arm.

Gabriel steps forward. "Actually, that might have been my fault."

Gary waves a dismissive hand. "Nah, I knew what I was getting myself into. I thought I could come up here and talk some sense into God, y'know, try to get him to help out down below."

She raises her eyebrows and cocks a thumb backward. "Who, that guy?"

Gary laughs and runs his hand over his head. "Yeeeeahh. That guy. Pretty dumb, eh?"

She smiles and nods. "Yeah. Pretty dumb. But that's you to a fault. Selfless and willing to sacrifice anything and everything to help others. It's why you are the purest soul I know." She grabs his face and kisses his forehead and Gary smiles, closing his eyes and welcoming the Divinity that comes with it.

Opening them again, Gary looks back and smiles at Jacob, Emily, and Tony, then turns back to Charlotte. "So, I guess you're moving in for the kill then, the final battle so to speak."

Pursing her lips, she nods.

"And Judas, where is he?"

She gives a small laugh. "Without doubt raising merry hell right now, kicking ass and taking names I suspect. But I need to get down there as soon as I can so that he doesn't go too far."

"Too far?" Gary says, frowning.

"Yeah. It's a long story," she stares at him for a moment and then looks past him to his family, "and I'll fill you in on the details ASAP."

He opens his mouth to say something and shakes his head.

Her eyes bead with tears, and she places her hands on his shoulders. "I'm sorry, I'm so, so sorry, but I need you... I can't do this without you."

He shakes his head, his own eyes glistening, the emotion threatening to spill out. "Of course you can. You're Charlotte Hope, you can do anything. You don't need me."

"But I do. And I'm so sorry – I really am so very sorry."

He takes an emotional breath. "I just got here. I haven't seen him in... well, I just got here."

She moves her hands from the tops of his arms to the sides of his face. "I know. But they will be here for you and you will see him again. That's a promise."

He lowers his head and wipes away a single tear with the back of his hand, then looks back up at her. "But I'm dead."

She smiles. "Say goodbye to them. Then we get to work."

Michael, dressed in full battle armor, stands atop a large set of white stairs that lead down to a mustering area for Heaven's army. Below, thousands of angels line up in perfect formation, awaiting the command from their leader. As Gabriel approaches, Michael calls them to attention and they respond in precise unison, the sound of their stomping feet crunching loud.

Gabriel nods at Michael and is about to say something when Michael pre-empts him.

"My Captain. We await your command."

Gabriel regards him for a moment and then Raphael and Raguel also, who stand to attention and nod at him with inconspicuous smiles. Taking a deep breath, Gabriel descends the stairs, followed by the other Archangels, and strides onto the platform with purpose, where the gathered troops create a pathway either side of him.

"Ready?" Charlotte asks, as Gary walks back to her having said his teary goodbyes to his family.

"Yeah. Yeah, I'm ready."

"How'd they take it?"

He looks back at them for a moment and then to her. "Fine. They understood. They know how important this is. I think Jacob was pretty impressed that I get to be your right-hand guy."

She smiles. "Right-hand guy?" She offers a breathy laugh and shakes her head. "Sweetie, you are so much more than my right-hand guy." She smiles again. "See ya very soon." She places a finger in the center of his forehead.

Gary sits bolt upright and exhales hard.

The young female medic who had just finished covering him up in the med-bay screams, flailing her arms in the air and jolting backward into a cart full of metal pans and glass beakers.

He turns toward her, an arm out to try to calm her. "I'm sorry. I'm so sorry. Where's Nathan?"

She doesn't answer, instead continues to try to catch her breath while bent over, her hands on her knees.

Hopping off the table, Gary strides over and grabs hold of her, straightening her up, and she screams again. "Where's Colonel Taylor?" he says, this time with more urgency.

Marching through his troops, pieces of Gabriel's armor fly to him and mold onto his body. His arm and shin guards, the breastplate, the pauldrons all attaching to him with a clank. Then his battle helmet, covering not only his head but his neck, fits around his skull. And finally he holds out a hand to receive his impressive looking long sword, and upon gripping it he twirls it around and seats it on his back between his shoulder blades.

His stride turns into a jog, and then a sprint, followed by Michael and his team, and as they pass them, the ranks of angels break from their rows and file into place behind him, matching their speed as they race toward the Earth-drop.

SIXTY-TWO

"You, my friend, were dead. No heartbeat, no pulse, no breathing, just... dead," Nathan says, counting the clinical symptoms on his fingers.

Gary smiles. "Yeah. Yeah, I was but now I'm back."

Nathan regards him for a moment and then laughs, semi-maniacally. "So what happened? What was that all about?"

Pursing his lips, Gary scratches the side of his head vigorously. "Ahhh, it was kinda mine and Gabriel's idea. Go upstairs, talk to God, try to convince him to get involved."

There is a brief pause. "And?" An amused Nathan prompts him.

Gary laughs and looks to one side. "Not me, buddy. I couldn't get through to him. But she sure as hell did."

Nathan nods. "So that's where she went."

"She was here?"

"Yeah, she was here. Brought the kids back."

"Kids? What, Sarah and co?"

He nods again.

"From where?"

Nathan laughs, "Oh, you're gonna love this. From Hell."

"HELL?"

"Yep. Hell."

Gary's mouth opens and closes, trying to find the right words. Raising his hands, he shakes his head, then looks down, his mouth still agape.

"Listen, man," Nathan says, his eyebrows raised, "it's a tale for another day. I guess if she hasn't told you about it, then have more pressing matters to attend to?"

Gary slowly nods, returning his attention to Nathan. "Yeah. Yeah, we do. We need to get everyone together—"

"I'll just stop you there, buddy," Nathan says, holding up a hand. "It's already done. She said muster everyone, so that is what I did."

"Right. Right, excellent. Well then, let's waste no time. Where are they?"

"On the apron outside hangar four."

"Okay, cool. Lemme grab my gear and I'll be there in five."

"All right. See ya soon." Nathan turns to walk away and then stops. He glances back. "I'm really glad you ain't dead, Gary. Really glad." He nods.

Gary smiles. "Thanks, man," he says, nodding back.

A knock causes Gary, who is finishing clipping up his body armor, to turn his attention toward it to see Sarah smiling in the doorway.

"Hey," he says, smiling back.

She enters the room. "So how does it feel to be a modern-day Lazarus?"

He laughs. "To be honest," he pauses and then laughs again, "it feels strange. Very, very strange."

She laughs back, then walks over and picks up his weapon, cocking and checking it, sighting it with one eye, then lowers and hands it to him."

He looks surprised. "Wow, someone's become a badass overnight. Since when did you know about guns?"

She smiles. "Hardly a badass. But Nathan says we are all going to have to fight if we are to save our world."

He turns away from her for a moment, closing his locker with a clank, then taking a deep breath, he turns back. "You don't have to come you know, you could just—"

She holds up a hand. "No! This is bigger than anything the world has ever faced in all its centuries of troubles. Besides, what am I if I'm not prepared to fight for my home?" Her eyes harbor a yearning coupled with sorrow and she looks down, then up as she tracks him walking toward her.

"Look. Not everyone need be a fighter to play their part, and believe me you have done more than enough up to now. No one would think any less of you."

She looks down again for a moment and licks her lips, then swallows hard. "I would," she says, looking back up.

He sighs, sympathizing with her. "Vengeance… it's a powerful thing Sarah. It can change a person, make them something they're not. It's the planting of a seed within you that should be avoided at all costs, because it will grow at a rapid rate and consume everything about them."

She shakes her head a little. "This isn't about revenge. I have come to terms with the loss of my sister. This is about doing what's right. For everyone."

He admires her, the courage she displays, knowing exactly the sort of fight she is moments from entering, yet she is unafraid, determined even. He screws his mouth up into a smile and sighs. "Come on," he says, placing a hand around her shoulder and leading her out of the door, "let's go save the world."

"Oh my word," she giggles, "that was so corny."

He laughs.

Nathan strides over to Conrad as the big Ukrainian ushers people around outside the hangar. "Are those the only birds we have left?" he says, pointing to two Apache gunships in the process of initiating their rotors.

"No sir, have more craft but not pilots. These two only ones survived attack."

"Shit," he says, looking to his left. "All right, it will have to do. Looks like a ground-heavy campaign anyway."

"Sir," Conrad says, lowering his voice and moving toward him while pointing at the gunships, "these will not last long. Surely there will be flying demons, and much more maneuverability they have."

Normally, this would be the point where he would have inspirational words for him, to rally and give him cause to think that death is not waiting for them, that their skill will see them through to fight another day. But he cannot. He knows it would be a lie and that Conrad would see right through it. After all they have been through, the big man deserves to know his true feelings. He sighs. "Conrad. In truth, I don't think any of us will last that long. But this is what we do. This is who we are. We are soldiers, and absolutely everything is at stake here. And I for one want to stand at whatever gate is determined for me, and know before I am judged that I did everything I could to prevent the end, if that is what is to be our fate." He motions toward the helicopters with his head. "And I am sure those fellas will feel the same as well, as will every man and woman here. They are not stupid people. They know what they are getting themselves into."

Conrad smiles. An action that takes Nathan aback, as in all the time he has known the man he can't ever remember him doing so. Sure, he has seen him laughing maniacally as he tears into demons, but never a smile of heart-felt emotion, his hard-exterior peeled back to reveal his softer core.

"You are right, Colonel Taylor. No matter what, it has been my honest and genuine pleasure to have met and have fought with you. You are finest man I have ever known. It would have been honor to serve with you properly back in day."

Nathan takes a moment to consider a response, then smiles, deciding to say nothing at all. He simply holds out a hand to Conrad and exchanges a firm shake with him.

The moment is broken as Gary and Sarah approach, closely followed by Isaac and Daniel, with Jonesy bringing up the rear.

Gary nods at Conrad who responds by smiling and giving him a thumbs up.

"Holy shit," Gary says, his eyebrows raised. "He does smile."

Nathan laughs. "I know, right. He did it to me a second ago, now I can't get the big daft bastard to stop."

Conrad offers a loud and over-exaggerated laugh. "I go now. Make sure all is ready with men."

"Ahem," Sarah says, "there's women in there too you know."

"You know what I mean," he says, as he walks away with his back to her and waving a hand.

"So this is it?" Daniel says, clapping his hands together while moving closer to them. His mood may be playful, but his tone suggests otherwise. He glances at everyone, a distinct nervousness in his eyes.

Gary nods while looking at them all. "Yeah, this is it." He smiles and then looks across the apron to where the forces are gathered. His heart sinks. "Is that all that's left? All that survived the attack?"

Nathan sighs and pats him on the back as he walks past him. "We will make it count where we can."

Gary looks at Sarah, who offers him a doleful smile, and he then turns toward Isaac, who takes a deep breath. His attention flits between them. "No matter what we stick together, okay? We will get through this. I promise."

"I believe you," Isaac says, his attitude toward Gary the least hostile it has been since the pair met.

Gary holds out a hand and Isaac gives it a firm shake.

They say nothing, as there is nothing more to be said. Whatever happens next will shape the outcome of the world forever, and each person knows it. They all know how important their role will be in the fight no matter how small it may be.

The group remains silent for a moment, each contemplating what the next hour or so will bring.

Their musings are brought to a sudden halt by the sound of a powerful portal opening on the tarmac a short distance from them in the direction Nathan walked off into. From out of it strides Charlotte, heading toward the gathered troops.

"Come on," Gary says, setting off toward her, "it's time."

Nathan acknowledges her as she approaches and she smiles at him.

"Gary?" she says, raising an eyebrow.

Nathan points behind her in the direction from where Gary and the others approaches.

"Okay, good," she says, turning back to him. "This it?" she says, pointing at the troops.

He glances over his shoulder and sighs. "'Fraid so."

She takes a deep breath and exhales, nodding as she does. She smiles at Gary as he moves to her side and he returns one of his own. "Okay then," she says, "let's see what we got."

As she approaches the 60 or so men and women gathered ahead of her, they begin to acknowledge her. Those sitting get to their feet, and others who were engaged in conversation cease their chatter and focus their attention upon her.

Scratching her head, she appears agitated, looking back at Gary and the others as they gather around, and then back to the group. Peering into the faces of those who are to be entrusted with the survival of humanity, she feels her stomach knot. Public speaking has never been her forte, but neither has a lack of having anything to say. But she knows the words she must offer before they enter battle, the inspiration she must spread, has caused a nervousness in her that she hasn't felt in a long time. She sighs, once again turning to Gary in the hope of receiving inspiration of her own. He winks, and she smiles within herself. It was enough. She turns back to the people and takes another deep breath.

"My name is Charlotte… although I guess most of you know that." She smiles. "I'm not the President of the United States, and this isn't a cheesy movie about aliens taking over our world."

A small amount of laughter ripples out from the group.

"But I do feel that there is a need to say a few words before we do what we all know must be done. You all deserve that much. You deserve to know what your sacrifice will mean to our world when we succeed in taking it back. And we will succeed."

A few people smile and straighten up, her opening words having an immediate effect.

"What awaits us will be terrifying. This much I cannot and will not lie to you about. But you must be strong. You must be resolute. Although it feels that the world is gone, that we are the only ones left, that simply is not true. Many others still survive however they can, fighting their own terrors day by day. But what we will accomplish today will set them free. It will set us all free and allow us to come together, finally as one people, knowing that at the end of days, in our darkest moment, we stood together as brother and sister – as equals, irrespective of our faiths or beliefs. That what we did mattered, more than anything else has ever mattered in the history of the world. However, not all of you will make it back. We can't. But I have no doubt in my mind that if you pass, you will awake anew in a land free from pain and suffering, and that I will see each of you again someday."

She wets her lips and takes another deep breath, looking out over the faces of the people stood in front of her, some determined, others with their fears evident. She wonders if telling them the blunt truth is wise. Whether it is inspiring or doing more harm than good. She shakes it from her mind, deciding to carry on regardless. They deserve to be treated with respect and to know exactly what awaits them.

"So I ask you now to take up arms, maybe for the last time ever, and stand with me as we push back against the darkness. As we show the terrible creatures that await us that we will not fear them and that they do not define us." She smiles and takes another deep breath. "You are all my friends, and the admiration I have for you cannot be measured. I am proud to fight for and stand with each and every one of you." She smiles again.

There are no cheers, whoops, or fists pumping the air. The gathered troops simply look to one another, and exchange silent marks of respect, handshakes, and hugs.

Gary places a hand on Charlotte's shoulder to congratulate her on a job well done, just as a young soldier steps forward.

The young man raises a hand as if he were in school. "Charlotte," he says, a boyish nervousness to his voice, "I'm with you." He looks around, "we... are with you, of course. But," he looks down, and swallows hard, then back up, "is this it? Are we to do this alone?"

She smiles, nods, and walks over to him, then places her hands on his shoulders. "No. Not alone."

From overhead, an immense explosion splits the sky, the loudest thunder that there has ever been, and a single fireball blazes across it, quickly joined by three others, each with loud booms of their own. Then, the entire early evening sky illuminates as thousands more appear with sonic booms so loud it causes everyone but Charlotte to cover their ears and startle.

Striding away from the young man, furious intent etched into her face, Charlotte thrusts out a hand, clenches it into a fist, pulls it back and rips open a massive portal, at least 100 feet high and just as wide. And without breaking stride, she glances back at everyone and then walks through it.

END OF DAYS

His grin stretches the handprint scars left by Charlotte, an expression that is equal parts smug and evil as he stands in the middle of the post-apocalyptic New York City street, immaculate in his black suit and long black overcoat, his legs apart, arms behind his back as he faces the massive portal that has opened in front of him. Glancing up, Lucifer sniffs, unconcerned with the thousands of pluming fireballs streaking down from Heaven, and his eyes drift over his own army, present in their tens of thousands, every variety and size of demon he has at his disposal lined up on every ruined building, in every side street, among the rubble and devastation, and perched within the broken and leaning skyscrapers. They are everywhere.

Springing up and down on his toes, growing impatient, he turns toward Samael and nods at him then returns his smug gaze to the portal, and from out of its center strides Charlotte, causing him to burst into a surprised laugh. "Wow," he says, glancing at Samael once again and then back to her, "you, young lady, are bloody hard to kill. I am seriously impressed!"

Although his voice is at a normal level and he is a great distance from her, she hears him as though he were right in front of her.

Performing a slow handclap that causes Samael to smile, Lucifer frowns, then leans to his right, looking over her shoulder, the action symbolic. "What, no Judas?" He laughs. "I'll be honest, I thought the portal was his."

Charlotte halts a short distance away from the anomaly event behind her, and throws her hands out to her sides, her swords flying into them.

She has had enough. Enough of his smug and talkative ways, of him being in her life for so long, keeping her in fear and on the run, and she will very much enjoy beating him into the ground. She knows, however, that destroying him would be problematic and is hoping that Gabriel and his team will have a solution, but in the meantime, she aims to kill as many of his demons as she possibly can, and then beat his ass senseless.

She looks around at the demons, their numbers too many to count, and then back to Lucifer. "Talk, talk, talk, talk, talk," she says with a sneer. "That's all you do, Lucifer. You talk and you talk." She stares at him for a second. "No matter, because after tonight you won't feel like talking for a very long time."

He laughs and looks to Samael again, shaking his head. "Is this bitch for real?" He looks back at her, and sniffs. "Ahhh, fuck it," he says, clicking his fingers, and materializing Beelzebub through a fog, who walks toward him slowly. Lucifer's attire then changes into battle armor, but not like any he has previously worn. His assimilation of The Book and The Seals has seen a formidable infusion of Light-Divinity and his devastating dark energy, granting him access to something previously out of reach, a power he has sought for an eternity, and the sleek, black armor that crunches itself around his body reflects his new level and standing within the universe. He holds his hand out to his side. "Makarus, it is time."

Changing from stroll to sprint, Beelzebub then transforms into the massive great-sword, its blade red in color, somersaulting and landing in Lucifer's hand and he strides forward with it, his powerful feet crunching into the dirt, the ground cratering underneath each footfall. No other demon moves. None dare until they receive the command from their master.

Closing and opening her eyes, a deep breath between the action, Charlotte holds her swords up in front of her face horizontally and buffs them with Light-Divinity, causing them to glow a brilliant white that illuminates her face, and as her eyes peer over the blades, they narrow and she charges at Lucifer, thrusting her swords down and back to streamline her movement.

Behind her, Nathan and Gary's forces charge through the portal, their battle cries filling the night air, and above Gabriel and his army complete the final few hundred feet descent, swords drawn and pointed at the horde of demons below. And they cry out for battle also, eager and finally grateful that they are unshackled and allowed to tear into the forces of Hell once again without fear of punishment from above. And Gabriel knows that this battle will dwarf even that of the last one he fought against Lucifer.

Lucifer roars, his voice deep and booming, and his horde explode into action.

However, he does not charge at Charlotte as she thought he would. Instead, massive demonic wings sprout from his back and he powers up toward the Heavenly forces screaming toward him, closely followed by Samael.

From varying positions around the Tonada building other winged creatures burst upward, taking flight and following the trajectory of their master, screaming and screeching as they race into aerial combat.

"SPARE NONE. SHOW NO MERCY!" Gabriel roars at his forces, and they return with further battle cries of their own, increasing their velocity into attack.

The crimson night sky is illuminated by powerful energy waves, light and dark alike as the forces of Heaven and Hell collide, erupting into fierce battle. As they meet, demons and angels rain down and the carnage claims its first victims. The other angels not facing an enemy land on the ground in their thousands and begin their attack, crunching into demons as they race across the terrain to meet them.

On the ground looking up, Charlotte growls and screws up her face, annoyed at being denied engaging Lucifer personally. She returns her attention to the battlefield and the onslaught of demons raging toward her and so, shifts into shadow-step and tears into them. Thrusting her swords forward, she ripples a wave of Divinity at them, exploding the first to approach, then sweeps her swords outward destroying dozens more with the same technique. The lingering force of the second divinity wave is so potent the ones behind those first dispatched run into it and explode.

She is unstoppable. A force of holy retribution, a cyclonic killing machine allowing nothing to stand in her way as she dispatches scores of demons foolish enough to attack. Her fighting speed is too much, and her power is too great as she moves between them at an insane velocity within shadow-step, and they are unable to see her as she moves among them, hacking them to pieces.

However, for everything she accomplishes, for every demon she slays, even more portals open in the ground, with more joining their hellish brethren and bolstering their numbers. Raging, she drives through, slicing them, and any that dare get too close she smashes them in the face with the hilts of her swords so hard it causes their heads to explode. Yet still more come, and before long her position is overrun with nowhere to shadow-step to. And she stops as a large group encircles her.

Ahead, five Demon-Knights charge toward her, the ground shaking beneath their feet, their bone armor clunking with each powerful stride.

Charlotte spins her swords around so that the tips of the blades point toward the ground and grips them hard, her face contorting as she concentrates and pours a mixture of Light- and Dark-Divinity into the weapons. And as the horde and Knights close within striking distance of her, she screams while driving her swords into the ground. The area around her erupts with multiple geysers of Divinity, their energy exploding demons into the air and obliterating them. Her face looks maddening as the mixture of dark and white light illuminates it, her ponytailed hair raised and strands flapping upward from the blast wave.

Gary, Nathan, and the other soldiers slide to a halt and shield their eyes from the magnificent and terrifying plumes of energy.

"Jesus!" Gary says to himself, "just what the hell did you learn down there Charley?"

Then Gary and the others flinch as to their right a gigantic demon explodes out of the lower section of a ruined skyscraper. Many of the soldiers stumble backward, preparing to run from the terrifying sight of its green scaly body covered in sharp and curved horns that protrude out of its torso and head. It roars, fierce and loud, a heat wave from its mouth distorting the air. In its hands it carries a gigantic battle ax that it now raises into the air, readying to swing down at them.

"Fuck me!" Gary says, his eyes wide with fear.

"RUUUUUUN!" Nathan shouts and the forces scatter as the ax sweeps down behind them, carving up the ground and rocketing soldiers to their screaming deaths.

Amid the confusion, they split up with Nathan, Conrad, and Daniel moving in a different direction to Gary, Sarah, and Isaac as they sprint to safer areas of the battlefield. But no matter which way the parties run to, each are faced with a gauntlet of rubble and smaller demons to contend with and they open fire at the hellish creatures while trying to maintain their footing.

From out of Charlotte's portal, the two Apache gunships roar right into the path of the enormous demon swiping its ax across the ground ahead of them.

"GUNS, GUNS, GUNS!" the lead pilot screams and his gunner, sat in front of him, engages the beast with the 30mm chain gun. The second aircraft follows suit, rippling large projectiles into the demon's body, causing it to turn and focus its attention upon them and away from the ground forces below.

"EVADE! EVADE!" the second pilot shouts as the demon rages at them, preparing to swing its ax in their direction.

The roar of the rotors intensifies as the gunships bank out of the way with almost no time to spare under the demon's ax as it swings it at them. However, the enormity of the weapon and its slow speed affords them maneuverability, and they spin around and into hover to continue peppering the gigantic creature with their cannons. Staggered whooshes join the noise of the chain guns as each aircraft launches laser-guided Hellfire missiles that explode on impact, knocking the demon backward but not off its feet.

"Holy shit!" the left aircrafts pilot screams, throwing his cyclic to the left, hard, to avoid the demon as it leaps at them, its sudden shift in agility and speed almost catching him off-guard. His aircraft screams as it moves through the air and he fights with the controls to try to stabilize it as a multitude of alarms sound within the cockpit.

As he regains the aircraft's composure, his gunner is about to engage the creature once more when the helicopter jerks violently to the side from the impact caused by a flying demon wrapping itself around the cockpit. Both gunner and pilot scream as the creature head butts the canopy several times, roaring with each strike as it works its way in. Shaking its head side-to-side, it finally breaches the canopy and tears into the gunner with huge, razor-sharp teeth clamping into his head, severing it just above the mouth and blood erupts within the aircraft. Frantically the pilot scrabbles to release his sidearm strapped to his left hip, but cannot due to the uncontrollable spin the aircraft has entered.

Removing its head from within the cockpit, the demon rises into the air and cackles with laughter, then pushes off the helicopter, powering itself back into the sky with massive wings, its turbulence sending the aircraft spiraling down where it explodes on the ground.

The winged demon then spins around, turning its attention toward the remaining aircraft.

In the sky above the carnage, Lucifer and Gabriel engage in fierce aerial combat. Each attempts to gain the upper hand, their attacks relentless as their powerful swords smash against one another, metal upon metal chiming in the night sky.

Working his way to an advantage, Lucifer spins left to right, and his sword whistles through the air and into Gabriel's, the Archangel having anticipated the move, and their weapons explode together to form a quivering cross.

Lucifer laughs.

"It has been a long time since we did this, brother," he says, "but you are no longer the stronger of us. I now hold the key to everything and it resides within me. Even now, that power is too much for you and still it continues to grow. Soon, it will be too much for father as well. Your kin are minutes away from their dooms. I will end you and then soak the Earth in blood before marching to the gates of the White Kingdom and smashing down its doo—"

Sick of his posturing, Gabriel head-butts him and then punches into his chest with his sword arm, rocketing him to the ground. "She's right," he says, powering his wings forward and down in pursuit. "You do talk too damn much."

Below, Lucifer crashes into the ground in a giant plume of dust and dirt. But before the Archangel can take advantage, he is out of the dusty crater and streaming upward at Gabriel once more.

"Father's pathetic puppet," Lucifer roars, "I am going to enjoy ripping you to pieces." He screams again, his rage reaching new heights.

Despite his best efforts to block him, Gabriel is unable to and Lucifer punches into him with such force, it propels him back up into the sky another 100 feet. Before he has time to recover, the Lord of Hell is above and behind him, and he punches into Gabriel's back, hurtling him back toward the ground. And it is now Lucifer's turn to be the cat, chasing down his prey as he enters a power dive toward Gabriel. Upon reaching him, he slices his sword into his back causing the Archangel to cry out.

With Heaven's firstborn at the end of his weapon, Lucifer drives him down and into the ground, where it once again explodes from their impact, spraying dust and dirt everywhere.

***

Archangel Michael rolls out of his hard landing into a sliding halt, with his sword out to his side and his other hand steadying him across the ground, feet wide apart and his body low. Ahead, Samael lands with control and into a small hop to counter the effect of doing so. He has his back to Michael as he talks to him, his red powerful-looking body glistening with sweat.

"So this is it my brother, my old commander. The final battle." He runs a hand over one of his horns that sweep down from the front and sides of his head. "I kinda like 'em, you know? I think this look suits me." He laughs, deep and guttural.

Michael moves into a standing position. "I suppose this is the part where you tell me it was all my fault that I never listened to you or paid you enough respect, huh? Spare me the sermon, Samael. I've heard it all before from the one you now call master."

Samael roars with laughter again. "Master? You think I would call anyone master? No, my erstwhile friend, no one is my master. True, I will aid the Dark One in his pursuit of power and then, when it suits me, I will take it for myself." He laughs again. "This isn't the part where I tell you it was your fault. This isn't the part where I say you never paid enough respect to me. And this isn't the part where I confess to the pain of the absence of the Divine. This, my brother, is the part where I kill you."

Samael roars and charges at Michael, who responds in kind.

***

Sarah screams as she shields her left side from another lava ball that lands much closer than the previous one. She cries out again as Isaac wraps himself around her and throws them both into a crater as another ball of fire splashes into the ground behind them.

Isaac turns to Gary, who had gotten there a fraction of a second before them. "We're getting slaughtered here. We're not making a difference." His face harbors the same anger and aggression as it has for most of the last nine months, their situation enraging him.

Gary grips him by the shoulder. "It matters. Everything we do matters, because it keeps more of those things' attention on us and not her. We are here more for distraction than offense, so you better start dealing with that." He then flinches and pushes all three of them back into the wall of the crater as another fiery projectile lands above them, spraying lava near their feet.

All three drag their limbs back to avoid being touched by the volcanic material and Sarah focuses her attention on Gary, her voice raised over the noise of the battlefield.

"We need a better spot. We gotta get out of here or we won't be around to matter at all."

"Can't argue with that," Gary says, searching for a viable escape route. "There," he says, pointing at the open foyer of a partially destroyed building. "In there – it should provide us with cover while we try to regroup." He looks at each of them in turn, breathing heavily. "Run as fast as you can, and not in a straight line. Keep 'em guessing. Got it?"

They nod vigorously, almost in unison.

"Okay," Gary says, looking ahead and mentally preparing himself for the run. "Three... two... one... GO!"

He screams the last word as they race over the destroyed landscape, trying to maintain their footing as best they can while heeding his advice and running fast, zigzag lines.

At last they reach the building, having dodged, ducked, and weaved their way around the bombardment of fire, and they bundle themselves inside, their lungs burning, screaming for air as they suck down as much as possible.

With a grunt Gary gets to his feet, his weapon raised as he assesses the area, aware they have raced into it with no notion of what might be inside. Edging through what he believes to be a lobby, he trains his weapon from side to side, ducking down to see under obstacles, ensuring that nothing terrifying awaits them ready to pounce. Satisfied the area is secure, he motions to Sarah and Isaac. "Okay, come on," he says, keeping his voice low, not taking any chances that there may indeed be a hidden presence. "Let's see if we can find a way out of this and then get back into the fight."

"You wanna go back out there?" Sarah says, whispering, a mixture of alarm and surprise in her voice.

Gary looks at her for a moment, then sighs and walks over to her. "Let's find somewhere safe for you two to hole up and wait this out. You guys have done more than enough, you've been through a lot and there's no need to get involved any further." He holds up a placating hand as Isaac starts to protest. "Look, I appreciate that you wanted to do your part, but I told you that this would be terrifying, and I for one think it's time you two sat this out."

"No way!" Isaac says, with a frightening amount of determination.

"Isaac!" Gary says.

"No way."

"Isaac!" He repeats, this time forgetting that he is supposed to be keeping his voice down.

They look around for a second, concerned that something may have heard their little spat and, satisfied nothing has, stare at each other for a moment.

Eventually Isaac breaks the silence.

"No! I'm not giving up. I don't care! I won't stop until I have killed every last one of the bastards that took Abigail from me. Every last one of the fuckers!"

The pain of the loss of his little sister at the hands of Samael hits Isaac again, and he sobs, turning from left to right, not sure of what to do or where to go and so he slams his back into a wall, banging his elbow against it a few times. He slides down into a crouch, dropping his weapon and putting his hands over his face.

Sarah rushes over and wraps herself around him, pulling him in tight as his muted sobs drift up from within her arms.

Staring at them, Gary's eyes puddle, empathy for Isaac's emotion hitting him hard. The understanding of how long the anger and pain of Isaac's sister's murder must have been eating away at him inside, unlike Sarah who, despite missing Abigail an incomprehensible amount, had somehow managed to let go of those emotions and come to accept her passing, knowing that where she ended up was a place of peace and contentment. But for Isaac, the responsibility that had been placed upon his young shoulders to keep both of his sisters safe had clearly weighed him down and his failure to protect the younger of his siblings had destroyed much of him inside, even though there was very little he could have done to prevent it. In all this time, Gary had believed that Isaac had blamed him for Abigail's death, when in fact he now realizes that he had been nothing more than a focal point for his own guilt, and that he blamed himself. He also realizes everything the boy had suffered in the last nine months had been unfair, and now looking at him he hates himself for not trying to counsel him better. He moves over and kneels beside them both as Sarah continues to comfort her brother.

"Isaac. It's time to let go of that guilt, to stop blaming yourself. You did everything you could to keep her safe, and you did a damn fine job at that. If anything, I was to blame for Abigail's death. I should've done more, I shouldn't have left her, no matter what. It's something I'll have to live with for the rest of my life, but you shouldn't have to. Especially because you have another who needs you. Sarah needs you right now. She needs your strength. She needs the brother that you were when we first met. Calm and calculating, reasonable and compassionate. It's time to let all this go and bring yourself back to the person you once were." He stands and holds out his hand. "Come on. Let's find a way out of here."

Sarah lets Isaac go and stands, and he looks up at Gary. Regarding him for a moment, he then wipes his face, grabs his rifle, and takes the man's hand, accepting the help to get back on his feet. Wiping his face again he sniffs, then looks at Sarah and smiles as best he can under the circumstances. He looks back to Gary. "Thank you Gary. But you're wrong."

Gary raises his eyebrows.

"You were not to blame at all. You did everything you could. Conrad told me what happened that day. He told me that even though you were tied up, somehow you still helped Abigail escape. The fact that you managed to get her out of that room at all, in the condition you were in, was something of a miracle." He sighs and looks down, then back up again. "And I don't want to let all of this go. I want to keep hold of some of the emotions I feel for that day. I'll have to learn not to let them get the better of me," he half-laughs, "if we even survive today, but I need it to keep her flame alive inside me. I can let go of the blame, but not the passion."

Gary smiles and nods. "Welcome back, Isaac."

"But I still want to fight."

"Then so do I," Sarah says, before Gary has a chance to speak.

He regards them both for a moment. "Right. Good." He smiles. "Okay, let's get out of this damn building."

***

"DOWN!" Conrad shouts as the helicopter explodes and a rotor blade clanks across the landscape toward them.

Daniel screams, high-pitched and feminine, as he dives to the dirt and throws his hands over his head. He feels a rush of air pass over him and wonders just how close the thing had come to splitting him in two. He pushes the thought out of his mind, as getting to his feet and away from the burning wreck behind him becomes his top priority. He knows the helicopter may still explode and he doesn't want to be anywhere near it should that happen. He is about to stand when he is hauled to his feet by Conrad, the big man having grabbed the back of his body armor.

"We go! Now!"

Daniel nods and follows, his head swimming with terrifying emotions. Battle and combat isn't something he will ever get used to, and at this moment he feels like he is more of a hindrance than help. Although he hates being such, he knows there is nothing he can do about it and so chases after Conrad so that they can catch up with Colonel Taylor. Wide eyed, Daniel then freezes and calls out in panic. "My gun! I've dropped my gun!"

"Forget it," Conrad says, without looking back at him, continuing to forge on. "Won't make difference for you anyway. Come now. Hurry."

Although he feels hurt by the statement, he knows Conrad is right and so he forgets about his weapon and races after the man, scrabbling up and over the rubble ahead of him. Clearing the top of the mound he sees Colonel Taylor ahead, wrestling a smaller demon onto the floor and getting the better of it. The Colonel then pulls a large knife from a sheath on his leg and stabs into its head many times, and he then drops to the ground with a grunt, as the creature bursts into dust, dissipating beneath him.

"Holy fucking shit," Daniel says and then jolts forward as Conrad grabs the top of his vest and yanks him toward him.

"No time to admire the man, must go. Keep moving."

"This way," Nathan says, beckoning them forward. "Look. Down there."

Daniel follows the sight line of his pointing finger to see a blur of light weave between groups of demons, exploding them into dust. He barks a sharp laugh.

"That's where I wanna be," Nathan says, looking back at them, "fighting with her. It will increase our survivability rate by a factor of 10 at least. Come on."

"Damn straight," Daniel says as he staggers over the uneven ground, following Colonel Taylor and Conrad who are already on the move.

Dammit, she says to herself as she dispatches another group of demons only to see more portals open around her, throwing more of the damn things back into the mix. She takes a deep breath and scowls. *Is this a benefit Lucifer has gotten from The Book? Auto-recall? Dammit. Are they coming back out of the pit instantly instead of years later?*

She remembers Judas once telling her that demons never truly die, instead they return to the pit of creation in Hell where they remain for an unknown amount of time. He once suggested that in his experience killing them with the Katanas of Destiny kept them down for much longer than normal, but they always returned eventually. However, she now muses whether Lucifer's increased control over Hell, afforded to him by assimilation of the completed Book, is bringing demons back the minute they are dispatched.

She vociferates her annoyance. She doesn't know how much longer she can keep this up. This is a battle that cannot rage for eternity, and she needs to find a way to put these things down for good. She glances upward. *I'm open to suggestions you know!* Her eyes dart left and right, waiting, hoping for a response. Nothing comes. *Figures,* she tells herself as more demons rush toward her, and visibly she deflates with a sigh, then shadow-steps to them and into attack.

Nathan hunkers down as a series of portals open in front of him, the crackling and fizzing of their electrical arcing overpowering every other sound, and demons pour out of them. He grunts and grits his teeth. "Where the fuck are they all coming from?" he says, his tone venomous. "For every one of them she fucking murders, more come back. It's rapidly descending into a war of attrition she cannot possibly win." He looks up to the sky, raging with angels and demons locked in battle as small bursts of dark and light energy spike out amid their skirmishes.

"Hell… I think you'll find, Colonel," Daniel says, sliding down a pile of rubble toward him.

He turns to the boy, his movement sharp, his demeanor screaming 'I'm not in the mood for this,' and Daniel holds his hands up, quickly changing his flippancy to reason.

"What I mean to say, sir, is that I think it's the same ones coming back repeatedly. Look!"

He points to Charlotte, as she splits a large fire-breathing demon in half, one with distinct characteristics and no sooner than she has, a portal opens a short way from her and the same demon rears up from within it and attacks again.

"And I think I know why," Daniel says, pointing to the large tower in the center of the battlefield. "Look, toward the top of that tower that I assume is Lucifer's fortress. Do you see it?"

Conrad squints his eyes. "See what? I don't get it."

"I do," Nathan says, his vision fixed on the tower. "I see it." He turns back toward Daniel. "You, my boy, are a fucking genius." Grabbing him by the sides of his face, he kisses his forehead with force.

Daniel screws up his face and squirms. "Well, obviously," he says, pulling away, "and ewww, by the way." He wipes his forehead with the back of his hand.

Conrad continues to look puzzled. "I still don't get it. What is boy genius for?"

Nathan grabs Conrad's arm and pulls him to his position. He points to the top of the tower. "There. See it? A ring of what looks like light."

Conrad squints. "I no have glasses. Cannot see that far."

Nathan looks at him, his eyes wide open. "Oh, my friend, you are just full of surprises today."

The side of Conrad's mouth twitches into an 'almost' smile.

Nathan turns back toward the tower. "Close to the top of the tower, about three-quarters of the way up its superstructure, there is a ring of light and I think Daniel's right – I think that is the source of their regenerative power. I can't quite make out what's under the light… demons maybe?"

"Here," Conrad says, "use these." He takes out a small pair of pocket binoculars and hands them to Nathan, who regards him with even more confusion.

Taking them, he shakes his head at him. "Why didn't you just use these?"

"I no have glasses," he replies, with a shake of his head in return. "Would make no difference."

"Then why do you have them?" Nathan asks, with a deep frown.

Conrad shrugs. "For now. Seems was good call on my part."

Letting out a spiky laugh, Nathan then turns his attention back to the tower, observing it through the binoculars. "Yep. Spot on Danny boy, spot on! A ring of demons, holding staffs in the air, and the circling light is emanating from them. I am willing to bet my life on it – that's the source of the regeneration." He folds the binoculars away and hands them back to Conrad, who, despite his statement a moment ago, unfolds them, raises them to his eyes, squints and then shakes his head while putting them away.

"Question is," Nathan says, turning to face Conrad and Daniel, "how do we get up there to deal with it?"

A demon appears at the top of the crater they are hunkered in and screams, its arms spread, spittle spraying out of its wide-open and teeth-filled mouth.

"Shit!" Nathan says, scrambling to raise his weapon.

Conrad is about to open fire, when a sword pierces the creature's head and exits through its face, and it is then lifted into the air and flung far away. Charlotte then ambles into view.

"I thought I could hear you guys in here," she says, nodding at them, "which means so can they." She motions back with her head. "Come on. Let's make a tactical retreat and get our shit together."

Opening a portal beneath Nathan, Conrad, and Daniel, causing them to fall through it, she jumps down and follows them, landing on the roof of a small building a short distance away from where they were, and one overlooking the battlefield.

"Thanks for the warning," Daniel says, as he gets to his feet, rubbing his backside.

"Yeah, well, sorry about that," she says, turning toward Nathan. She points to the tower. "We need to shut that down."

Nathan nods. "Uncanny, we were just talking about that."

"I know. Like I said, I heard you."

"How we get up there?" Conrad asks, dusting himself down.

Charlotte smiles and winks. "Gotta love portals." She thrusts her hand forward while focusing on the tower and then clenches it into a fist, pulling her arm back to her body.

Nothing happens.

She tries it again.

Still nothing.

"Goddamit!" she says, screwing up her face. "Goddamn Thŭramré's."

"Thuram–what?" Nathan asks.

"Thŭramré. A Divinity-binding curse… look, it doesn't matter, point is, I can't portal up there. We need to find another way."

Nathan checks his weapon, then looks at the tower. "Get us as close as you can to the fucking thing and we go in on foot and work our way up."

Daniel's eyes open wide as he points at it. "You wanna go *inside* that thing?"

"You got a better suggestion?"

425

"I might," Charlotte says, pointing at the gigantic demon, swinging its massive ax at the remaining gunship close to the tower.

All three men look at her, their mouths open.

"How?" Nathan asks, raising his eyebrows.

She smiles while biting her bottom lip and raises her eyebrows, then tries to open a portal above the massive demon. She screams in frustration, flicking her hand forward as the portal fails to open. "For crying out loud, what's the radius on that damn thing?"

"The Thurmare?" Nathan asks.

"It's Thŭramré – and yeah, seems the big bastard is either within its sphere of operation or has one of its own. I can't portal onto that either."

As if cued by her statement, a group of angels swoop down toward the ax demon and try to attack it, only to plummet to the ground as they draw close, their flight terminated. The demon roars at them and then stomps them into a soggy mess as they attempt to scramble away from it.

"Jesus," she says with a frown, and then, examining it closer, she points at the creature. "Yep, look – it's got one of its own. One of those mage things on top of its head, in between its horns. I thought that energy was fire, but it's a localized Thŭramré beam to prevent anything getting close to it from the air. Clever bastard." She looks around over the battlefield while taking a deep breath. "Gonna need another solution." Her gaze focuses on something. She smiles and points. "And some bait."

Following the path of her indicating finger, Nathan smiles and then nods. He turns toward Conrad and Daniel. "Okay boys, it's time for some trickeration."

Daniel looks confused. "What?" he says, frowning.

"Is football term," Conrad says, nudging him, "means trick play."

"Great. Sports," Daniel replies, his voice monotone.

The sound of something landing on the roof behind them causes everyone to spin around, with Nathan and Conrad snapping their weapons up in front of them.

"Ahhh, perfect timing," Charlotte says as Raphael and Raguel approach.

"Charlotte?" Raphael says, nodding at her, "you okay?"

"I'm fine Raph, but I need an escort." She points to the demon who has finally caught the remaining Apache gunship with one of its ax swings, exploding it in half.

"Goddamit!" Nathan shouts, turning away in anger.

Charlotte sighs and lowers her head for second then looks back at the Archangels. "I can't portal onto it, it's got a friggin' Thŭramré so the guys are gonna lure it to that building over there," she points to it, "and I'm gonna catch a ride from that point. Would be nice to have an escort so I can concentrate on the jumping and not the fighting." She smiles.

Raguel closes his hand into a fist, thumps it against his chest and bows his head. "It will be our honor, my Lady."

"Oh my God," she says, placing the tips of her fingers on her head and pushing them backward, "you must stop with that 'my Lady' shit."

***

Lucifer pulls Gabriel up and out of the ground, still attached to his sword, and flings him to one side, where he rolls and crashes into the side of a building.

Grunting while pushing himself out of the rubble, Gabriel holds his hand out to his side and his sword scrambles across the ground, and flies into it. He takes a deep breath and cricks his neck from side to side as the wound in his back closes and heals.

Lucifer laughs. "I should've known. No one possesses regeneration like His first and favorite."

Gabriel regards him with contempt. "ENOUGH OF THIS! Stop this brother. You have gone too far this time. This will spell the end of you. Your realm may not be a place that you wish to be, but it will still see you alive. If you continue down this path, there will be no coming back from it. He will lock you away in a tiny box this time if you don't stop this."

427

Lucifer shadow-steps into Gabriel and punches him, smashing him back into the wall. "I WILL STOP NOTHING! This world will soon be mine. I will send you below, and father along with you. And there you will rot until the Alfather sweeps everything away."

With a retaliatory roar, Gabriel powers out of the wall, his wings driving him forward, and he grabs Lucifer and throws him across the battlefield.

Without losing balance, Lucifer lands cleanly on his feet and slides backward, his knees bent and, upon coming to a halt, rushes at Gabriel once again, swinging his sword at the Archangel.

Entering a swordfight of high-speed and powerful strikes, their blades ring out against one another as each repeatedly tries to gain the advantage. In between strikes, one will lash out with a fist or a kick and catch the other off-guard only to recover and slip in a deceptive blow of their own. The fight is fast and furious.

After a while, Lucifer loses patience and throws his arms out to the side, expelling a powerful energy wave that pushes Gabriel backward, forcing him to wrap his wings around himself while burying his head into the back of them, using them as a shield, his feet skidding through the dirt.

Then the Lord of Hell throws his arms down and to his sides and concentrates, his head bent forward, his face concealed by his battle helmet.

"Stop this brother," Gabriel shouts to him again, "this power will consume you."

But he isn't listening. He calls upon as much energy as The Book and Seals will give him, and his new form of Dark-Divinity flows out and surrounds him in immense quantities.

Attempting to take advantage of Lucifer's distracted power-up Gabriel rushes him, his sword held in both hands, and he swings at Lucifer, his plan to knock him out of the process and to then somehow subdue him. But as he approaches, Lucifer shadow-steps behind him at a speed that even Gabriel cannot see.

With his back exposed, Lucifer kicks Gabriel at the rear of his knee, unbalancing him and then slams the hilt of his sword into the nape of his neck, dropping him to his knees. Driving the massive sword into Gabriel's back, he pours Dark-Divinity through it and into the Archangel who screams, his arms thrust outward and dropping his sword.

Lucifer holds Makarus in place for a moment and then slides Gabriel off it with his foot, sending him sprawling to the ground with a thud. He flicks the blood off the blade and then stomps toward him.

***

Raphael signals to a large group of angels and they swoop down, engaging the demons around the area that Charlotte is preparing to portal Nathan and Conrad into.

As the men walk toward Charlotte's anomaly, Daniel steps forward only to be stopped by her. "Not this time Daniel. Stay up here and find a good hiding spot."

He frowns. "But I want to help!"

She smiles. "You already have, sweetie. More than you realize."

She strokes the side of his face and Divinity washes over him. He takes a wonderful deep breath, and leans into her hand, placing his on top of hers.

She smiles once again, removes her hand, then walks over to Nathan. "Ready?"

"Ready," he replies, looking at Conrad who screws his mouth up and nods.

"Let us fuck shit up," the big Ukrainian says.

"Or at least run away from it," Nathan says.

Conrad blurts a haughty laugh. "Is good also."

They step into the portal and exit on the other side, not too far away from the massive ax demon, but far enough to be on the periphery of the Thŭramré. Ahead, angels swarm down near the beast, then rush over the ground toward it and attack the demons.

"That's our cue," Nathan says and races off toward the target, followed by Conrad.

429

They sprint in and around the warring super beings, dodging sword swipes and demon claws where they can, peppering others with gunfire at every opportunity, the holy water-infused bullets rippling through and destroying their foes. As they get to within striking distance of the ax demon, Nathan fires a volley at the creature that hits it in the top of its arm and it turns toward him.

"Got your fucking attention, have I?" he screams. "Let's go, big boy."

The demon roars and pulls its ax out of the side of a building then charges at them.

"Oh shit!" Conrad shouts as both men turn and run.

Overlooking the scene, Charlotte opens a portal on the roof of the target building as the demon makes its way toward it and then turns to Daniel and smiles, who smiles back. She looks at Raphael and Raguel. "Okay boys, here we go."

She is about to step into the portal when the demon launches its weapon at the fleeing men and the ax whistles through the air in a sideways, circular motion.

"DOOOWN!" Nathan screams, glancing back at the sound of something large moving through the air, and he and Conrad collapse to the ground.

The ax whizzes over their head and into the building in which Charlotte was intending to jump from.

"SHIT!" she shouts upon seeing it collapse, and then looks around quickly. She rips open a portal in front of another building, the trans-dimensional gate serving to act as a beacon to Nathan and Conrad as well as her exit point.

Hearing the sound, Nathan looks to his left as the portal opens in front of another building a short distance away. He looks up to the roof from where they came to see Charlotte running into her entry portal and turns to Conrad. "Change of plan. This way."

Scrambling to his feet and followed by Conrad, he sprints toward the rippling energy and sees Charlotte and her escorts exit and race into the building, followed by a multitude of demons drawn to their position and flooding into the doors behind and up the sides of the building.

"We need to buck, Conrad."

"Am coming. Do not wait for me."

Behind, they hear the enormous demon charge, the earth quaking beneath its feet with each powerful stride. Once or twice they almost lose their balance, such is the impact, but they remain determined and forge on. However, the creature is too large and too fast and within seconds it is almost upon them.

Conrad ducks as he hears a massive hand swoop in overhead and crunch into the ground at Nathan's position. He screams to his Commander upon hearing the man's angered cries as he is lifted into the air and thrown away from his intended destination.

Nathan falls to the ground with a vicious thud that hurts a lot, crushing his ribs as he lands awkwardly on a jutting piece of rock, air exiting his lungs with a painful 'ooft.' He groans, turning over onto his back and holds an arm up as the demon picks up a large piece of rubble and launches it at him. Terror floods through him as the massive piece of rock hurtles toward him, but the sensation is overshadowed by surprise as something grabs hold of his body armor and quickly drags him to the side away from the trajectory of the gigantic missile. He grunts in pain as he is rolled over onto his front, then again onto his back and ends up looking up into the blood-streaked face of Jonesy. He offers a short, sharp laugh as best he can.

"Fuck me, Jonesy. You are fucking impossible to kill, ain't ya?"

Jonesy laughs. "Just lucky I guess sir. Hold still, don't make it any worse."

"It won't matter in a minute buddy when they see where we are and swarm the area. Get out of here and find some cover while she does her thing."

Jonesy raises his rifle, readying himself for anything that might attack. "With all due respects sir, how about you get fucked instead." He glances back down at Nathan and grins, and the Colonel returns the gesture through bloodied teeth, then flops his head back onto the ground.

Conrad gets back to his feet in time to see the gigantic demon prepare to launch another attack in the direction where Nathan went down. "Hey. HEY! Fuckface. Here. Here. Come get me!" He pulls his sidearm from out of its holster and fires a volley of bullets at it. The 9mm rounds mean nothing to the creature, but the noise serves to grab its attention and as it does, Conrad turns and runs toward the building that Charlotte raced into, the demon having taken the bait and is now thundering after him.

He sprints as fast as he can, sucking down as much air into his lungs as possible, determined to get the thing to the right spot, but with terror building in him fast. His anxiety rises and he is panicked at not being sure how close the beast is. He is about to dive for cover feeling that he may just be in the right place for Charlotte to do her thing, when the demon slams a massive fist down on top of him and crushes him to death.

Inside, Charlotte, Raphael, and Raguel scale the stairs and move through the building with fierce determination, mounting two at time. Behind them they hear the screams, gnashing, and salivations of demons skittering up the staircase and walls.

"How far up?" Raphael shouts.

"I dunno," she replies between breaths, "30 floors maybe?"

"Then why didn't we portal to the top?" he suggests.

"Because I needed Nathan and Conrad to understand our plan, so placing the portal at the entrance was wise."

"Okay fine, but why are we now running like humans?"

Smiling, and without an answer, she shifts into shadow-step and the Archangels follow suit.

Eventually, they pass a sign for the 30th floor and go up one further flight, then crash through the door leading out of the stairwell, blasting the thing off its hinges, and moving into what seems to be an executive office.

Ahead, and through large panes of glass, she can just make out the top of the demon's head as it raises a huge hand and then slams it down into the ground.

"NOW!" she screams, powering toward it, this time at human speed, fearful that she might over compensate the jump if her velocity is too great.

Around them, through broken and open window frames, demons flood in, howling and screaming, and Raphael and Raguel unsheathe their swords, killing any that draw close as Charlotte leaps over hurdles of overturned office furniture and equipment, ducking the strikes of demons, and punching any that get too close.

As she reaches an open window with the demon below, she leaps out of it, into the air, followed by the two Archangels and, throwing her arms to her sides mid-flight, she catches her swords, while to each side of her Raphael and Raguel spread their wings wide to control their descent. Behind them demons cascade out of the window and fall to their deaths.

Charlotte lands on the demon's head, closely followed by the Archangels right next to the demon mage controlling the Thŭramré, much to its surprise. Before he has time to react, Raphael slices him in two as Charlotte slams her swords down into the beast's head, and gritting her teeth streams Light-Divinity into it with a roar.

The demon screams, rocking its head backward and throwing its arms up into the air, attempting to grab at whatever landed upon it. But there is nothing it can do about the invasive parasite that is Charlotte's Divinity, and before it has chance to even realize what is going on, she invades its mind and its eyes turn pure white as it falls under her control.

She looks up, her eyes also a brilliant white.

"Right you bastards, time for a game changer," she says, and powers the beast forward, using her swords to steer just as she did with the Mazorakor.

***

Michael and Samael trade blows, ducking and slipping each other's sword swings and connecting where they can.

433

Catching Samael off-guard, Michael punches him with his non-sword hand, then spins and slices him with his weapon.

With a shriek, the blow cutting him deep, Samael retaliates and knocks Michael back a short distance, then his face contorts with rage and he charges at him, but the Archangel shadow-steps to his right and then left, slicing at Samael with each move, carving further deep wounds into his chest.

Coming to a sliding halt a little further away from Samael, Michael points at the wounds. "I can do this all day, Sammy – I'll keep slicing you up until there's nothing left. Surrender now and throw yourself on the mercy of the Creator."

Samael throws his head back and laughs hard as his wounds fully heal, then stomps toward Michael. "Don't make me laugh, Mikey. I am but toying with you. Lucifer has bequeathed some of his gift to me as he thinks of me as his new favorite. And I have been happy to accept those gifts," he slices at Michael, who dodges the attack, "as I will then use them against him later."

He slices again, but Michael isn't quite quick enough this time and the blade catches him, drawing blood.

"What's the matter, Mikey? Not used to getting cut?" Samael laughs and then shadow-steps and grabs hold of him, powering Michael into and through the side of a building. Twisting his body, he launches the Archangel into the air and through another wall, where he smashes out of it and back onto the street, landing next to a startled Gary, Sarah, and Isaac.

Racing to his feet, Michael urges them to run away as fast as they can, then turns to face Samael who breaks through the remainder of the wall and into the open, a maniacal grin upon his face.

"YOU!" Isaac blurts upon seeing the huge red demon. He raises his rifle and launches a hail of bullets at him.

Samael throws a hand up to his face as the holy water-tipped rounds ripple into him. Although they don't hurt much they are very annoying, and he snarls at the boy and stomps toward him.

"MOVE!" Gary shouts, grabbing hold of the back of Isaac's body armor and dragging him away upon seeing Samael rage toward them.

434

Michael roars as he charges into and bundles Samael to the ground, whereupon he rains punches down on him.

Grabbing hold of the Archangel, Samael launches him over his head toward Gary and the others, causing Michael to adjust his position mid-flight and arc himself around using his wings to stop himself from tumbling into the humans. Then, holding his arm out, he wills his dropped sword back into it and charges at Samael once more.

***

Charlotte guides her demon toward the tower, using it to batter startled creatures out of the way below her, much to the amusement of Raphael and Raguel.

"Never have I seen such a thing before," Raguel says, a broad smile upon his face. "You truly are something to behold, my Lady."

"Rag. Pack it in, will ya?" she says, closing her eyes briefly and sighing.

"Sorry, my La— I mean Charlotte."

She points at the tower. "Okay. We get to it in a minute, and I use this big bastard to scale the wall and take out the mages, then we jump down and stomp on every little shit we find and they shouldn't regenerate. Sound like a plan?"

The Archangels nod and smile.

***

Samael uppercuts Michael with his non-sword hand, a blow that sends him flying into the air and landing on a pile of rocks. Then, at his side, the humans open fire again, forcing him to raise a hand to his face to protect it. He snarls. "Bothersome creatures. I will enjoy killing you as I did your little bitch sister."

Michael gets back to his feet and charges again.

Samael's speed and new-found power has Michael surprised, and for the first time in the fight he is wondering if he will ever gain an advantage over him. As he closes in, another devastating punch rocks him to the side, knocking him over and causing him to let go of his sword again. *How is Samael doing this?* he asks himself. *What power has Lucifer bestowed upon him?*

Samael chuckles, his demonic voice booming. He flicks his sword down by his side and it ignites into fire with a fierce glow that makes the blade appear as though it had just been pulled from a furnace. "Gabriel may be a forever creation, Michael, but let's see if you are," he says as he slowly approaches the downed Archangel, struggling on the floor and in difficulty. Another hail of bullets causes Samael to stop, as the boy charges at him, screaming. "Ahhh, the brother," he says, not bothering to shield himself from the bullets anymore, "with his guilty rage."

Samael flicks his sword at Isaac and the fiery blade slices through his arm, cutting it in half and causing the weapon and the detached limb to fall to the ground where it still pumps bullets from the gun.

It takes Isaac a few seconds to acknowledge what has just happened and so his screams of pain are delayed. But come they do, and he drops to his knees while staring at his severed arm, cauterized by the fire-sword.

Samael throws his head back with maniacal laughter and continues toward Michael, who is trying to get back to his feet. He grabs the Archangel by the throat and lifts him into the air. "Any last words, Mikey?" he asks, with a grin.

***

Lucifer stands over Gabriel with his sword Makarus held out to his side, admiring it. "You should be grateful, Gabe. You will be my first catch of the day. This will be talked about for eternity." He holds the sword up. "Poor Gabriel," he says, mocking him with false pity, "Heaven's greatest warrior."

Beneath him, propped up on one elbow, Gabriel offers a pained laugh, causing Lucifer to hesitate and look at him in surprise. "Oh, dear brother. I'm not Heaven's greatest warrior." He motions behind with his head toward the tower. "He is."

The upper half of the Red Keep explodes with Dark-Divinity.

Charlotte throws a hand up to her face as the tower ahead detonates, and a loud, booming voice screams, "LUCIFER!"

From out of the ruined side of the tower, she sees Judas leap out, his legs and arms flailing in the air and as he hits the dirt, the ground exploding around his impact point from the force. He then races out of the dust cloud, sprinting toward Lucifer who she can now see on the other side of the battle field, stood over what looks to be Gabriel.

"Gabe!" she says, turning the demon around and moving it into that direction, the plan to take the tower now a useless one.

As she brings the beast around, she sees Lucifer break off and race toward Judas, both warriors trailed by massive dirt clouds behind them and as they close in on each other, she hears them both roar and then sees them leap into the air, readying their swords to strike at one another.

THE FINAL BATTLE

Judas breathes heavily while looking at the ruined upper stories of the Keep. Holding up his hands, he clenches them into fists and closes his eyes tight, then grits his teeth. The power coursing through his body confuses and disorientates him and he blinks a few times to try to clear his vision. He then shakes his head as multiple voices race through his mind, calling over one another and getting in the way – the three Horsemen and other demons. He staggers.

"What's going on Ika? Why am I hearing the other two in my mind?" he asks his sword, still embedded in the ground next to him. "I only absorbed Famine into me through you. Not War and Death. So why am I hearing them and the others?"

"You're hearing them through me, Judas. We are now connected, with our symbiosis having been growing stronger and stronger over the last few hours. The increase in both our power is due to the two gem pieces, and the many demon souls I have now absorbed, and our minds communicate to one another. Is it not wonderful? Do you not feel true power?"

He does. He feels every bit of the incredible and terrifying energy, and he clenches and unclenches his hands again while closing his eyes and taking deep breaths, his body taut, attempting to take control of the electricity within. He then looks out of the exploded tower to see the devastated New York City skyline, and the battle that rages above and on the streets below them. Feeling Lucifer's presence, his face reddens and he grits his teeth, summoning Ikazuchi into his outstretched hand, the weapon slicing out of the ground and spinning into his grip.

"LUCIFER!" he screams, as he leaps out of the tower and drops 200 feet, exploding into the ground below, dust and dirt pluming up into the night air. Streaking out of the cloud he sprints toward his enemy, approaching him fast. His arms pump up and down hard with Ikazuchi rising and falling as he throws everything into the run, his sprint now almost as fast as shadow-step. As he nears Lucifer his eyes narrow, focusing on the creature he means to tear apart. He holds Ikazuchi out to the side and leaps.

Lucifer does the same – the two titans, streaming through the air, their weapons raised and ready to connect.

The resulting shockwave from their swords colliding pulses outward with massive force, exploding a blinding sphere of energy – a potent mixture of Dark and Light Divinity.

"HOLD ON," Charlotte screams to Raphael and Raguel as the shockwave reaches their position and, hunkering down, she makes her demon do the same, slamming its massive ax into the ground to act as an anchor. But it is to no avail, as the energy wave is too powerful and as it hits it knocks the beast off its feet and the three of them off the top of it. The blast is so strong that Charlotte must construct a Divinity shield around herself seconds before she smashes into and through the side of a building, then through multiple walls, tumbling into a messy heap in what appears to be a ruined foyer. She staggers as she attempts to get back to her feet and touches her wet forehead, then brings her fingers in front of her eyes. Blood. She blinks and looks down at her hands taking a few breaths. Then, thrusting them out to her sides, she holds them there. A short distance away, she hears the pained roar of the giant demon and, seconds later, her swords whistle through the hole she left in the building and into her hands. Taking another deep breath, she grits her teeth and shadow-steps outside.

"I said, any last words Mikey?" Samael repeats, standing over the downed Archangel who is attempting to sit up.

Michael glares at him. *He is beaten? How could Samael possess so much strength to do so?* He screws his face up in defiance. "This isn't over Samael. Not by a long way."

"Oh, I know," Samael says with a raucous laugh, and he is about to drive his sword down when the Red Keep explodes, its position just visible from in between the buildings where he stands. He snaps his attention toward it, and then turns back to Michael as a scream draws his focus.

As she holds her downed brother, Sarah feels a powerful rage burn within her and she turns toward Samael who is laughing as he straddles Michael. Then to her right, the massive tower explodes and she flinches, but the creature who has hurt her family so much refocuses her attention and, turning back toward Samael, who has turned to face the explosion, something inside her snaps, an aggression she has never experienced before or indeed known existed. And so she lets go of Isaac and races toward Michael's sword, laying on the ground a few feet away, and behind her she hears Gary scream her name, urging her to stop. But it's too late, she is committed and very determined. And then another sensation swells within her, one she has felt very few times in her entire life – pure, unadulterated hatred. As she scoops up the heavy sword with both hands, it being almost too heavy for her to lift, the emotion reaches monumental heights and she screams while driving it into Samael's side, relishing his deep cry of pain.

She stumbles as he turns to face her, a terrifying rage burning in his eyes, his mouth filled with razor-sharp teeth screaming and he raises a clawed hand to her, causing her to hold up a terrified hand to her face.

Through a pained expression, his regenerative healing still in its early stage, Michael leaps up at Samael so fast that the demon has no chance to react, and, drawing the sword from his ribs, spins to his right, raising it up and around in an arc, taking Samael's head clean off.

The demon explodes with such force it blasts him over and sends Sarah scraping backward over the ground.

Gary lowers his arms, thrown up in front of his face to shield from Samael's demise and scrambles toward her. "Sarah, SARAH! Are you okay?"

She struggles on the floor, dazed and confused, then blinks at him, coughs once, and nods.

Then Gary snaps his head up toward the sound of a massive metallic explosion from somewhere on the other side of the building in front of them. "DOWN!" he screams and throws himself over Sarah as the huge shockwave smashes into the building and erupts out of any opening it can find.

The speed at which they attack one another is staggering, battling within a spherical maelstrom of fizzing and crackling Divinity of both Light and Dark manifested in electrical arcing and spiking all around them. Metal clashes against metal, and each sword of power screams with glee, happy to finally be locked in battle with each other and, unlike Judas' first encounter with Lucifer, him outmatched and the fight one-sided, this engagement is an entirely different affair – and Lucifer knows it, their swords locking together once more.

"My, my Iscariot, you have grown powerful, haven't you? This might even prove to be of some entertainment for me."

Judas pushes against him, moving Lucifer away enough for him to strike with a powerful overhead swing, forcing the Lord of Hell to raise his sword to block it. The blow hits with such force it pummels Lucifer down into the ground, which buckles and crunches around him.

"NO!" Judas shouts, "there will be no talk, only your destruction."

Lucifer roars, immediately powering up and out of the crater, throwing his wings back and streaming toward Judas and he punts into his midriff and rockets him upward.

The energy field around their warring bodies ceases, as they streak out of it and explode into the upper floors of a huge skyscraper, then separate and tumble through the desolate office space, smashing through internal walls, desks, and furniture.

Regaining his footing, Judas skids backward, knees bent, and one leg forward as Lucifer gets to his feet as well and turns to face him with a scowl. Offering him no quarter, Judas shadow-steps to the side of Lucifer, grabbing him, and then lifts him into the air and slams him into the floor. Lifting him up again, he then hurls him forward, where he tumbles out of control, careering through the building and smashing through the remains of a plate glass window and over the edge. Judas is on him in seconds, diving out of the window, and chasing Lucifer as he falls, powering downward with a powerful thrust of his wings to grab him.

As they plummet, they exchange punches, viciously beating one another, and approaching the ground, Judas roars his rage and rains in continuous and powerful blows into Lucifer's face.

They crash into the wasteland again, causing another explosion of dirt and rubble, and Judas is the first to gain control, righting himself and lifting Lucifer up, then throwing him to one side where the Lord of Hell screams his own rage while tumbling over the ground. Then, correcting himself, Lucifer charges at Judas again, his feet pounding into the ground and his sword held high.

"Oh God. Dad!" Charlotte says, as Judas and Lucifer rocket upward and into the side of a building shortly after coming together, then turns her attention toward the position she last saw Gabriel and sighs, relieved to see him back on his feet and destroying demons. She then looks up at the war still raging in the sky and then over the battlefield that offers the same view – death and destruction everywhere. Her attention snaps to a group of soldiers who by some miracle are still alive, taking cover in front of a building behind a Humvee, and peppering demons with the vehicle's .50 machine gun. She curses as above them a large group of demons scramble down the building's wall, attempting to get behind the team and take them by surprise.

As Charlotte shadow-steps toward the skirmish, Raphael and Raguel land on the side of the building and, sprinting at them, obliterate the descending demons by running along the wall and cutting them down.

With one problem taken care of, Charlotte changes her angle of attack and moves to the horde confronting the soldiers from the front, and with a scream she tears into them. This time, with the tower and its mages destroyed, they don't come back.

***

Michael lifts a large slab of concrete from Gary and Sarah and throws it away effortlessly. He then helps them both to their feet and looks them up and down while taking a deep breath. "Are you okay?" he asks, breathing out through his nose.

They cough while nodding, their faces dirty, clothing torn in places. Satisfied, Michael moves to Isaac who is unconscious on the ground, truly fortunate not to have had any substantial pieces of masonry drop onto him following the shockwave. Picking him up, Michael examines him.

Scrambling over uneven ground to get to his side, Sarah sobs. "Oh no, oh my God. He's dead – he's dead isn't he?"

"No," Michael replies, "he's not dead, but he is very badly hurt." He examines the charred and blackened end of his severed arm, then looks to the ground to see if he can find the rest of the limb. He cannot. "He needs medical attention urgently."

"Can't you help? Can't Charlotte help?" Sarah asks, tears streaming down her face.

Michael looks over to the battlefield, beyond the buildings that they are in between. "I do not possess those gifts, and the one who could is locked in combat. There is no time. You need to go now." He opens a portal to the side of him. "I assume you left medical staff back at the base?" he says, turning to Gary.

"Yeah," he replies, nodding.

"Good. Then get these two back and get him help."

443

Gary shakes his head. "I'm staying." He looks at Sarah, "I'm sorry. Look, you've done enough. Get Isaac out of here and get him help."

Sarah steps up to him and touches the side of his face. "Don't die," she says, then takes Isaac's weight and, with help from Michael, drags him through the portal.

Michael watches them go through it, then turns to Gary. "Okay, let's finish this," he says, grabbing him around the waist and powering into the air toward Charlotte.

***

Separate my brother from him, Judas, Ikazuchi says within his mind. *Let me defeat him and then Lucifer will have no choice but to accept me on my terms.*

No. I intend to kill him, he replies, while trading sword blows with Lucifer, moving over and around rubble, the uneven ground proving no hindrance to the pair.

That is madness, Judas. Let us see my plan through, it will be better for us both. Trust me, I beg of you. You can still beat him into submission without me. That will be your reward.

Judas grunts, then punches into Lucifer's sword arm, it being midway thorough a downward swing, and parries the strike, sending it back and up. He then punches into his face with the hilt of Ikazuchi, rocking Lucifer backward and allowing him enough room to slice up with his sword and sever Lucifer's arm just below the elbow, sending his hand and forearm, still gripping his sword, spinning away. As Lucifer screams with pain and rage, Judas hurls Ikazuchi toward Makarus. "IKAZUCHI, ENRAGE!" he screams, and the sword transforms into its giant serpent form, with Makarus doing the same, and the two fly into one another, tumbling out of control and into the side of a building.

Presenting his severed arm to Judas, Lucifer smiles as his rapid repair system paints a new one and he flexes his fingers upon its completion. Then they circle one another. "So Iscariot, this is how it is to be? You think your weapon will defeat mine and then Azazel will offer me a choice?" He laughs.

"I don't care about any of that," Judas says, his face blazing with contempt. "I only care about beating you to death, and I told you: NO MORE TALK."

He shadow-steps toward Lucifer, punching him in the chest and launching him back and upward into the building they had dove out of moments earlier. He continues to shadow-step into the building and toward Lucifer who, having corrected himself upon crashing into the skyscraper, moves likewise and back to Judas, where he trades blows and defends himself from Iscariot's relentless attacks.

Throwing a combination of punches, Lucifer overreaches himself and Judas ducks under and into him, throwing a massive uppercut into his jaw, rocketing Lucifer upward through another ceiling and into an office space in the floor above.

Transforming into the mass of ravens, he flaps after and engulfs Lucifer, changing course and smashing out of the side of the building, where he then releases the Lord of Hell to the ground to bounce over it and crash to a halt against a large slab of concrete.

The building groans and creaks, with masonry crumbling everywhere, accompanied by large shards of glass, the damage sustained from both the Red Keep's rising and the two warring titans having caused the structure to become perilously unstable.

Ignoring the teetering building, Lucifer roars and gets back to his feet, then sprints toward Judas. He digs down deep within himself, calling forth more power from The Book and Seals, and greater amounts of Dark-Divinity envelop him, swirling around as he moves, and this time it is his turn to out-maneuver Judas, zipping to his left and then right as his opponent struggles to maintain focus on his position. Materializing on Judas' left-hand side, he punches into his head, blasting him to the right and then zips to the other side of him before he crashes to the ground, and punches him back to where they started.

With a wild swing, Judas tries to anticipate Lucifer's next move, but he isn't there, instead he has powered behind him and punches into his back, launching Judas across the wasteland. Getting to his feet, Judas repeats his attempt to connect with him, but again there is no Lucifer – this time he appears in front of him and throws another vicious punch, knocking him to the ground. With Lucifer's shadow-step proving difficult for him to get a fix on due to his speed, Judas ceases his pointless, uncontrolled attacks and waits for him to strike.

He doesn't have to wait long as Lucifer repeats his attack pattern. However, this time Judas reaches into himself and, calling upon Death's gift, moves into trans-dimensional space, the Horseman's ability now inherent in him having been absorbed by Azazel.

Lucifer grunts with anger at Judas' disappearance into the tear in the fabric of their reality, and his fist connects with nothing but the residual energy as it wisps away to nothing. "Impossible!" he says, looking around, his face reddening with fury beneath his armor-plated helmet. He snarls through jagged teeth, "No one could've have come to terms with the Horseman's gifts so quickly. No one!" He turns in circles attempting to pinpoint Judas' re-entry, eager to sense any energy spike that would signal his return. Instead, he calls out in surprise and anger as he is gripped by two of the spikes on back of is armor and thrown toward another building where he crunches through the wall, obliterating everything in his path, then out of the other side where he rolls across the ground uncontrollably. With yet another cry of fury, he thrusts a hand down into the ground to act as an anchor, and brings himself to a sliding halt with his body so low to the ground he is almost laying upon it.

Reappearing in front of Lucifer, Judas' attention then snaps to the building behind them just as something large smashes into it causing it to crunch down, its various supporting struts sustaining too much damage for it not to obey gravity, and it topples.

Lucifer moves from bended knee to a standing position as the disintegrating building leans toward them and masonry and debris drop all around as they stride toward one another slowly.

"So, these are to be the final moments whatever the outcome?" Lucifer says, as more of the building showers down around them.

"These are to be the final moments," Judas repeats, his facial expression blank and emotionless.

The two vocalize rage as they charge and leap at one another, their fists raised, and the building collapses on top of them.

***

Serpent Azazel sinks his fangs into his brother's snake body, then lifts him into the air and throws him to one side. Then, transforming into his human form, he walks toward the dust cloud, with debris peppering down around him, and stops 20 feet away as Beelzebub ambles out dusting himself down.

Beelzebub smiles. "You underestimate me brother. I can see it in your eyes. You think that this fight will be simple, that you will defeat me with brute force and rage alone." He chuckles. "I have been the Lord of Hell's weapon for eons. I have helped him strike down countless usurpers within the kingdom and any angel that was foolish enough to challenge him. I have tasted his power and he has given it freely to me. No brother, this will *not* be a simple fight." He laughs once again.

Azazel grins and then charges at him, transforming into a gigantic, winged demonic entity and as he gets within striking distance of him, Beelzebub also transforms into a similar creature and the two smash into one another and then take to the sky locked in battle.

They screech, each trying to work around the other so they might clamp their massive fanged mouths into necks and gain valuable purchase, and spotting an opening, Azazel beats his left wing hard, barrel rolling and moving into position at Beelzebub's back. He digs his claws in, causing Beelzebub to cry out and spin in the air, which in turn causes Azazel to lose his grip. The force of the spin throws Azazel down and away, and correcting his flight, Beelzebub thrusts his wings back and streaks toward his opponent just as Azazel turns mid-flight and faces his brother.

Crashing into him, Beelzebub hurtles them both to the ground and Lucifer's weapon roars with laughter into his brother's face.

"We are battle, brother. We are war and conflict. We are everything that causes the world fear, pain, and suffering. Release yourself from this pathetic Iscariot. Kneel to us, and together we will rain down fire and death upon all."

Azazel snarls. "I think I would rather do that on my own... brother." He disappears into the same trans-dimensional plane that Death used.

Beelzebub calls out in pain as Azazel rematerializes at his back, clamps down with huge talons, and slams him into the ground, then shifts into giant wolf form and sinks his teeth into the back of Beelzebub's long neck. Lifting him, he throws him into a building ahead.

Crashing through the skyscraper's ground floor, Beelzebub's destruction causes it to crunch down and begin to collapse. Then while still in wolf form, Azazel charges into the building and attacks Beelzebub who has now chosen a massive humanoid demonic form and is getting to his feet, smashing his way upward through the building, causing more catastrophic damage.

The wolf crunches into him, and Beelzebub grips it by its snarling snapping head as it slides him backward and out of the building.

Turning toward the sound of the skyscraper's bottom floor exploding and seeing its demolition get underway, Charlotte slices off the demon's head she is fighting and points in its direction, drawing the Archangels' attention to it. "MOVE. WE NEED TO MOVE. GET EVERYONE OUT OF HERE."

Having joined them a few minutes earlier along with Michael and Gary, Gabriel opens a portal to the side of the forces and the remaining soldiers scramble through it.

Shadow-stepping toward Gary, Charlotte grabs him and zooms him away just as the building crashes down onto the spot they were standing on not a fraction of a second before.

Although they are to the side and little further away from the crumbling skyscraper than Charlotte and the others are, Jonesy and

Nathan hunker down, making themselves as small as possible, their vicinity to the collapsing building still vulnerable to fragments that would rain down as shrapnel onto their position. They both call out as the structure crashes down and the ground thunders around them from the impact, spewing dust and debris into a cloud.

***

Exploding up and out of the ruined building into the air before crashing back down to the ground, Judas and Lucifer yet again engage in fierce hand-to-hand combat. After a few attacks, Judas' rage piques and he roars, drawing upon more of the Horsemen's energy stored within him and he rains in blow upon blow into Lucifer's face.

Trying to fight back, but forced into defensiveness, Lucifer struggles to contend with the magnitude of his relentless opponent. The power exhibited by Judas is a clear and evident mixture of his fury and the infused essences of the Horsemen he has defeated, and it is proving too much for him to contain. He cannot believe that the betrayer is getting the better of him, that the pathetic creature he so easily devastated in the early morning glow of the New Mexico desert sun a few years back now displays more power than he possesses, and that it could be enough to defeat him. He is starting to wish he had followed Samael's advice and taken care of Iscariot while he mourned The Light's supposed death. He glances to his right to see Azazel towering over Beelzebub, both in their human forms, Azazel's attention fixed upon their position and calling to Judas. He then grunts as he is picked up again and hurled to the ground, skidding along it on his back and thudding to a halt in a crumpled mess.

***

Still in their wolf and giant demonic humanoid forms, Azazel and Beelzebub erupt from out of the ruins of the skyscraper and tumble out of control through the debris. Azazel once again clamps his jaws around Beelzebub's neck and bites down hard, causing him to scream.

449

Feeling the pressure from the bite, Beelzebub beats at the top of wolf-Azazel's head as hard as he can but is unsuccessful in lessening his grip. He is being subdued and running out of the strength needed to fight the animal. He never thought this was possible. He was sure that the power Lucifer gained from assimilating the relics would have proven too much for Iscariot and his brother, and he cannot believe it has not been. He grunts in frustration, and glances toward Judas and Lucifer as the angel straddles his master, delivering brutal punch after punch into his face and he knows they have lost, that the dangerous symbiotic nature fueling both Judas and Azazel has been too much for them. And no matter how powerful Lucifer is or had become, Iscariot's burning rage at the loss of the girl, coupled with the benefits he received from the Ancient Ones, has been the deciding factor. He is about to be destroyed by his brother, and Azazel will take his place at Lucifer's side once his capture is complete, knowing the Lord of Hell will succumb to his demands and there is nothing he can do about it. They have won. He will die and return to limbo, and they will have won. They really should have destroyed Iscariot in Hell when they had the chance.

Azazel growls with glee as he clamps down hard on his brother's neck one final time and, feeling the energy drain from him, releases him, and raises his head up, Beelzebub's black blood dripping from his mouth. He stares at his hapless and defeated opponent. "Neither you nor Leviathan have ever been my equal… EVER!" He growls again, this time with rage. "Your time is at hand brother. Time for me to take back what is rightfully mine, and for you to enjoy the Nether." He shifts back into his human form as Beelzebub does the same, diminishing from the giants they were into regular-sized people.

As Beelzebub gurgles, clutching at his throat, his life force oozing from it, Azazel looks toward Judas who also has his fight under control. He glances back down at his brother, then turns to Judas and calls his name as the man picks up Lucifer and hurls him across the battlefield.

Grabbing Beelzebub, Azazel hurls him the 100 yards to Judas where he lands and bounces to a halt at his feet. Staring down at Beelzebub, Judas then glances at Azazel who motions to his own chest with a closed fist and, looking back down and gritting his teeth, Judas punches into Beelzebub's chest and the demon screams as a burst of energy explodes from the wound and shoots out beams that radiate outward at different angles. Pulling his black blood-soaked hand out, Judas admires it while holding it out to his side, with the red glowing gem, much bigger than the previous two, pulsing within it. Then, as Beelzebub crumbles into nothing at his feet, Judas shadow-steps to Azazel and slams the gem into his chest a fraction of a second before Azazel transforms into Ikazuchi, and Judas grabs hold of the sword as it vibrates violently within his hand. His arm tenses as a devastating power pulses through, and Ikazuchi glows blood-red, and Judas screams from the pain of electric energy coursing through his weapon as it regains all its power. Shaking, he brings the sword around to his front and takes it in both hands, his face illuminated by the brilliance of its red glow, his appearance that of an insane man, with eyes wide and teeth gritted into a maniacal grin.

After a few seconds the reaction subsides, and he takes a deep breath, exhaling it through puffed lips. He then looks to Lucifer.

Staggered and unfocused, Lucifer scrabbles against the concrete slab he was hurled into, shuffling his feet in the dirt as he tries to gain purchase enough to stand, trying to work out why his repair system is working as slowly as it is. He gives up, flopping against the slab, and sliding back down as Judas leaps through the air and lands at his feet.

Lucifer then removes his battle helmet to reveal his face, a blackened bloodied mess. He chuckles through the pain. "Oh, how the mighty fall, eh, Iscariot?" He laughs again. "It seems our roles are reversed, and it is now I that cannot heal from your damage. I wonder if someone is tipping the scales of fate a little, hmmm?" He glances upward with another small laugh, and Judas follows his gaze, but not all the way, returning his attention to his defeated foe. "So what will you do now, betrayer?"

Ikazuchi's voice drifts out from the sword. "Okay Judas, well done. It is now time for me to do my part. It's time to negotiate."

Lucifer laughs again, once – hard and sharp. "Negotiate? So you do wish to become my weapon and give Iscariot an out?" He stares at

Judas for a few seconds while struggling with his breathing. "And what are to be the terms? To leave you alone, to not hunt you for the rest of my days?" His face screws up into a snarl. "If you give me that sword, Iscariot, I will gain power in comparison to yours and I will never stop hunting you. I will *never* stop hunting her."

Judas frowns. "I will not allow you anywhere near the White Kingdom, so you will never touch her."

Lucifer laughs again while coughing. "And why would I need to go there when I can hunt her here in this plane of existence?" He looks past Judas to a part of the battlefield not too far from them.

Judas follows his gaze and his eyes open wide as he sees Charlotte helping a stumbling Gary to his feet and, sensing that he sees her, she looks toward him and smiles, her shoulders heaving from a deep breath and holding up a hand. His breathing quickens and his eyes glisten. His mouth twitches into a smile. *She's alive. And I didn't sense her. Why didn't I sense her?* He looks down for a moment and then understands. Through all his rage, his focus on defeating Lucifer, he hadn't sensed she had been here all along, that his anger and hatred had overwhelmed him. His smile wanes. Or had it been that he has gone too far, that he has taken too much of Azazel and the Horsemen into him, and that allowing Lady Famine into his soul had been blocking the bond he shares with her? Had he allowed himself too much movement toward darkness? He lowers his head and then looks to his sword, holding it up and turning it in his hands. In the dark recesses of his mind, he feels Lady Famine trying to communicate with him, the Horseman sensing their collusion weakening. He closes his eyes and grits his teeth, forcing her back down – he doesn't want to talk with her.

"Judas!" a concerned Ikazuchi says. "Forget her and release me now. Let me discuss our terms with Lucifer, it doesn't have to end this way. I will ensure the Horsemen leave this existence. I will remove them from you myself and send them back to the Alfather."

Lucifer snarls. "It does have to end this way Iscariot and the very second I get that sword, I will be upon you. I will be upon her. I will never give this up. I will never ever stop. *Ever.*"

Judas' eyes snap open and he stares at Lucifer, then looks back at Charlotte.

He looks down at the ground and closes his eyes again.

Opening them, Judas takes a deep breath and looks at her once more.

***

"You okay?" she says, helping Gary to his feet, him wincing at the pain in his leg as he tries to put weight on it and stand unaided.

"Yeah. I think so. Took a bit of a fall as we came to a stop." He looks down to the wound on his thigh and grunts at the pain as he yet again tries to put weight on it.

"Gary!" she says, drawing his attention. "It's Judas! It's my dad."

She smiles and holds up a hand up to him, knowing that he sees her.

"He's done it," Gary says, laughing through a smile. "He's only gone and bloody done it. That man is something else."

Her smile wanes. "No. No he can't. He can't defeat him."

"What?" he says, as she slips from under his shoulder and walks away, leaving him to hop to gain stability. "Wait! What do you mean?" he says, hopping to a large piece of rubble and leaning against. But she isn't listening.

She quickens her pace, the concern growing within her, then takes a sharp intake of breath and holds it as he turns toward her once more, smiles and mouths the words, "I love you. I'm sorry."

Charlotte screams at him to stop, and then breaks into shadow-step.

His heart pounds within his chest and his eyes puddle with tears, his emotions at a stalemate. His overwhelming happiness at seeing her alive has him wanting to run to her and scoop her up into his arms. He wants to imagine her as the scared six-year-old little girl she was when he met her, and squeeze her tight, her fatherly need for him greater than anything else. But he cannot. He knows that Lucifer speaks the truth. He will never leave her alone, never stop hunting her, whether she be on Earth or ascended. And so there is only one thing he can do, one final act of love for the person he cares most about. More than any other living creature he has ever cared for in his 2000-year lifespan.

He takes a deep breath and looks down again, his mind racing with reason. Maybe he can retain control, at least for many years to come, to give her the break, the rest she deserves, a chance to rebuild the world and make it better. Maybe. But maybe is better than nothing at all, and if he leaves this to chance, if he allows the creature at his feet access to his weapon and lets him go, he knows that the only outcome will be the very thing they have been fighting to stop for the last two years. He cannot and will not allow that.

Judas looks up at her, tears now filling his eyes. He closes them, and they spill out, slaloming down his cheeks. And through it all, the emotion and sadness, a memory hits him hard. A picture of her as a little girl lying in his lap in a field while he gently rubs her scraped knee. The picture gains movement and sound.

Then I will become strong and look after you, she says within the memory, smiling at him.

With a sharp intake of breath, he opens his eyes, looking at her as she strides toward him.

He smiles, and more tears cascade down his face.

"I love you. I'm sorry," he says to her. Then lifts Ikazuchi up into the air.

Charlotte screams, "No!" as she streaks forward into shadow-step.

Lucifer roars with deep demonic laughter.

Judas Iscariot swings his sword and decapitates Satan.

The blast wave that knocks her backward and out of shadow-step is second only to that of Judas' scream, one that contains countless others within it as he is violently hauled 20 feet into the air, Ikazuchi alongside him. The scream intensifies, piercing and shrill causing her to throw her hands up to her ears and bury her head in her knees as she curls into a fetal position where she landed.

Away from her, Lucifer's headless body spasms on the ground, and then black liquid erupts from his severed neck, a thick, rippling black torrent, moving of its own volition, and it encircles Judas just as three beams of light erupt out of him and rocket upward into space. The black liquid then wraps around him at every possible point. Weaving in between his arms, legs, and around his head as all the while he continues to scream. Then, rising like a wave, the river of blood sweeps over and into him via every opening it can find, permeating into every part of him and he gurgles and splutters as it enters his mouth to silence the screaming. And then he explodes, into thousands of pieces and in every direction. But the pieces do not scatter, as each remains attached with fibrous strands, and as they reach the edge of their elasticity, they halt for a moment, then zip back to his bloodied skeleton, slapping together piece by piece and rebuilding him. To his side, Ikazuchi continues to circle in the air, awaiting the final transformation. And then with all the pieces back in place, he lowers to the ground, the action graceful, while holding his hand out to receive Ikazuchi.

As his feet touch down, he opens his eyes to reveal a fierce orange glow burning within them, and he stabs his sword into the ground.

Charlotte pulls herself to her feet, and looks behind her at Gary as he tries to do the same, his injured leg causing him much more issues in accomplishing it than her. She looks toward Judas, standing perfectly still, his hand on his sword resting in the dirt. She smiles a little and then starts to make her way toward him but stops as he holds a hand out to her and ticks a finger left and right.

Her smile wanes.

It isn't him, not all of him at least. She knows it isn't. It may look like Judas and there may be much of him that she can still detect, but there is something else in there.

A new Lucifer has been born.

Judas-Lucifer looks to the ground at The Book and Seals scattered at his feet. Turning his non-sword hand over, the relics lift into the air and into it, The Book first, followed by The Seals, all stacking on top of it each other with a click. He glances down at them and then sends them to her through the air.

She reaches out and takes them as they get within touching distance, then looks at them with a frown and back up at him.

His mouth twitches as though threatening to turn into a smile, and he then lifts his hand into the air and clenches it into a fist and portals open everywhere, all over the battlefield, sucking demons into them, all of whom had ceased battling with angels to witness the birth of a new master. Some scramble and claw at the ground, unwilling to go as they are dragged screaming back into Hell and the sky illuminates with pockets of red as the winged demons are also returned. And then, as quickly as the event came, it stops and the night sky returns to a welcoming black, the red haze having dissipated.

Glancing at her one final time, Judas-Lucifer opens a portal beneath him and descends.

She shakes her head, and her shoulders heave, then she drops to her knees and tears flood down her face as she lets the relics fall from her hands.

Gary drops to his knees at the side of her ignoring the intense pain he feels in his leg and wraps himself around her as she howls in inconsolable misery.

They remain that way for a time, with her struggling to bring her grief under control, her face buried deep in Gary's shoulder, her life having just collapsed in front of her.

Eventually, the tears subside to a whimper, and then stop altogether, and Gary hugs her tighter.

"A fucking asshole," she says, wiping the remaining tears away, with the back of her hand. "Those were my last words to him. I called him a fucking asshole. Oh God, Gary. Oh my God!" She begins to sob again.

Gary struggles to speak, his own grief and sadness getting the better of him. He smacks his lips together and swallows hard. "He… he knew you didn't mean it. He loved you more than anything in the world. He wouldn't have done something so selfless otherwise. He did it for you, Charley. He did it for you. To keep you safe."

She cries further and buries her head into his chest and they remain that way, locked in an embrace as the Archangels approach them, their heads bowed.

"Let me take those," a despondent Gabriel says, reaching down and collecting The Book and The Seals, and then opening two portals, one after another. "Take her from here, Gary. Take her from this place. You both deserve some rest."

Gary looks around, panic creeping into his eyes. "Nathan! Where's Nathan?"

Gabriel nods to appease him. "He's fine, both he and Sergeant Jones are fine. A little beaten up, but okay considering."

Gary sighs.

Gabriel regards Charlotte for a moment. "I am so, so very sorry Charlotte," he says, sighing, then walks through the second portal, followed by the other Archangel's who in turn offer nods of condolence before departing.

Getting her to her feet, Gary walks Charlotte through the portal and it closes behind them.

SIXTY-FIVE

11 months later

Charlotte takes a deep breath and sighs as she walks, then runs her hands over her pure white, three-quarter length hooded jacket, straightening it. She repeats the action on her white, tight-fitted trousers, ensuring they are free of any detritus.

She has been adjusting her clothing for half the morning, and Gary turns around to her as he walks ahead accompanied by Nathan.

"Quit it," he says, scowling, "you look fine."

She scrunches her nose up at him and then turns around to Sarah and Isaac, with the four Archangels and Daniel behind them, and raises her eyebrows at Sarah.

"He's right. You do look great," Sarah says, with a smile, then looks down at her white, flat-soled boots. "And I love the boots, so nice!"

"I know, right?" Charlotte says, opening her eyes wide, "when I saw them I just thought, Charley, you just have to—"

"Ladies!" Gabriel's stern voice interrupts. "This is an important event, not a chance to chitchat about a shopping trip."

The girls exchange a quick glance between them, each with a small smile and Charlotte faces her front, continuing to follow Gary.

Everyone is dressed impeccably for the dedication ceremony they are en route to, with Sarah in a beautiful dress, her hair tied up, and the men in suits, although Daniel continues to fiddle with his as he walks, in particular the crotch region as the trousers are not fitting quite right.

At last, they approach the end of the wide corridor leading to the building's exit and walk outside through large glass doors that slide open as they approach, and Charlotte makes her way to a dais ahead of them, shielding her eyes from the glorious sun.

The street ahead is almost unrecognizable from how it was 11 months ago, the very spot upon which they battled Lucifer and his forces to secure humanity's freedom.

Following Lucifer's defeat, word had spread like wildfire across the planet and people had once again started to come together, safe in the knowledge that it was all over – that they could move from place to place without fear of being ripped apart by demons. Since that fateful day, not one of the creatures had been spotted nor a single incident reported, and the world had at last allowed itself to believe that the worst was over, that they could return to normal life. And so the cleanup began, expedited in no small part to Gabriel and his angels' help as they worked tirelessly to restore the planet's basic requirements for power, clean water, and crop plantations, many of which had been destroyed by the Hellrot that had gripped the world. Within a few months things had gotten back to a semblance of normality and people of all backgrounds began moving to places they felt they wanted to be, without the fear of territoriality, borders, or tribalism. Indeed, an unexpected benefit of Judas taking demons back to Hell was that he had also taken the worst the world had to offer with him. As reports from various places told of strange portals opening under torturers, cannibals, murderers, and others.

And so many months on, the world has come together as one people with mutual respect for each other's beliefs, in a safe environment and it looks a much better place than it had prior to the Apocalypse.

Clearing her throat as she approaches the podium, Charlotte looks out over the vast crowds that have gathered outside what used to be the Tonada building, now rebuilt and renamed Hope's Beginning, where records of the Apocalypse are kept, the story told through tributes to those who gave their all to see the planet recover its freedom so that they may never be forgotten.

It had been Gabriel to suggest this area should be one of the first to be cleaned and restored. He said the site of humankind's greatest victory should be where we remember all of those who contributed to it. And Charlotte agreed.

With the world's eyes upon her, desperate for her opinion, and hailing her as their new leader she had to make many decisions in the first few months, but eventually she had set them straight, refusing to let anyone refer to her as a savior, or worse, ruler. She was clear in stating that the world needed a return to law and government, with an emphasis this time on honesty, integrity, and looking after each and every person with no succumbing to the enticement of wealth and power. And, given her reported supernatural abilities, even if some were exaggerated (flying like Superman being one of them), few had wanted to argue with her – not least since the terrors of the Apocalypse has sated humankinds desire for war, and people had welcomed the warm glow of peace.

Charlotte lowers her hand from her forehead, and as she takes her place behind the podium a middle-aged man scurries forward, adjusts the height of the microphone sat on it and she stops him with a smile, telling him it's fine, that she doesn't need it, at which he edges away, frowning. She takes a deep breath and exhales, then looks around at Gary and the others taking their positions around her.

Gary smiles and nods at her and she returns the gesture.

She looks back to the crowd and addresses them without the need for amplification equipment, her voice carrying to everyone as though she were stood right next to them.

"My friends. Thank you so much for coming to this brief yet very important ceremony. We are gathered today to honor a man who gave everything so that we may live and continue on as a species, learning to

460

respect and love one another again." She pauses and swallows hard, feeling emotion build inside her and she fights against it. "The history books would tell us he was a villain, a betrayer, but nothing could be further from the truth." She smiles, still fighting back tears. "He was a hero. A savior. A protector and a warrior." She pauses. "He was a brother," she looks at Gabriel and the other Archangels who smile at her, and then glances at Gary, "and a friend." She says, and he smiles as well. "But most of all," she struggles with the tears again and takes a deep breath, "most of all… he was my dad."

She blinks back the tears, then moves away from the podium, toward a large object covered in a white cloth. Pulling at it, she removes it to reveal a large statue of Judas, holding the katanas of destiny, with her as a little girl in front of him holding Mr. Tumbles her old teddy-bear, the sculpture having been created at her request and from her memories but, upon finally seeing it, the emotion becomes almost too much for her and she breathes in, attempting to stifle her tears.

Not wishing the crowds to witness her sorrow, Gary steps to her side. "Not here," he whispers and steadying her as she sways on her feet.

And it is Gabriel who provides the final bit of help by getting down on one knee to honor the memory of Judas. The sight of the highest-ranking angel kneeling causes everyone around him to do the same, including the gathered crowds and so they pay their respects to Judas Iscariot, the man who had saved all their lives.

***

Charlotte walks ahead of the entourage, down the wide corridor that leads to a large circular room. Their footsteps echo against the highly polished marble floor as they traverse the vast chamber, the place tranquil, its walls a calming shade of cream. A handful of people are dotted around, most of who are engaged in the area's construction. They stop what they are doing and acknowledge her with a bow, to which she holds up a humble hand and offers a slightly embarrassed frown, suggesting they need not do such a thing.

First in line behind her is Isaac, and he grips her sheathed swords in each hand, his lower right arm a robotic prosthetic created for him by Daniel. He takes a deep breath as his attention flits between being focused on what he is doing and keeping an eye on the civilians and workers. In truth, he very much enjoys the status that being a close friend of The Light gives, and his stern face reflects the officialdom.

Behind and flanking Isaac stride Gary and Nathan, closely followed by Sarah, Daniel, and Jonesy with the Archangels bringing up the rear.

As they progress further into the room, the wall's construction changes from cream plaster to a black polished granite and Charlotte glances down to her right at an elderly gentleman and his helper, with the old man sat on a small stool, his attention focused on a wall in front of him as he etches another name into the memorial wall with a small sandblasting machine.

His helper taps him on the shoulder, causing him to look up, and then shut off the noisy contraption, his attention flitting from his helper to the entourage, and sitting up straight he nods at Charlotte who in turn smiles back at him.

She casts her eye over the thousands of gold leaf stenciled names, neat and precise, stretching from the old man's position and around to the left, all the way across the crescent-shaped wall forming the end section of the corridor. She follows it around as she walks and lets out a thoughtful sigh.

As they near the end of the corridor, she raises her hands into the air, palms uppermost and her swords elegantly float from their scabbards, away from Isaac and then past her, drifting ahead and twirling in the air in a beautiful and poetic dance, leaving delicate trails of Divinity as they go.

Muted chatter and sounds of amazement flow from the onlookers as the weapons near their intended target, a granite pedestal with a flat wide top and intricate carved shaft, attached to a large base sitting atop a slightly larger plinth.

The bulk of the group comes to a halt before reaching the pedestal that is just a few feet away from and dead center of the memorial wall, and Sarah eases her way past them, leaving only her and Charlotte to approach the ornamental piece as the swords ease their way on top of it, rotating at angles, and their tips floating a couple of inches above its surface. Closing her eyes, Charlotte raises her hands into the air and clenches them, pouring vast amounts of Divinity into the swords, causing them to glow white. Opening her eyes, she exhales and nods to Sarah who returns the gesture and walks over to the pedestal. Reaching out, she attempts to retrieve the swords and her face contorts with focus as she struggles to move her hands toward the weapons. Her scowl deepens as she pushes harder against an invisible barrier, her hands trembling a few inches from the weapons, and at last gives up with a grunt, then turns toward Charlotte and smiles.

Satisfied that not even Sarah, who she deems one of the purest human souls on the planet, can retrieve the holy swords, Charlotte smiles and then sighs as she looks up.

At just above head height, and interspersed among the engraved names arcing around the room, sit large portraits of those she felt a strong emotional attachment to that lost their lives, aiding her in the fight against the darkness, painted from her memory by a talented artist she'd been introduced to.

On one side, Sister Marie Anesta, Abi Colter, Conrad Bzovsky, and Lewis Porter. And on the other, the Archangels Uriel, Jophiel, and Zadkiel, with Abigail Fisher, detectives Pete Stillman, Martin Dowd, and Captain Banks to the side of them.

At the head of the room and the center of all portraits, sits the beautiful painting of her mother Talia Vaez, her sacrifice ensuring Charlotte's survival, proof that one's past need not shape their future.

Charlotte approaches the portrait and leans against the wall with one hand beneath it. She looks to the ground and her body fills with emotion. Her shoulders shudder and she can contain it no more. She whispers, "thank you," and the tears come.

Nathan holds a hand up into the air and turns it in an anti-clockwise direction, signaling everyone to turn around and let Charlotte have her moment and leave her to her grief.

A few people around the room misunderstand the gesture and stare at each other for a moment and then comply, getting the message as

Charlotte's entourage, including the Archangels, about-face and bow their heads in reverence.

Tears drop onto the floor beneath Charlotte, and she cries in a way she hasn't since the day of Judas' passing.

Having taken her time to grieve and visit every portrait, admiring each one in silent contemplation, she walks back to her gathered friends and allows other people who have begun to gather at the memorial to move in and view the paintings and pay their respects in their own way.

Gary turns toward her as she approaches, him being the closest, breaking off his chat with Nathan. "All done?" he says with a smile.

She smiles back. "Yeah, all done." She breathes out deeply, then glances at Nathan. "So, mister in-charge-of-the-world's-security-council," she smiles, "what's next for you?"

He laughs a little. "You know that's not true, I'm not the head of anything."

She scrunches her nose up at him. "Yeah, I know, I just love messin' with ya." She smiles again.

He scowls at her playfully, then raises his eyebrows. "Well then, miss in-charge-of-the-whole-planet…"

She smiles, conceding his touché moment.

"…I have a few people to talk with, make sure that Daniel's demon defense initiatives are on track, y'know – just in case," he glances toward Daniel, who is stood laughing and joking with Sarah and Isaac, "and then I'm all yours," he says, returning his gaze to her with a smile.

She frowns. "You not gonna take it easy, enjoy the rest of your days away from the maddening crowds and hassle?"

"You're kidding! Where you go, I go." He winks at her.

She laughs and then leans in and kisses him on the cheek. "Thank you, Nathan, for everything."

His face grows a little more serious. "No. Thank you, Charlotte. For everything." He nods.

She hugs him tight and then walks away.

"Oh – and tell Isaac I want to see him, will ya!" he says, calling after her. "That boy's been idle long enough, he can start helping me on a few things."

She holds her hand up in the air as she walks and waves it without turning back to him.

Gary smiles and pats him on the shoulder, the gesture returned by Nathan, then follows her.

"So," Charlotte says, approaching Sarah, Isaac, and Daniel and pointing at Isaac's prosthetic limb, "this is the version 2.1 I have been hearing so much about then, yeah?" She smiles.

Isaac holds up his robotic hand, "Yup," he says, rolling his fingers in sequence, "this guy right here is a bloody genius."

Daniel squirms, feeling undeserved of the praise. "Well, I wouldn't say that. I just altered an already pretty great design from stuff I found in the new lab. Someone else deserves the credit for that." He points at the limb.

"Yeah, well," Isaac says, continuing to admire it, "they ain't around, are they! So you're getting the kudos, simple as that." He smiles at him.

Daniel shrugs. "All right, if you insist on lauding me as your God." He holds out a hand as though he means for Isaac to kiss it, to which Isaac gives him the finger and shakes his head.

Charlotte laughs and looks at Sarah. "Is it always like this?"

"Yeah," she replies, "always." She raises her eyebrows sharply.

Charlotte laughs again. "Poor you." She looks at Isaac. "Okay you. General Taylor's looking for ya."

He looks toward the man then back at her. "So it's General now?"

She smiles. "It is to you, soldier." She winks.

Isaac smiles and nods curtly, then hurries off toward Nathan.

Charlotte watches him walk away then turns to Sarah. "Come see me later for some girly time?"

"Yeah, of course," she says with a smile.

Taking a deep breath, Charlotte walks away with Gary in tow.

"Strange day," she says without looking back at him.

"We've had stranger," he replies, with a small laugh.

She laughs also but says nothing more, as ahead Gabriel approaches.

"So," Gabriel says, "all things are now in their place and your calling is at hand. Are you ready, my child?"

"Just about I think," she says, jerking her mouth downward.

Gabriel smiles and places his hands on her shoulders. "You will do great things, Charlotte Vaez. Great things indeed."

She places a hand on top of his, her eyes glistening, filling with tears that don't quite swell enough for them to spill out and down her face. She embraces him, burying her face in his chest, and squeezes tight, holding for a few moments then peeling away.

He strokes the side of her face, smiles, and walks away.

"You are something else, you know that?" Michael says, as walks up to and hugs her.

"You too, Michael," she says, with a smile, "you too."

"Whenever you need us," he says, separating from her, then glancing upward.

"I know," she replies, patting the side of his arm gently as he walks away.

Raphael and Raguel follow suit, offering a warm embrace and kind words, then they too take their leave, following Gabriel and Michael.

Turning toward Gary, she takes a deep breath, exhaling rapidly. "Uggh, that's quite enough of all that. Let's go get some sun, shall we?" she says with a smile.

They walk through the building and out of the exit, her arm linked in his, laughing and joking with one another, and as they leave the sun's brilliance hits them and she raises a hand to her face, shielding her eyes from its glare, then closes them and removes it, allowing the warmth of the sun to wash over her.

"So what do you want to do now?" Gary asks, grabbing her attention.

She turns to face him, contemplating her answer, then looks down at the ground briefly and back up at him. "What do you think he would want me to do?"

Gary flicks his eyebrows up. "Well… he would want you to get out there and heal the world." He smiles and takes a deep breath. "But, what do *you* want to do?"

She looks up to the sky for a moment and then back at him. Relinking her arm with his, she smiles. "Well then, Gary… let's get out there and heal the world."

Charlotte Vaez and Gary Cross walk down the stone steps leading up to Hope's Beginning and into a crowd of people.

EPILOGUE

Within a new fortress in Hell of his own creation, Lucifer sits upon his throne, wearing a contemplative dry grin. Although he is one being, he feels the presence of another deep within him, a powerful soul, a man working hard to prevent him from making the full transition he knows he is destined for. The presence calms him, soothing his innate desire for carnage and destruction, and keeps him in check, stopping him from resuming the crusade the previous incarnation of him had waged.

Centuries have passed since that time, although within the fabric of his reality it has been nothing more than a few months. The land above that the previous Lucifer had tried to conquer was now changed beyond recognition, having embraced the peace afforded to them by the sacrifice of the one within him, and moved forward allowing religion and science to share equal standing for the betterment of all. Yes, it is a much better world above thanks to Judas' sacrifice.

But now he is getting better at not listening to Iscariot's voice, at not taking his advice, and at not allowing him the space in his mind he has occupied over up till now. And as Judas attempts to speak to him again, he closes his eyes, subduing his voice and forcing it down until it is nothing more than a whisper, a ghost in the darkest recesses of his mind. Then, it ceases altogether.

Lucifer opens his eyes. "Ahhh, that's better," he says, a wicked smile upon his face.

Behind and to his left, Azazel taps him on the shoulder, and the appearance of a visitor causes Lucifer's smile to widen.

"Malphas, you old dog," Lucifer says, standing, his arms outstretched as the demon ambles toward him through a gauntlet of Hell's denizens stood within the expansive throne chamber, his eyes glancing around at them nervously and his demeanor skittish as they eye him with contempt.

As he gets within a few feet of the stairs leading up to the throne, he looks up at Lucifer, his head still lowered. He swallows hard and glances around again while wetting his mouth and licking his scaly lips. "Master!" he says, holding out his hands.

Malphas is about to get down on bended knee when Lucifer shadow-steps into him, exploding the former General, showering body parts and black blood across the throne room and its occupants go wild with whoops and cheers.

Shadow-stepping back to his throne and taking a seat, Lucifer clicks his finger and from the side and out of a crowd of demons the Lord of Sand approaches. And Lucifer addresses him without looking in his direction.

"Seems you played a great card during our fight some time back." He now turns his head toward him, slowly. "But remember, I am not Iscariot so don't you ever disappoint me... General."

"I don't intend to, master," he says while bowing and backing away. "I don't intend to at all."

Behind and to the side of him, Azazel smiles victoriously and places a hand on Lucifer's shoulder.

The adventure continues

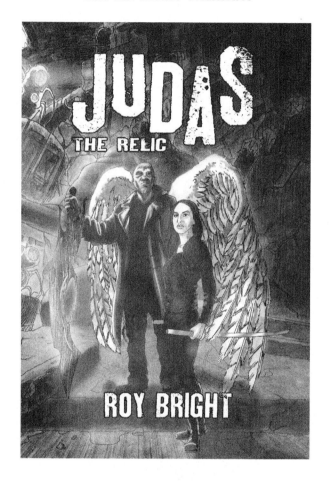

Available now from Amazon

Visit the author's website and sign up for the newsletter to be kept up to date
with all future releases:
www.roytbright.com

ABOUT THE AUTHOR

Roy Thomas Bright was born 22nd October 1971, in Manchester and grew up in Burnley, East Lancashire, the son of Edwin and Bridie Bright.

He received his secondary education at St Wilfrids C of E High School in Blackburn and upon leaving decided to join the Royal Navy as a gunner. The need to patrol some of the worlds 'hotspots' allowed him to travel the globe extensively, and he was very fortunate to see a vast number of exotic countries and different cultures.

In 1998, Roy decided to leave the Royal Navy to pursue a career as a professional musician. Having been a musician since the age of six and able to play a plethora of instruments, Roy went on to experience many highs in his first band 'deponeye' until that ended in 2004. In 2005 Roy started his second band Exit State, which enjoyed great success touring all over the UK and parts of Europe, a No.1 video on Kerrang TV's Most Requested show and sharing the stage with the likes of Michael Schenker, Blaze Bayley (Iron Maiden), Esoterica, Dave Evans (AC/DC), The Black Mollys, Forever Never, Black Spiders and Neil Buchanan's Marseille.

Following a successful tour with guitar legend Michael Schenker in 2012, Exit State were delighted to be invited to become Patrons of the Children's Hospice Arts charity chARTUK, an organization Roy is still a proud patron of, whose amazing work aims to enrich the lives of children and young people with severe disabilities and life-limiting conditions in hospices through the creative, performing and literary arts, enabling individual expression, creativity and communication.

It was in late 2012 while enjoying touring downtime that Roy decided to pursue one of his other creative passions – writing. The idea for Judas had been sitting deeply within his psyche for some time and the amalgamation of the original idea fueled by the lyrics in the rock song What Have You Done by Within Temptation finally saw him put pen to paper. A massive and steep learning curve followed, but he was fortunate due to connections made from his time within the music sector to receive exceptional advice from a number of sources. An introduction by Exit State's manager Mark Appleton to Stephen Clegg, the author of Maria's Papers, proved to be an invaluable one as Stephen's help and guidance was key in ensuring Judas was worthy of being published.

In 2012, Roy published Judas via Whiteley Publishing. He then re-published a second edition of the novel via self-publishing in 2016 and hasn't looked back since.

Roy is thoroughly enjoying writing more and more, including screenplays with his screenwriting partner Mike Harris and has penned a number of original scripts, including the Judas stories. He has now begun work on the fourth novel in the Judas saga - a 'Book Zero', which details events happening in and around the same timeframe as the first story.

Roy has three children, Reece, Tyler and Lily.

Printed in Great Britain
by Amazon